THE BREAKING
OF A WAVE

Fabio Genovesi

THE BREAKING
OF A WAVE

*Translated from the Italian
by Will Schutt*

Europa
editions

Europa Editions
214 West 29th Street
New York, N.Y. 10001
www.europaeditions.com
info@europaeditions.com

Copyright © 2015 by Mondadori Libri S.p.A. Milano
First Publication 2016 by Europa Editions

Translation by Will Schutt
Original title: *Chi manda le onde*
Translation copyright © 2016 by Europa Editions

Library of Congress Cataloging in Publication Data is available
ISBN 978-1-60945-387-9

Genovesi, Fabio
The Breaking of a Wave

Book design by Emanuele Ragnisco
www.mekkanografici.com

Cover photo © Delpixart/iStock

Prepress by Grafica Punto Print – Rome

Printed in the USA

To my mother and father

To myself I seem to have been only like a boy playing
on the sea-shore, and diverting myself now and then
finding a smoother pebble or a prettier shell than ordinary,
whilst the great ocean of truth lay
all undiscovered before me.

—Isaac Newton

THE BREAKING
OF A WAVE

PART 1

The breaking of a wave cannot explain the whole sea.
—VLADIMIR NABOKOV

HI, I'M TAGES. WHO ARE YOU?

There's this Etruscan farmer digging holes in a field and since he's Etruscan he's doing it like three thousand years ago. No tools, no nothing. The poor guy's really doing it the hard way.

By accident he digs one hole deeper than the others and the earth below begins to move. A hand pops out, then an arm, and in the end a whole child emerges, a kid with white hair who leaps in front of the farmer and says, "Hi, I'm Tages. Who are you?"

The man doesn't answer. He doesn't breathe. He's shaking so bad you can't tell whether he's shaking or dancing. He opens his mouth but the only thing that comes out is a terrified scream so loud the whole Etruscan population hears it and races to see what's happening. And what's happening is this crazy thing that the Etruscans saw for real and that I only heard about from my brother Luca. And I know it sounds absurd and out there but I totally believe it.

Then again I believe everything. My name is Luna and I'm thirteen years old and up until last year I still believed in Santa Claus. At first he even scared me. Because let's face it, this story about a stranger who sneaks into your house at night and brings you a bunch of presents, well, it sounded weird to me. I mean if someone gives you a present he'd want you to see him, right? That way you can thank him and tell him he's awesome and he'll be happy. But Santa Claus, he enters through the fireplace when everyone's asleep and then he runs away.

That's not good guy behavior. That's burglar behavior. In fact, the morning after, while the rest of the children in the world were racing to see what Santa Claus had brought them, I was checking the rooms to see if he'd stolen anything.

Like that time I'd begged with all my heart for a new bike, the blue bike I'd seen in the window at Santini's. But on Christmas morning, there was no bike under the tree, there was Mom and Luca, all serious and bummed out, and Mom started saying, "I'm so sorry, Luna. Things are tough this year and we can't—" I stopped her right there. It wasn't her fault, I told her. I knew that sooner or later Santa Claus would steal our presents, and who knew what good my bike was going to do him up at the North Pole.

But he would usually bring me a couple of presents. In the end I even grew to like him a little. Until a year ago when I was in seventh grade and the last day before Christmas break the teacher gave us a homework assignment called "The Big Little Disappointments in Life: How I Felt when I Found out Santa Claus Doesn't Exist."

I wrote it down in my journal, I read it, I read it again, I looked around the room to see if the others were shocked too or if it was just me. But it was just me.

"Excuse me, Teacher, I don't understand."

"What don't you understand, Luna?"

"No, I mean, what do you mean Santa Claus doesn't exist? It's not true. I hate to break it to you but it's just not true. Is it?"

The teacher didn't say a word. Neither did my classmates. For a minute it was so silent you could hear the custodian cursing at the coffee machine in the hallway, then the whole class burst out laughing, calling me the meanest words in the world. The teacher said, "Quiet, quiet, everyone, or you're all getting an F." But no one listened. Instead they started launching crumpled paper balls at me and erasers and pencils and other heavier, harder things, but I ignored them because all I could see in front of me was Santa Claus waving goodbye, leaving for good. He and his elfin pals were disappearing along with the house at the North Pole and the eight reindeer from his sleigh. Comet, Donner, Prancer, and . . . I can't remember the others but who cares, it's not as if they're real, they're just nonsense made up to make me look like an idiot, and the only thing real in the world were those hard pointy things my classmates were firing at me.

But Tages is another story. Tages has nothing to do with Santa Claus. He really did exist. Sure, the story of a kid with white hair who popped out of the earth may sound weird, but so what, everything in the world is weird. A man meets a woman, puts his penis in her and after nine months a baby comes out of her tummy—is that any less weird? To tell you the truth I think it sounds more normal for someone to pop out of the earth like, you know, a flower or a mushroom or a whole bunch of other stuff around us.

And if someone says there's no such thing as a kid with white hair, that means there's no such thing as me either, since that's exactly how I was born. I have white hair, white skin, and my eyes are almost transparent. I have to be careful the sun doesn't burn me and what little I see of the world I see weirdly. But that doesn't mean I'm make-believe; I'm an albino. It happens. There are albino birds and albino fish and albino crocodiles and monkeys and whales and turtles. Even plants can be albinos. Even flowers. It's totally normal. But not for people, no sir. People always complain that life's all the same and flat and boring. But if someone a little different walks by they spaz, they freak. Like my classmates, who think I'm the Devil's daughter or a vampire, as if I could put a curse on them or maybe infect them with this thing and suddenly they'd all turn white like me. I don't know what exactly they're thinking. I only know it hurts when they pick on you because you're different. And it hurts even more when they're scared to pick on you and keep their distance.

Anyway, all this just to say there's nothing weird about the story of Tages. Tages was just an albino kid who turned up one day and started talking to the Etruscans.

"Hello, people! I've come to teach you how to read your fate," he says. And I'm positive they all looked at him then looked at each other and then somebody raised his hand. "Pardon me, Tages, but what's with the white hair?"

Tages gets upset. He pounds on his leg. "Really? I come all this way to talk to you about your fate and you ask me about my hair?"

"Yeah, well, it's weird."

"There's nothing weird about it."

"Actually there is. It's white. I mean, if you were old it wouldn't be weird, but you're not and it is."

Tages shakes his head and doesn't answer. Luckily there's a woman in the crowd who does. "Wait a minute, guys. You're being unfair. If you ask me, Tages isn't weird. He's just a dwarf. An old dwarf who looks like a kid. Isn't that right?"

"No! I'm not a dwarf and I'm not old. I was born with white hair. Do you have a problem with that?"

"No, no, of course not. But look, frankly, it's pretty weird."

Tages lowers his eyes. He looks at the hole in the field where he came from. "You people are a bunch of dicks. I've got a mind to go back underground without teaching you squat. I should have gone to the Egyptians or Babylonians. But I'm here now so cut the crap and keep quiet. We don't have much time. I mean I do because I'm immortal but you are not, so listen up."

Tages takes a deep breath then starts to explain. And for a minute the Etruscans continue to stare at his white hair. But his words are so mesmerizing they begin to listen to him for real. Some even take notes. Tages talks about lightning, earthquakes, and other weird things that happen in the world. He tells them they're all signs sent from heaven. He tells them about the flight of birds, about statues that catch fire and sheep born without hooves, and the more he talks the more they realize that this guy really knows his stuff. And maybe that's why his hair is white, because he might be a kid but he's as wise as an old man.

Only an old man who's in shape, who has his head together. Not like my Grandpa Rolando who thought he was an American soldier named John. Me and my brother Luca would ask him how come, if he were American, he didn't speak the language, and he would say a bomb had exploded next to him and he was still in shock. In fact he couldn't even say the word "shock." He said "sock." And every evening me and my big brother would listen to him tell the same old story about the day he found himself alone staring down the whole German army and he had to flee on foot from an enemy plane chasing after him. At one point Grandpa saw a gigantic tree that he hid behind and there he found a dead soldier holding a rifle. The rifle had only one shot left so Grandpa waited until the airplane was right on top of him, took aim at a bomb under one of the wings and at the very last minute fired. The airplane exploded.

The German pilot ejected just in time, descended slowly on his parachute, then began running toward him with a pistol. Except instead of shooting him, the German shook his hand and said something. And here, at the end of this story that Grandpa told us every night, the same way every time, he always had the German say something different.

One time he said, "Dein aim ist equal to dein courage, Herr John." And another time: "Today you have taught me what courage is, dear John." Or: "John my pal, join me at the bar, I'm buying this hero a beer . . . "

Whatever he said was always new and always beautiful to

hear, but then I wondered aloud how the German knew his name was John and where the two of them had managed to find beer on a battlefield . . . That's when Luca would squeeze me hard and clamp a hand over my mouth. "Come on, John," he'd say, "it's late. Time to hit the barracks. The two of us'll keep watch tonight."

Grandpa would say yes, it was time, salute us military-style, and wander off to bed. Exactly the same night after night, year after year. Then in September Grandpa died.

Just like that, in his sleep. When he went to bed he was alive and when he woke up he wasn't. A couple of elegant men arrived to place him in an open casket and arranged it in the living room so that people could come see him. Except no one came.

Every so often Mom would go in for a bit and I would go with her, except I'd stand by the doorway because I was scared to look Grandpa in the face. I kept my eyes down and looked at his hands resting on his tummy, and since I don't see too well they seemed all one thing to me, white and frozen and fake. Then I looked up and there was Luca beside the coffin. He'd stayed with Grandpa all day and all night.

At dinnertime I stuck my head in the door to ask him if he was going to eat with us. "Coming," he said. But he never came. So Mom sent me to fetch him again.

"You coming? We're having fish sticks and peas."

"Yum. I'll be right there. I'm just going to finish saying goodbye."

"You're saying goodbye to Grandpa?"

"No, I already said goodbye to him. Now I'm saying goodbye to John and the German soldier."

"Ah," I said, "I see," even though I didn't see very much.

"I was just thinking, do you know the German soldier's name?"

I shook my head.

"Me neither. Grandpa never said. Why didn't we ever ask him?"

I thought about it, didn't know what to say, said nothing.

"Too bad. It'll remain a mystery," said Luca in that calming voice of his. Then he went back to chatting quietly with all the people he was saying goodbye to in the coffin.

I nodded as if I'd thought that stuff about the German myself. But I hadn't thought about it at all and suddenly in my head I could see all these people together, waving goodbye and leaving for good. Grandpa, John, the nameless German. They were all going where Santa Claus and the elves and the reindeer had gone, where Grandma had already gone, and where my first goldfish had gone, too. (His name was Signor Vincenzo, and in reality he was more black than gold.) I saw them going round and round, fast, like in a vortex, becoming smaller and darker and finally vanishing.

Then I felt this stinging around my eyes. I ran to the kitchen, buried my face in Mom's sweater while she was setting the table, and hugged her hard. And she said, "Oh no, Luna, cheer up, don't cry . . . " but from her twisted, broken-into-tiny-pieces voice you understood completely that she was crying too.

It's normal, I think. Sometimes things happen that you can't do anything about, you can only have a cry and go on, waiting for something different to come along. Like the Etruscans, who in my opinion cried a whole bunch at the end of that afternoon, when Tages stopped talking and waved goodbye and then went back underground same as the setting sun. And in my opinion they returned to that spot every day and the farmer who discovered Tages continued to dig really deep holes all his life, hoping that sooner or later he'd find him again.

Because Tages had taught them a lot: how to read the will of Heaven in what happens on Earth, how to read your fate in the world around us. Great, thanks, Tages, but why are you leaving now? What's the point of recognizing fate and the things that come your way if you can't avoid the bad stuff, and the good stuff, even if you hug it tight, slips off into the vortex of the past? Like you and your Etruscan friends who are all dead and have left nothing behind but smelly, dusty tombs. Like Santa Claus and Signor Vincenzo and Grandpa. Like everything that blows in and blows out, and where it all ends up I don't know.

The Happy Explorer

I t's Saturday afternoon and I'm trying not to fall asleep while Mr. Marino is talking about the mystery of the Holy Trinity, the mystery of mass, and a bunch of other mysteries in the faith. But the biggest mystery of all is why on earth every Saturday Mom forces me to come to catechism.

Normal parents I get. That's just how they are. They complain about having to look after the house or keep up with work and having no time to do the things they like, and meanwhile they force their children to live like them, school and homework all week, and Saturday and Sunday, which could be free, really aren't free at all because of catechism and mass. But Mom, she's different, sometimes almost too different: When the sun's out, for instance, she doesn't wake me up. She says it's too pretty out to shut yourself in a dark, stinky school. Say I have an assignment due in class that day, or my teacher is planning to quiz me. Instead I open my eyes and it's already ten o'clock. I call the shop where Mom works and tell her I'm ruined. Tomorrow at school the teacher is going to kill me. That's just for starters. And over the noise of the hair dryer and her customers' chatter she answers me all upbeat: "What's the fuss? You won't go tomorrow either. Problem solved, right?"

No, problem not solved. That may work for Luca, who gets up in the morning, slips into his wetsuit, and heads to the sea with a surfboard tucked under his arm. He only goes to school every once and a while, when there aren't any waves, just to do something else for a change. He takes his seat and everyone crowds around his desk, all worked up and happy to see him. Then he earns a string of great grades and it's thanks a bunch and catch you later.

In fact, Luca doesn't even have to show up to school. He got a good grade this week even though he's off in France surfing with his friends. Yesterday, he told us, the philosophy teacher was supposed to quiz him, but since Luca wasn't there, the teacher gave him a B+, on faith, saying that Luca would never earn anything below a B+. Luca can breathe easy. I swear that's what happened. He himself sent us a text about it, and Mom and I laughed long and hard.

Although honestly it's not fair. I mean I'm happy for Luca, since I may not know what philosophy is but you can bet he does. He knows about everything in the whole world. What I mean is it's not fair when teachers do that. And it's not fair when they mark you down for misconduct if you show up late to school or don't do your homework, while when I do that, unh-unh, with me they smile and tell me not to worry. They think my white skin makes me frail and weak and that even though I'm in a normal class I'm not at the same level as everyone else and if I make a mistake it doesn't matter, the important thing is I tried.

They even want to assign me a special needs teacher. Every year they tell me so and every year I tell them I don't need one. Sometimes they insist. That's when Mom takes over. She tells them I don't need any help, that what they should do is hire someone to clean up the bathrooms—they smell like roadkill. They also want to give me a computer because the print in books is too small for me; I look at the pages and seem to see several straight rows of ants lined up next to each other. But I use a magnifying glass made for that very purpose. I slide it over the lines to enlarge them, and even if it's heavy to carry around and makes my head spin a little, with the magnifying glass I can read for half an hour a sitting, which may not be long but it's a hundred thousand times longer than a lot of my classmates.

At any rate, it's not fair that I need a magnifying glass to read. It's not fair that they treat me better or worse than the others. None of it's fair. But what is really unfair is that today is Saturday and the beach is two minutes away yet I can't go because for some mysterious reason Mom makes me come to catechism.

So here I am, in a dark, damp room that stinks of boiled potatoes, sitting at a desk identical to the ones at school. The catechist reads stories from the Bible and afterward we have to summarize them and write down what we think about them, which is practically the same assignment we get in literature class, except about God.

The Bible stories describe either the life of Jesus or stuff that happened way before him—that stuff's called the Old Testament and it's way more exciting because God is always getting angry and destroying cities with balls of fire or sending killer insects to eat people.

With Jesus, on the other hand, there's never any action. I like him, I do, but sometimes, as a character, he resembles me so much he gets on my nerves. People treat him like dirt and he says nothing, just stands there and never retaliates.

Mom is always watching movies with a Chinese guy named Bruce Lee, and the stories of Bruce Lee begin just like those of Jesus. You see him walking down a street or in the middle of a marketplace. At a certain point some thugs turn up and start bothering him. But he keeps walking with his head down. Then one of them goes too far, pushes him or insults his mom. That's when Bruce Lee loses it. He lets out this weird scream and flattens two guys with one kick. He hurls another at the rest of the gang. Then he knocks the dust off his pants and heads back out onto the road with all these people massacred behind him.

Not Jesus. He's the son of God and if he wanted to, he could bring down a river of fire from the sky. He could turn his enemies' hair into a bunch of cobras or vipers that bite their necks a million times. Instead he just stands there and takes it and never fights back. In the end the only move he makes is when he turns the other cheek. Some feat. The catechist says that next year we'll be confirmed and confirmation means joining Christ's army. But what's a guy who never fights need with an army?

If you think about it, though, things could be worse, a lot worse. In place of Mr. Marino we could have Mother Greta for catechist. She's from Trentino and looks like a very old, very ugly man dressed as a nun. She has a massive jaw and one eye larger than the other, which, when she looks at you, aims a little above your head. She's not the only nun with this defect. There are at least three. Maybe it's because nuns always keep one eye on earthly things and one on those saints up there.

Anyway, Mother Greta is everyone's worst nightmare, and after catechism she waits for us outside in the convent playground. Which is really just a stretch of asphalt with a single seesaw and a crooked bench. As of a few weeks ago there's also a heap of deflated truck tires that the nuns use for a new game they came up with called "The Happy Explorer": they line up the tires in a row, snugly, one after another, so that they form a kind of tunnel, and the goal is to crawl in one end and slither out the other. But the tires are all dirty and hard and uneven, and the tunnel is narrow and smells like pee, and even if many of my classmates are pleased to play "The Happy Explorer," I wonder what there is to explore in there. I'm especially curious to know how this is supposed to make us happy. Confined spaces scare me. In fact as soon as I see the sisters pick up the tires I tell them I want to go pray and then disappear into the chapel. But last Saturday Mother Greta caught me. With her, my prayers don't stand a chance.

"Where do you think you're running off to?" she asked, stopping me in the middle of the schoolyard, with that voice all gravelly dribbling down her double chin.

"Excuse me, Mother, I'm going to chapel to say a Hail Mary to the Virgin."

"Save it for later. Come, we're playing 'The Happy Explorer.'"

"I really wanted to pray right now."

"You can pray later. The Virgin is in no hurry. Mary has many virtues and patience *is* one of them. I, on the other hand, have no patience, so go on, get in the tunnel."

But I couldn't get in. More importantly I didn't want to. I only wanted God to help me, to rain down fire from the sky or send locusts to eat Mother Greta. If God were too busy, a saint would do fine. Just as long as Jesus didn't come. Please not him. I already knew what he would say.

"Luna dear, go on, get in the hole."

"But Jesus I don't want to!"

"I know. But get in the hole anyway. And remember to forgive them."

"I have to forgive them too?"

"They know not what they do."

"That's not true. They know exactly what they're doing. They're hurting me!"

And Jesus would have looked at me, smiled, and raised his eyes to heaven. Then he would have crawled in the hole with me to keep me company and do a bit of suffering together.

"Go on, little girl, move it!" insisted Mother Greta, while all the kids jumped up and down, shouting, "Move it!" Unlike me, they couldn't wait to get inside.

"Don't you see you're ruining the game for your friends? Why is it they play along and you don't? Do you think you're special? Do you think you're different? Don't you see you're the same as all the others? Come on, kids, give the wimp a hand!"

That was exactly what they'd been waiting for. They dove on top of me, took hold of my arms and the hood of my sweat-shirt, and shoved me into the tires.

I was chest deep in the tunnel. They kept shoving me in by my legs. Someone even untied my shoelaces. In my mind I kept repeating the thing I always think of when I suffer some abuse: it could be worse, I could have been born in Africa.

In Africa being an albino and steering clear of the sun is hard enough. But the real problem is that down there, albinos don't last long. There they are in their villages walking around without a care when a jeep arrives and guys with giant knives hop out, kill them, and carry them off. All because witches concoct magic potions with albino legs and hands and hair and blood. Any piece will do. When an albino dies, the family has to cover them with bricks, otherwise at night someone will dig them up and rob the parts he needs until bit by bit there's nothing left. And if you're a girl like me, then it's even worse, since men with AIDS think that by sleeping with an albino woman they'll be cured. So they rape you, infect you with AIDS—and goodnight.

In other words, look, this is just to say that things weren't going so badly for me. They were pushing me into the tires where I might catch some infection, sure, but I definitely wasn't catching AIDS, and instead of chopping off my legs they were only untying my shoelaces. So inside the tunnel I kept saying to myself, "You could be in Africa, you could be in Africa . . ." Then they started to bang real hard on the tires with their fists and feet. From inside it felt like a lot of bombs exploding all around me, like the German ones that almost killed Grandpa, back in the days of soldier John, when he went into shock after all that bombing. Maybe I would wind up the same. Maybe I would come out of that hole and go crazy and think I was someone else too. It actually didn't seem like such a bad thing to crawl out the other end and not be me, since, from where I stood—stuck in the dark, smelly old tires—my life really sucked, and the one good thing about being in there was that no one could see me when I stopped fighting, lay my head on the rank rubber, and started to cry.

So that explains why the sound of the bell signaling the end of catechism sends a shiver down my spine like a diabolical serpent and I begin to shake. Last to leave, I get to the schoolyard and brace myself for what has to happen. But when I take a look around, I realize immediately that I won't run into any more trouble: in the playground, for the first time ever, is Zot. I'm spared.

Zot's in the same class as me. He arrived last month. The principal brought him in one day and told us his name was Zot, that he came from Chernobyl, and that it was our job to make him feel at home. I looked at him. He kept his eyes down but maybe for a moment he looked at me too, and it was clear that for me the worst was over, that Zot had come to save me. Short and scrawny, he had on a giant pink wool sweater so long it looked like a dress; extra wide, worn-out loafers; an old-guy gray checked jacket, and a hat crowned with a feather set crooked on his rug of curly poodle-like hair. I put on my glasses and took a closer look. It was clear that from that day on I could breathe easier at school, because if an insult were flown, or a gob of spit or a punch, they were all headed for that boy there, like bugs to a light bulb.

But Zot had yet to be seen at catechism and I had thought that because he came from Russia he was a communist and an enemy of religion. Yet here he is, already being manhandled by some boys and shoved inside the tunnel and screaming, "Scoundrels, quit it! You're making me perspire! You're ruining my cardigan! Mother, I implore you to come to my aid! Bring these people to their senses!" in his thin little voice and the flawless, grandaddy Italian he speaks.

They continue to push him in by his feet and poke fun of his worn-out loafers, which I can see now too, since I'm standing just a foot away. I smell the odor of the tires and feel something boiling up in my legs and chest, like a force growing bigger and warmer and driving me to move, to stop them, or at least try to, to scream that they suck and deserve to burn in the depths of Hell. Maybe Jesus himself is making me boil, to jolt me, to urge me, "Go on, Luna, don't be afraid of your convictions, don't be scared of what they'll do to you. It's the right thing to do. Do it for me . . . "

But I stay put. I shake my head and say, "No way, Jesus, forget it. I'm not doing that for you. You're the Son of God and you could stop them in a second. You could send locusts or make frogs rain down or change the playground into a lake of fire and only save Zot and me. You could let us fly far away, to a place where we'll be left in peace."

But as usual Jesus does nothing, just makes my arms and chest shake and stands there reminding me what I should do. The only day things went my way and I could return home without a care in the world, practically problem free. Yet here I am, opening my mouth, talking, trying to do something.

Besides, if I wait for Jesus—goodnight.

DUPLEX

S andro comes home and tosses his bag on the kitchen table. It's full of books and weighs a ton. Shouldering it aggravates his headache. But even breathing aggravates his headache, and every heartbeat is a hammer blow between his eyes. Thank God school lets out at noon on Mondays, otherwise today he really would have died in class.

"Sandro," calls his mother, lost in the steam coming off the stove, "don't put your bag on the table, we're about to eat."

The water is boiling in two different pots, one for rice and one for pasta. Cooking the same thing for everybody would be more practical, only this morning Sandro left a note saying he wanted rice, and his dad doesn't want rice because he says the Chinese are invading us and soon we'll all be forced to eat rice every day, so for as long as he can he's binging on spaghetti.

"How was school?"

"Same old, same old."

"What did you do?"

"Nothing."

"Nothing? What do you mean nothing?"

"Same old, same old, Mom, bored my balls off, what do you think we did!" Sandro makes the mistake of shouting. When he shouts his head explodes. He yanks his bag from the table and knocks over a plate, which vaults off a chair, hits the ground, and shatters. The sound penetrates his ears and a hundred thousand minuscule, pointy shards stab him, one by one, in the brain.

He lets his bag fall too. Fuck it. He clasps his temples, runs to his room, jumps on the bed, and plants his face in the pillow.

He was the same when he woke up today. Doesn't even know if he had breakfast and can't remember how he got to school. He took his seat and didn't open his mouth, didn't listen to a word, at some point he even fell asleep and awoke to the laughter of the class staring at him. And that's no good, that's seriously bad. A student who falls asleep in class can get a mark for misconduct. Imagine if you're the teacher, like Sandro.

It's his fault for carrying on with this Sunday-night-out nonsense.

Saturday used to be his big night out, then high school kids elbowed their way into Saturday, and he and his friends settled for Friday. But over time, the kids expanded their operation and hijacked Friday as well, forcing them to hang tight till Sunday evening. Which, in effect, makes sense: Saturday is convenient for high school kids, since they don't go to school on Sunday. Friday is for college kids, since they don't have classes on Saturday. Sunday night, on the other hand, is for those who have nothing to do on Monday, or the rest of the week for that matter; it suits Sandro and his friends perfectly.

Except this absurd thing happened last month. Now Sandro has something to do. He became a teacher. Or rather, a sub. Actually, lower than a sub, if such a thing is possible. If in the darkest depths of the social ladder there exists a rung beneath subs, then that's right where Sandro stands. When a teacher feels sick and the regular sub can't fill in, and on his way to school the regular sub's sub drives his car into a tree, that's when they call Sandro. He'll never be a real teacher because he didn't take the exam or earn a teaching certificate. Sandro never did dick all.

He didn't even fill out the application for these lousy substitute jobs; his mom did. On the sly. The sister of a friend of

hers works at the teaching agency. They orchestrated everything without saying a word to him. Then last month he
received a phone call and for a little while now Sandro has
been teaching English at a high school.

At *the* high school, actually, the only one in Forte dei Marmi,
the same Math and Science Academy he studied at twenty years
ago. He always hated math and is still trying to figure out what
physics is, but there were no other high schools in town, and in
order to get to bigger schools, like in Viareggio, he would have
had to wake up a half hour earlier. So he spent five crappy years
studying shit subjects, but at least he did them here, at the high
school where by some miracle he now teaches.

Happiness has gone to his mom's head. She goes to the
supermarket and says, "Slice me half a pound of ham, the good
stuff. It's for my son the teacher." While talking to a friend
she'll suddenly stop and say, "Oh God, look at the time, my
son the teacher will be getting home soon." In other words,
now the whole town knows, and everyone finds it unbelievable. But it seems even more unbelievable to Sandro, especially
on Monday mornings after his Sunday nights out.

"Sandro! Come eat! It's ready!" his mother yells from the
kitchen. Sandro says he's coming, only under his breath, into his
pillow. He rolls onto his back and tries to breathe. His head
throbs and an acidic nausea mounts in his stomach and creeps
up his throat. He scans the ceiling, the shelves that wrap around
the room and reach all the way up there, warped under the
weight of his records and CDs and rock magazines. As soon as
he has a little time he has to organize the magazines by month
and year and put the records in alphabetical order by the name
of the band. Like it used to be, when he was sixteen years old
and alphabetical order meant everything. Sometimes he would
buy a record just because the band name began with a letter in
short supply in his collection. Then one day he came home with
a new record and realized he already had another yet to be

shelved, and because Marino had been waiting for him outside, Sandro placed the new record on top of the old. "Whatever," he said, "I'll shelve them tomorrow." But tomorrow became the day after tomorrow, and then the day after the day after tomorrow, and the number of records to shelve rose to three, to fifty, to a hundred, piling up one on top of the other and weighing on him, awaiting the day when he would put everything back in order.

The problem is that the day never comes—not for records, not for any of it. One summer night Sandro was crossing the pine grove in Versiliana to grab a beer with friends when he saw something red hanging from the branch of a pine tree and took it down. It was a tattered piece of rubber with a string attached and at the bottom of the string a note. The note read, "Balloon set free in Reggio Emilia on May 10 by Ivan Cilloni, 2B. If you get this message, send me a postcard from wherever you live. As a reward you'll get a drawing of a rhinoceros made by me. They're my strong suit. Bye, Ivan." Then the address. Sandro almost cried. That balloon had flown all the way from Reggio Emilia and landed in his lap—just think how happy this kid would be when he got a postcard from Forte dei Marmi! So he brought the card back home and set it on the nightstand as a reminder to himself to buy a postcard, write a note, and stick it in the mail. And the note-to-self is still there, waiting for that famous right day that never comes, after nine years. Motherfucker. Nine years.

But now that he thinks about it, tomorrow he has the day off from school. In the morning he's going to pick mushrooms with Rambo and Marino, but the afternoon might be just the time to finally set everything straight. Sure, like that, tomorrow Sandro will stay here and organize everything and mail a beautiful postcard to Reggio Emilia. Tomorrow, yes, tomorrow . . .

"Sandrooo!"

"Coming."

"Your rice is getting cold."

"Who cares."

"It's not good when it's cold."

"What do you mean it's not good? You always make cold rice in the summer."

"That's different! That has capers, mushrooms, olives, bits of tuna, bits of ham, bits of—"

"Enough! I don't give a shit!"

Sandro shouts, and the words come out all gnarled due to a sharp pang that runs across his skull and mangles his mouth. Every noise, every movement, is a merciless thrust of the blade. Including the creak of box springs and, worse, this *beep-beep* coming out of nowhere.

It's the cell phone in his pants pocket. They say you shouldn't keep it near your balls or your heart or your head— where should you put it then? Sandro sees he's got a new message, and even the little screen light is like a glaring needle being thrust into his eye. But then he reads the message and a smile crosses his lips.

1:10 P.M.: Hey teach, this place rocks! I'm seeing everything, tasting everything, experiencing it all, just like you told me to. And I'm doing it all for you too. L.

The L. stands for Luca, his favorite student. Sandro knows teachers shouldn't play favorites, but then students shouldn't be so different. A kid this smart and hip shouldn't exist among all those mean little shits. Right or wrong, he favors Luca, who's the spitting image of himself at sixteen.

Exactly the same, only smarter maybe, more alert, better looking, more— All right, maybe they're not exactly alike, but they have the same inner spirit, the same mortar of passions that can wipe out this dismal puny world. And to hell with this little town we were born in, to hell with parents, to hell with school and grades and designer clothes and Saturday afternoon strolls downtown to see and be seen and all the other bullshit around here, slowly closing in on them, growing narrower and narrower until the day they clamp a hook around your neck and before you know it you've become a slave like everybody else.

"Sandro!" Now his dad joins in, his mouth full. "I'm starting without you, you hear!"

"Knock yourself out, old man."

Case in point: lunchtime, the mindless fear that the food will get cold and his dad will start without him and the world will come crashing down. One of the thousand bits of horseshit that pile up and pound you into the ground. And Sandro fell for it. Maybe Sandro let himself be fooled. But not Luca, Luca still has time, he can save himself.

Right now he's in Biarritz, France, for a week, sleeping in a camper and surfing with friends. A fairy tale, one of those trips when you're happy because it seems as though at that moment your real life is spreading out before you, that it's just a step away and waiting for you in all its splendor. But then time passes and you realize that life wasn't spread out before you, that that there was life, those very days, those nights, you thought it was a step away and instead it was right in front of you. You thought it was just a taste, a warm-up before you reached that incredible age when you're fully grown and you don't have to obey anyone and everything's grand. You wait, you hope, and you don't realize that true bliss is this right here, and by the time you understand that, it's already past you and you're left alone to remember how things once were.

That's why Luca had to go surf in Biarritz. His mother hadn't wanted him to go. She'd said now wasn't the right time, that he was still underage, she trusted him but not the world. And then there was the matter of money—he'd need money to go— and at that moment they had none . . . That's what Luca's mom had said and that's precisely the problem: there are always loads of perfectly good reasons that lead to making the wrong decision, to taking a kid full of talent and potential and opportunities on the horizon, a young eagle with talons poised to take life in his clutches, and plucking him one feather at a time, slowly, imperceptibly, so as not to hurt him, so he doesn't even realize, until one day that hawk has been transformed into a farm-raised chicken, ready to be roasted on society's spit.

It's happened to many people. Maybe it had even happened to him. But Sandro doesn't want to think about it now. He'd rather think about the fact that in the end he'd convinced her otherwise, Luca's mom, Luca's beautiful mom. She'd come to the parent-teacher conference and he'd told her what the deal was. Thanks to him Luca's now in France conquering the ocean and French girls, with their bright skin, their buttery bodies, their dazed eyes that wander at random but always land on the right spot. It's thanks to Sandro if tonight Luca's laying one down on the beach and pouncing on life, tugging on those soft yet firm breasts swelling with possibility, plump with the future.

But better than any French girl is Luca's mom, Serena, the most mesmerizing woman Sandro has ever seen in person, or, for that matter, in the photos and dirty movies he's watched over the years, and that's a lot of years, a whole lot of movies. But he had actually seen her before. She had gone to the same high school. Then for a long time their paths hadn't crossed, and now here she is, more beautiful than before. And this is an incredible sign. It means that there's hope, that beautiful things can happen even when you no longer expect them to. Yes, Sandro, maybe there are always beautiful things awaiting you, maybe your chances haven't dried up, maybe even when your own horizon looks drab and dispiriting and you think there's nothing left to see, that's when the surprises ambush you and turn your life upside down . . .

But a deafening ring right beside his ear crushes that thought, like a slipper pulverizing a mosquito in the night. This time it isn't the cell phone, it's the landline on the nightstand, and it rings again. And again.

Sandro never answers the landline. It's always either someone looking to sell you junk or an old ballbuster asking for his mother, and if Sandro answers they'll ask him how he's doing, if he's found a job yet, if he has a girlfriend. Only the phone beside him continues to ring and it's drilling a hole in his head, so he picks it up and spits out two words.

"What now?"

" . . . "

"I said, what now?"

"Uhm, yes, hi . . . " A woman's voice. Pretty too. "I'd like to speak with Sandro Mancini." He can't believe it, but he believes it a little. Because, goddammit, sometimes it really does happen: you're thinking of a person and that person calls you. It *is* her. Luca's mom. She wants to thank you for having convinced her to send her son off, that it was the right thing to do, that the problem with her is that she never knows what she ought to do, that life is tough and she lacks confidence, she's alone, she has no one beside her to give her advice, to get close to, and—

"Yes, speaking, this is Sandro. Hey, Serena!"

" . . . "

"Serena? Can you hear me?"

"Actually I'm calling on behalf of RAI."

"RAI?"

"Yes, Italian Radio and Television. I'm calling about your TV subscription. Your bill is overdue."

"You're not calling about this bullshit licensing fee again, are you? You're killing me. I already told you, I don't owe you anything. My mother already paid for it!"

"There's no need to raise your voice, Mr. Mancini. I'm

practically calling you of my own volition. I'm under no obligation to call. But I asked you to send a fax to my attention and—"

"In fact, I sent it."

"Yes, you did, but what I'd asked for was a sworn statement declaring you live with your parents. All you sent me were recommendations for new programming. And insults."

Sandro doesn't answer right away. First he tries to remember what he wrote in the fax, but it's a total blank. He only knows that he'd been edgy that day. He had gone with Rambo and Marino to deliver supermarket flyers, and lots of people had shouted from inside their homes that they didn't want them, not to stuff their mailboxes with trash. Many gave him the finger. And while he was writing the fax he got more and more pissed off about living in a country so backward and crusty that people still use fax machines, just because well-connected people legacied into public sector jobs don't know how to read an email—some progress, some fucking progress we were making—

"Sandrooo!" His mother from the kitchen again, increasingly plaintive. "It's getting cold!"

Sandro grits his teeth, takes a deep breath, and continues. "Look, I don't remember exactly what I wrote, but I'm sure I put down that I live with my parents."

"Yes, but there's no address, there's no information about your parents. No dates, no fiscal code, no RAI subscription number. Nothing."

"Shit, look them up yourselves. Where did you mail the letters you sent me asking for money? To my house is where. Therefore you already have the address. And can't you see that it's the same address as my mom's, who's only been paying you your licensing fee for, like, a million years?"

"True, Mr. Mancini, true. All you need to do is send me a fax declaring that you reside with your parents and I can take care of everything. I assure you I'm going out of my way to make this call. But I understand your point and am trying to help. You send me this fax declaring that you live with your parents, that you don't have a place of your own but still occupy your little room, and you'll see—"

"Whoa there. Let's not get carried away. That makes it sound like I'm ten years old."

"I apologize, that wasn't my intention. But isn't that your situation? In other words, if you live at home with your parents, then I imagine you have a room."

"Yeah, but you called it 'little,' for Christ's sake. That makes it sound like I'm some dumb kid."

Again his mother from the kitchen: "Sandro, the rice is cold. I'm putting it in the bain-marie!"

"Not the bain-marie, I hate the bain-marie!" he shouts, clutching his throbbing head. "Hello?" says the woman from RAI, "Hello? What was that?" Sandro no longer has the energy to keep up appearances, but he tries to save himself all the same. "I said, it's not a little room. It's a private room with its own bathroom. It's separated from the rest of the house. I'm free to go as I please."

"Ah, interesting. So you're saying it's a home with separate living quarters?"

"Right, exactly, separate living quarters."

"Well then, aha, Mr. Mancini, aha. That changes the situation. That explains why we billed you. Living with your parents is one thing. But, if I've understood you correctly, I would categorize your situation as a duplex. Does it by any chance have a kitchenette, Mr. Mancini?

"No, there's no kitchenette, but I could have one if I wanted."

"You see? Then that fits the description of a duplex to a T. I'm afraid that means you'll have to pay a separate TV licensing fee."

"What? You're joking. How's that possible?"

"You don't live with your parents, Mr. Mancini. You may live in the same building, but there are two different residencies inside the building. Therefore you must have a TV subscription for your parents, and another for what I imagine you have in your duplex."

"But I don't have a TV in my room."

"No, but perhaps you have one in your kitchenette, or your private bathroom."

"If I don't have a TV in my room, do you really think I have one in the john? And I don't have a kitchenette. I don't have the money for one and I'll never have it if you steal my money for some stupid unjust licensing fee."

"That's the law, Mr. Mancini, you own a duplex and therefore—"

"Knock it off with this duplex nonsense, knock it off! I live with my parents in one house. There's a kitchen, bathroom, hallway, and two bedrooms. My parents sleep in one and I sleep in the other. There's not even a living room. There's nothing. Happy now? Don't make me shout again, my head's about to explode."

"I'm the one who should be asking you not to shout. And that you address me properly. I'm a doctor. Dr. Catapano."

"Oh, a doctor, shit. Well, I've got a title too, believe it or not. I'm a professor. Chew on that. Professor Mancini. And where does that leave us? Does that make an impression on you, in your little world of M.D.s and esquires and bullshit titles?"

"All right, Professor, at this point I've gone above and beyond. I'm hanging up now. I suggest you fill out the form and go to the post office to pay your bill and your late fee, since you're past due. At this point your late fee amounts to—"

"Yeah right. I'm not going to the post office. I don't have time to waste."

"Of course you don't, Professor, I imagine you're a very

busy man. You better run off to lunch now, your rice is getting cold and mommy's upset."

Just like that. That's exactly what that bitch said. Sandro blinks, wrings the phone like it were Dr. Catapano's neck, opens his lungs to capacity to suck in all the air he needs to gun down this moron with insults. But just as the first "fuck you" reaches his lips, he hears the dry, merciless *click* of the line. The bitch hung up.

And so Sandro, with all the air and rage left in his breath and the pain in his head shuttering his eyes, slams the phone down. But that's not good enough. He picks it up again and slams it harder. He picks it up once more and pounds it into the cradle so powerfully that he hears a mix of buzzing and cracked plastic and doesn't need to lift it to his ear again to know that the telephone has split in two.

His mother, from the kitchen: "Sandro, what happened?! Have you hurt yourself? Sandro! Sandrino!"

YOUR NAME IS SERENA

Your name is Serena but Serena doesn't suit you.
So what your parents named you that—what did they
know? Your mom died when you were over thirty,
your father this September, and they still hadn't understood
you. Fat chance they had a clue what you were like when you
were born.

Sure, they might have picked a less risky name, but that's
what happened and now you're stuck with it. Like women
named Joy or Gay. Like your friend Allegra who's been
depressed all her life. Like your cousin, who may go by the
name Angelica but she's the biggest slut on the coast from
Genoa to Orbetello.

But it doesn't matter. Nothing matters on a day as sunny as
today. Some people couldn't care less about the weather; the sun
could shine or rain fall for a month straight and they'd hardly
notice. They're relaxed or edgy for reasons of their own devis-
ing, impervious to water and a lot else that turns up in the sky.

Not you. Today the sun's out and that's enough to make you
smile. Plus it's Tuesday, and Tuesdays you don't work, you go
fetch Luca and Luna from school. All the other hairdressers
are closed Mondays. Maybe because women only want to get
their hair done for important functions, and nothing's ever
going on around here on Monday night. Subtract two months
of summer and nothing's *ever* going on here, not on Tuesdays
or Wednesdays or any day of the week. So Miss Gemma can
close shop when she feels like and pray the place will ride

things out, otherwise Gemma's Hair Studio will be converted into yet another hole-in-the-wall with tinted windows where people play video poker and slot machines, and for you, Serena, every day will be a Tuesday: the whole week free to spend with your kids, parked on the curb, clutching an accordion, a hat turned up for handouts.

But it hasn't come to that yet, so there's no sense in thinking about it. The only thing that makes sense is to hang a right for Luna's school, even though you're in the habit of driving straight and stopping at the high school to pick up Luca first. Luca's not there today.

Luca's in France. You think about it and it feels weird. You're happy because he's happy. He sends you these amazing text messages that, like a fool, you spend your nights rereading, but then you imagine him up there facing the ocean, no, in the ocean, in the middle of the cold, gigantic waves, and you're seized by fear. He's only seventeen, you could have told him no. But how can you say no to Luca? Everything he does is always so perfect and natural. Saying no to him is like saying no to the arrival of spring. You can stand in the middle of the road and say, "Stop right there, Spring, don't come any closer," and try to block every bud from blossoming on the branches, to squeeze shut every flower opening in the parks, but Spring doesn't even hear you, she scatters to the winds and warms the air and colors explode and animals go nuts and in five minutes she's caught hold of you too.

Enough is enough. Luca is happy and you have to be happy too. Now go get Luna, order a pizza, and eat it someplace out of doors. That is, by the sea. Luna always wants to go to the sea, just like her brother. Even if she shouldn't, even if the sun is really not good for her and she has to wear a hoodie and sunglasses on top of a thick coat of sunscreen . . . of course you left the sunscreen at the house. You'd set it on the kitchen table so as not to forget it, and then you forgot it there.

You ass! You airhead! How is it possible you're always thinking so much you never remember a thing? An ass and an airhead, an airhead and an ass . . . Meanwhile you've arrived at school, but you're so busy putting yourself down that for a moment you neglect to notice something's off: no one is outside, the schoolyard sits empty, the front door on the far side of the building is closed.

Oh God, maybe today is one of those idiotic national holidays. Maybe they've evacuated the school in an emergency. Or perhaps they'd recently relocated and Luna had told you as much but you forgot. Who knows, anything is possible. Crazier things happen in the world every day. In fact, you look at your watch and realize something even more incredible: you're early.

Ten full minutes, almost a quarter of an hour—the effect is disorienting. Inside, the teachers are still lecturing, the gate's shut. Just now the custodian is opening it. She sees you parked out front and waves. She's not all there, permanently grinning from one corner of her mouth and toting a small pink backpack over her shoulder, the contents of which no one knows. She keeps waving at you, touches her forehead, and gives you the A-OK sign, her way of saying your bangs look good. You smile and thank her. "Not too bad yourself," you shout. She bursts out laughing, covers her face with her hands as if to say no, it's not true, tucks her hair behind her ears, and finishes opening the gate.

Who knows why she's so obsessed with your bangs. She's been complementing you on this cut for ages, ever since you began picking up Luca from middle school. You've had a fringe cut for twenty years and changing it is out of the question. Because you work with hair and every day you encounter these girls and women who want to change their lives and hope to start by getting a new cut, color, coif. They quit straightening or curling their hair, they quit streaking it, and they think the same can be done to their habit of trusting everybody, of trying to make everyone happy by saying to hell with their own happiness, of pretending their situation is perfectly fine when it's really not fine at all. "Not anymore, Serena, that's right, as of today that's all going to change," they say, sizing themselves up in the mirror as locks of hair fall this way and that. And in the end nothing changes aside from their hairstyle, which feels weird for a time but after a while they grow used to it, just as they've grown used to loads of other things they don't like about their lives, things that by now seem neither good nor bad, simply normal.

In the meantime other cars pull up to the school bearing other mothers inside. Each stays shut inside her gigantic vehicle and waits, checking her cell phone or staring ahead into the emptiness beyond her windshield. So you open the door and step outside, because if sad people serve a purpose it's to remind you of what you must never become. You light a cigarette and lean against the car, crossing your arms and eyeing the squat, square school in front of you.

Repainted, it's still the same as when you attended. Except in those days it was an elementary school, and when you see it, you always think back to your first day of school, which lasted a mere half hour.

You hardly thought of it as the First Day of School. To you it was the only day. You hadn't understood it was a permanent thing. You thought that morning was a fluke, that your mom had things to do and had dumped you in this old room with cracked walls along with a bunch of kids you'd never seen before, who looked each other over, bewildered, and played at staying seated behind a gray little table, wearing a pink or blue smock, while an old lady at the head of the room ran through the rules to this stupid game.

Which, by the way, is a total snooze: standing still and listening to this lady talk about pens, notebooks, and other stuff you're supposed to bring with you. You don't listen. You just rest your head in your hands and your elbows on the little table that this lady calls a desk. And you want to stay like that until your mom finally comes back for you.

Except you have to pee.

You've had to for some time now, just a little. Now you really have to go. Your legs start to wiggle, you look around, you try squeezing hard to push it back up, but you can't hold it for long. What should you do? You have to go to the bathroom. But where is it? Is there a bathroom in this dump?

The woman is explaining how this room is your classroom, that you're Group B. But she says nothing about a bathroom. Maybe she already mentioned it and you weren't listening. Your legs shake more violently, you begin to sweat, you feel the pee has reached the gate and is ready to break on through. It knocks. "Open up, open up!" it shouts. But you can't do that in front of all these people here, so you open your mouth and cry, "Miss, I have to pee!"

The lady stops, purses her lips, and stares at you in disbelief as if rather than speaking you'd lobbed a stone at her.

"Serena, you must raise your hand before you speak."

You nod your head and think to yourself this game is *super* tiresome and full of ridiculous rules. You raise one hand, then the other.

"One hand will do, Serena."

"Sorry, Miss, I raised the other so it would equal the first one I raised."

"Ah, that's all right then." For whatever reason she starts laughing. "But please don't call me 'Miss.' I'm your teacher."

"All right, teacher, I have to pee," you say, and maybe the pee heard you calling, because now you've got to go even worse.

"That's not how we ask. We say, 'May I go to the bathroom?'"

"May I go to the bathroom?"

"Can't you wait till recess?"

No, you can't. You're not exactly sure what recess is, but you're sure you can't wait for it. "No, teacher, I have to go now or I'll wet my pants."

The other kids start laughing as if they'd never had to pee before. But everyone has to pee all the time, that's why there are bathrooms everywhere: restaurants, movie theaters, cafes. Here too, let's hope.

"All right, but make it quick."

You nod and shoot up from your seat. And if before you really had to go, now that you're standing you're about to burst. A little leaks out, you feel your underwear get warm, but you squeeze your stomach and hold it in. And you stand still next to your desk as the teacher stares at you.

"Well then, Serena, going or not?"

"I . . . I don't know where the bathroom is."

"Oh, I apologize, I hadn't thought about that. Stay there a second while I finish this important lesson and then I'll take you myself—actually, hold on." The teacher goes to the door, opens it, and in a loud voice calls out a weird name, Derna or Terna something, then comes back into the room. "The custodian will be right in and she'll take you, all right?"

She sits down and resumes talking about pointless stuff, lined notebooks and graph paper notebooks, and you really have to pee and your stomach is full of it and maybe your head is full of it now too—that's why you can't think of anything but peeing. And a little about Derna, or Terna, who's a no-show.

For the time being you sit back down, since when you were seated you didn't have to go as badly. Or so you think. On the contrary, now you can't even breathe, every time you let a little air in through your nose, a drop of pee slips out. You can feel it trickling down your legs. It's warm and spreading to your coveralls. And the more you feel, the harder it is to hold it in, and the part still inside you says, "How can you let that other pee out and not me?" And if you let that pee out too, at some point you feel the back of your knee getting warm, it kind of tickles, and you think it can't get any wetter than this, so you stop squeezing and let it rain.

You take a breath and for a moment you're in heaven. Then you look down and nearly die of shame. On the floor is a lake, a huge lake all around you, which spreads wider and wider and is about to touch the feet of the kid at the desk next to yours. She turns, looks down, and, realizing what's what, leaps to her feet so quickly her chair tips over and everyone swings round, and this dumbfounded girl points at the lake, then points at you.

The teacher quits nattering and hurries over, and in comes a fat lady who must be Derna or Terna, and all the other kids jump up and shout, "Pisser! Pisser!" And the teacher shouts over them, "Cool it! Sit down and behave or I'll extend the lesson so long we won't be done till next century!" But no one knows what the lesson is, or a century for that matter, so the ruckus continues. And you cry and close your eyes and don't open them again, not even when the giant arms of Derna or Terna gather you up and slowly lift you to your feet and lead you out of the classroom, where she should have led you a long time ago.

She tells you not to worry, what happened was really no big deal. You open your eyes a tad and see a hairless woman standing next to her wearing a black apron and examining you. Derna or Terna tells her to fetch some sawdust and you start crying again.

"No, please, not sawdust," you say. Though you don't know what it is, the word sounds so much like a saw that you're afraid they'll punish you by sawing off your legs or some other limb.

"No, no, don't worry. Sawdust are woodchips for soaking up the liquid under your desk," says the custodian, and she takes you to the bathroom and hands you a giant roll of toilet paper while she calls your mother to come pick you up right away.

That's how your first day of school ends. And it may only have lasted a half hour but during that time you learned two important lessons: Firstly, what sawdust means. Secondly, and more importantly, you discovered that when you really have to do something, you don't have to ask permission. You get up and go.

Finally the bell rings. Loud. It reaches all the way to the street and calls you back to the present, to this Tuesday when you're almost forty and have two kids and you've come to pick up your youngest, and you have to admit that all in all you didn't turn out so badly.

A trauma like that could have done real damage. People weaker than you might have really lost their heads. Traumas of that nature turn serial killers into serial killers, who murder people and eat them. Screwing up your mind takes next to nothing. The crazy-fuse is short and silent, and when it's lit, it's goodnight.

The gate swings open and the custodian yells, "Slow down! Slow down!" but no one listens. Kids spill outside in a phosphorescent stream of sweatshirts and knapsacks and spiky hair, war cries and curse words and ringtones crackle with energy that has been crammed behind a desk all morning and now explodes wildly. The stream expands in the schoolyard, then contracts again to pass through the gate, and the contest to be first one out is decided by sticks and stones.

And there, way in the back, all alone and propped against the far wall of the schoolyard, is Luna.

She catches sight of you, lifts her head, smiles and waves.

She says she posts up there so that you can spot her immediately and not waste time searching for her in the mob. You keep saying that it doesn't matter, were she surrounded by a hundred million kids you'd still be able to spot her. "Because I'm the only one with white hair?" she says. "No," you reply, "because you're the only one period." "Thanks," says Luna, "next time I'll go with the other kids." But she never does.

She's so different from Luca, who, when he gets out of school, is always at the center of it all. Without wanting to be, Luca is still the center. Everyone else forms a circle around him. His classmates trail after him, as do his teachers, and though the girls stand back, they still gaze at him from afar and fix their hair. Luca doesn't even notice. He stares straight ahead and smiles serenely at some mysterious glimmer of a thought. Then he sees you in the car, smiles wider, picks up his pace, approaches you, and kisses you on the cheek, then bends at the waist, since the Panda is small and he's almost six feet tall. He gets in and you start the car and close the door and shut out the world, which remains back there, empty and sad to see you go.

Today however is different. Today there's only Luna, who's still at the far end of the schoolyard because the mob of kids at the gate won't settle down. In fact it has begun to swarm around a kid who, trying to get out, is met at every turn with a shove or a punch or a foot in the ass.

You hope it's not him, but who else could it be? So short and with that floppy straw hat on his head. Who else could it be but that luckless kid who landed in Versilia as part of the relief program for children from Chernobyl? At one point they collar him and lift him sheer off the ground, tossing him out front like a trash bag, and his knees hit the ground so hard even you wince. But he says nothing, doesn't defend himself, merely hangs on to his hat for dear life.

Matters decline when this enormous kid, Damiano, turns up, the son of this dipshit dentist who lusted after you in high school. Damiano's in the same class as the Russian boy and Luna yet he already sports gut rolls and a mustache. Give him a comb-over and he'd pass for sixty. He steps up to the Russian boy and, after administering a few kicks and punches, tears off his hat. That's when the boy finally reacts. Except his reaction is to cry, "You brute!" while flailing his arms in an attempt to retrieve his hat.

Meanwhile everyone laughs and shouts as Damiano wipes his butt with the hat, flattens it, sings, "Shit hat, shit hat . . . " Then he wrings it out like a rag, spits in it, and finally palms it Frisbee-style as if he'll fling it a hundred yards in the air.

"That's enough! Give it back! That hat's rather precious! Treat it with respect! Lowlife!"

"Me, a lowlife? You've got some nerve, dickbrains." Damiano winds up as if he really is going to throw the hat, taking aim at the tall blackberry hedge dividing the street and school from the neighboring grounds, where there once stood a pine grove that they tore down to build some villas, a project temporarily stalled by permit issues. Now it's just a stretch of mud and cement bags and rats.

"Hand over my Panama. I'm asking you to do me this courtesy. It's my grandfather's. It has considerable sentimental value."

Damiano barely listens. He laughs and the others laugh with him. Two teachers walk by, a man and a woman. They see what's happening, shake their heads, and keep walking. You on the other hand? You draw closer, Serena. At first you simply meant to retrieve Luna, who's still standing back there surveying the scene. You hadn't given one thought to meddling in this business. But as you pass by, your feet swerve of their own accord, and suddenly you find yourself standing between Damiano and the Russian boy.

"Give him his hat back," you say.

"Huh? What do you want?"

"Give him his hat back immediately or I'll tell your father."

"Big whoop. My dad's a dickhead."

"True, but you still need to give him his hat back."

"Why? What'll you do if I don't?" Damiano stares at you and smiles with that chubby mouth of his, his lips wet and his teeth hidden behind the braces his dickhead dad installed himself. Again he winds up to launch the hat.

The kids standing around spread out to give him room, and even if no one dares say so out loud, it's clear that they're all dying for Damiano to throw it, to see what will happen next. For the same reason, you're praying he won't.

"Listen to the lady, scoundrel!" says the boy, who has taken cover behind you and in order to talk peeks out just a little. He comes up to your stomach.

"Shut up," you tell him, then turn back to Damiano. "And you, give him his hat back."

"And what'll you do if I don't?"

"If you don't, you're going to regret it."

Everyone turns serious save Damiano. He keeps laughing, winds up, pretends to throw the hat, then stops, and just when you think he's only pretending and doesn't have the courage to do it, he lets out a cry, a piggish squeal, and throws it for real.

The hat goes flying, spins and flies. It rises in the air, which is filled with his cry and the eager cries of his classmates, sails over the hedge, and disappears forever, out of reach, somewhere in the mud around the closed construction site.

Damiano turns to you, blows a kiss, and sticks out his tongue. Except it's not like a kid sticking out his tongue. It's much creepier, more revolting—him dragging his tongue across his chubby lips and the thin hairs of his mustache. To top it off, he winks at you.

"Now what are you going to do, lady? Touch me and I tell."

You grit your teeth, breathe, shake your head. You put your hands up and take a step backward to send a clear signal to him and to the mothers who've begun to form a crowd that violence is not part of your world, that for you, violence doesn't exist. Besides, he's a kid—what is this, the Dark Ages? It's not as if we can solve everything with sticks and stones, right?

Then he looks at you, smiles and touches your shoulder with those fat, oily fingers of his. "Atta girl, it's not worth the risk. If you touch me they'll lock you up, and your daughter will have to go back to the freak show where you found her."

He laughs and everyone laughs as he imitates a freak, holding his arms out in front of him, opening his eyes wide and exhuming from deep in his throat an animal call: "Arrrrggh, arrrgggh." Suddenly his playact comes crashing down, he doubles over, a third "arrrrggh" escapes his lips, except lower this time, wounded; you've planted your shin between his legs, a sharp and precise kick so hard that, if this boy's balls have dropped, let's hope he took a good look at them, because it'll be a long time before he ever sees them again.

Everyone clears out. Damiano remains on his knees, unable to breathe and trying to learn how again, while the Russian boy stares at you wide-eyed and pulls away a little, and Luna finally reaches you at a trot. You look at her. Even behind her sunglasses you can tell by her expression how royally you've screwed up.

You keep looking at her, not knowing what to say. You'd like to tell her that you did it for her, because this jerk said something awful, because these kids aren't innocent, they're the mini version of the assholes they'll turn into in a few years. Plus Luca's not being here puts you on edge. Tomorrow is his birthday. He's turning eighteen and it would have been nice for the three of you to celebrate together. And then you remembered that day at school when you wet yourself, and that always rankles you, so all things considered you had a shitstorm in your head and have caused a shitstorm here with this hateful fat boy.

But conveying all that with a look isn't easy. Besides, Luna has turned away from you. She's raised her head and is staring over your shoulder. You turn around, and next to one of the teachers and the custodian is Damiano's mom, who has just arrived and is trying to get out of her SUV but struggling to remove her seatbelt, as if it were a giant octopus tentacle, and the whole time she's sweating and tugging and shouting, "Bitch! Bitch!"

"Get out of here quick," you say to Luna and the Russian boy.

"But Miss, my hat—"

"Don't call me Miss. Your hat's gone. Besides, it looked ridiculous. Now go find your mom."

"I don't have a mom. I take the bus."

"Oh, right, sorry. Then get on the bus."

"Usually I prefer avoiding the bus and going by foot. Three-quarters of an hour and I'm home."

"Wow. You must like to walk."

"Not especially. But if I take the bus I can expect ten minutes of being beaten. Hence my preference for walking."

What's sad is the way he says it, as if that were the most normal thing in the world. Poor kid. Beatings at school, beatings on the bus, perhaps beatings when he gets home—what must go on in his head? Those forty-five minutes on foot may be the best part of his day.

But you don't have time to feel too sorry for him. Damiano's mom has freed herself from the seatbelt and is running toward you with her double chin and big flabby breasts bobbing this way and that.

"Go with Luna. Get in my car. I'll take you home. Hurry!"

"Far be it from me to offend you, Miss, but I don't know you. I don't know if I can trust you."

"What do you care? Worst-case scenario is I beat you up. But everyone beats you up, so what's the difference? Get in the car with Luna and wait for me there."

"It just doesn't strike me as being a prudent decision—"

"Go, damn it!" You grab him by the arm and push him away. Luna calls him over and the pair of them finally takes off for the car just as Damiano's mom arrives with her enormous ankles and her bottle-blond hair that in any serious country would be outlawed. She pushes aside one teacher and another teacher tries to reason with her but she says if he touches her she'll have him locked up. She stands facing you, spreads her arms out, and lunges at you with all her weight.

And you, Serena, you stand your ground, one foot in front of the other. You wipe your bangs out of your face and narrow your eyes, taking your time, sizing her up, poised to strike where it hurts.

Your name is Serena. And Tuesday is your day off.

THE KING OF PORCINI

"Come in, over. You find anything? Over."

"Hey, Rambo, which one of us are you talking to?"

"Both of you. You find anything? Over."

"Not me," says Sandro.

"Come again? Not one? Over."

"No. Why? How many have you found?"

"None. Over. How about you, Marino? Marino, you there?"

" . . . "

"Yo, Sandro, I'm getting worried. How can he not hear me? Why are you the only one answering me? Over."

"I'm an idiot is why. And cut this 'over' crap out."

"I can't. It's the international code for ham radio operators. When someone stops talking they say 'over.' Otherwise you talk over one another and it's total anarchy. Speaking of which, after you receive my communication you're supposed to say 'Roger.' That way we can be sure—"

Rambo's words get swallowed up by an electric gurgle as Sandro turns off his walkie-talkie, sticks it in his pocket, and continues his search free of Rambo's crackling voice in the air.

The walkie-talkies are a new thing. They bought them yesterday so that if someone gets lost, like last time, they don't have to spend all night searching for him. Or so they hope. Just as they hope to find lots of porcini, which sell at thirty euros a kilo and could yield serious bank. Even if thus far all they've done is spend money—on walkie-talkies—and have spotted exactly zero porcini.

But that's inevitable. You have to be connoisseurs, expert mushroom hunters, specialists who know the good spots and the right days. They're not experts, they're specialists in zippo, three friends following a dream to make enough money to bid their parents farewell and go live on their own. Well, not exactly on their own. Together, like off-campus students, which is a little sad when you're forty but it still beats living with Mom and Dad.

Marino has a sort of ramshackle fixer-upper in Vaiana, the least affluent suburb in Forte dei Marmi and the farthest from the sea. But they don't give a shit about affluence, they'd be happy just to repair the place and stay there. It's a dream they've pursued since back in high school, yet today, more than twenty years later, it appears even farther out of reach than it did then. But things can't be this way, this is some sort of trick of the eye. Sandro, Rambo, and Marino have to persevere, keep their heads down and their chins up, stand firm and believe in themselves and keep finding new ways to earn a buck. Technically speaking, Rambo works at his parents' newsstand, Marino is an on-again off-again traffic cop, and Sandro's now subbing—but those jobs aren't enough and there aren't any others to be had. For them, there is no clear and open road for the future. So they're trying to pave one for themselves, to beat unbeaten paths in the middle of the mysterious jungle of destiny, all twisted and aimless, and the three of them are condemned to wing it for eternity, jackasses forever.

Like today, when they haven't seen a mushroom yet and Marino may have fallen in a ditch and so long, Marino. Nonetheless, Sandro is happy to be hiking in the mountains. It beats spending the morning at school, all those hours behind his desk struggling to make it to lunch. The best strategy is the translation exercise: you feed them a phrase in Italian, the kids write it down in their notebooks and then have to translate it into English. When they're done, you call on one kid at random and make her read aloud. Then you feed them another, then another and so forth, until the bell rings. But the real trick lies in the amount of time you allot for translating the phrase: ten long minutes, maybe even a quarter hour. The kids jot down their completely wide-of-the-mark translations and then sit still, more or less behaving, minding their own business, while he reads the paper, fires off some texts, or simply closes his eyes and sleeps, sort of.

To think that when they had called him about teaching, despite flipping out at his mom, Sandro had felt kind of happy. The first day, he was running ten minutes late and had rushed off to school on his Vespa with his leather bag—a never-before-used graduation gift from his aunt and uncle—between his legs while a movie played in his head. It opened with him entering the classroom. The kids' jaws dropped when they saw this professor—so different, so cool. He tossed his bag on the floor, slid behind his desk, and told them the deal. "Hey, I'm Sandro Mancini, I teach English. And I don't give a damn about deadlines or grades or schedules. I only care about the heart. Lend me your hearts, kids, and I'll lend you mine."

Yes, just like that. And perhaps it was the freezing air on his face, or the hour of the morning, a time that hadn't seen him on his feet in ages, but Sandro had rushed off to school completely convinced that he'd enter the classroom and immediately form a special bond with these kids. To the boys he'd be big brother; to the girls, forbidden fruit, a kind of fascinating guru who crash-landed in their lives and changed them forever. And that's how, as he shook these kids out of their torpor, as he taught them to take life by the horns and bow to no man, Sandro would discover his true calling.

Which had not been the guitar, nor poetry, nor a combination of the two, which he had tried, becoming a low-fi singer-songwriter called Total Darkness. (No one ever actually called him that.) He sent demo tapes to record companies, rock magazines, even venues that booked Toto cover bands. Radio silence. Not a word back. Sandro blamed Italy for being a small, sanctimonious country where, if you don't know the right people, you'll never become anything, where real talent goes unrecognized and the same old bullshit keeps getting spun. But that was a lie. The truth is that music wasn't his calling. Sandro Mancini was born to teach.

Well, that's what he'd thought anyways, gunning down the back road on his Vespa, passing one warehouse under construction and another just shuttered, and the closer to school he got the more he believed it.

But between the custodian's welcome ("Classroom's over there. Get going, you're late"), the expression of the few kids who had deigned to sit up when he walked into the room, and the whiff of chemicals coming off the radiators running full blast, he knew it wasn't meant to be. He may have sucked as a singer-songwriter, but as a teacher he was Total Darkness too.

Not that he doesn't know his stuff. Sandro speaks English a hundred times better than the full-time faculty, the doddering old guard who spend a month explaining the difference between a wristwatch, a wall clock, and a cuckoo clock, so that when the kids travel abroad they can't even order a sandwich. It's that he doesn't know how to convey to others all the things he knows. And even in the rare cases when someone learns something thanks to him, Sandro—why pretend otherwise—doesn't give two shits. He'll be in that classroom for a month tops and that's that. He knows it and the kids know it too. They're like two passengers boarding a train, and one is already preparing to get off at the next stop.

In fact, if a leprechaun or magic dwarf or something of that kind were to pop out from behind a tree right now and offer him a hundred euros for every one of his students' names he could remember, Sandro would still be broke. He could call up a few faces, especially the girls' faces, but zero names. A few kids he couldn't even say for certain are Italian, and he still hasn't figured out whether one of his students is a boy or a girl. And you're asking him for names?

There's Luca, of course, but Luca doesn't count.

They'd struck up a conversation on day one, during recess, while Sandro was by himself leaning against the wall in a corner of the hallway where neither students nor teachers ever hung out. He was stroking a pack of cigarettes in his jeans pocket and cooking up a way to duck out for a smoke without being seen.

"We smoke in the bathrooms, but the teachers sneak off to the teachers' lounge," said this kid who'd appeared out of nowhere. Tall, with long blond hair, he wore a faded blue T-shirt with a picture of a palm tree. He was the kind of boy that girls wind up taking pills to forget, that makes men uneasily recall the time when they were fourteen and realized that one of their classmates seemed handsome to them, really handsome, and so they tossed and turned all night, terrified they might be queer and ahead of them lay years and years of lying to their parents, of people's petty jokes and perhaps a few gay-bashings by gangs of suburban Nazis.

"Thanks for the information," said Sandro, stifling a smile. "And the teachers' lounge is where?"

"Top floor. It's the only one with a door in one piece. How long you here for?"

"Here where?"

"School. How long do you have to stay here?"

"I don't *have to*," said Sandro, and he was about to break into a speech about the special role that teachers play in society, about the importance of his occupation for the future of the country. But he didn't feel like saying that bullshit, and the calm expression on the kid's face led him to understand there was no need to. Instead they started talking about music, the big acts Sandro had seen live, and Luca went wild at every name he dropped, couldn't believe Sandro had really seen so-and-so play, and Sandro felt simultaneously badass and prehistoric.

Then they started talking about other concerts slated for that summer, about how Luca had no money but still wanted to go. How he wanted to travel to Biarritz the following week to go surfing with his friends who had rented a camper. Only his mother might not give him permission to go.

That word, "permission," drove Sandro crazy. How could you suffocate a kid like this? How could you keep him caged up with the excuse that it's still too soon, with that shitty lie that one day he'd be able to do as he pleased? That day never comes. So he told him, teacher to student, what the deal was. How at forty years old he'd come here to teach at his mother's bidding. Which is crazy stuff, right, and even crazier to admit to a kid who was supposed to consider him a beacon of light. But Luca listened carefully. It seemed like he cared, like he even understood him, so Sandro carried on. He told him about the time his mother called him because she had heard an ambulance pass by and had gotten scared, about the time she'd made a vegetable quiche and written his name on top with a slice of Kraft and drawn a little heart next to it. He was even going to tell him about how he comes home at night to find his mom has laid out his pajamas on the radiator . . . but fortunately the bell rang, like an explosion of metal over their heads, and Sandro remembered where he was and what he had to do. He stopped talking, and each hurried off to where he was meant to be.

The same thing is happening now, in the dense woods. A loud noise brings Sandro back to reality. A sharp cry from the sky. A buzzard circling around and around, hunting for prey. The noise makes him shiver, and he realizes that for a while now he has been wandering aimlessly in the middle of the woods with his head in the clouds—not the ideal method for finding mushrooms.

He looks around and sees only trees and stones, stones and trees. He could either press forward a bit and see what happens or head back to where he'd started, but which way is forward and which back is anyone's guess, and the more he thinks about it the less he can be sure, and the only thing that's clear among all these stones and branches is that, motherfucker, Sandro is lost.

He checks his cell phone but there's no coverage, there's never coverage up here in the mountains, otherwise like hell they'd buy these walkie-talkies. He turns it on. "Help, guys, I don't know where I am. Where are you?" But all he hears is a confused noise, like a swarm of wasps struggling to bust out of the transmitter. "Can you hear me? Rambo, can you hear me? If you can hear me, please say something . . . over."

Nothing. Not even "over" works. So Sandro stops walking and posts up under a massive tree, much wider and taller than the others. He sits down and stays put. In a situation like this the one thing to do is locate a landmark and cling to it. Moving around makes things worse. A lot of people think getting lost is a black-and-white, cut–and-dry matter: you either know where you are or you don't. On the contrary, there are a thousand gradations of lostness. Each of us is always a little lost. But if you aren't aware of it and keep walking around at random, you risk getting really lost and ending up all alone in the dark of night, where you can't see anything and the only sound you hear is the soft drop of drool from the mouths of approaching wolves.

Not Sandro, he won't make that mistake. He may know nothing about mushrooms but he's a pro at getting lost. He leans his back against the trunk of the tree, closes his eyes, and tries to relax. But hearing the *beep* of his cell phone, he jumps to his feet. In the silent woods it sounds like music from Mars. Coverage! He's saved! Maybe this tree works like an antenna, picking up the few radio waves in the air and channeling them down here.

But no, Sandro checks his phone. No coverage, zippo. Then he checks to see who sent the message and everything becomes clear. It's Luca. Sandro had been thinking of that magical kid and his dreamy trip to Biarritz, and at that moment Luca had been thinking of his awesome teacher and written him a text, which would arrive with or without coverage. Because when things are meant to be, they have great powers, they defeat impossible odds, they plow forward at full speed and simply happen.

2:07 P.M.: Hey teacher, everything's tops here. As always you were right. Did you find what you were looking for? Keep trying. You're almost there. L.

Sandro reads and smiles, shaking his head as though Luca could see him. No, he hasn't found what he was looking for. He doesn't even know what he was looking for, and on top of that he's lost. But that's okay. Everyone talks nonsense now and then. Even Luca.

Luca, who's in France, having fun with his friends, riding the waves by day and, who knows, talking game to girls by night. Girls here hound him so much he has to duck for cover. The most hard-up devise ways to corner him. They loiter by the women's bathroom waiting for Luca to pass by, and if he's not careful one day they'll take him by force, drag him into the bathroom, and whatever happens happens . . .

The buzzard shrieks again, circling the sky, and its cry doesn't even give him time to imagine that scene, with all those girls in the women's bathroom and himself in Luca's shoes. The call brings him back to reality, long on trees and stones, short on group sex.

Sandro looks up and sees it circling and circling, scanning the ground for something to catch to live another day. In this sense the buzzard isn't that different from him and his friends.

Only it flies high in the sky and never stops, while he is sitting here, bewildered, not doing dick.

He grabs hold of the trunk and lifts himself up—he may not know how to fly but somehow he has to get out of this stony, leaf-blown hell alive. But first he points his telephone at the buzzard and tries to take a photo of it to send to Luca along with the message: "I haven't found what I'm looking for but I'll be damned if I'm not looking."

Yeah, that's it, what a line. Placed in the right spot in a song, it'd be real tight. Maybe he'd finally write a new track and call it "Buzzard." But before that he has to get this godforsaken bird to stand still so he can take its photo. On the first shot he only catches a wing, on the second the sky, on the third he drops his phone. It hits the ground, rolls a few feet downhill, and vanishes in the tall grass beside a boulder.

Shit. Sandro pounds his thigh, hurting both leg and hand in the process, then runs downhill and kneels beside the boulder. He reaches out his aching hand and is about to rummage in the tall grass when he hears a hissing noise, like someone exhaling, and quickly pulls back. Great. Perfect. That shithead Marino had put the fear of snakes in him. All morning he'd kept on whining about how nuts it was to hike in the mountains without antivenom or knee-highs or walking sticks. In his opinion these mountains were oozing with snakes.

But were they to heed Marino they'd never do anything in this life, let alone find work. They go forage for mussels around the jetty piers and Marino's scared that the harbormaster will nab him or that he'll catch a cold. They go dumpster diving and he's scared he'll get bitten by mice and infected with leptospirosis. They go steal pinecones in the pine grove and he's scared the warden will find out and never call him back to traffic duty. That's no way to live—that's not living—that's dying in slo-mo.

Sandro shouldn't pander to Marino's ridiculous fears. Sandro has to hang tough. Again he hears that same shrill noise in the leaves, but he doesn't care. He takes a deep breath, raises his hand, and plunges it into the leaves, into that damp dark mystery. First he feels the cool grass, then the cold ground, and finally the hard plastic of his telephone. He's about to pull it out when he feels something else next to it. Something smooth, puffy, much bigger. He brushes aside the grass, removes the stones, pokes his head under the boulder, and almost faints at the mind-blowing spectacle before him: the largest porcini in the world. His whole life he's never seen one this big, neither in person nor on the screen. (Come to think of it, he's never seen porcini in a movie before.) It's enormous, so perfect it doesn't seem real. But it is real. It's gigantic. It's the King of Porcini.

"The King of Porcini! The King of Porcini!" he shouts, pulling it up from the ground, gently at first and then, seeing as the King won't surrender, giving it a hard tug. But it has to surrender to him; he found it and he's taking it. Yes, he found it, Sandro found it! He's got to tell the others. Luca too. Hell, the kid was right, he said he was about to find what he was looking for, and motherfucker here it is! Here it is!

He extracts it, lifts it in the air, and studies its perfect and gigantic profile against the sky, where the buzzard's still flying around with nothing to show for it.

He shakes the King at the sky, hoping the bird will see it and bow down to him and his bravura. "Hey buzzard, check this out! Up yours!"

He waves at the animal and gives him the finger. Then he cradles the mushroom like a newborn and starts running downhill in long, reckless strides.

Since the upshot of not knowing where you are is that you're free to look both ways and take the easiest road out.

GIFTS FROM THE SEA

L ately the sea's been really angry, all black and frothing, crying so loud that I can hear it from my room at night. Why it's all worked up I couldn't say. The sea's a big place. Maybe it's upset about something that happened on the other side of the horizon, in Corsica or Spain or even farther away. But this morning it has calmed down and it sparkles in the sun with all these bright little squares that I have to look at from behind tinted glasses or else they'll make my head spin.

But I'm smiling, too, because I love the sun to death. Literally. I shouldn't be in the sun at all. Otherwise I'll get burned and covered with blisters and risk dying. I always have to stay in the shade, or, better, in the house, and not come out until sunset. But I put on a sweater and sunglasses and a pound of sunscreen and go outside anyways. It's better to take a chance and die outside than stay home and let sadness kill you.

Besides, it's so nice here. I listen to the waves lapping at the shore and forget all about eating my slice of pizza, which is good, but the taste mingles with the smell of sunscreen on my face and neck and hands and arms and all over. Before going for pizza, Mom and I stopped by the pharmacy to pick it up, then we came here to the sea, sat in the shade of the cabanas, and sent a message to Luca telling him he's missing out on pizza-by-the-sea Tuesdays and that he better hurry home soon. But he hasn't written back yet. He's probably on the top of one of those really tall waves in the ocean, looking at the world from up there, which must be like heaven, and if he doesn't tell me every little thing about what he saw when he gets home, I swear I'll punch him in the nose.

But Luca always tells me what he sees. Even while we're walking together he tells me what's around us, since I don't see too well, especially things at a distance, which look like a blur of color. Say I see a green-and-red river. He tells me it's a forest full of trees, birds in the air, blackberry bushes. Then I say, "Let's go," and we go. When I'm close up I can make out some dark, round shapes, reach my hand out, pick one, and put it in my mouth, and it really does taste like blackberries. So I tell him it's delicious and Luca laughs and says, "Did you just say blackberries are good? Hold the phone, Luna. Let me alert the press. It's sure to make the front page." I laugh and shove him, only gently. He laughs and pretends to bop me on the head. Anyways, all of that's to say that it would be great if today, on pizza Tuesday, my big brother were here.

Instead there's Zot.

We were giving him a ride home when Mom asked him what he'd had for lunch, and I didn't see the look Zot gave her, but Mom must have seen it in the rearview mirror, because she pulled a U-ie, and we all went for pizza together.

"Has Luca written back?" I ask.

Mom checks her phone again and shakes her head. "He must be in the water. He'll write back after."

"We can't call him?"

"I wish, Luna. I'd call him every minute if I could, but we promised . . . "

True, we had promised not to call him. It had been hard enough convincing him to take his cell phone. We'd given it to him for Christmas, and he never uses it. "But no calls, just texts once in a while. Otherwise what'll I have to tell you when I get back?"

"But Mom, I think we have to call him. It's an emergency."

"An emergency?"

"Yeah, I mean, you going to jail is an emergency."

"Excuse me? Why would I go to jail?"

"For before. At school."

"Listen, drama queen, they don't lock you up for kicking someone," she says. She eats the last wedge of her pizza and wipes her hands on the blue wood of the cabana. Then she spreads her army shirt out on the sand, lies down, and doesn't say another word.

Zot and I stay seated, he on his white cotton hanky, the kind old guys carry. He had it tucked into the pocket of his heavy, baggy, gray, old-guy jacket.

"Why aren't you eating your pizza?" I ask. For the last half hour he's been chewing the same tiny piece.

"I'm savoring it slowly."

"Tell the truth. You don't like it."

"If you must know, I'm relishing it. But I want to make it last."

"Look, you don't have to eat it if you don't like it. Leave it. Besides, you ordered the Neapolitan and that comes with those super salty anchovies."

"It happens to be my favorite."

"Come on, tell the truth, I know why you ordered it."

"You do? And why's that?"

"Because you were standing there and couldn't make up your mind, and the man at the pizza place told you, 'There's always the Neapolitan. It's a classic.' And you're a sucker for all thing classic, so that's what you ordered."

"That's preposterous."

"No, it's the truth."

"It is not!" Zot lets out this weird cry that sounds like a mouse being picked up and squeezed.

"Keep it down or you'll wake my mom! She has to rest as much as possible, because if she goes to jail, we're in for stress big-time."

Soon as I say it, Mom springs up. "I'm not going to jail. Cut that nonsense out, I'm not going anywhere! Look around you. This place is paradise. Now be quiet and enjoy the day a little." She digs around in her shirt pocket, pulls out a pack of cigarettes, and lights one up.

And me, I can't wait any longer. I stand up and tell her I'm going to the shore to get my gift.

"What gift?" Zot asks, but no one answers him. Like clockwork, Mom tells me to pull my hood on tight, keep my sunglasses on, and not take too long picking out a gift, because the sunscreen wears off.

"Miss," says Zot, "if it's not too rude, I would like to go to the shore and see this gift too." I spin around, but fortunately Mom knows that it's something I have to do on my own. "Don't call me 'Miss,'" she says, "and yes, you are definitely being rude. First finish your pizza and after that you have to tell me what your deal is. Who you are, where you're from, the whole shebang."

Zot doesn't say anything, just opens his mouth, tries to shovel another hunk of pizza in, and stays put while I head off to the shore.

With every step I take, the sea shines brighter and the wind blows harder, and in no time I'm taking faster, longer strides. Without meaning to I've started to run.

The sand on the shore is dark and cool, my feet sink a little, and it's only now I realize that it's made up of a lot of tiny pebbles, which are rolling over my toes and tickling me. I smile, partly at the tickling and partly at the waves gently lapping at my feet now and again. Even if the air outside feels almost like summer, the water is real cold. I set out along the water's edge.

I come here almost every day. After all, it's only five minutes from home. My smile vanishes pronto when I think that pretty soon that won't be the case. On the day of Grandpa's funeral, some relatives I'd never seen before showed up. At first all they said was that they were really sorry. Then they must have changed the subject, because Mom stopped nodding. Actually they fought. As they were leaving she shouted, "You have no right! You have no right!" But it turns out they did have a right, since afterward there appeared a sign on the fence with a telephone number and a message saying that anybody who wanted to buy the place had to call that number. In Italian as well as this weird language that's all over town these days. It's how the Russians write.

And I'm really sad we're giving it to them. It sits on a pretty road, small and narrow and closed-off at one end. A lot of people used to live there year-round, then gradually everyone sold their house and now ours is the only normal one left, the only house someone lives in. The others are giant villas that the owners visit one month out of the year, and when they buy our house they'll tear that down too and build up another villa, and we'll go live in a place far from the sea and when I miss our house I won't even be able to come look at it from the outside, since my house will no longer exist.

In fact, I got mad and made a fuss about it. Luca, on the other hand, didn't say anything. Nada. Yet ever since the day they put the sign out front he stopped showing up for lunch. In the morning he goes to the beach and he stays there till dinner.

I get it. I'd like to stay here till dinner too.

I stroll beside the sea, which after all those days of being angry has now calmed down and sends me the last little transparent waves that sound as if on top of their curly edges they were carrying a bunch of leaves that rustled in the air. The waves come slowly and cover the sand, and before going back out they leave something behind. They leave gifts on the shore.

A million, maybe a billion of them, things it hides on the sea-floor, under all that blue, and every once in a while it picks one and sends it to dry land. A lot of people don't even notice, maybe because they can see everything around them and get

lost looking out at the horizon and sailboats and seagulls fishing and the coast and the mountains up there that disappear
into the water. But me, I can't see these things, and if I keep
looking up at the sky I'll go blind. I walk with my hood over
my head and my eyes on the ground, and in the end it's no
wonder I noticed this really weird stuff that the sea scatters on
the shore. All the things that wound up in the sea ever since the
world began, from the time of dinosaurs to this morning,
things born in the water or that fell from ships or were torn
from the land by overflowing rivers. They're on the bottom,
dancing this way and that, and every so often one of them
catches a current, latches onto a wave, and, before you know
it, reaches the sand, waiting to surprise me.

Of course green crabs and hermit crabs and seashells are
normal findings. And sadly sticks and plastic bags are normal
too. But what's a toothbrush doing on the shore? How far did
this doggie-paw slipper or that remote control travel to get
here? And there are shoes, too, and license plates and dolls'
heads with their hair all disheveled and speckled with seashells
and one eye open and the other shut, boxes of chocolate and
Band-Aids and soda cans with super weird labels, which could
come from anywhere, India or Japan or a whole other planet.

I don't know. But I spend days studying these treasures. I
make a note of the pretty things in my journal and the prettiest I carry home with me. Not too many. Mom tells me I can
take one a day. I pick them up and place them in my room.
One time Luca entered and asked me: "What gifts did the sea
bring you today?" And ever since then that's what we call
them: gifts from the sea. By now the room is stuffed with
them—on top of the furniture, under the bed, on the win-
dowsill, in the corners, even scattered on the floor. Gifts
everywhere.

Today's the same. I ask myself where each thing comes
from, how it got here, and how long the getting here took. And

I don't feel the sun creeping up my sweater and finding my skin. I don't feel my eyes begin to sting or the tears running down from behind my glasses and blending with the sunscreen that keeps fading.

I do, however, hear Mom's deafening whistle. She sticks two fingers in her mouth, like a shepherd calling in his sheep. I turn toward the cabanas and see a blue upright shape. That's her. She yells at me to come back. Already? I was here for such a short time . . . Maybe something happened. Maybe Zot choked to death on his pizza. Maybe they've come to take Mom off to jail. I don't know. But just in case I grab a gnarled stick that looks like a duck, thank the sea, and head back, gift in hand, to see what's happened.

"Sorry Luna, I couldn't stand it on my own any longer," Mom says. She wraps her hands around her neck and pretends to strangle herself. "Look at me. My heart's so heavy I can't breathe. Your friend Zot told me the story of his life. I've never heard something so sad."

Zot is still sitting on the wooden railing and holding that slice of Neapolitan pizza in his hand, which looks even bigger than before.

"I'm sorry, Miss, but you asked me to tell you."

"Stop calling me 'Miss.' And how was I supposed to know it would be so depressing?"

"Why," I say, "what's his story?"

"Never mind, Luna, don't ask, not ever. Spare yourself. I'm begging you. It's not to be believed."

"I don't find it so sad," says Zot. "There were good days."

"Believe me, kid, I hope every day for the rest of your life is a good day, starting today, but you don't know the first thing about good days. If I think about that one Christmas and the puppy with a spot over its eye, or that story about the shoes stuffed with—enough, don't make me think about it!"

"Thanks a lot, Mom, I thought you'd called me over because they were taking you to jail—"

"Again with this jail business? I told you, I'm not going to jail!"

"I really hope not. But you beat up Damiano. And his mom."

"I didn't beat them up, drama queen. I kicked each of them once. Big whoop!"

It's true. One kick apiece and that was that. The same spot-on kick in the same place, and both of them hit the ground. Then she ran to the car and while she was hurrying to start the engine she looked at me and told me to always remember this one important thing: Not only does a kick between the legs work on boys, but, delivered hard enough, it can take a woman down too. "Got it, Luna?" I nodded. And maybe one day that info will be of real use to me but I sure hope not.

"If you do go to jail, can I still live at home with Luca?"

"I don't suppose so," says Zot. "They'd probably place you in an orphanage. But perhaps they would pick one close to the prison."

"That's enough!" Mom shouts. She jumps up, grabs her purse, and takes out her cell phone. She dials a number and cradles the phone while fishing another cigarette out of her army shirt, which used to be Luca's but doesn't fit him anymore, so now it's hers, and even if it's for boys, it looks good on her. Everything looks good on Mom.

"I've had it up to here with both of you, let's settle this thing. I'm sick of hearing about it . . . Yes, hello?" Her tone suddenly changes. "I need to talk with the doctor. No, right away, tell him to stop whatever he's doing. Tell him it's urgent. No, wait, tell him Serena wants to speak with him."

She looks at me and winks. Ten seconds later she's back to talking, only this time she speaks in this soft, low voice I've never heard before.

"Hi Giancarlo. How are you? You've already heard. Just as well. I know, I mean, that's why I'm calling. I just want to tell you how sorry I am. I screwed up. I acted like an idiot and I'm very sorry about your son. But not about your wife. That was self-defense. She jumped on top of me. What are you supposed to do when you see someone her size coming at you? I know, I know, she's right to press charges. It makes perfect sense. She deserved it but Damiano didn't. He can't help it if he's not the nicest kid . . . Look, Giancarlo, I don't know how to say this and maybe I shouldn't say anything at all, but when I look at that boy, it's like coming face-to-face with the emblem of your life with another person. And I know you've built something important with her, that it's too late for . . . Anyways, I don't know, I thought I didn't care, but this morning I saw him and this feeling came over me—all this anger, disappointment, pain . . . I'm an idiot, a fool. No, no, Giancarlo, it's true. I made a mistake and I know it. Just telling you these things is a mistake. I'm probably better off keeping my mouth shut. I know, I know you can understand me . . . You and I don't need words to understand one another. We have a spiritual connection, you know. But I shouldn't be saying these things to you. You have your life and family, it's not my place to . . . Forget it, Giancarlo, I'm begging you. My life has always been a disaster and I don't want to ruin yours too. And who knows what'll happen when the court and lawyers get involved? I can't even afford a lawyer. I don't know what I'll do. But that's as it should be. I screwed up and have to pay the price. No, no, Giancarlo, this is how it ought to be, and maybe even these thoughts, these screw-ups, will help me stop thinking about it so much, about how I really feel about you. Maybe we're better off that way, you know? No, no, don't do anything, don't you dare. Don't mess things up with your wife. Really, I don't want you to. I can't ask you to . . . Go back to your patient, Giancarlo. You do good things for people. It's a beautiful thing. It's a calling. I don't deserve your kindness. I don't deserve you. Forget me, Giancarlo, my sweet Giancarlo. Au revoir."

Mom hangs up and puts the phone back in her purse. "All settled. Happy now?"

I'm not sure I understand what just happened. As a matter of fact I don't understand it one bit. But given the tone of her voice and the groan she makes right after, I decide to tell her I am.

Mom finishes her cigarette and uses the end bit to light up another. Then she lies down on her shirt again.

And I go lie down next to her, like we do in bed at night, since there are only two rooms at home and one is Luca's and she and I sleep together in the other one.

"Zot, why don't you lie down for a while?" Mom asks.

"No thank you, I'm still eating."

"I told you, you don't have to finish it. You can throw it away."

"No, really, I like it . . . besides, I can't digest properly if I lie down on a full stomach. Once, when I was at the orphanage—"

"No, please, I can't take another story about the orphanage."

"But it's not a sad story, it's—"

"No, no, I don't care. I'm positive it's heartbreaking."

Zot tells her it's not, and maybe they drag on like that or maybe they change the subject or stop talking alltogether. I don't know because I fall asleep. Words cease to exist. They bleed into the sound of the sea coming and going, coming and going, and everything is one long swishing sound, then that swishing sound becomes a clear, quivering light, before that, too, disappears, and me along with it.

RETIREES DO AS THEY PLEASE

The morning mushroom hunt is taking longer than expected. It's almost ten p.m. and they're still on the road back. Outside the car it's too dark to see anything, especially the end of this narrow windy road that rises and falls as it cuts through the thicket of trees, like something out of a horror movie Sandro saw when he was six years old and will never forget: a guy is driving his car through the middle of the countryside, heading somewhere, maybe for work, but he ends up pulling into a remote little village where everyone is kind and hospitable until it turns out they eat people. In fact, they try to eat him. But he manages to escape. He hops in his car and for a minute the car won't start, but when it does, he takes off full throttle down those mountain roads. And he keeps turning and turning but he doesn't know where he's going, and as a consequence of all that turning, he finds himself back in the same little village where the cannibals have been biding their time and they lunge forward and eat him.

So what if you've never heard talk of cannibals in the Apuan Alps? There are towns up here where, in the cemeteries, you'll find at most three different family names on the gravestones, and when you're forced to marry your cousin who knows what tricks your mind'll play on you. To be safe, it's better to go during the daytime and return home before dark. But they were in the woods till late. For hours they went around in circles looking for one another and now they're fried.

No sooner had he found the King of Porcini than Sandro shouted into his walkie-talkie, "This thing is unreal! It's humongous!" Shortly after which he heard Rambo's voice and a little later Marino's. They told him to hurry over so they could take a look. He said it'd be better if they came to him, since he wasn't exactly sure where he was. But neither did they. All of them were lost.

For a while the only sound Sandro heard was the crackling of the walkie-talkie, and when they began talking again they all started in at once, blaming each other. They wandered the woods haphazardly, firing off fuck-yous, fighting, trying to remember whose genius idea it was to buy walkie-talkies, which may be useful if one person gets lost, but if all three of them get lost then this plastic piece of shit is only good for insulting one another while roaming through the woods in the direction of some wild beast just waiting for sundown to skin them alive.

But in the end no one died and by dinnertime they were all standing around the car. Rambo told them he'd gotten his bearings when the stars came out. Marino had crossed paths with two retirees, mushroom-picking pros, who had escorted him to the car and practically saved his life. The last to arrive was Sandro, who had found his way back to the road by following the music coming from a karaoke bar: for the first time in his life he'd been happy to hear a track by the Pooh.

And when the two retirees saw him carrying the King of Porcini in his arms, they couldn't believe their eyes. Not even these guys had seen anything like it. It was mind-blowing, a giant, the kind of trophy that turns you into a legend overnight.

Sandro nodded and tried to act bored, as though for him plunder of that caliber were the norm, while Rambo hugged him and Marino squeezed them both and kept repeating, "All for one and one for all, brothers. We're saved. Nature's made us stronger. No problems, no fear, no women." Meanwhile the two retirees sized up the mega mushroom, shared a look, and didn't even ask Sandro if he wanted to sell it or how much he was asking. Nope. They just fetched out a hundred-euro bill, a hundred, and reached for the King with their liver-spotted hands.

Sandro hugged it closer to his chest and took a step back. He'd busted his ass to find that mushroom, risked his life in more ways than one, and all he wanted was to go home and show off this bad boy to his dad, who the night before had poked fun of him for a whole half hour: "Where do you think you're going all of a sudden? Do you know the right spots? Do you have a permit? Boots? A basket? Just where do you think you're going?" For his dad, as for dads the world over, any endeavor, from flying to the moon to fixing a bookshelf, is a job that requires eons of preparation, empire-building organization, and every tool in the toolbox.

But real life isn't like that. Oftentimes the important thing in life is to believe in yourself so badly that things can't help but conform to your will and fall into place. Without too much preparation and precaution. All one needs is a kick in the pants to take the air out of all these should-and-shouldn't diatribes and spur one to action. Yeah, that's it, and today Sandro had proved it by finding the King of Porcini. No maps, no boots, nothing whatsoever. And now he was heading home to rub this mind-blowing trophy in his dad's face.

Only the retirees had seen it and decided they had to have it, and when it comes to retirees, the game's rigged. They've worked for years, back when, for kicks, people used to toss money in the air instead of confetti, and even now, when they've stopped working, the checks keep rolling in each month. Retirees are an economic power, and they wander among young people like westerners vacationing in the Third World, laughing at the cost of stuff and frittering away money just to empty their pockets of loose change. If they want something, retirees

won't take no for an answer. In fact, after a brief show of resistance, Sandro caved, pocketed the hundred euros, and handed
over the King of Porcini.

Then he jumped in the car and told Rambo to step on it.

He didn't want to spend another minute with those two old
billionaires who had already placed the King on the ground,
sprinkled a little grass on top to make the scene look more convincing, and with the latest iPhone were snapping thousands of
photos of themselves in poses of astonishment and triumph.
Photos that in the next five minutes would circulate among
their friends and acquaintances, and because these two retirees
were technophiles, in no time the photos would wind up on
forums for mushroom hunters—Sandro's never seen them but
he's positive they exist—to officially break the news world-
wide: it wasn't him who found the King of Porcini but these
two geezers swimming in cash.

Sandro is mulling it over now, at ten at night, curled
uncomfortably in the passenger seat of Rambo's army jeep,
while they continue to search for the road home.

He looks out the window at the thicket of trees that light up
as the car passes then fade back into the single dark wall on
either side. He feels tired. Sure, all day he trekked up and
down the mountains, but it's not that, it's a different kind of
tiredness. It's the tiredness of another day lost to getting lost,
this time in the mountains. But if it's not the mountains then
it's the pine grove where they steal pinecones, or the parking
lot at the mall, or the streets that all look the same where they
deliver phonebooks and flyers announcing store sales and
menus for the next county fair, the pointless roundabouts built
in no man's land that send you every which way but lead
nowhere. How can you get lost all the time if you don't even
know where you're going?

Sandro doesn't know. He doesn't even want to think about

it. He closes his eyes, leans his head against the dewy window, and prays the motion of the car will put him to sleep. Like when he was young and the car trip home took no time. He'd wake up in his mom's arms in the driveway and everything would be over, all would be well. One time he slept five hours straight, from Madonna di Campiglio to Tuscany, in 1985, that banner year his parents were convinced they were rich. Or at least not at the bottom of the ladder. Or, even if they were at the bottom, then it meant that the whole ladder was pointing to better places, and even a gardener's family could afford a ski trip.

"What the hell," his father had said, "I've worked hard all my life and this is one reward I want to reap." Him and Mom in his aunt and uncle's ski suits. They'd even sprung for a new one for Sandro along with a pair of red Moon Boots, whereas two years prior, when a little snow had, incredibly, fallen in Forte dei Marmi, his mom had sent him outside with his shoes wrapped in plastic bags cinched round his ankles with rubber bands.

None of them knew how to ski. His mom spent the whole time keeping toasty in the motel. His dad rented a sled and went up and down a hill in a parking lot. But for Sandro they'd purchased lessons. "You've got years of skiing ahead of you, consider it an investment," said his father, who by then had morphed into an entrepreneur, the kind of guy who saw far into the future, in an era where everything seemed possible and you could climb the social pyramid like it were the sweet snow-capped mountains of Madonna di Campiglio.

On the trip back from that miraculous week, Sandro slept soundly, deep in a dream he still remembers clearly. He was super rich and lived in a mansion on a mountaintop, where people were always asking him for help and his money was the solution to everyone's problems. But too many people came begging and he couldn't get a moment's peace, so Sandro hopped on his private helicopter and fled to the North Pole, and while he was dreaming of that arctic flight he could really feel the propeller blades above him, they shook him and shook him, until finally the blades turned into the hands of his father in the car, shaking him awake now that they'd made it home. A five-hour drive blew by in a dream.

But here on the hard seat in Rambo's derelict army jeep he can't sleep a wink. He thinks back to Madonna di Campiglio, how they never went back after that year, how they never put on another pair of skis again, never scaled another mountain let alone the social pyramid. 1985 remained a mind-blowing one-in-a-million year, a thing of the past, gone forever, just like the King of Porcini, the greatest source of satisfaction he'd had in these dark times, and he'd just sold it for a hundred euros.

But even if he didn't have these thoughts knocking around in his head, it would be hard to sleep with Rambo beside him raining down insults on Marino.

"Are you retarded? The law establishes limits, and those limits are clear and should be respected. And if the law says the limit is eighteen, that means if you meet a girl who's eighteen you're well within your rights to fuck her."

"When was the last time we hung out with an eighteen-year-old?"

"Whatever, I'm speaking hypothetically, obviously!"

Indeed, any time they spoke of women it was pure fantasy: neither Rambo nor Marino had ever succeeded in getting his hands on one, not ever. As for Sandro, who had dated a girl from Calabria for two months in college, and another girl for three months, and who one time at the beach had been taken practically by force by a tourist from Switzerland, well, next to them he looked like an international playboy.

"Besides, that isn't the point," says Rambo. "The point is, now that our friend Sandro is making the rounds of the schools, he's got a serious opportunity. He's surrounded by those fresh, lively young girls, who are of age, I might add, and if he plays his cards right, I bet he can tap a couple. The law's on his side."

"I know, Rambo." From the backseat, Marino's reedy voice is nearly swallowed up by the noise of the car. "But, it's just, I'd feel weird doing it with a girl who's eighteen."

"Here we go again. And why's that?"

"Because they're too young. Or we're too old. Heck, we're more than twice their age. Eighteen's too young."

"And how young is old enough?"

"I don't know. Twenty-three? It's still pretty young, but twenty-three's better."

"Twenty-three? You retard! Italian law says eighteen, where do you get twenty-three from? When you're driving in your car and the sign says—"

"He doesn't drive," says Sandro flatly, without lifting his head off the window, without opening his eyes. "Marino doesn't have a license."

"Oh right, I'd tried to erase that fact from my memory. How pathetic. Anyways, license or no license, you can still get me. So, say you're on the road, and the sign says the speed limit's thirty miles an hour. What do you do? Go ten because thirty feels too fast?"

"What does that have to do with anything? That's different."

"No, no. No way is that different. It's the law. And the law's the same for everybody. For you the driver going thirty an hour, and for Sandro, who, if he capitalizes on this opportunity, gets to fuck an eighteen-year-old. We're all good, law-abiding people. And they say no one grows up in Italy. Well, obviously. If they treat you like a baby when you're eighteen, what're you supposed to do? Besides, Marino my friend, these eighteen-year-olds today would make your head spin. Just ask Sandro here. He's snowed under every day. Right, Sandro? Sandro? Yo, Sandro!"

Rambo reaches his hand out and slams him on the back—two, three, fifty times—but Sandro doesn't answer. He keeps looking out at the dark road, so narrow that branches scrape the windows.

"Yo, Sandro, go on, tell him, would you? What are the girls like at school? Sluts, right? What are they like, huh, what are they like? Go on, tell him, go on . . . "

"I don't know," he says after a while, "more than the girls, there are some knockout moms."

He answers robotically, with no intonation, just to make Rambo shut up. Rambo, on the other hand, yells louder and tells him to go fuck himself, that moms are everywhere, you can find them in the supermarket, at the doctor's—who gives a shit about moms when you're at school? And then Marino says if a woman is a mom, it probably means she's also married, and therefore it's not right to do her either. To which Rambo yells, "Marino, you don't like moms and you don't like daughters. In my opinion, you don't like pussy period!"

And Marino, on cue, swears he does, and Rambo says he doesn't. Do too, do not, do too . . . But Sandro's stopped listening. He's already drifted off: talk of pretty mothers was enough to send him back to that glorious afternoon last week during parent-teacher conferences. A beautiful moment, a sliver of life so luminous that, to think back on it, it doesn't even feel like part of his private collection. And yet it is, and simply remembering it, he feels something warm in his throat, in his chest, even his head resting against the dewy window.

As if to warm himself by that roaring fire, Sandro inches forward and leaps into the flames of life and emotion and, yes, why not, the flames of love.

And he begins to remember everything exactly as it happened.

EINSTEIN COULDN'T TIE HIS SHOES

On top of it all, Sandro hadn't even wanted to go to school that afternoon. He'd presented his case to the principal: he'd just started working, the kids hardly knew who he was, what was the point of talking to their parents? And the principal replied, "Don't be afraid. Just say what you can. Don't overdo it. Err on the side of vagueness and you shouldn't run into any problems."

But the problem is that Sandro can't stand vagueness. Even worse is seeing the disappointed looks on these mothers' faces, nearly all of them well groomed and decked out for the occasion, anticipating an afternoon unlike all the others, a special moment in their monotonous lives of set schedules and disenchantment round every bend, and instead one by one they yawn in your face while you tender the most meaningless statements in the world: Your son's not doing badly but neither is he doing great. Your daughter makes an effort but could make more of an effort . . .

Sandro talks while they listen with one ear, watch the clock, and finally walk away, their eyes bloodshot with boredom thanks to this bland, inept teacher who in five minutes will fade from their memory.

And Sandro won't accept that. He doesn't want to fade. He wants these moms to like him. He wants to bypass their heads and reach their hearts and from there enter their bloodstream and spread to their entire body. He wants them to return home eager to tell their husbands about this fabulous young teacher who in just two weeks has understood these kids better than their parents. He wants some hidden corner of their minds to burn bright with the thought that a teacher this perceptive might understand them too—their doubts, their needs, everything that the rest of the world has never known how to see. And, who knows, were they not married, were he not their kid's teacher . . .

Yes, that's what Sandro wants. That's what all serious teachers should want. Otherwise, if you lack passion, you're merely stealing money from the state. So, when another mom walked in with her head hung low, humiliated by her previous conferences and resigned to endure yet another, saying, "Sorry, I'm Erik Conti's mother, sorry," Sandro had had enough. He leapt to his feet, swung round from behind his desk, and shook her hand.

"Ah, Erik's mom, finally! Great kid you've got, Miss."

She peeled her eyes off the floor and looked up at him, confused, like someone expecting to be pummeled and being kissed on the mouth instead. "Sorry? You mean my Erik? Erik Conti?"

"That's the one. What an intellect! Highly unusual, sure, but very lively."

"Honestly the math teacher just told me he's the one reason her class is behind."

"Oh, that's typical. Teachers who don't know how to run their classes always blame the kids. Besides, between you and me, do you really expect someone who teaches math to understand a thing about life?" Sandro winks at her. The woman lets slip a timid smile, tries to conceal it, doesn't succeed.

He should stop there. He's gone far enough. But that smile, that look . . . It's the first time Sandro has felt good at this school. Actually it's the first time he's felt good in months. So his mouth runs on autopilot: "Don't worry, miss, you'll have lots to be happy about in the future. You might have to swallow some bitter pills today, but one day you'll be walking down the street with your son and all these people will have to eat their petty words."

"Are you sure about that? I love Erik and all, but I don't see this great intellect you're talking about."

"Clearly. But his is an original, brilliant, unconventional intellect. Van Gogh was a genius, and you'll recall he cut his ear off, just like that, to pass the time."

"That's true, I heard that."

"And Einstein? Did you know Einstein couldn't tie his shoes?"

"Really?"

"Yep. His sister tied them for him. And if his sister wasn't around, Einstein would leave the house in slippers." Now that he's gotten going there's no holding back. What does it matter if he's not sure Einstein had a sister? What matters is that Erik Conti has a mom and now that mom is happy. And she's listening to Mr. Mancini with her hands on her chest and passion in her throat. She's trying to stay cool but it's clear she wants to hug him hard and love him till it hurts.

"Neither does my Erik, Mr. Mancini! Erik doesn't know how to tie his shoes either!"

"Excuse me?"

"Nope, he can't put on his pants or brush his teeth by himself," she says, her voice now swelling with pride.

Sandro nods and smiles, though his smile is starting to wane. It's slowly beginning to dawn on him who Erik Conti is. He's the "problem" student in sore need of a tutor but after cuts to the budget they'd decided he could go without just fine. And while Sandro conducts his lesson, this boy spends the whole hour at his desk scratching his forehead with his index finger and squinting while muttering under his breath something that sounds like "councilor" but maybe—let's hope—isn't "councilor."

That's who Erik Conti is. But by now Sandro has spoken,

overdone it, ignited a happiness in this mom she hasn't felt in years. She smiles, giggles uncontrollably, snatches the teacher's hand and won't let go. Maybe she doesn't really believe all these wonderful things about her son but they're beautiful to hear and she'll hang on to them for at least the time it takes to travel home from school. A dream, once begun, can last a lifetime or five minutes. It doesn't matter which. A dream always begins by lasting an eternity.

Erik's mom bids Sandro goodbye and heads for the door, walking backwards so she can continue to gaze at him and say thank you. And once she's gone, Sandro feels a tad disheartened when no one else comes in after her.

He'd like to keep this up till tomorrow. He'd like to feel this way his whole life. Indeed he stays there, sits back down at his desk, and waits. But nothing. So he gathers the pencils and papers he'd used to draw circles and lines while he was talking, as if those symbols were an extension of his precious thoughts, and puts them in his bag. He grabs some pens technically belonging to the school but which no one uses, puts them in his bag as well, gets up, and heads for the door.

And just as he's about to leave, a wave crashes down on him. It sends him reeling. He drops on the floor like a wet sock. Sandro barely has time to close his eyes. He no longer knows where the floor begins and the ceiling ends. Everything is spinning, him most of all, and when he hears this sharp crack at first he thinks something far off has shattered into a thousand little pieces before he realizes it's his tailbone.

Splayed out on the floor, he massages the bone, while a voice above him keeps repeating, "Sorry, sorry, sorry. I'm so, so sorry!" Sandro shakes his head, picks himself back off the ground, and slowly catches his breath. He looks up, sees what almost killed him, and gasps all over again: standing before Sandro is the most beautiful woman in the world.

"I'm sorry! I know I'm late but there was this old woman without an appointment who wanted a perm and then I couldn't find my car keys or locate the right classroom and I swept into the room and I found you! I'm really sorry. But, look, I never come to teacher conferences. This is my first time and I specifically came to see you. So even if I almost killed you, you can take it as a compliment, I think. Don't you?"

He doesn't answer, doesn't even nod or shake his head. He can't. He's staring into her eyes, her big, dark, totally uninhibited eyes under her chestnut-blond bangs. Had someone asked a minute earlier, Sandro would have said that bangs suck, that it's a haircut for stupid kids or goths obsessed with the Middle Ages. But now he realizes it's the best haircut in the universe, hands down, the perfect fit for a face like hers, a body like hers (hot even in jeans and an army shirt), two eyes without eyeliner that still manage to dazzle after a day's work, that give the whole cosmetics and fashion industry a spanking.

"Mr. Mancini, listen, you're the expert here and I wouldn't dream of telling you how to do your job, but maybe we could take a seat?" The corners of her lips curl into a half smile.

"Yes, of course." Sandro bolts for his desk, indicates a chair, sits down, and pops back up again, waiting for her to take her seat before sitting down himself. He looks at her. He knows he has to say something intelligent, say anything, but how can he? They're so close, and she continues to smile that smile, to have those eyes. Eyes that Sandro now realizes he recognizes: the eyes of Serena, the prettiest girl in school, whom he had spent his entire adolescence thinking about and never once mustered the courage to talk to. Holy shit, here he is, mustering it, by accident, twenty years on.

"Listen, I came because my son won't stop talking about you. 'My English teacher this, my English teacher that . . . ' I figured I'd come see the famous Mr. Mancini for myself. But if it's too late and you'd rather not talk, just say the word."

There's a touch of regret in her voice. Maybe she's disappointed. Yet her smile hasn't vanished. Suddenly Sandro gets it, this amazing and terrifying thing: that's no smile, that's her natural look, not some momentary marvel but a remarkable condition that goes on and on. The man who loves this woman gets to see that his whole life. All he needs to do is turn around and there it'll be, even on hard days, even when things don't go as planned, a reminder he has at least one gigantic reason to be happy.

And Sandro envies him, this man, even if he must have sweat blood to be with someone like her. Because you have to give up your life to be with this kind of woman: no crew of friends, no personal hobby, no concert-binging and crap of that kind, just a life committed to being with her and making sure she doesn't slip away. Good God, what he wouldn't give to be that man.

And this thought, half-hope and half-desperation, so addles his brain that when he finally manages to speak, instead of saying something beautiful or profound or, if nothing else, rational, Sandro asks her the most pointless and obvious question there is: "Sorry, whose mother are you?"

And of course she opens her lovely mouth and says, "Pleased to meet you. I'm Serena, Luca's mom."

Of course. Who else could the most beautiful woman in the world give birth to but the most exceptional kid in the world? Sandro almost apologizes for having asked. He takes a breath and unleashes a cascade of compliments, not much of a challenge after extolling the virtues of Erik, the kid who can't tie his shoelaces. With Luca it's a breeze. Except while telling Serena how marvelous and intelligent and magical her son is, Sandro realizes all too well there's no point. He can hear it in her voice and see it in her eyes; she hears these compliments every day. By now they probably bore her. So, after checking off the thousand wonderful things Luca does and the million wonderful things he'll one day do, Sandro arrives at the one thing Luca can't do: the trip to Biarritz she refuses to let him take. Because it's patently unfair, and helping Luca is very important to him, and the discussion only inadvertently serves the purpose of making a good impression on Serena, of showing her that he's a teacher, true, but also a man, a real man who lives life to its fullest, who takes the bull by the horns and bites bullets and knows what's best for himself and others.

"I know it's none of my business, Serena. Luca is a minor and you can decide whether or not to let him go to Biarritz. The choice is yours. But I'm asking you, are you positive you can choose for him?"

"What do you mean?"

"I mean in my opinion you can't. In my opinion you can't decide for Luca. A kid like that, you can't stop him or push him. He exists on a different plane, he's up here, doing his own thing. I don't know how to explain it, it's as though . . . hmm, I don't know."

"I don't know either, but it's true."

"Well then, you can spend your whole life wondering whether or not to let him go, but it's not as though you can really decide for Luca. It's more about you just trying to do something, like Wile E. Coyote and his umbrella."

"Huh?"

"You know the cartoon, Wile E. Coyote, the one who chases after the Road Runner."

"Yeah, sure."

"There's this thing he does all the time. He winds up in a ravine or canyon or someplace like that, looks up, and sees a giant boulder hurtling toward him. And instead of stepping aside, he whips out an umbrella. Remember? A really small umbrella that he opens and huddles under. Then the boulder comes crashing down and crushes him."

"Yeah, so?"

"So I think by trying to stop Luca you're doing the same thing Coyote does with the giant boulder. You can open your umbrella, but it won't do you much good."

Serena looks at him, sinking her marvelous, liquid eyes into his. "All right, teacher, you're saying I should let him go, huh?"

Sandro nods firmly, as if he's a firm man—firm and full of wisdom—someone who knows what's best in life, and lucky the woman who finds herself by his side.

For a moment Serena says nothing. She gets up, goes to leave, then turns back. "That cartoon always pissed me off."

"Me too," says Sandro.

Serena snorts and makes a face. She doesn't want to smile but she does. And that smile stays with Sandro even after she's left the room, even after he, too, leaves and goes home.

Even now, as he thinks back on it, and his heart skips a beat or two.

LIKE HELL I'M CALLING HER LUNA

S erena had those two kids herself. She's not into men, so she went to a clinic in Switzerland and picked their daddy out of a catalog."

"Serena bought those two kids from Gypsies who abducted them in the market. They charged her half price for the second one."

But this is your favorite: "Serena had those two kids with a priest, a young handsome priest who was prepared to give up the priesthood to be with her. But when the second kid was born that white he thought it was a sign from Heaven and repented. Now he lives in a monastery in the mountains."

Those are the rumors around town, those and a thousand worse. New ones crop up every day and sooner or later they reach the ears of Miss Gemma, who relays them to you and you laugh long and hard. Because they're not born of spite. They grow like mold in the wintertime, when there's no one around in Forte dei Marmi and if you want something to happen you have to make it up yourself. The kids fall back on drugs or find more imaginative ways of wriggling free of the world. Men go hunting or fishing and spend the night playing video poker or—to save a buck—picking up trannies. Women don't go in for hobbies that involve getting your hands dirty and they don't know where to procure drugs, so if they're decent-looking they have affairs and if they're not they pass the time making them up about other people around town.

That's the way it is. That's the norm. And a young woman with two kids and no man in sight is almost asking for it. That there are a thousand ridiculous rumors circulating about Luca and Luna's dad is inevitable. The only rumor that doesn't circulate is the truth, since you're the only one who knows that, Serena.

And it's much more ridiculous than any of the tales you've heard.

Spring, 1996. You're twenty-two. You finished high school without a single fail and enrolled in pre-law, just like all your friends. And for a few years you manage to plow ahead, mornings on campus, afternoons studying, but every once in a while you look up from those millions of minor laws policing minor issues and think you owe an apology to the hours spent in doctors' waiting rooms or in line at the post office, to homebound Sundays sick with fever, to afternoons Mom sent you kicking and screaming to flute lessons and you sat in a room with the blind instructor who smelled like piss. You owe an apology to all the worst things in your life, because now that you're studying law, you realize they were hardly the worst. This is the worst. And continuing any further is impossible. You can't do it. Your mother always told you that you'd never amount to anything in life because you never saw things through to the end. Sure, you may be partly to blame, but so are things that suck, and instead of seeing them through you just want to drop them. Or rather, instead of abandoning them all at once, you do what you do, setting them on the ground for a minute, pulling away just a tad, staring up at the sky, and taking one step, then another, then another, continuing to get farther and farther away from them, leaving them to wilt on the side of the road.

You do the same with college. You don't drop out or withdraw or do anything as drastic as that. You just decide to find a summer job to pay for your loans and books, and then a friend of your dad offers you a weird job working the county fair circuit.

Your dad's a butcher and the guy who supplies his meat slicers and scales has a side operation selling other weird equipment at county fairs in Tuscany and Emilia. He needs someone young, someone who can stand on her feet all day and has a way with words to call people's attention to the Super Mondial 2000 and convince them that this marvelous device for crushing garlic cloves, scaling fish, pitting olives, and slicing cucumbers will change their lives.

So you begin touring the country, traveling nonstop, a new town every day, like a starlet. True, rather than New York and Tokyo your bus pulls into Settignano, Ponte a Egola, La Rosa di Terricciola, Terranuova Bracciolini: bizarre places crammed between two intersections and comprising a couple of slanted houses, half a church, and a bar with an arcade in back. Places so godawful on the big day of the trade show, with its riot of people and kids and bands, you shudder to think what they're like the day after, when the streets have cleared and paper, torn plastic, and bean skins spin around silently in empty space. Lucky for you, you're gone the day after. The day after you're already at another town fair, telling a new yet totally identical public about the miracles this stainless steel tool performs.

Old ladies lured by the power of garlic presses, sniveling kids, men only interested in the snug, low-cut shirt you're forced to wear ("A skirt'd be nice but it's not obligatory. You're behind a table so your thighs barely show"). To avoid facing them, you look down at the Super Mondial 2000, take a breath, and fire away:

"Ladies and gentlemen, I hold in my hands something you could call a garlic press or a meat tenderizer or a fish scaler or an olive pitter. You could call it many things. But it's actually something much simpler and more significant. What you see in front of you, folks, is the Future. And the Future will save you a lot of hard work, a lot of time, and a lot of useless gadgets."

Meanwhile you slip two or three cloves of garlic (four won't fit) into the special groove, crush them, and exhibit the pungent pulp that has slid through six holes in the front grid. Then you reopen the utensil and hold up the two empty skins in your fingers.

"How many times have you had to crush tons of cloves, ladies, while also pitting olives and scaling fish? And how confusing are all those contraptions? And who's going to clean them? You are, clearly. Because even if you pray your hubbies will handle it . . . "

The women shake their heads, smile bitterly, volunteer their own comments: "Yeah, right." "Fat chance." "Dream on."

"And just look at how sturdy and powerful this tenderizer is, ladies. It works well for pork chops and scaloppini . . . and your husbands when they're not listening."

At this point people start laughing and—you hope—someone decides to take this shitty hunk of steel home.

And so it goes, day in, day out. The names of the towns and fairs change, but everything else stays the same. Same spiel, same choreographed moves, same smell of roasted pork and sausage saturating the air, and that mix of garlic and fish you can't wash from your hands. Day after day after identical day. You talk, you demonstrate, you crush, you scale, you pit, you pray.

And then one June Wednesday in San Vincenzo he appears.

There he is, being shoved by the crowds in front of your stall yet still holding your gaze. He couldn't care less about what you're selling. He stares straight into your eyes. Arms crossed, a flimsy shirt that looks made of canvas, ripped jeans, bare feet. No flip-flops or sandals or anything—he's actually barefoot. You haven't a clue how he manages to get down the street. All you know, Serena, is that he can't take his eyes off of you.

He looks straight through you, so deep that for a second you stop speaking. It's not the look of someone staring at a person but of someone scanning the horizon. Only you're the horizon.

Your legs shake, just as your friends always said, those ditzes who come to you for advice when they're in trouble because they know they'll find someone who'll advise them: "Tell him to go to hell, forget about him, don't waste a minute on that guy." Giving advice about certain things is so easy, comes so naturally, sounds so true. But it's not true now. You put down the Super Mondial 2000 and keep looking at him, and maybe it's all that talk under the blazing sun, or maybe you're tired after waking up at five, but whatever it is, you're not yourself. You're another person, someone you don't recognize. You don't know what kind of girl she is. You only know that this girl wants to tell the fish, garlic, olives, and old folks to fuck off, them and their questions about how much this stupid gizmo costs and how come the last olive wasn't properly pitted. This girl wants to kick over the stall and go to him.

But there's no need. He comes to you. He pushes past your audience, which is slowly breaking up, unsatisfied. You try to clean your hands with a towel, but he takes them in his. He's taller than you but not too tall. He smiles but it's not the smile of someone who's into himself. It's the smile of someone who's into you. He touches your skin, your throat, your wrists, travels up your spine, down your ribs, and, it goes without saying, reaches your heart.

Which is beating fast, but not as fast as you're moving. Neither of you has spoken a word yet already you're in the pine grove behind the square. People pass by on their way to the beach, and children chase after each other screaming, but there are several bushes to hide behind, and you're on the ground, undressed, him on top of you, inside you. But talking is impossible. You tried to at first. You said, "But I, I . . . " and he pressed his lips against your lips and you began kissing, him kissing you and sucking on your tongue, nibbling your lips, pulling your hair and drawing you close, and he plunges deeper and deeper into you, to a place you never knew existed, but as soon as he gets there it wakes up from its eternal slumber, trembles and melts, and you feel this gigantic wave, as powerful as the waves you rode at the beach as a kid, that spun you around till you no longer knew up from down, and for a moment you felt you were drowning, then finally, breathlessly, you resurfaced, ready to ride another.

You don't know how much time passes. An hour, a century, a second. And you stay there, lying on your back, him on top of you, his breath warm and salty in your hair, on the nape of your neck. You could stay this way forever, mushrooms could sprout on top of you, insects build a nest between you, it wouldn't be a problem, go on, grow, just as long as you can stay like this forever.

But five minutes later he draws back, stands, pulls his pants up, and looks at you with his green, almost watery eyes. And you hear his voice, raspy and deep. All he says is "Call him Luca."

He pulls a cigarette out of his pocket before vanishing in the pines like smoke. And you'd like to get up and run after him but first you have to put your clothes on. You can't find your shoes, and when you find them you no longer know where he went, or maybe you do, but you don't know what you'd say to him.

You don't even know what those three ridiculous words mean: "Call him Luca." Call who Luca? Maybe you misheard him. Maybe he said, "Call me Luca." If only it were his name. You made love to a man in a pine grove in the middle of a fair and you don't even know his name and you don't understand a thing.

But a month later you do. And you call the baby Luca.

There. That's the true story of how your son was born. And if a more ridiculous story in the world exists, you haven't heard it. Actually, there is one that's even crazier, and it's the story of how Luna was born five years later.

Five years that could have been beautiful had it not been for your mother. Every day you saw in her eyes the shame and scandal of having a daughter with a fatherless child. As if her eyes didn't say it all, your mother felt compelled to tell you so, with a hand on her heart and horror in her voice.

Yet one night, five years later, rather than fight about it, you leave Luca and go out with friends. Some are still struggling to graduate, some work as paralegals for this or that law firm, others are clinging to a different line of work. Like you. You no longer work the fair circuit. You do shampoos and dye jobs at a salon and are just beginning to cut hair. The clientele tell you how good you are while the men mostly stick to remarking on your looks. And to get them to leave you alone you tell them you have a kid. Only they don't leave you alone. They stand there like they've been bludgeoned, then come back for more. So you tell them you're into women. Even after that a lot of men don't quit. Actually they get turned on. So then you tell them you have AIDS, which isn't kind and may in fact be a horrible thing to say, but hell, it works. The room clears out immediately.

And that's fine by you, since the one man you need is always by your side. Luca is five years old and hasn't cried once, never thrown a fit. It used to make you sad the way every mom thinks her kid is the best thing going on the planet, and all it takes is one "Me go poo" to make her think she's given birth to a genius. Yet sometimes Luca says stuff so intelligent it scares you. Like yesterday, when you were coming back from work and struggling to steady the bike on its kickstand and he was sitting on the grass in the yard with his back against a sycamore, staring into space. He stood up, walked over to you, and said, "One of these nights you have to go out, Mom. You're young. It's only fair you go out with your friends. I'll keep an eye on Grandma and Grandpa."

So that Saturday you go out. Your friends couldn't believe you'd called. They're thrilled and you're all excited and you plan the ultimate night out: cocktails, dinner, dancing at a nightclub by the beach south of Viareggio, in an area called Costa dei Barbari, one long strip of bars and clubs, clubs and bars. And it's like a party, Serena's party, your friends say so and you say so too. You clink glasses loaded with ice and cocktails and everything is peachy: the jokes, the laughs, the talk of men whom one of them likes but can't have, or who don't like her enough, or who like her but she likes someone else. There's the smell of evenings when summer's on its way with a glass in hand and the music bumping. There's the breeze that picks up the scent of jasmine from who knows where and carries it all the way to a bar crowded with people drenched in sweat.

To top it off, he's there. Out on the street.

You're about to enter the nightclub, and he's there alone, smoking by the entrance. He sees you; you see him. For five years you've rehearsed this scene, which for all you knew may never have happened. At first you thought that if by some stroke of bad luck it did happen, this asshole would have to get comfy and endure what you had to say for hours and hours, your pure venom, screeds spit up from your throat and chest, where all your hatred had been left to ferment, all your rancor for this man who shows up and takes what he wants and disappears and leaves you with a belly on the brink of exploding and shards of a life you no longer know the shape of. But then Luca was born. Luca began to walk, talk, look at you in such a way as to make you feel the reverse, that the world was all wrong and you two, you two alone, were right. So then you decided that if you saw him, you wouldn't attack him, you wouldn't even yell at him. No, you'd pretend not to see him. You'd pretend to be someone else. What was important was that he never come near you nor that beautiful boy you call your son, *your* son, whom he doesn't even know exists. What are the odds he'd comprehend what a marvel the kid is?

But then you pass him and tell the others, "Go on ahead, I'll be there in a minute," and you're not sure what you want to do. Maybe you've returned to your initial idea: acting the adult is all well and good but nothing's ever gained by it, so maybe you'll go say something, briefly, and you'll spit every word, and every word you spit will be a slap in the face. You walk up to him in strides so long your skirt strains underneath, head down, teeth clenched in anger. But he just smiles at you. He smiles calmly, cigarette in mouth. He takes a drag and tosses it. And just as you're about to lunge at him he opens his arms and you wind up hugging him. You don't know how or why. If you did, you might at least have a clue about what would happen in the next five minutes (five minutes!) before stretching out on the sand behind some resort beach chairs left out in the sultry night air, with the lights of fishing boats off the shore and a few couples cuddling. You don't waste time cuddling; no sooner do you get there than he's wiped out all the bitterness inside you with a kiss. He cups your face and looks at you in this puzzling manner that still takes your breath away. A minute later you feel his hand pulling your hair, turning you around, tugging your dress so hard he almost tears it, while with his other hand he squeezes your side and presses you against him. Another minute and he's on top of you, inside you, everywhere. And there are people who can hear you, there are a million reasons you shouldn't be here, yet you feel like screaming, and you yourself don't even know what you want to scream, and fortunately you'll never know because he sticks his fingers in your mouth and you feel like biting down on them but instead start sucking them, they taste like cigarettes and something else you like but you don't know what, you don't know anything anymore. Every thrust is harder and deeper, a step closer to a world where it doesn't matter who you are, what you want, right from wrong. And it goes on, this time out of time that lends everything meaning, and you wake up every day and dress and tidy up and leave the house because you know that occasionally, amid the blur of days, a sliver of this moment will surface and justify everything else.

And everything else includes the beach, the sand beneath your knees, the half-torn skirt, his breath on your neck that tastes like smoke and maybe pine trees—that clear, sticky, sweet resin that won't wash off once it's touched your skin.

You stand up and look at him, not wanting to be seen like this, disheveled, sweaty, sand all over, your shirt ragged and your face red. You especially don't want him to see the waves of pleasure running through you, which you can still feel breaking inside you, the brief, slight shocks you can't make stop.

Suddenly he pulls away and you catch sight of the enormous round moon in the sky. If someone were to ask, you'd say it wasn't there before, you would have noticed. It's almost like a pale sun, low-slung and close by. It casts light on the beach while he wipes the sand off his legs, lies down on top of you again, brushes your ear with his lips, and whispers in that rough voice, that voice made of resin, "Call her Luna."

At the time it didn't even occur to you to think, "Like hell he's knocked me up again." You didn't even think about fetching that pill which, when you're in doubt, resets everything.

Not you, Serena. You thought: "Like hell I'm calling her Luna."

What a stupid name, a name for seventies-era hippies, you'd never call her that. Especially when it turns out your friend Susy knows him. What he looks like anyway. He was a friend of a friend of her boyfriend, but she hasn't seen him in a century, ever since he went to jail, for drugs or something, people beaten till they had brain damage. His name is Stefano but everyone calls him the Guillotine on account of a tattoo on his chest, a black guillotine with the blade falling, about to finish the job. And when she tells you, you nod, although you don't have a clue whether it's true, you've never seen the chest of the man who fathered your son and this other baby on its way. And you still don't know if it's a boy or a girl or if you'll even keep it. All you know is you're not calling it Luna.

Actually, no, there's another thing you know: you're done with men. You're intelligent, practical, sharp, and always clear-headed when it comes to what other women should do with men. But if you think about the men in your life, well, what a horror show. Were you the kind who gave it up to every guy she met, the kind who went home with a different someone every night, or two someones, or three, at least then you could understand. With large numbers it's normal for there to be a dope, a dick, a mental retard—that's the price of so many generous acts, of so much action. But not you, Serena, you never give it up. Then one night every thousand years for some mysterious reason it happens, and you give in bad. To men with hang-ups, men who, at forty, still have their mothers lay their clothes out for them so they won't be baffled about what to wear. Men who tell you every little detail about the getaway weekend they want to spend with you yet can't find a minute to inform you they have a wife and kids. Men who don't do anything for work but follow their big dreams to become artists and hang around the beach all day sculpting their abs into their own private symbol of infinity . . . The treasure chest is terrifying. And now, perhaps, complete. All you were missing was a drug-dealing ex-con who has probably already forgotten you.

And that's just fine. He doesn't remember and you don't want to. He doesn't exist. Nothing this shitty should exist for you two, it's just you and Luca and this little girl—that's right, a girl—who will be joining you soon, although for now she's just a belly so big she could easily have swallowed your feet last month and you wouldn't have noticed.

Then one day you open the newspaper, out of boredom, to shut out your mom's voice, to not have to see her shaking her head and thumping the space where her heart should be, and there in the paper is a picture of him, Stefano the Guillotine, next to an older man and a woman staring daggers with an Eastern name. Kaput below the exit ramp for Lucca, at the bottom of the canal. Witnesses say another car was chasing them. The police investigate but everyone has a rough idea about what happened, and you don't want to know any more than you already do. You cut out the Guillotine's photo and place it in a drawer. Then one night you take it outside and burn it in the yard, letting the sea breeze carry away the ashes while life carries you away, as only life knows how, randomly and as far away as possible.

And you call her Luna.

GIANT PORCINI IN GARFAGNANA TOWN TO CELEBRATE TWO RECORD-HOLDING RETIREES

SERAVEZZA. Two expert mushroom hunters from Seravezza, Gualtiero Stagi and Walter Francesconi, hit the jackpot yesterday. In an area whose location has for obvious reasons been kept secret, the two retirees discovered a porcino mushroom (*Boletus aereus*) weighing a whopping 3.2 kg.

Connoisseurs have come from all over Italy to catch a glimpse of the record-breaking mushroom, including a representative from the Italian Mycological Union. The University of Pisa has also made a bid to examine the magnificent specimen. Understandably, the two stars of the event are elated.

"We were heading home after a pretty dull day," said 65-year-old Stagi, a former stonecutter, "when we noticed this weird pile of leaves. We couldn't see the mushroom just yet, but we've been doing this for years, we knew we had to check it out. It was the most beautiful feeling of my life."

70-year-old Francescani, a former councilor in Versilia's Public Works Department, hopes their find will help send a message.

"The same day we found the biggest porcini on record, us 'geezers' helped save the lives of three boys who'd gotten lost in the mountains, probably after a night of partying. I'd just like to say to all you seniors out there, 'Never say die!' As for you kids, 'Say no to drugs.'"

For those interested in learning more, the two lucky hunters will recount their adventure tonight at 9 P.M. in the Town Hall Council Chambers.

—Teresa Bartolaccini

"Sons of bitches," says Sandro. But Rambo's already said it a thousand times, as has Marino, who never curses because he's afraid he'll let one slip in front of the kids at catechism.

"I say we go there tonight and tear them a new asshole," says Rambo, leaning against the newsstand window. The giant porcini is the leading story in *Il Tirreno* and appears in *La Nazione* right below a help wanted ad for five jobs at a large household appliances warehouse.

Rambo had called the others as soon as he saw it. Marino arrived immediately. He'd been riding around on his bike and still had on his traffic uniform. Sandro had been stuck in a teachers' meeting where he'd said nothing and heard less, but eventually he'd shown up too. They look at the giant photo of those two goddamn geezers holding the King of Porcini in one hand and giving a thumbs-up with the other. "Sons of bitches, sons of bitches!" In their rage they wring the pages of *Il Tirreno* as if it were the necks of those two goddamn old guys.

"Easy, boys," says the newsstand lady. "If you crumple it like that I can't sell it anymore!" Rambo tells her to take a hike.

The lady happens to be Rambo's mom, and Rambo's mom happens to own the newsstand. She and Rambo's dad bought it with the money they made selling their chicken shack to the Esselunga supermarket. Rambo's sister, Christina, is seven years his junior and lives in Boston. She's a researcher for medical equipment, the pride of her parents. The only thing that kept them up at night was this older pigheaded son of theirs who was permanently dressed for the trenches. So, with the money from the chicken shack, they acquired the newsstand and a location. And what a location: right in the center of Forte dei Marmi, a hub of foot traffic where even in the dead of winter they stand a fighting chance, and during summer they could spit in their customers' faces and still turn a profit.

Rambo might not go so far as to spit on customers, but he comes close. That's just how he is. He blows his top easily. He foams with rage when people come in at sunup looking for the paper before it's arrived, or in the evening when he's sold out, or ask for a copy of *Corriere della Sera*—not today's but yesterday's—or *La Repubblica* without the insert, or the insert without *La Repubblica*. In the end Rambo goes berserk, and if some out-of-towner asks if he happens to stock *Yachting*, he starts yelling at him to pay his taxes and sends him running for the door. Once, when a notary from Florence purchased *Beautiful Homes* and asked for a ten-cent discount, Rambo responded that the guy's wife was giving discounts in the alley out back.

Since then, his parents man the register full time, his dad in the morning and his mom in the afternoon. After a lifetime of working, they'd bought the newsstand thinking they'd no longer have to worry about their son. Now they work even harder than before. And all they ask of Rambo is to steer clear of the shop, a job he'd excelled at until today, when he dropped by on his way to the shooting range and froze upon spotting those two old bastards with the King of Porcini.

"Let's crash this thing and stir shit up," he says.

"I can't, I'm on duty," says Marino, his blue uniform big as a bathrobe.

"Me neither. I have homework to grade."

"Not now. Tonight, at the meeting, in front of everyone! We'll show up and tell people what really went down."

"Who's going to believe us? We have no proof," Marino snivels.

"Actually, I got off a shot of the mushroom," says Sandro. It's true, he'd taken a photo to send to Luca. "It's hard to make out but you can see it."

"Attaboy, Sandro, that's the mother of all proof! We'll take that to Seravezza and rip them a new one. Come on, let's go get it blown-up poster-size and—"

"But I'm on duty."

"And I've got homework to grade."

"You guys are a couple of limp turds," says Rambo, slamming the paper on the ground. Just then an old lady exits the newsstand, loses her balance, and almost falls over. Rambo rushes to her aid, catches her, and holds her steady.

"Oh dear, thank you, son. My knee gave out."

"No worries, ma'am, it happens."

"It does when you're my age. Getting old is awful, boys. Enjoy yourselves while you're young and carefree. Happiness dwindles."

"We'll try, lady."

"Then again, did you see those two men from Seravezza? We might be old but we're a lot tougher than the next generation."

The lady says so and then nods approvingly at her own remark, seeing as the three boys don't. She takes a few more tentative steps, grabs hold of a tricycle with a basket in back, and struggles to straddle it.

She pushes it to the curb and stops to check for cars, even though it's the off-season and she could cross the road with her eyes closed. Hell, if she wanted to, she could lay a blanket in the middle of the road and eat lunch there. But just when she's finally made up her mind to blast off, a jeep comes tearing down the coastal road, honks, starts to brake, swerves into the other lane, and just brushes past her, then continues on its way, delivering a few fuck-yous with its horn.

The lady doesn't even notice. She looks down, checks to see if her tires have enough air in them, then leisurely rides away.

Rambo picks *Il Tirreno* off the ground and smooths it out with his hand. "Pity."

T he tires of the Graziella are flat. As usual. They've got holes and need replacing, but her husband says they're old is all, they may lose a little air but as long as he pumps them up every morning, they'll do.

Maybe so. But now they're flat, and Ines pedals with difficulty, late for 5 o'clock mass and taking the long way round to boot. She usually passes by the little square with the grocer's and the mobile center, but not when she's on her way to church. Because the mobile center used to be a bakery, and if she passes by there, she'll start thinking about the summer of 1952 when she was twenty-two and her husband was still her boyfriend and had gone to work in Emilia for a roofing company so that he could come back with money to burn and they could get married.

While she waited for him back home, she gave her mother a hand with her needlework, and every day that summer— every single day, without fail—right after lunch Ines would go to the bakery, knock gently on the shutters, and the baker's assistant would lead her to the back of the shop where they'd make love.

His name was Luigi. A rail-thin kid from Liguria, he didn't talk much, but she was crazy about him nonetheless. The day they met she had shown up late to buy a loaf of bread and it was just the two of them in the bakery. He handed her the bread and dropped the change on the counter, and as Ines collected her coins Luigi snatched up her hand and told her,

"Come back at two, I'll make you feel good." Just like that. Ines still remembers every word, the serious look on his face, the way his lips curled slightly on one side when he'd stopped talking. She remembers the way she answered him too, abruptly and out of breath and implausibly: "All right. Till then."

It went on like that all summer, every day at two, even on Sundays. Then Luigi went back to Liguria, her boyfriend returned from Emilia and by October became her husband, and for the next sixty years of Ines's life nothing that intense had ever happened again, perhaps nothing at all had happened to her. To this day, when she passes by the square on her bike, those blistering, sweaty post-lunch trysts come back to her and she can feel his hands on her, how they held her tight, how they let her slip away. She doesn't mind thinking about it. Some days she passes by there on purpose. Some days she pedals really slowly just to linger a moment longer.

But not on her way to mass. No sir, not then. Even if her tires are flat, even if she's running late, Ines takes the long route by way of the avenue, arrives at the church, locks her bike to a tree, and goes in.

She hopes that the cool dark will help her forget the heat of those hands, that the smell of wax and old wood will carry away the smell of wet flour, sweat, and all those things that may be wrong yet feel so miraculous.

"Lord, why hast thou forsaken me?"

Father Ermete had been so happy. No one had come to church and he could skip the 5 o'clock mass and return to the sacristy. Then we heard these soft taps that turned out to be the footsteps of a lady who'd just walked in. The Father looked up to the heavens, consulted with the Lord, then with me. "Put your cap on, Luna, we're getting started."

I nodded so hard I felt dizzy a minute, since I was as happy as he was sad to see that lady arrive. For the last year I'd asked him why girls can't serve mass, and for a while his only answer was, "Because." Then he figured out that that was no kind of answer for me, so Father Ermete told me that girls can't serve because the Gospel says so. Only that turned out to be untrue. Luca and I divvied up the Gospel and read the whole thing. Well, we might have skipped a few parts that clearly had nothing to do with it, like the end, when they put Jesus on the cross. It was pretty unlikely that between getting whipped and being stabbed in the chest Jesus would stop and say, "Oh, I almost forgot, make sure girls don't serve mass, would you?" Anyway, Jesus never said such a thing, not on the cross, not ever.

"You sure about that?" said Father Ermete.

"Yep."

"Weird. Maybe it's in the Old Testament."

So we started reading that too, and meanwhile every Sunday the altar was swarmed by altar *boys* fighting over who got to serve mass, since the one who'd served the most masses by Christmas would win a "beautiful prize." Then the other day Father Ermete let slip that the prize is a statue of the Virgin covered in seashells. The next mass, he found himself alone. Ditto the one after that and the one after that and so on till today, when I ran into him in the square on my way to the beach and he told me, "Luna, I'm still convinced girls can't serve mass, and Jesus would agree, but if you come serve at five o'clock today, we'll both turn a blind eye."

And I'm so happy I'm shaking. True, it's not an important mass, but it's a start. And seeing as it's just me, I get to handle everything: the chalice, the communion plate, the bell, the tray, the cruet for water, the cruet for wine. Even collecting alms, although clearly there won't be many today, since I might not see very well from a distance and the church may be dark, but all the pews and the seats on the sides and in back look empty to me. There's just this lady, a black streak with a bit of white on top, and I want to tell her thanks, I want to ask her her name and tell her it's beautiful even if it's ugly, because she's the reason I get to serve mass.

Mom should be on her way as well. I called her first thing and she said she was leaving the shop and coming to see me. But maybe there are too many customers and she can't get away. Maybe she forgot. I don't know. All that matters now is that this lady showed up. Otherwise the church would be empty and Father Ermete would have run off to the rectory to watch his documentaries.

They're his real passion. He talks about them all the time. Because even if the documentaries tell the story of the lives of millions of plants and animals, in his opinion they all say the same thing: God exists. Beavers chop down trees and build perfect dams, therefore God exists. Migratory birds have compasses in their heads that guide them from one continent to another, therefore God exists. Whales talk to each other by singing this song that's so loud you can hear it from one side of the ocean to the other. Therefore God exists.

In fact, as at every other mass, Father Ermete begins with the normal prayers and psalms and then five minutes later launches into his fixation.

"Everyone here admires buildings, admires skyscrapers," he says, even though he's talking to just one person. "Paintings and sculptures you find extraordinary, though they are very simple creations. But when you walk down the street you take no notice of the heavenly perfection to be found in . . . in a leaf, for example. When in fact you should know that nature herself is the most awe-inspiring building, the most remarkable painting. Not for nothing did Saint Francis love nature. You know, I'll let you in on a little secret: had television existed in his day, you can be sure Saint Francis would have loved documentaries. Did you know that fireflies use light to make other fireflies fall in love with them? And bees? Shucks, bees are at least ten or twenty miracles put together. Last night I was watching a documentary on flies—our dear brethren—flies! Say you're standing around admiring a sculpture and while you're distracted, you crush some fly that's bothering you. What you don't realize is that no sculpture in the world can hold a candle to the miracle that is the fly. Not to mention dragonflies. Not to mention . . . "

And he goes on this way, no readings, nothing that the missal says you should say. But pretty soon we'll get to the most important part, where I have to go to the sacristy all by myself and fetch the chalices and the host, and I really hope by the time I get back Mom will have arrived.

Maybe she's just finishing combing a customer's hair or running a few errands for Miss Gemma. There's still time. Father Ermete has moved on from flies and is now talking about octopi, and when he starts talking octopi it means there's at least a half hour to go.

"Did you know that octopi can open cans? Did you know octopi change color a hundred times faster than chameleons? Did you know octopi latch onto fishing nets and pretend to be dead, and when a fish swims by—bam!—they pounce."

Therefore God exists.

WHEN IN FACT

1:59 P.M.: Hey pretty mamma, how are you? How's my sister? It's colder this morning but the waves are perfect. Could you pick up today's paper for me? Don't work too hard, don't get angry, and tell Luna she's a dork. (Then tell her I'm just kidding.) Don't forget the paper. L.

Five minutes. Had Luca's text arrived just five minutes earlier, you could have bought the paper on your lunch break. Instead you had a ham sandwich, drank a coffee, smoked a cigarette, had another coffee, and your phone didn't go off until after Miss Minetti walked in for her dye job and began enumerating for you how much she hates her sister-in-law.

You had just enough time to tell her you had to go pee, then ran to the bathroom, took your notebook out of your purse, and copied out Luca's message.

It's become a habit since he left. Every time he sends you a text from France you copy it out in this notebook along with the date and time. Maybe you're doing it for him. Read all together, they form a kind of diary, and he may not appreciate it now, but in a few years he'll be glad to reread the things he wrote on his first trip with friends.

And if he doesn't, then you can keep these messages for yourself. You've read them so many times you know them by heart. Some are really amazing and others a bit more practical, like this one about the paper, which is really peculiar. Luca never reads the paper nor shows any interest in the news on

TV. Every so often, when the closing music kicks in after the weather report, he asks you, "Anything happen anywhere?" You shake your head and he goes back to doing the mysterious things he does in his room. So if today he's asking for the paper that means you have to find a copy.

Easier said than done. On your lunch break maybe, but at 5 o'clock the newsstand next door has sold out. During the summer they're flooded with copies. They even carry regional papers from the mid-north for out-of-towners keen on keeping abreast of what's happening back home. Then in the winter the distributors stop delivering papers altogether. They figure no one's left in Forte dei Marmi, and even if some savages have stayed behind and are living in the pine groves or under bridges, there's no way those animals can read.

The newsstand downtown, the biggest around, might have something left. And so, even if Luna's serving mass for the first time and you're already running late, you take a slight detour and stop there. Besides, you've never been able to say no to Luca. What are the chances you're going to start on his birthday?

Today he comes of age. Your son is turning eighteen and, as with any mother, that fact has a strange effect on you. Only you have the opposite reaction. Most mothers are taken aback to see their son become a man. In their minds, he'll always be a kid. What surprises you is that Luca's only now officially an adult. Luca was born an adult. He was eighteen when he was five. And now that he's turned eighteen he could be your father. Easy.

But what's there to say, Luca is turning eighteen and not being able to hug him on his birthday feels strange. So what if he'll be back tomorrow? It's not the same. And although you're happy he's happy and having lots of fun, when he gets back, there'll be no escaping. He got his week with friends, now he has to spend the next one with you and Luna, and tell you all about it, every little thing, from morning to night, until he's talked so much he loses his voice.

In the meantime, you have to hurry. The mass has started and you want to see your daughter up at the altar, and she wants to see you down in the pews.

You've almost made it, and the nice thing about this place in the off-season is that you won't waste a minute looking for a parking spot or waiting behind anybody else to buy the paper. But now you're stopped by a traffic light, which couldn't care less about what's going on around it. It doesn't care if the intersection is dead silent, if no one's driven past in a week. It stays red for a certain number of minutes and you have to sit there. Humanity has razed mountains, mastered the skies, conquered the moon—why should you submit to a red light? You don't know, but you can't cross, you shouldn't. Those fucking cameras are there, watching, spying on you. Only by some miracle do you manage to make it to the end of the month with all the regular bills and expenses. You can't afford another ticket. To calm yourself down, you take out the notebook with Luca's messages and reread a favorite.

9:19 P.M.: Hey pretty mamma, today it was sunny. No wind, no waves. Instead of surfing I swam. There's this huge wood shack on the beach covered with palm branches. You'd love it. And it's perfect for Luna to sit in the shade. All three of us could hang out there morning to night. Maybe one day, if we have the money, we can come here together. I think we c—

Drrring! Drrring!

You're interrupted by a weak, rickety noise from another planet. Someone in front of you is ringing a bicycle bell. You only realize what's going on when a voice shrieks, "Lane! Lane!"

A tricycle is heading toward you, trying to squeeze

between your car and the curb even though there's no room. Ines, a friend of your mother's, and like your mother, a total bitch. She could easily pass on the other side of the street but instead keeps pedaling in the wrong direction, driving a wedge between you and the curb. You swing around, flip her the finger, park the car halfway on the curb, and run for the newsstand.

You pass three guys arguing, one dressed like a traffic cop. Great, all you need now is a ticket. "Don't look at my car," you shout, "it's parked illegally but I'll be out of here in no time. Don't pull any fast ones or I'll be pissed!"

The lady at the newsstand greets you, smiles, waits for you to tell her what you want, and it dawns on you that you don't know; Luca didn't tell you which paper to get him. But it doesn't matter because everything's sold out except a copy of the *Gazzetta di Parma* that had been delivered in the off-season by mistake.

You buy it. Flashing a smile, you thank the traffic cop, who hasn't budged. And only now do you see him. Only now do you realize that one of the guys is Mr. Mancini from the parent-teacher conference, the English teacher Luca likes so much.

Come to think of it, you don't dislike him either, and now he looks even better, in jeans and a faded shirt, with that air of someone who doesn't have a thing on this planet to do. You smile, and he smiles back and waves, flapping his hand as if rather than nearby you were standing on a ship that was pulling away from a port at night, headed out into the dark sea forever.

You look at him. What could you see in a guy like this? He's neither handsome nor charming, and if he happens to be interesting he's pretty good at hiding it behind that bewildered, baffled air of his. But the answer's simple: you like him because you're a fool. In fact, you're better off giving men a wide berth,

Serena. A party of one may be bad, but a party of two can be twice as bad. A lot of women fill their days with men just because they're unsatisfied with their lives. But no one can enrich her life by adding just anything; you have to add something good. Take your mother for instance. She would dress everything in olive oil, and olive oil makes you want to puke. She used to boil carrots and drown them in oil. You'd get pissed and she'd say, "What are carrots supposed to taste like if I don't add oil?" And you would try to explain to her that boiled carrots might not taste like much, but there's no point in trying to improve them by dousing them with something that makes you retch. Yet you'd stop yourself midsentence, seeing as your mother wasn't listening. She kept spreading her disgusting oil on top, trying to make those bland carrots taste like something, the way women waste their lives on imbeciles.

But you resist. You have to resist. Who cares if you like this Mr. Mancini? Everyone in his rightful place, everyone cool.

Still, you smile as you pass him to exit the newsstand. He replies, steps closer, extends his hand, withdraws it, doesn't know what to do with either hand, and finally sticks both in his pockets.

"Good evening," he says. "What's with the *Gazzetta di Parma*?"

You hold the paper up and look at it. It's not for you, you say.

"Is your husband from Emilia?"

"No, why?"

"No reason. I have some friends in Parma and was just curious—"

"You were curious to know whether one of your friends was my husband?"

"No, no, I—"

"Well, I don't have a husband from Parma, or anywhere, if that's what you wanted to know."

He raises his hand and shakes his head as if to say no, but then you smile, and his lips curl into something resembling a smile. Or palsy. He stares at the ground then looks back up at you, and the confusion wavering in those brown, average eyes of his stirs something inside you—confirmation that you, Serena, have to give men a really wide berth. Because you couldn't care less about stable men who always have a handle on the situation. And men who always know what's best and risk simplifying your life you find sad. But this guy here, this bewildered klutz standing in front of you, holding his arms as if they'd just been presented to him and he were searching for a place to set them down, this guy whose life is so clearly screwed up that it could easily rub off on yours, well, just what pressing reason could you have for liking him, and liking him so much?

Maybe because, like him, you're an idiot. Actually, strike "maybe." Look at you, instead of jumping in your car and running off to church where your daughter's waiting for you, you're still here. Luckily, where your brain fails, your phone rushes in. It's Gemma calling. Maybe you have to go back to the shop, maybe some nag has come in, the kind of customer who insists only you can dye her hair.

"Excuse me a minute," you say, as if the call had interrupted a conversation. "Hello?"

"Serena, where are you?"

"I'm on my way to church to see Luna. Why? Do you need something?"

"No, no, just come home as soon as you can . . . I'll be waiting outside your house."

"My house? Why? What happened?"

"Nothing, nothing at all." Her voice sounds weird, strained. "Just get here as soon as you can."

"Did you and Vincenzo have another fight?" Last month, her husband had taken up video poker again, and Gemma slept at yours. "What's that moron done now?"

"No, no, nothing."

"Then what are you doing at my place?"

" . . . "

"Gemma?"

"All right, O.K., Vincenzo and I had a little fight."

"Ha, I knew it! Don't worry, the gate's unlocked and the keys are under the vase next to the kitchen entrance. Let yourself in, I'll be there soon."

You hang up the phone and drop the paper. The teacher dives to pick it up. You thank him and look at him and there's no need to say anything. Clearly you have to run. It's so clear even he gets it.

"Well, see you soon, I hope," he says.

"I hope so too." You say it because you mean it, because it's true. You say it because you're a total fool.

But now's not the time to dwell on that. Now there's a mess to clean up, and you're excellent at cleaning up messes when they're not yours. A minute ago you may have been clueless about the teacher, but with Gemma you've already drawn up a deft plan. You'll run home, put the kettle on, and console her. You could do this for a living. All your friends seek you out when this stuff happens to them. They're the reason you keep tea in the house. As far as you and the kids are concerned, tea is bitter black water.

All around you the streets zigzag and unravel, utterly empty, while you drive fast in the direction of the church and Luna. You leave the car in the square, where you shouldn't, but who cares. You enter. The church is empty. Maybe mass has ended already. Motherfucker.

Wait, no, the priest is still talking. Only the worshippers are missing, except for the blue head of an old woman in front. And there's Luna, partially obscured by the priest, standing next to him at the altar. You think to wave, but maybe that's against the rules. Besides, she's so far away she'd never see you.

Her hair is pulled back, her skin whiter than usual underneath her black cap, but she does great: all earnest, answering the priest's prayers, kneeling exactly at the right time—she's a professional altar boy. And now you regret having missed the start of mass. As the priest winds down the Lamb of God prayer and starts talking about real lambs, about how intelligent sheep are, about a documentary on the miracle of wool, you stop listening and concentrate on your daughter.

And in that darkness, trembling faintly with electric candlelight, in that mushroomlike warmth, amid the smell of old wood, something very strange happens. Suddenly your thoughts fade, your worries abate. Out of nowhere, you feel just fine.

Sure, Gemma may have problems, but they're her problems, and the mass will end shortly and you'll go hug Luna tightly. Gemma can tell you everything when you get home, but not now. Now you take a breath and lean back. You make yourself comfortable on this stiff uncomfortable pew and let the muffled sounds of mass echo off the walls and inside you, as if nothing else existed, as if the world outside were a film everyone was talking about, and maybe one night you'd go see it, but not now. Not now.

"At what point did you see me? At what point did you get there?"

"I told you, at the beginning. I mean, not right at the beginning, but close," you say, speeding home.

"But why did you sit in the back? You could have sat up front."

"I didn't want you getting all excited. I didn't want you to flip out."

"I didn't flip out."

"I know you didn't. You did great. Actually, we should celebrate. I'm just sorry Gemma is waiting for us and needs consoling. Are you going to help me? Shall we console her together?"

"I'm not sure I'm any good at consoling people."

"You're my daughter, of course you're good at it. It's a curse, Luna. Remember that."

"Why a curse? Isn't it a good thing?"

"Yeah, sure, fantastic. Except everyone wants you to help them with their problems and no one ever pays a thought to yours, not even you."

"Ah, so I'll try not to console too many people."

"Smart girl, give it a shot."

For a while you stop talking. And the feeling that came over you in church, that flush of well-being, still lingers inside you as you drive down the sunny streets lined with pine trees.

"Why's Lady Gemma sad?"

"She had a fight with her husband."

"Again? Why are they together if they fight all the time?"

"Beats me."

"What are they fighting about this time?"

You don't answer. You don't know. You don't care much either. Besides, you'll be home shortly and Gemma will tell you everything. And even if tonight she's sad, you have to celebrate all the same, because Luna deserves it. You do too, a little. And Luca will be back tomorrow, and the day after that you'll all celebrate together. You don't know what time he's getting back. Nor does he, probably. And yet you want to know, right now. Crazy as it sounds, you want to know the exact hour and minute.

Instead you start to sense something else, something strange inside you that has bypassed your head. It passes your throat, your heart, the invisible holes in your skin, and by some mysterious route enters your bloodstream. Your breathing becomes labored, you sweat, Luna asks you something but you can't hear her. All you can sense is this thing gripping your insides and spreading, crowding everything out, even the air that struggles to get in, and shortening your breath. It constricts your throat, extinguishes your voice.

You turn onto the narrow cul-de-sac no one but you lives on. But now there are three cars parked out front. Make that four. Too many. And people outside, a carabinieri jeep, an ambulance. And Gemma, who sees you and starts walking over . . .

You stop driving. You take your foot off the gas, let go of the clutch, and place both hands on the steering wheel. The car trudges along for a minute, hiccupping forward, and then stalls and sputters out. And here come Miss Gemma and another lady from the neighborhood alongside the carabinieri.

"What's going on, Mom? Are they really taking you to jail?"

Luna's voice trembles as she asks, trembles, and then she cries.

You, on the other hand, smile. Actually you laugh. And you nod, yes. Yes, that's it! They're taking you to jail for kicking someone at school. Two people, actually, and one of them a little boy. Of course! They're taking you to jail. That's why they're looking for you. That's fair, yes, totally fair.

By now the people are surrounding the car. You roll up the windows, lock the doors. Luna looks both ways. You don't know how well she can see outside, if she can see the faces mouthing for her to open up, to get out of the car, the dark shapes of the carabinieri saying, "Make room! Make room!" All you know is that your daughter is crying. A moment ago she was standing next to the priest at mass, and you were watching her, happily, and now she's crying, and nothing about this is fair, and you shake your head and you shout, "Go away! Go away! Shut up and go away! Go away! Nothing happened! Nothing happened!"

When in fact.

PART 2

Maybe it's the music of the sea
that stirs your heart while you stand by.
All ships return and you don't want to.
What bitter tears are shed, are shed by you.
—NICOLA NISA SALERNO

H ad you been asked before what pain was, you would have said some vicious beast that swoops down and slashes you, bites you, tears you limb from limb. And that would have been bullshit.

Because that's not pain, Serena. At most that's a monster in a scary movie. But what could you have known about it. You've seen plenty of movies, but as for real pain, you've never felt that before.

It saturates your life. Wait, no, you don't have a life, pain is your life, and now you know it doesn't swoop down on you like some beast. Pain's in no hurry. It advances so slowly that for a while you look around, confused, and wonder, "Well, where is it?" And it keeps creeping closer and closer until it pounces, and by the time it reaches you it's beyond escaping. Monsters in movies climb through a window or pop out from under the bed or behind a gravestone, and you have a shot at escaping, you slip into the woods and run as far as you can, then turn to see if it's behind you. You trip and fall, get back up, start running again, limp off to who knows where, and you run and scream because it keeps getting closer and closer, until that last horrible scream when it's got you and in a minute it's all over.

Real pain doesn't emerge from a particular place. It engulfs you, like the sea at high tide, deep and dark and full of towering waves coming at you from all directions. The current carries you, a little here, a little there, then a bigger wave comes crashing on top of you and pulls you underwater, and you can't breathe and you don't know where you are anymore, or up from down, or what these soft, slithery things are, fastening onto your wrists and legs and dragging you under. So you surrender, sinking down endlessly, and everything spins faster and slower at the same time. In your ears you hear your heart beating slowly and you stop breathing, and just as you're about to drown, the wave settles and you find yourself with your head above water, breathing, still here, wherever here may be. You look around for something to hold onto but there's no point, the bulge of another dark wave is mounting, blacking out everything, and soon you'll be dragged under again as the sea tightens its embrace, constricting your throat, crushing your chest, driving you downward.

The same sea took Luca away, the very same dark waters made your son disappear, waters so vast his friends hardly realized what had happened. Only later did they notice his blue-and-red board and paddle over. The leash strapped to his ankle was attached to the board yet Luca was still underwater. The doctors found nothing, no bruises, no injuries, no drugs or alcohol in his system. They declared it a natural death. A seventeen-year-old boy (eighteen that day), tall, strong, in perfect shape—how the hell could they call his death natural?

He'd never had any issues, never once been sick. When you or Luna came down with a cold—and during winter Luna has a permanent cold—Luca would ask what we meant by a stuffy nose, what it was like to blow your nose and feel mucus drain from your body, because he'd never, not once, had a cold. Then how can you imagine Luca playing in the sea with his friends and all of a sudden, poof, he's extinguished, and they find him hooked to his surfboard but still underwater, his green eyes open, staring up at the sky above. How can you call that natural. It's as if, as if . . . you grope for something comparable, something as crazy or terrifying, but come up short.

All you feel is the sea mounting once more, dragging you down, deeper and deeper.

You try to rise but once again the blankets are too heavy this morning; they pin you to the bed and you lie there staring at the ceiling. You don't know what time it is, but the light cutting through the slats would suggest it's at least eleven. You prefer the rain, listening to the patter of water on the roof; it makes it easier to stay in bed, listening, waiting for tomorrow. You sit up, slide your legs out from under the blanket, and feel for the floor with your feet, but it seems like an impossible height to climb down from, so you turn your head and lie back down again. Maybe your low blood pressure is to blame, all those liquids and pills you take to calm down or perk up—you don't know which and it hardly matters.

Just lie back down, close your eyes, and wait for the light to fade from the curtains, for the arrival of another night, your favorite part of the day, since no one is shocked you're in bed. Except it's morning now and according to the rest of the world you should be on your feet.

But what the hell do you care what the rest of the world thinks? I mean, it matters a little bit, a little, a bright white bit called Luna, and if she weren't here you could easily . . . you could even up and . . . who knows, you don't know that, you know nothing. Besides, Luna is here, so it makes no sense to think about what you would do were she not.

All that makes sense is for you to get up, get dressed, go shopping, greet everyone on the street and not give a damn about the pained looks they give you while they inquire how you are, buy something to eat, and return home to prepare lunch for Luna before she goes back to school.

Yes, school is back in session today. You hadn't realized. Luna woke up early and brought you breakfast in bed and your medicine. You asked her what she was doing awake and dressed so early, and she answered that she was going to school, and the whole thing seemed ridiculous to you. How can Luca be dead and school start again? How can the bus pick up the kids, one by one, and how can they board the bus, the nerds up front and the troublemakers in back, and laugh and poke fun and throw things at one another, if Luca is dead? Are the teachers really there opening their roll books and taking attendance and beginning a new school year if Luca is dead?

No, it's not possible.

In fact that is exactly what keeps the pain at bay at first, the fact that it is simply not possible.

That afternoon in March, the last day your world existed, you returned home with Luna, everyone gathered together, and Gemma told you what happened to Luca, that one moment he was in the water with his friends and the next they didn't see him anymore, only his board floating and . . . and then you covered your face with your hands, you stayed that way a minute, and then you removed them, looked at everyone staring mutely at you and broke into laughter.

Yes, laughter. And surely they all thought you had lost your mind or hadn't understood. But the problem wasn't with you. They were the ones who didn't know Luca. And Luna was laughing too, a little, while you hugged her hard. "Luna! Everything's fine, Luna, don't worry. Do you remember that time there was that yacht offshore and Luca swam out to it and they ferried him to the Island of Giglio? Do you remember that day he went out for ice cream and when he caught sight of the snow in the mountains decided to hike up to the top of Mount Pania instead? And he ate the snow and got back home at . . . what time was it? Midnight? One?"

"Even later than that, Mom! Even later!"

And you nodded, yes, and you laughed. Because it was clear that something of that kind had happened this time too, anything else would be impossible.

The ambulance workers in their ridiculous orange uniforms formed a circle around you, and Gemma held your hand while you pictured Luca riding the waves, out there in the ocean, and maybe a French girl had caught sight of him and fallen in love and swum out to him. If it happens to him all the time here, then you can bet it happens in France, where people are more open-minded. They took a shine to each other, she asked him to go home with her, and Luca had left the surfboard behind and gone. Or maybe not. Maybe while he was surfing he'd run into a school of dolphins and he'd straddled one and it had carried him to a wonderful island, a secret and miraculous place, and in a little while he'll write you to come meet him and you'll all go live there.

That's why, when they told you these things, you started to laugh and squeezed Luna. They all looked at you like you were a madwoman. Sorry, you said, but they were wasting their time, nothing had happened. You wished them good evening and walked into your house with your daughter and Gemma. You went to your room, stood up on the bed, took down your suitcase from on top of the wardrobe, and began stuffing things inside.

"Let's go, Luna, give me a hand. What are you going to bring? Summer stuff, huh, and a bathing suit, you'll need a bathing suit."

"Where are we going?"

"To be with Luca, where else? You'll see. The sun will be bright. Grab your sunscreen. And your sweatshirt with the hood."

Luna nodded and began opening her drawers too, but slowly and without removing anything, while Gemma tried to stop you, tugging on your arms, asking you to sit down a moment.

"I don't have the time, Gemma. When we get back we can talk all you want. And you can tell me what Vincenzo did this time, okay? Do you want a tea for now? Luna, make a tea for Gemma, would you?"

"No thanks, Serena, I don't want tea. But stop a second, I'm asking you to please hear me out. Luca hasn't disappeared. He was by his surfboard. I'm terribly sorry, Serena, but they found him. Do you understand? They found him."

"Gemma, bear with me, I can't listen to your problems just now. We're leaving. Do me a favor, Luna? Bring a pair of jeans and a sweatshirt for Luca—he packed practically nothing and I bet he could use them."

Everything you found you threw on top of the suitcase, a mountain of stuff: underwear, socks, shirts, boxes of mothballs, moldy old embroidery your mother had made. And you would have kept on until you'd cleaned out the whole house, who knows what you would have done next, but suddenly your arms became heavy, you bent over, you heard a noise in your head, like a swarm of bees caught in a wind, a strong wind that picked you up and flung you down. And Luna and Gemma must have seen you falling because they ran to catch you before you hit the ground. But you fell faster.

You hit your head on the floor, though you don't remember that. You didn't feel any pain. The same thing happened in the ambulance on the way to the hospital, and you stared up at the white ceiling pitching back and forth. The pain still didn't come. Maybe it was so great it needed more room and had to empty out your insides first: gone the French girl who'd invited Luca home, gone the dolphins and mysterious island, gone Luca's eighteenth birthday party with just the three of you. Gone his green eyes, his smile, his way of telling you, "Don't worry, Mom, what's the big deal? You don't have to worry about anything. Ever."

From then on it felt like an enormous hole had opened up into which everything fell and was lost: day and night, the hours, lunch and dinner, this meaningless light cutting through the curtain slats. There's not even a point to rising and fixing Luna something to eat. Soon she'll be back, saying she was wrong, that school hasn't started back up, that she had gone there and found the gate locked and a sign saying school was over, that school would never reopen again.

Because there's nothing to reopen, no reason to go on, nothing makes sense anymore. And you lie here in the dark, catching your breath, between one wave and the next.

JIMMY PAGE'S DOUBLE NECK

The cranked-up sound of an electric guitar at full volume—that's the great dividing line, the axe stroke that splits humanity in half. Six billion people, thousands of different colors, thousands of different languages, thousands of different hairstyles—in an instant you can separate them into just two groups: those who love the cranked-up sound of an electric guitar and those who hate it. There's no middle road. There's no one out there who can listen to a blistering solo and remain lukewarm or indifferent. And if by chance those people do exist, Sandro couldn't give a fuck about their kind.

He loves the electric guitar. It's the sound of life, so raw and strange, full of melody infused with hissing, magnetic stuff looping around the notes, with desire and rage and abandon, wrong turns and first shots and total disorder all mixed together, stuffed inside a piece of wood with six strings pulled tight across it and fired into the air at full tilt.

Yet today the sound makes him nauseous.

Perhaps because it's three in the afternoon and he's just woken up. He hadn't woken up by himself, either. He'd heard someone calling, "Maestro, maestro," and opened one eye and saw this boy with longish hair holding a guitar. It took a few seconds for Sandro to realize where he was and in what era, then he pulled a sweater on over his pajamas, sat on the bed, and began the lesson.

Now he has to sit and listen to the same pentatonic scale

being played over and over, the same shrill, creaky notes penetrating the fog of his mind one by one and getting lost there, after a night spent half asleep and half staring at the white ceiling, and the ceiling business is the better of the two, because whenever he goes to sleep he dreams of Luca.

For the past six months it's been like this, with the exception of the first few days. The first few days he hadn't slept at all. He couldn't even lie down without feeling as though he were drowning, so he sat up and read every article in the local papers, all the farewells Luca's friends and acquaintances posted on Facebook and blogs and every other e-dump where people offload their thoughts.

They keep publishing remembrances of Luca and photos of him walking down the street, slipping into or out of his wetsuit on the shore, swimming, picking up a seashell off the beach. And underneath each photo a volley of comments like, "Luca, since you've been gone the world's not as beautiful," and, "Luca, as of today a brighter star burns in the sky," and other crap people always feel the need to write out of that repulsive instinct to make everything about them.

Stupid clichéd crap—all alike in its effort to be unique. Nonetheless, as soon as a new one pops up, Sandro rushes to read it and spends hours studying it. He doesn't know why, maybe simply out of a desire to make himself feel bad, in the hope that some small part of his brain will register a significant detail, that Luca had gone to Biarritz because he wanted to see a girl he really liked or because he had gotten into trouble here and wanted to hide out awhile or maybe his friends had nagged him so much that in the end they'd practically taken him by force. For Sandro, anything but the truth would do. Because the truth is he killed him.

There are only so many ways to put it. Actually, there's one way and that's it. He killed him. And maybe it would have been quicker to use a gun or a knife or a chainsaw, but there are ways of effectively killing people without getting your hands dirty. Enter Sandro. He encouraged Luca, urged him to go, practically pushed him into taking that ill-fated trip by force.

"You've got to go to Biarritz, Luca. I'll lend you the money if that's the issue. If your mom's reluctant to let you go, look, go anyway. Mothers are society's first line of attack, and society has one goal and one goal only—to keep you prisoner forever. You don't realize it because it operates slowly. It starts out like this huge fence, so huge you don't even see it. But it keeps closing in, until one day it turns out to be a cage and at that point it's too late. Lights out. So, now that you see that fence closing in, you have to take aim, wind up, and knock it down. Knock it down, Luca, break on through and run!"

That's what he'd told him, word for word. Had an adventurer, a daredevil, a rebel who lives on the edge and takes great big bites out of life been the one to tell him, well, it still would have been hot air. But out of Sandro's mouth it was a total joke. At forty years old he still lives at home with his parents and has never once taken a risk in his life—never, never, never.

"Can't you see it's the thing to do, Luca? Go on, don't be afraid, man up!"

But manning up sounds easy when someone else is taking the risk. There's nothing manly about it. It's called being a dick, period. To add insult to injury, when Sandro had met Serena he acted the philosopher, spouting all that bullshit about a force that can't be stopped, about that boy's great destiny, about Wile E. Coyote's umbrella . . . Sandro shudders at the thought. What an imbecile! What an idiot! No, Sandro is a killer.

"Keep going, maestro?" asks his student, briefly taking his fingers off the strings and blowing on them to relieve the pain. The mini amp beside the bed sizzles like a deep fryer. His student is sucking back the saliva from his braces. He must have been playing the same scale for fifteen minutes. Sandro had told him to keep going until he said stop. But who gave any more thought to that?

"That'll do. Now play it backwards for me."

"I was playing it backwards."

"You sure? Then go back to playing it normally. But give it more oomph, more verve, more love."

The boy grips the guitar neck again with his slender, bent fingers, while Sandro returns to thinking about Serena. In the last few months he'd tried to see her but it had been impossible. She never shows up to work at the salon. They say she doesn't leave the house anymore. The last time he saw her was at the funeral. Yet Sandro didn't have the courage to face her that day. Instead he spied on her from a distance. The number of people there had made hiding the easiest thing in the world. He positioned himself behind a group of girls carrying a banner that said "You'll always ride the waves of our hearts" and watched her following behind the coffin, eyes on the ground, hair disheveled, ushered by a woman who had wrapped an arm around her waist and was whispering into her ear. On her other side, a little pale girl wearing giant sunglasses and a black sweatshirt with the hood up.

Sandro watched her arrive and had wanted to be the one to embrace her, to say something, yet—what with all his courage—when she passed him by, he stepped back and let the crowd swallow him. What can you say in such painful circumstances? Nothing makes sense. Every word sounds as stupid as that banner advertising waves of the heart. Besides, the truth is, Sandro was afraid. Afraid that extraordinary woman's dulled look would suddenly ignite with life again, with a hateful light that stabbed his eyes, and she'd lunge for them and try to tear them out, or worse, open her mouth and tell him what was what. "Hey teacher," she'd say, "you killed my son. Happy?"

So Sandro stood back and watched the coffin from behind the people shaking their heads as if to say it wasn't fair, and he imagined Luca's perfect body in there, his long hair around his face, his eyes closed, total darkness. He had told him to go, to not let himself be confined by fences. Now he's confined to a wooden box. Take a chance, he'd told him, live your life. And he'd shipped him off to die.

Since then, every time Sandro manages to lie down, he thinks of Luca laid out in the coffin, and if by accident he falls asleep once in a while, he dreams about him.

But in his dreams Luca's not underground or floating life-lessly in the waves. No, that would be a relief. Instead Sandro's dreams are terrifying, soul-crushing. He sees Luca jogging happily or with his friends at night, drunkenly laughing about nothing, or behind a paddle boat at the beach with a girl he'd known all of ten minutes. He dreams of him sleeping with one, two, three women at a time—a blonde, a brunette, a redhead. He dreams of him holding a pen and notebook, leaning against a motorcycle on a dusty back road in the middle of Mexico, under a wild blue sky where the stars pop like popcorn. He dreams of him shaking hands and collecting his diploma, then the diploma turns into a trophy, then into a newborn baby, and so on and so forth, all these beautiful things Luca was bound to have done, which were awaiting him just a little farther down the road of his twinkling life. But on his way he came across a blockade, a blockade in the form of a shitty substitute teacher, and Luca's road ended there, and Luca along with it.

Sandro wakes up from these horrible dreams covered in sweat, his heart rate a hundred. He stands and looks around, unsure where he is until he sees the walls papered with records and magazines, the guitar in a corner, little Ivan's letter that landed here from Reggio Emilia on a balloon nine years ago and is still awaiting a reply, and the shame kills him. Except he doesn't really die. Sandro's still here. For no just cause his sorry ass life goes on.

"Maestro, can we play a different scale?"

"Sorry?"

"Could you teach me another scale? I know this one pretty good."

Sandro stares at his student, trying to bring him into focus. Then he turns to the door and shouts, "Coffee!" He waits a minute before shouting again. His mother doesn't answer, but the sound of things being moved around in the kitchen implies she's heard him.

"It's too soon," he tells the boy. "The pentatonic scales are very important. We'll do the second once you've nailed the first. Go on, start over."

The boy nods, sucks back his saliva, and looks down at his instrument again. But before playing he raises his eyes a moment and observes Sandro. Even from that angle, even for just a second, Sandro recognizes that look under his pimply forehead and knows the moment has arrived for this kid. Sooner or later the moment always arrives. It depends on how sharp the student is, how gifted, yet it's always just a matter of time. Even if for Sandro time didn't do shit.

He's been playing guitar for twenty-six years. Twenty-six! How pathetic! He started playing in junior high after his uncle Roberto told him about Jimmy Page. Uncle Roberto had long hair and wore a leather jacket and skull T-shirts he picked up at a place in Florence called Hell 'N' Suicide. Nineteen years old, he aspired to be a rock photographer so he could tour with bands and hang around the music scene he loved to death. The one thing he owned more of than skull T-shirts were records. Had he spent less on accessories and purchased an actual camera, he might have become a photographer. But he wound up doing landscaping with his dad. The two of them would climb to the tops of trees to remove pinecones. One day he fell from a branch, no safety rope, and now he's stuck in a wheelchair. Twice a year he travels to Medjugorje. He's never seen Our Lady but he met a one-legged woman from Antignano there and now they live together and build giant crèches year-round, with waterfalls and mountains and figurines that run by themselves.

But back then Uncle Roberto was a wild man. They were having dinner at his grandmother's that night to celebrate his birthday and Uncle Roberto showed him a photo of Led Zeppelin that he kept in his wallet. There was Jimmy Page holding this insane double-neck guitar.

"Jimmy Page slays a ton of pussy. Jimmy Page slays so much pussy that every night he walks into his hotel room and finds twenty or thirty chicks who want to sleep with him because they know that if they sleep with him, at the next concert Jimmy Page will dedicate a song to them. And Jimmy Page sleeps with all of them—three, four, seven at a time—never the same number—that would be bad luck—while the rest wait on the floor and get it on with each other. But afterward at the concert Jimmy Page can't play enough songs to dedicate one to each. Led Zeppelin's songs are never-ending; they play ten, maybe twelve a concert, when there's, like, minimum thirty chicks a night, and Jimmy Page is a man of his word. He attaches importance to dedicating a tune to each chick. So what does Jimmy Page do? Jimmy Page gets a double-neck guitar, and he plays one neck a little and the other a little, so that every song counts for two and he can kill two pussies with one stone. See how sly Jimmy Page is, Sandro?"

Sandro didn't have an answer ready. He sat there, speechless. But he understood perfectly: he had to learn how to play guitar.

He started out playing a used Eko acoustic. Every day he practiced and studied, and even if at first it was all burning fingers and notes as derelict as the instrument they issued from, Sandro smiled and persisted, confident he'd get good over time, that his hair would grow out and he'd get an electric guitar and finally the moment would come when he'd have a double neck to keep up with all that pussy dying to drop into his arms.

Except things didn't go down that way. This here has nothing to do with math, that bogus realm where one plus one always equals two, where playing ten years automatically means you'll be ten times better than when you started. Not music. Because besides practice and hard work and determination, there is this totally unfair, malicious factor that worms its way in and couldn't care less about dedication or hard work. And that factor goes by the name of talent. And Sandro, poor bastard, had none. He was utterly hopeless. Years went by, enough time for his hair to grow long and short again and fall out, and yet Jimmy Page's double neck never materialized. Sandro's slow and clumsy fingers struggled to find the right places on one neck, never mind two.

Yet his students must not know that. He has been giving guitar lessons since his college days; every kid in the area gets his start in Maestro Sandro's room. That's what he tells them to call him: maestro. He knows it's pathetic and, technically speaking, untrue, but it keeps the kids in check. As do his stories about playing gigs in London back in the day, when in fact he's never been to London because he's scared of flying. You heard it here, an English teacher who's never been to London and a maestro who can't play music. But bullshitting is a requirement, because if the kids raise their heads, if they dare to look the facts in the face—even for a minute—they'll see immediately how third-rate their maestro is. Because this kid here, who started taking lessons last month and has played the same pentatonic scale nonstop, must not imagine for a second that after over a quarter century Sandro would have a hard time playing it this smoothly and accurately.

But it's out of his hands, it's only a matter of time. Sooner or later the terrible moment comes when the boy lifts his head and looks at him the same way this kid just looked at him, sucking back his saliva, saying, "Sorry, Maestro, I tried to do some things on my own at home. I know you told me not to, but there was a how-to on the Internet for the 'Master of Puppets' solo. I tried following along but I'm not sure I've got it right. Can I play it for you a second?"

Sandro doesn't even say yes. He doesn't do anything except lean back against the wall behind the bed and brace himself. Happens every time. If it's not Metallica's "Master of Puppets" than it's Ozzy Osbourne's "Miracle Man" or "Rust in Peace" by Megadeth or another of the thousand killer anthems Sandro has tried to play for years and ultimately filed under "Things That Are Humanly Impossible."

But as this kid demonstrates, they're far from impossible. Two months he's been playing with a third-rate teacher yet he attacks the solo, his fingers fly across the strings and, aside from a little drool, the whole thing comes out perfect and fast, just like the original. When he's finished, Sandro will say good job and then go on to explain that it's not his style, he isn't the maestro for him, and he'll hand him the number of a guy named Manuel who teaches in Viareggio. For every student Sandro sends on, Manuel buys Sandro a beer.

He's done it a thousand times; one more shouldn't be so tough. But this time he starts to think of Luca and it is tough. Luca didn't know him well enough or long enough to see him the way this kid has seen him. Or maybe he did. Maybe just before he fell, before he sank to the bottom, before he closed his eyes forever under the weight of the ocean, Luca thought of him, saw his reflection in that dark water, and understood who Sandro Mancini really was, what mettle he was made of, how sad his life was. From a thousand miles away he, too, for a moment, had given Sandro that same look, his eyes filled with salt water, foam, and disappointment.

GHOST HOUSE

It's really hot out today. It was the first day of school and everyone was wearing short sleeves, apart from me since I have to protect my arms from the sun, and apart from Zot, who has on a fur-lined hat and a wool jacket buttoned to the collar.

I mean really, he comes from Russia, you'd think heat here would kill him. But maybe the place he comes from is an unusual place and nothing like Russia. In fact, Mom once asked him where he was from. He said he was Russian and she smiled. Then he told her he came from Chernobyl and she covered her nose and mouth, gave him this really scared look, and began backing up, dragging her daughter away by the arm. Maybe Chernobyl is a weird place, and Zot is even weirder. Not to say other people count for normal. Nowadays nothing's normal. For the past six months not one normal thing has happened. What normal looks like I can hardly remember.

Regardless, we walk home together because for us the bus is dangerous. Not on the way to school. Everyone is tired then and leaves us in peace. But on the return trip we're better off on foot. We walk slowly toward my house, since Zot wants to see Mom. This summer he came over and said, "Good morning, Miss," and she smiled but only with her mouth. She didn't look up at him or even warn him that if he calls her "Miss" again she'll crack his skull open. Yet he still wants to come back.

"She's the same as when you saw her last."

"Fine by me, Luna."

"She might not even say hi."

"Not a problem, I'll say hi to her. It pleases me to see her, and in my opinion, it pleases her too."

"I don't know about that."

"Oh, yes, yes, definitely! Were you not happy to see me this morning?"

He asks and I don't answer. As a matter of fact I was, but I can't manage to say I'm happy anymore. I don't even know whether it's right to be happy. I keep my mouth shut and walk straight ahead. That's just how things are now. Over these last crappy months I've been totally clueless. Everything happens at random and I don't get why. I just watch it happen.

Six months is a lot of months. That's twenty-four weeks, almost two hundred days during which people around the world have woken up and gone to work or around town or wherever they feel like, and then returned home and eaten dinner and watched TV and fallen asleep only to do it all over again the next morning. Airplanes have taken off, ships floated in all sorts of weird places, spring come and gone, school ended. Somehow I even advanced to the next grade. Then summer came and now that's nearly over too. In fact, school has started up again. A lot has happened in the last six months.

But not for Mom and me.

Nothing happens to us anymore, nothing exists any longer, not even the days. We eat when we remember to and sleep when sleep comes over us, without saying, "I'm going to bed." One minute we're awake, the next we're not. In bed I hear the sound of the sea growing mad, like it's calling me, asking, "Luna, why don't you visit me anymore? Don't you want my gifts anymore?" No, I don't. I don't want any more sticks or dirty broken stuff that serves no purpose. Instead of giving me all that junk the sea could have saved my brother.

But the sea isn't the only place I've stopped going. I don't go anywhere anymore. In six months I've left the backyard a total of three times, for checkups at the hospital. Miss Gemma takes me, and after the checkups she always asks if I want to get ice cream or poke my head into a store, but all I want is to go back home to Mom and lie down next to her in the dark and stare into empty space.

Except this morning I went out. School reopened and like all the other kids I went. Not that I had a choice. I just woke up and went, even though I don't have the books and have become unused to people passing by and talking really loudly, to all this light, this really glaring light, light everywhere. Except here, I think, as Zot turns left onto a dark narrow street that I never take. And don't want to take now.

"Not that way. This way, Zot. Come on."

"Why?"

"We'll get there quicker."

"But I have to stop at home for a second to tell my grandfather I'm going over to your place. Then we can go."

"Fine, whatever, but let's not take this street."

"Why?"

"Because there's that house," I say. And I think of that house at the end of the street, sort of surrounded by a forest. They call it Ghost House. The name alone makes my voice tremble. But Zot doesn't listen. Without turning back, he heads down the dark street, and I follow pretty far behind him. You can already see those tall, dark trees down there splayed with branches that hide the house.

One time Grandpa told me about this night during World War II when he saw five people hanged there, swinging from a pine tree. I asked if they had killed themselves or if someone else had done it, and Grandpa said that the Germans did it, that during the war you fought to survive every day—there was no time to kill yourself.

Another time this lady whose hair my mother cut told me

that one night, around dinnertime, she was walking by the place when she heard a noise. She turned toward the woods and saw an old woman with a shovel burying something, or someone, there in the middle of the woods.

Story or no story, the sight of Ghost House is enough to freak anyone out. The neighboring houses are all new, huge, cream-colored. Their owners only come for August but the houses look tidy all the same: the grass is neatly cut and the yards have zero trees in them or at most a few palm trees, since palm trees don't make a mess. Ghost House, on the other hand, disappears behind a forest of thick, crooked trees that look like they're about to fall over. Probably the only reason they're standing is because they lean against one another, inter-twined and tangled up, and underneath there are brambles and thorns and it's always dark, even now, at lunchtime, and I'd rather run past it and not stop till I've reached home.

Zot doesn't run. On the contrary, he actually stops in front of it. He walks up to the rusty gate and peers in. After a minute he opens it and I swear he enters and begins to make his way through the haunted woods.

"Zot, what are you doing? Are you crazy? Get out of there! Run!"

"I told you. I have to tell my grandfather I'm going to your place!"

I just look at him, stunned. It's not possible. Of all places, Zot lives here at Ghost House! I stop in the middle of the street. I can't believe it.

"Come on, Luna," he shouts, halfway there. I shake my head briskly and hang back by the gate, above which hangs a sign written in large letters on a piece of wood, as clear as can be:

BUZZER BROKEN. DON'T RING. GO AWAY.

"Come on, Luna, are you scared?"

"No. But I'll just wait back here."

"All right, but if you're scared, I should point out that the gate is the most dangerous spot. That's where the rifle is aimed," he says, disappearing into the overgrowth.

I look around. I can hardly see a thing but I hear a lot of weird noises and a sharp crack that could either be Zot stepping on a branch or a rifle being cocked. So I grab hold of the bars of the gate, breathe deep and take the plunge. I can't believe it. Here I am, in the woods of Ghost House, branches crisscrossing around me, and I put my hands out to feel my way forward.

"Zot! Are there dangerous animals here?"

"No," he says in the dark. "Just snakes and spiders."

I swear that's what he says—snakes and spiders. I get stuck and try pushing aside the branches using just two fingers. I'm really scared. Like I was when I entered this place, and like this morning when I left home and freaked out about the road, school, whether or not the teachers would ask to see the homework we did over break, when I didn't even take a break, never mind do the homework for break. And now I'm scared to return home and find Mom still lying in the dark, or in the bathroom crying softly on the toilet, and when I get there and greet her, she startles, as if I were a robber.

The same thing happened this morning when I picked up my backpack and told her I was going to school. She didn't answer, yet I know it was the most ridiculous thing in the world to her. Luca's dead. Why go to school? Why leave the house? So you can be frightened by snakes and spiders?

Maybe I'm the problem. Maybe I'm stupid or cruel, since I continue to disobey her, and some things scare me and other things I still like. I keep shaking as I push the branches with my fingers, as a cobweb lands in my face. And past the trees I actually leap in the air when this phlegmy cry comes out of nowhere. "Hands up, bastards! Hands up! Prepare to meet your maker!"

"Hold it, Grandfather. It's me!" says Zot, even if his arms are up too.

"Ah. And who's the old lady?"

"She's not an old lady. She's in my class."

"What's with the white hair?"

"She was born that way, Grandfather. Her name is Luna. I told her to come."

"That was a mistake."

"Sorry, Grandfather."

"I'm not your grandfather. And sorry cuts no muster!"

Zot nods, then turns to me. "Don't be fooled by his uncouth words, Luna. Grandfather is actually an exquisite person."

Could be, but I keep my hands up anyhow, stock-still save for my heart beating in my throat. From inside come the sounds of wood and iron, some swear words about the Virgin Mary, and the *click*, *clack*, and *click* of the door opening, just a bit, then the phlegmy voice again, saying, "Get in. Quick."

Zot runs inside but no way am I going in there. I hang back, unsure what to do, until someone grabs me and tosses me inside. Inside Ghost House.

What a stink of old rugs, old clothes left for years in drawers, of wet dog and rainfall from two or three winters ago. I take my dark glasses off and see a table with two plates on top, possibly broken, a fridge with the door missing, and in the corner, at the window, Zot's grandfather stealing another glance outside.

He has on plastic slippers, pajama bottoms, and a tank top so baggy and beat-up he might as well be shirtless. On his head is a blue beret with something written on it I can't read. Oh right, and a rifle in his hand.

He shuts the window and looks at us. Strike that. Just at me, with a face covered in deep scarlike wrinkles and a puckered mouth, like he'd just bitten into a lemon.

"Where do you come from, white stuff? You radioactive too?"

"Sorry, what did you say?"

"I said, you from Chernobyl too?"

"No sir, I'm from here. But I'm albino. It has to do with genetics, which means—"

"I know what it means. One time there was this albino pheasant up in the mountains above Sillano. Totally white, even its beak. All winter we tried to nab her, but she was white as snow. Now you see her, now you don't. Normal pheasants we picked off gradually, but the albino pheasant got through winter unscathed." He rests his rifle against the wall and turns toward me. I nod and smile a little at how beautiful this story about the white pheasant is.

"How many years ago was that, sir? Is it still up in the mountains?"

"What's that?"

"The white pheasant. Is it still where you said it was?"

"Please. Once winter was over, the snow melted, and the white pheasant shone in the woods like a lightbulb. We found her in a field. She tried to fly away but we shot her. The second shot took her head off, and she caught six total, one after another. She was so mangled we couldn't eat her. Practically never hit the ground. She exploded in the air, rest her soul."

I stop nodding and try to smile a little more but can't.

"So, are you two boyfriend-girlfriend?" Zot's grandfather asks, standing with his back against the wall and the rifle set on the floor like a cane.

"No!" I blurt. "We go to school together!"

"Well, whatever, listen carefully all the same. I'm going to teach you something important. People say that shacking up together is a scam, that it's only good at the beginning, that the first two or three months are rosy but then it turns into a living hell. But that's a lie. Don't believe them . . . Not even the early days are rosy. Shacking up together is pain, period, from day one to the end of days. Got it?"

"Yes," I say, "but we just go to school together."

"Got it or not?"

"Yes, Grandfather."

"Good, that takes care of that. And knock it off with this grandfather nonsense. I'm not your grandfather. I'm Ferruccio. My friends call me Ferro, so you can call me Ferruccio. See, this gets back to my original point. I was just fine here on my own. I minded my own business and no one was around to hassle me. Then one day my dimwit daughter shows up and carries on about how she just has to have a kid from the Chernobyl Project. Chernobyl? No goddamn way, I told her. No goddamn way am I letting a Russian into my house. And a radioactive one at that! And she says to me, 'No, Daddy, this kid is really sweet and well behaved. I swear I'll take care of him all by myself.' Idiot thought he was a puppy. Understand? Eventually they really did ship this kid here. Only by then she'd forgotten all about him and left for Spain to go work in a bar with a friend twice as dumb. And who gets pinned with the radioactive kid?" asks Mr. Ferro. "This fool here gets pinned with him, this fool here." He twists his arm around as if to indicate he'd done it all by himself.

"I am very sorry, Grandfather. But I am not radioactive."

"That's what you say. And even if you're not, the fact is you're still a pain in the ass. And Russian. Christ, I have to stand guard 24/7 to keep them out, and they send a spy into my house. You people really are the devil. All those years you fed us that load of crap about the Soviet Union. I believed in it. We all believed in it, *Maremma Cane*. That you were thriving and happy and everyone—worker and doctor alike—was equal. That you didn't care about money, that money was driving us all bonkers because we were stoned on capitalism. We held demonstrations. We held gatherings for the Party. And what did we get? Shit all, that's what. A limp turd is what we got. Meanwhile you were waiting for the right moment, and as soon as we came to a bad—and I mean bad—end, you guys showed up and all of a sudden you were made of money, with your gold shoes and helicopters. You took away the country. Shitheads that we are, we sold it to you. But not me. With me it won't be pretty. You won't get my land, you hear me? None of it!"

Mr. Ferro carries on wagging his finger. Then he stops talking. No one talks. Only a death rattle rises up from the fridge, which I don't think works seeing as it has no door. In fact, the noise dies immediately. Ferro grabs a chair from the table, swivels it around, and sits down in it, like that, with the back facing forward. He looks at us.

"Well, what the hell do you want?"

"Nothing, Grandfather. I only wanted to tell you that I'm going over to Luna's and that you needn't fret about me."

"Fret?"

"I thought that perhaps if you didn't see me coming. Or perhaps you were preparing lunch and I hadn't . . . "

"What the hell do I care? Besides, there's nothing to eat. You didn't go shopping this morning and it's not as if I can go. Who would watch over the house?"

"I was at school. School reopened today. But I have to admit I am a touch famished."

"And I'm not? Too bad we don't have squat. But what does that matter to you? You're off to eat at your girlfriend's."

"We're not boyfriend-girlfriend!" I blurt. "And I don't think there's anything at my place either. Maybe breakfast things, like cookies or biscuits. If there's nothing for lunch, we could have breakfast again."

Zot raises his head and looks at me, and by the whiteness of his face I can tell he's smiling real hard, with all his teeth showing.

"Bravo, now get lost," says Ferro. "And while you're out, stop by the grocer's and pick up some stuff so maybe we can get some dinner around here tonight."

"All right! What should I get, Grandfather? Would you make me a list?"

"Bread, mortadella, spaghetti. And pecorino."

"Can we get cookies too?"

"Bread, mortadella, spaghetti, pecorino."

"And biscuits?"

Mr. Ferro doesn't answer and turns to me instead. "Do me a favor, kid. Would you answer this pain in the balls?"

I turn to Zot. "Bread, mortadella, spaghetti, pecorino."

"Thank God your girlfriend's got more brains than you. Now off you go, for real this time, I have to hit the crapper." He claps his hands, wipes them on his pajama pants, and lifts himself up off the chair with a few phlegm-filled groans. He picks up the rifle and walks off, bent in two and clutching his stomach.

"Are we going?" I ask, heading to the door.

"Yes, just a minute. I want to wait for Grandfather to return so I can say goodbye. I'd feel bad otherwise."

"What do you care? He'd be happier to find us gone."

"You don't know him. He can be a bit brusque, but deep down he's affectionate."

"Deep down where?"

Zot doesn't reply and I don't say anything else. The bathroom must be just on the other side of the kitchen wall, and the wall must be made of cardboard, cause it feels as if you were in there with him: you can hear the lid being lifted, the seat slammed, another groan like the one he'd made getting up from the chair. I think I even catch a whiff. I'm suffocating. If I stay here a second longer, I'll be sick.

"We've been here a half hour, Zot. Let's go!"

"Be patient just a minute, we'll say goodbye and then we'll go."

"Ugh, Zot, why did I come here? Why do I hang out with you?"

At first he doesn't say anything, just approaches the door. Then: "Luna, much as it pains me to say it, it's clear that you hang out with me because you are marginalized and no one else wants to be in your company." He says it normal, as if it were so obvious everyone knew.

"Hey, the same goes for you, you know?" I say. "You're at least as marginalized as me."

"I know, it's true. But I am happy to hang out with you. And that makes all the difference."

I turn and face him but fortunately he opens the door and the light outside engulfs me and keeps me from seeing, keeps me from thinking any longer.

THE THREE FACES OF SATURDAY NIGHT

Bye-bye, Bachelorette, Bye-bye

It's Saturday night and Cristina is dancing and laughing, and when she knows the tune she sings along with all the voice she's got, hugs her friends tight, takes a sip of her drink every time the deejay says, "Ladies and gentlemen, let's hear it for Cristina, tonight's her night!" She raises her glass and dances, sings, drinks, shouts. Because the deejay is right, tonight *is* her night. Her last night.

Tomorrow Cristina is getting married. In the little church in town called Our Lady of the Waters. She was born and raised here, and after the wedding she and Gianluca will move 200 yards down the road, into his parents' place, now converted into a two-family. Gianluca is the man of her life; they met when they were eighteen. He works in his uncle's electrical supply store and Cristina manages a shoe store in downtown Pisa. In the twelve years that they've dated— *twelve*—not a day has gone by that they haven't seen one another, apart from a weekend when he went to Sardinia for a car rally, and once when she went with her mother to the hot springs in Saturnia. Tomorrow they head for the altar, and Don Aldo, who presided over her baptism and confirmation, will turn to Cristina and ask her if she will take Gianluca forever, and she will say yes, till death do them part.

Her friends, on the other hand, tell her she's a fool. They

always tell her that, but tonight they really let her have it as they made their way to Versilia for the bachelorette party.

"How on earth do you do it? How are you not curious?"

Aside from Gianluca, Cristina has never been with anyone.

But who cares? What's the harm? That used to be totally normal: girls married the first guy to kiss them and carried on just fine, and the world with them. That's the way Cristina is, like her mother and especially like her grandmother Maria, the person who raised her, the person she loves most in the world. Almost more than Gianluca. Sure, it would be interesting to see how another guy is wired down there, to find out if there's a big difference. But look, she met the man of her life when she was eighteen and that man loves her and has never hurt her. Got something to say about it?

Yep, her friends do. They act all hip and superior yet for years they've been desperately bouncing from one asshole to another, and every time they get burned they say enough's enough, I'm through being a sucker, and all the while they're holding their phone and quaking in anticipation of the next text message or for someone to "like" the latest photo of them stretched out, soaking up the sun. So when her friends tell her she's making a mistake giving up all that, Cristina can't help but smile.

Only tonight her grandmother said it too. Cristina was making herself up in the bathroom for her evening out. She didn't even want a bachelorette party, but her friends had kept insisting, and yesterday Gianluca told her he was being taken to dinner at Caprice, a place in the hills where they serve meat and, more importantly, where Eastern hookers strip. "You know, for a lark," he'd said. So Cristina had said she was going out too, for a lark, and was looking at herself in the bathroom mirror wearing this skimpy, slinky red dress her friends had gotten her, and together they would all head out identically clad to see what was happening in Versilia.

She bent over the mirror then backed up to get the full view, and maybe it wasn't her place to say so, but she had a really hot body. And beautiful blue eyes. And full lips her friends made a lot of dirty jokes about. But those lips had a problem, a serious problem parked right above them—her nose. Too long, slightly humped, it sat right in the middle of her face, casting a shadow over her lips and burying her smile. Cristina stared at it and brooded.

Gianluca broods over it too, a little. Lately he keeps repeating, "Did you know that fox on TG1 had her nose done?" "Did you know the wife of that soccer player had her nose done?" "Guess what Gianni's sister had done?"

Finally Cristina told him maybe she should get hers done. But she said it to say it, in the expectation that Gianluca would immediately tell her she was crazy, that she was beautiful the way she was, that her beauty was natural and that he loves all of her, nose included. Instead he'd sat there silently for a second before saying it might be a nice idea.

Nice idea!

Tonight Cristina had studied her profile in the mirror, first normally and then with a hand over her nose. Who knows, maybe she would look better? Or maybe the problem was that Gianluca was an asshole and other, more sophisticated men in the world would love her for who she is . . .

Just then, without knocking, her grandmother had come in. She looked her over, from her high heels to her thighs to the morsel of flesh covered up by that dress. Then she looked deep into her eyes. "Cristina, you're a beauty," she told her.

"Thanks, Grandma, I love you too!" High on her heels, she bent over to hug her little grandmother, who, smothered in her embrace, added, "Beautiful and stupid."

"Grandma! Why would you say that?"

"Because it's true. If you were ugly I'd understand. But not this. I'm coming to your wedding tomorrow because I love you to death, but I'm telling you, I'm not happy about it."

"Why not? You don't want me to get married? You don't like Gianluca?"

"No, that's not the problem. Even if I did like him, you don't."

"Are you joking? I love him. He's the man of my life."

"Oh, shut up, what do you know? You ever try another?"

"Not you too, Grandma, I'm begging you. With my friends, I get it. But not you."

"Why not me?"

"Because, like me, you and Mom have only been with one man before."

"The hell I have!" Her grandmother looked over her shoulder and, seeing no one coming, continued: "Maybe your mom never, but I certainly supped my fill."

"Grandma! You were married when you were sixteen."

"True, but then there was the war. And, baby girl, you've no idea what war means." She shut the door and continued, softly this time. "Your grandfather shipped out to the front when I was eighteen. Three years I waited for him. Never even wrote. And I was pretty, young . . . I didn't know if he was still alive. I didn't know if I was alive. And at night I felt like I was on fire."

"So you slept with someone else?"

"Lower your voice," she said, nodding in the affirmative.

"Who was he?"

"You wouldn't know them."

"Them? How many were there?"

"I couldn't give you an exact figure. Ten. Eleven. Let's say ten and half."

Cristina stands there, leaning against the sink while this terrible scene plays in her mind: her grandmother as she is now— her close-cropped bluish hair, her legs wide as air ducts, her skin like a sheet just fished out of the washing machine—surrounded in bed by who knows how many men tugging her from all sides.

Instead it was her grandmother who tugged at her. She hugged her tightly and whispered in her ear, "Think about it, baby girl, think hard on it. I mean really hard. I'm not saying another thousand, not a hundred, but at least one, just one, so you know. Otherwise it'll stick in your throat forever."

She kissed her on the cheek and told her she loved her. Then she left and the bathroom suddenly became quiet and cramped, closing in around Cristina.

Who's dancing now, drinking, sweating in the middle of the crowd on the dance floor at Capannina's. She raises her head toward the ceiling, where men hover, looking out, looking at her. And Cristina laughs and waves and only occasionally thinks about shielding her nose, then hugs her friends one at a time.

They'd gotten her a gigantic black vibrator so big that at first Cristina had thought it was a baton, and seeing as she and Gianluca were moving to the end of a badly lit street, keeping a contraption like this in her purse when she returns from work at night might come in handy. Except it won't fit in a purse. It won't fit anywhere. In fact, a thing this big can't actually exist. Right? What does she know? Maybe it's not even that over-the-top. Maybe she thinks Gianluca is normal because the only one she's seen is his and in fact he's poorly endowed. Cristina is about to marry a poorly endowed guy and she's only going through with it because, fool that she is, she's never seen another. What does she know? What indeed?

Nothing. Not one nothing. And over the music and shouting she can hear her grandmother repeating: "I'm not saying another thousand, not a hundred, but at least one . . . "

Cristina shouts for another glass of champagne. Chiara runs to fetch it but rather than head for the bar, Chiara goes up, or down, or maybe Cristina is just drunk. Her head spins and all these strange men standing around her appear above her too, and below her, and almost on top of her.

There's a group of African guys—what're they like? Is it true they're so well equipped? What would sleeping with a blond be like? With someone who doesn't speak your language? She doesn't know. Cristina doesn't know anything. She doesn't know the feel of another person's breath on her skin, the taste, what happens to another man's eyes when he enters you, what he says to you and—

And if she doesn't know now, finding out the day after tomorrow will be a thousand times more difficult. Because tomorrow she gets married and marriage is sacred; after you're married it's a completely different thing—serious, inviolable. But that's after. Not tonight.

So Cristina dances, dances and laughs; her head spins but she doesn't feel sick. Actually, she feels great. Again the deejay calls out that tonight's her night then puts on a song she loves, one she used to hear on TV when she was a little girl and still knows by heart, especially the chorus:

Come on, shake your body, baby, do the conga
I know you can't control yourself any longer
Come on, shake your body, baby, do the conga
I know you can't control yourself any longer.

Cristina raises her arms and shakes her stuff as hard as she can. Her friends start pointing. They can't believe it. They shout that she's the queen, a legend, the hottest bitch in town! And it's true. In fact, men are circling her, clapping, edging in, attempting weird dance moves to get her attention. Weirdest of all is this boy in a white shirt, younger than her, hopping up and down and swaying, one hand over his heart and the other on his hip. She looks at him, smiles, and applauds. So he does a twirl then sidles up to her, real close, gets right in her face, puts his mouth to her ear and utters, softly yet resoundingly amid the confusion, the most beautiful words Cristina has ever heard.

Balmy and smooth, they enter her ear and massage her temples, slip down her throat and past her chest and reach her heart before trickling down to her stomach all the way to where Cristina's thighs meet, and they're so wet so quickly that she has to pull away from this amazing boy for a moment before wrapping her arms around him and clinging to him, to his unfamiliar scent, increasingly trembling, all lit up inside with the wonderful words he just uttered:

"Hey, I sure dig your nose."

El Cocktail del Amor

Godzunkle, it works! Godzunkle!

All summer his friends had given him shit for throwing away his money and wasting his nights in some rank gym. Dancing was for total fags, they told him. But man does it work—and then some. Godzunkle, it slays! Daniele was totally right to have taken Maestro Hugo Rose's Caribbean Dance Class at the arena in Fivizzano. The name might mean nothing to normal people but if you find a fan, you can tap that chick no sweat. It's like saying Legend taught you to sing or Bourdain to cook. When Daniele saw this half-naked girl start thrashing about to a salsa, he knew she was hip to it. So he showed her two or three serious moves, put his lips to her ear, and whispered those magic words, "Hey, I studied with Hugo Rose."

And, godzunkle, this girl lost her mind.

Actually, then and there she froze. She looked at him wide-eyed and said, "Are you kidding me?" He didn't know how to respond. Not only had she known about the class, not only did she know who Hugo "El Suave" Rose was, but she's such a big fan she couldn't believe she was standing face-to-face with one of his students. In fact, a minute later she jumped him and squeezed him tight. Thanks to his master's instruction, Daniele immediately took the situation in hand, pressed her to his chest, and started to dance.

Feel the fire of desire
As you dance the night away
'Cause tonight we're gonna party
Till we see the break of day . . .

She's over the moon. And she's hot too. Nice ass, nice tits. Too bad her nose is so huge it looks fake. Whatever. It doesn't matter. Daniele holds her nice and tight so he can't see it. Plus it's a scientific fact that girls with big noses have hot bodies. And his hands are all over that body as the two of them sway this way and that and back and forth, and the deeper he probes, the more she thrashes about.

Godzunkle, Maestro Rose really knew what he was talking about: "A woman changes her minds a thousand times a *segundo*. She thinks she wants one thing and then she wants another. *Pero* she gets it in her *cabeza* that she wants something else. When really women want just one thing: a man who's *seguro*, who's *presente*, who grabs her by the hair and makes her *bailar*."

Tonight that man is Daniele and an outing with friends organized at the last minute is turning into the colossal reward for a summer of lessons and exercises.

To think, he hadn't even wanted to come to Versilia. They'd taken his car and he'd wanted to go all the way to Montecatini, a place full of grannies. Time was, you had to pick them up in secret and pretend you didn't remember the next day, but now that they're no longer called grannies, now that they're called MILFs, you can talk a big game to your friends the day after. Right, his friends, who nevertheless nixed Montecatini. Tonight they were going to Versilia. End of story.

Thank God they did. Because now he's here and there's this girl with an enormous nose but with everything else slamming, who's rubbing up on him and he's had his hands all over her already and the time has come to make the most important move, what Maestro Hugo Rose taught him and him alone, during the last lesson, when he was the only one left in the class.

"Daniele, drive the woman wild. Make her *bailar*. And when she is really hot, you lift your leg and you stick it between her thighs. Hard. And keep it there. You keep it there hard and fast, *intiendes*? She needs to feel *la presencia*. The woman worries s*iempre*. She never know where to go. She go here *y* she go there *y* she only want *un hombre* to take her and hold her firm, with a hard, strong thing between her thighs. *Tu*. Make her feel *la presencia*. That is the most important move, Daniele. It's called 'El Cocktail del Amor.' If you serve her the right cocktail, you can be *seguro* there'll be dinner after. *Intiendes*?"

Daniele gets it, he gets it perfecto. And he has shown her a dance, twirled her this way and that, and she's laughing and shaking and letting out little squeals, but then all of a sudden she stops and becomes very serious, paralyzed, when he sticks his leg between hers and lifts both it and her dress all the way up into the warmth of that magic spot where her thighs meet. Daniele serves up El Cocktail del Amor and kisses her neck. She pulls her head back and stops breathing. Daniele stops breathing too, trying to figure out whether she's going to slap him in the face or press charges. But then he watches her draw near again, stare at him slit-eyed behind that gigantic nose, and shove all the tongue she's got down his throat. And they go at it for at least five minutes, continuing to kiss as he drags her away from the dance floor toward the little sofas.

They sit down, at which point Daniele wonders if he should offer her a drink. He disentangles his tongue from hers. "What do you want to do?"

And she replies, panting warmly, "Can I see what it's like?"

"Huh?"

"Can I see what your dick looks like?"

Just like that. Straight and to the point. A little slurred from the alcohol is all. Then she closes her eyes and goes back to kissing his neck. After that, Daniele can't see straight. He lifts her up and carries her to the ladies' room. And thank God, thank the Lord for granting him an unforgettable night tonight: as soon as they enter, the only other chick in the bathroom leaves. Daniele props her against the wall, unbuckles his python-skin belt, drops his jeans, and whips it out.

She stands there, motionless, her eyes crossed, one hand over her mouth and muffling her voice a bit, but he can still make out what she says:

"Is that normal?"

Daniele doesn't know what to say. So it's not huge, okay? It's not so small as to warrant making a scene like this.

"Whatever," he says, his voice wavering between horniness and humiliation, "it's not enormous, but it's all right. It's about average, see, not—"

"Are you telling me there are bigger ones than that?"

Daniele looks at her, sees the surprise and excitement in her eyes, and realizes there's no need to defend himself; what he needs to do is attack. "Bigger? Nah. This is as good as it gets."

She nods, bites her lip, and lowers her gaze again. She places her hand on top of it and rubs it slowly, as if she were scared it might bite her, and then—

And then all of a sudden the door swings opens and in come these girls singing and screaming. She recoils, almost falls backward. He buttons up his jeans. They hug one another again to hide their faces from these blue-ballers. And while they're hugging, Daniele racks his brain for a solution, a place to go—

"Are we close to the beach?" she asks him.

Daniele doesn't understand. "I dunno. I mean, yeah, it's just on the other side of the club."

"Do you know how to get there?"

"No. I'm not from around here, I never come here." He looks at her. Way to look like a doofus, like someone who doesn't even know how to get to the beach. Next thing you know she'll be turned off, this beast of an erection drilling a hole in your jeans will get no relief, and Maestro Hugo Rose will catch wind of what happened and disown you as his student.

But she keeps looking at him with those half-closed eyes. "You don't have a car?" she asks.

Yes, godzunkle, yes! The car!

He wraps an arm around her and walks her outside. They hold each other tightly, both tottering, she from too much drink and he from the pinch in his underwear. But all is well, Daniele knows that soon this discomfort will become comfortable, will become marvelous. And with their hearts beating faster than the music and pumping blood into every inch of their bodies, Cristina and Daniele step out of the club and into the arms of the warm night air, thumping with promise.

The Nightly Trials of Traffic Cops

Mustard pants, blue-short, sleeved shirt, orange vest and cap, reflective tape top-to-toe: Marino pedals down the dark coastal road, peering into every car window and trembling, because on a Saturday night in September this uniform makes him look like a Christmas tree, and for a traffic cop that's a death sentence.

The crazy thing is that the municipality makes them dress this way for their safety, so that cars can see them clearly and avoid running them over. But it's like hanging a stone around a scuba diver's neck so he can get to the bottom quicker, like dumping gas from a plane mid-flight so that it won't catch fire.

If the municipality really cared about its traffic cops, they would send them out in black flight suits and ski masks, like parking lot ninjas, and they could creep in the shadows with their citation holders, sling a ticket at your windshield, and disappear in the dark. Because for traffic cops, the real threat isn't being hit by accident but spotted by drivers who want to run him over on purpose.

Just read the dispatches from this past summer's war. There may be no mention of traffic cops being hit by cars, but four wound up in the emergency room with contusions and fractures, and last week a colleague was rushed to the hospital with third-degree burns after a tourist took a lighter to his synthetic orange vest—one spark and the vest burst into flames.

All told, the life of a traffic cop is demanding and risky. He's a destitute mercenary who risks his life for a few bucks while making a killing for the municipality. Like municipal cops. Actually, scratch that, a hundred times worse than municipal cops, since those guys get paid well and have a serious uniform, a radio if they need help, a sidearm if help can't wait. They may not be real policemen but you think twice before laying a hand on a municipal cop.

A traffic cop, on the other hand, is cannon fodder. Armed with a pen and citation pad and forced to go around dressed like a clown in a mash of factory overstock: they get their pants from bus inspectors and their shirts from plumbers. Their wide-brimmed caps are freebies from the annual senior citizen celebration; in fact, written across the front are the words "Forte dei Marmi Grandparent" with a patch over the word "Grandparent" that says "Traffic Cop." And seeing as this overstock is scraped together, everything comes in two sizes only—extra small and extra large—so that Marino is riding his bike around downtown tonight in socks as snug as tights and an enormous shirt blowing in the wind that makes him look like a kite on wheels.

And the image of his colleague on fire continues to torment him in the dark—lit up like a bonfire, like a pile of dry leaves, and left to burn. What is the world coming to? What is it coming to? Marino shakes his head and tries to muster some courage, gripping the handlebar and pedaling down the coastal road alongside the sweep of cars in the paid parking lots outside the nightclubs. But every shout, every horn, every set of high beams slapped across the dark makes him catch his breath.

Now, hey, tragedy may be inevitable, but if one struck him it wouldn't be fair. He's a catechist and has to shepherd kids through confirmation. God has to protect him, at least a little. But God has a lot on his mind, and maybe even he can't save you if you're tooling around in a uniform this bright.

Small wonder Marino is now pretending not to hear these shouts coming from the sidewalk. He keeps pedaling—speeds up a little, actually—as if the wind in his ears silenced the words of the citizen on the curb. "Get over here, dweeb! Stop!"

But Marino *can* hear those words. He can even hear the footsteps coming toward him on the sidewalk. So he springs up on his pedals and pumps with all his might to get out of there, only he's restrained by his tight pants, his shirt inflates like a blue parachute, he decelerates, and a hand snatches him, bringing an end to his flight.

Marino puts one foot on the ground, trying to steady himself and maintain a calm, professional tone, but his heart is beating in his throat. "Yes? May I help you?"

"Where the hell is my car?"

The guy's in his thirties. Not big but tall—check. And pissed off—double check. Behind him is a blond girl, her eyes down, tucked into a short, tight-fitting, and totally transparent dress. She's very pretty. Except for that gigantic nose.

"Hey, I'm talking to you, godzunkle, where the hell is my car!"

"Me, I don't . . . I don't know, sir. Sorry, I'm not a valet." Marino addresses him as sir—it's not like you're going to hit a guy who calls you sir, right? There's not enough intimacy. "Did you forget where you parked?"

"No, I know exactly where I parked."

"Then what's the problem?"

"The problem is it's not there anymore, asshole!"

The coastal road is one endless line of cars gunning for the nightclubs, people going in and out on foot, and this guy's shouts are drawing the attention of the Saturday night crowd who, deprived of love and sex and real fun, place what dreary hopes they have in assault and battery.

But not Marino. No, all Marino wants is to return home alive, and he tries to come off as meek as a medieval pageboy or a farrier greeting his lord atop a horse, riding crop in hand. He takes off his cap and holds it to his chest. "I'm really very sorry but I don't know how I can help you, sir."

"What do you mean? Aren't you supposed to keep an eye on the cars?"

"No, that's the job of a parking valet. A municipal cop at best. I'm just a traffic cop."

He tries to smile but clearly this is no laughing matter, so he apologizes another two or three times and remarks how scandalous it is, and if he keeps this up maybe he can calm the guy down while the girl in the red dress is touching his shoulder and telling him to drop it, to let it be.

"Help me understand a sec, dickhead," says the guy. "I work my ass off all week. I work. Godzunkle, I'm Italian." (Cue the applause, a couple "Right on"s and a faint chorus chanting, "Italia, Italia.") "Then I come here on Saturday night, I fork over all the money I've earned, and if I'm five minutes late you slap me with a ticket. But if some thieving Albanian or Romanian steals my car, you don't do anything to him? Is that it?"

"Like I said, I'm not a municipal cop. I cannot intervene. Besides, I didn't see anything, I just came on duty."

"Of course you didn't see anything, of course not. The car was right over there, how is it possible you didn't see anything?"

"Sorry, where?"

"There, dickhead, how many times do I have to tell you? There!"

The guy points to the only empty space in the line of cars parked along the edge of the road. Right in front of a large wrought-iron gate leading to a villa.

"Ah, I see," says Marino, continuing to turn his hat in his hands. "There's a gate over there. That's a driveway."

"So what?"

"So my guess is your car wasn't stolen. It was towed."

"Towed how?"

"Um, by a tow truck?"

The guy repeats the words "tow truck," and you can tell he has a whole slew of other things to say, which may be logical or may just be more insults to shower Marino with, but they catch in his throat. He stays like that, his mouth open, his eyes two pinballs bouncing around at random amid a thousand monstrosities, while the cars on the road honk their horns, trying to wheel past the knot of people.

The girl with the big nose comes up to him again and in a soft voice says she's cold, that maybe it'd be better if she went back to her friends. He whips around and shouts, "No! Wait! No, no—" He unbuttons his lily-white shirt, takes it off, and wraps it around her shoulders. He asks her if that's any better. She scoffs. "Not really," she says and stares back down at the ground. He looks at her for a minute, and then turns back, bare-chested, to face Marino.

And the people around start cheering again, as if by removing his shirt they were inching closer to a fight.

"You motherfucker. You had them tow my car, huh?"

"Me? What do I have to do with that? Towing's none of my—"

"Yeah, that's what you thought!" shouts someone from the crowd; by now a real crowd has formed and they expect a show. Applause. Someone smashes a bottle at Marino's feet.

Someone else shouts, "Kick that fucker's ass!"

The shouts grow louder and are so numerous they blur together, and rather than complete sentences they're an increasingly large welter of voices from which, every once and a while, a "shit" or an "ass" or a "dickhead" escapes. The girl with the big nose raises her eyes again, and only now seems to realize how many people have gathered around, guys who are loaded, kids with their hair shooting this way and that, plenty of girls like her looking on, looking at her, judging. She pulls her skirt down as far as she can, buttons his shirt to the neck, and says softly, "I'm going back to my friends, sorry," before stumbling off on her high heels.

"No, wait! Just a minute! I'm going to get the car back in just a minute, come on!" But she's already running and doesn't answer. "Or we could get a room. There are hella hotels! There are hella hotels!" But she doesn't turn around or stop, and this bare-chested guy watches her disappear. She's even more beautiful from behind: her butt lean yet round, her waist narrow, her soft hair swaying with each step. Plus, from the back you can't see that gigantic nose.

Just like the night's momentous opportunity, the woman ambles off and vanishes, materializing from nothing and retreating into nothing. It isn't fair, godzunkle, it's totally unfair! In a matter of minutes he'd lost his car and a hot date and, it was gradually dawning on him, his shirt too. No, nothing is fair in this life, it's one long spate of things that could go well but turn out for the worse. So, if other folks occasionally meet with a little injustice, tough shit. Tough shit, Marino.

"Happy now, motherfucker?" The bare-chested guy stares Marino straight in the eye, and after that everything happens with swift precision, like one of those chemistry formulas where you plug in everything they ask you to and it works. Take the late hour, the fatigue. Add excessive quantities of alcohol at the end of the night when the euphoric effect has worn off and all that's left is the bitter aftertaste. Add roused but ungratified hormones. Add people hanging around waiting for something big to happen. Add this guy's friends, who are just now arriving and discover him shirtless and themselves out a ride . . . If you don't want to see what spews from that nastiness you have to shut your eyes tight and keep them shut till you feel the first blow.

But it doesn't come. Marino feels no punches, no kicks, just the hands of this guy's friends pulling him off his bike. He tries to retain his grip on the handlebar but the bike drops to the ground. One of them jumps on it and the wheels cave, a fender cracks.

"Easy, guys, you're taking things a bit far," he says, trying to maintain a professional tone even in the hands of four or five guys who treat him like an old throwaway carpet. "That bike belongs to the town. It's public property."

Meanwhile Bare-Chest's friends hold Marino still. People kick him a couple of times. Someone from the crowd snatches the cap off his head.

"There's still time. You're an inch shy of the point of no return, but if you stop now there'll be no trouble," he says. But they must have misheard him. They strip off his neon vest and use it as a whip while Marino tries to shield himself. "Not my vest, guys! It's part of my uniform! Don't mess with it! You're assaulting a public officer!"

Bare-Chest bursts out laughing, and because he's a foot from Marino's face, it's a combo of laughter and spit. Marino smells the alcohol, feels little bubbles of acidic saliva hit his eyes. He's shoved on the ground like his bike before him, only now it's his bones making that clanking, cracking sound.

The cries of the crowd float up. Someone suggests kicking him. Another calls for a generic beating. "Hit 'em! Hi 'em!" Then comes a girl's voice, high and almost sweet, rising above the others: "Piss on him! Piss on that fag!"

Silence. Everything, even the road, even the world stops spinning for a moment and turns with the crowd to see where that voice is coming from. And there stands this tiny girl in a half-gray, half-pink dress, her hair pulled back, and a smile fading from her face.

Bare-Chest looks at his friends, at the wide- and red-eyed public beginning to cheer again. They collar Marino and hold him down on the ground, faceup in the middle of the road, the cars honking to get by, pebbles and shards of glass underneath his back, and above him Bare-Chest, a leg on either side of him. Pulling down his zipper.

The crowd screams. And, after tossing various epithets into the welter of that night, now they all scream the same thing. Clear, simple, urgent. "Piss on him! Piss on him!"

A prone Marino hears them but doesn't understand. His head hurts and he can barely lift it because Bare-Chest's friends are holding down his arms and legs. And he doesn't think or decide to speak himself; there must be an autopilot deep inside us that, when it sees we're about to crash and don't know what to do, takes the wheel without asking our permission. It opens his mouth and forces out the words. "Guys, I'm begging you, I have nothing to do with this! They pay me slave wages! While you guys are having a good time I'm outside doing this shitty job! I'm one of the kind ones, too. When I see a meter's expired, I wait. I make my rounds and don't come back till after a half hour, I swear! There are others who get a kick out of it, who write up tickets in advance, who lie about the time! If you'd like I can name names. They're here right now. One of them is Roberbluuurrgrrgrrgrgrrgh . . . "

After that nothing, just garbled noises rising up from his

stomach, under this steaming hot gush hitting his neck, his chin, and then, horribly, entering his mouth.

He chokes, as if he were swimming in the sea and had swallowed a wave. Only Marino isn't swimming, and this stuff may be salty but it's not seawater; it's piss filling his throat and lungs. He makes to rise and cough but they keep holding him down even as they pull back to avoid getting hit by the spray.

Around them the crowd hollers madly, people yell and jump in the air and hug each other as if Italy had just scored against Germany in the World Cup. The cry is so loud it drowns out the cars honking angrily behind them, stuck in the middle of the road, people who just want to go home or reach the last nightclub before it closes or mind their own business. All they can see is a tangle of people jumping and shouting, and don't realize that someone on the ground is almost drowning in piss.

But rather than drown, Marino leans his head to one side and vomits. As it went in, so now it goes out: hot and acidic. Totally awful, totally frightening.

"Fuck, gross!" One of the guys holding him down springs back, shielding his sleeve. He curses and walks off, the others pull away too, and Marino lies there on the asphalt, his eyes burning. He can't see anything nor does he want to. All he wants is to be left there, for everyone to go away and leave him to vomit some more.

Which is, in fact, what happens, after Bare-Chest lets out a long "Aaahhh" of satisfaction, as if he'd been holding it in forever. The crowd laughs, cheers, and starts retreating from the road, each shut up inside herself, so that what was a crowd has now become many individuals who had momentarily formed a single soul that wanted to see just one thing, and now that they had seen it they were walking away happy. And the cars are happy too. They give one last honk, rev their engines, and floor it down the road leading to the future.

But that road is seldom a smooth one. In fact, rather than sailing straight ahead, the first car to peel away jerks sideways after hitting something: a bump, a branch, a garbage bag that had rolled off of a dumpster.

Or Marino.

A Catechist Is Born

Luna, I implore you, don't talk to this rogue," says Zot, locking his bike to a lamppost.

The "rogue" is a black man, an African, the kind who hawks fake brand-name purses on the beach. But this guy's not on the beach, he's here in the hospital parking lot. When a car comes, he directs them to a free spot, waves, and, if they hand over some change, says thanks. He waves to us too now that we've ridden our bikes straight here from school, and all I have on me is a euro, which I give him.

"You're giving him money? Must I remind you what these people do to your kind?"

The black man looks at Zot, then at me, and says thanks for the euro. He doesn't understand. Unfortunately I do. Ever since I told Zot what happens to albinos in Africa he has been fixated on the two of us solving the issue. Me and him.

I tell him to shut up and head toward the hospital entrance. The road from school to here is long and sunshiny. Coming here by bike would have been tough without Zot. But once inside the hospital, given all the checkups and tests I have to take, I know by heart where everything is and hurry along in the hopes of losing him. Zot tries to keep up while continuing to talk breathlessly: "You shouldn't have given him money. You're just lucky that wretch wasn't carrying a cleaver, otherwise who knows what he may have done, who knows if you'd still have legs to run so fast."

We make it to the giant revolving door that doesn't start

moving until you're standing in front of it. There's always a group of old people flanking either side, trying to predict the exact moment when to dive forward and looking on with admiration at anyone who dares to enter. At the information desk Miss Franca greets me. I ask her how it's going and which room Mr. Marino—I don't know his last name—is in. "The one who got run over by a car Saturday night on the coastal road," I say, and Miss Franca knows who I mean, because on Saturday night they brought in three run-over people, but one is a girl and there's a funeral for the other this afternoon.

Second floor, room 153. We take the escalator and cross paths with two nurses who say hi and ask if Zot is my boyfriend. Three times I tell them *No*. They laugh. "See you soon," they say. And it makes me glad, although feeling at home in the hospital isn't such a great thing. Actually, the more lost in the halls you are and the less you know about departments and wards, the more it means your life is problem-free.

Take Luca, for example. The only time he was in the hospital was when he was born. Mom and I came all the time for my checkups and in the evening he would ask me how it went. He'd kiss me and say, "That's grand, Luna." One time he took me to the eye doctor. I don't remember why. All I remember is that the doctor saw me and wrote me a prescription for even stronger lenses, and since we were his last patients, he measured Luca's eyes too and told him he had 20/10 vision. 20/10. On a scale where 20/20 is normal, he had 20/10. I didn't even know that was possible. "Me neither," said Luca, laughing, and we left. And even if he did see so well, Luca never saw a hospital again.

Not even on his last day. My big brother didn't die in a white room with the heat blasting and the chemical smell and those machines beeping like cell phones whose batteries were dying. Luca died in the water, in the waves. Even when I don't want to, I often imagine him like that, floating faceup with his long hair drifting slowly above his head. Then it suddenly turns into seaweed, dark seaweed engulfing him, reaching his face and entering his mouth, his ears, his eyes, his beautiful green eyes with super vision and . . .

And luckily we reach the second floor, room 153.

"Luna, wait, where are you going?"

"Um, inside?"

"Yes, but wait. First we need a present."

"A what?"

"A gift, a little thought for our catechist: a bunch of flowers, a box of chocolates, at the very least a newspaper. Is there a newsstand in this place?"

"Yeah, below, but I don't think it's necessary."

"No, it isn't necessary, but it is courteous. I would be ashamed to walk in empty-handed."

I look at Zot, wobbling in the too strong, too vivid neon light of the hospital. I know they will never dim this light just as I know Zot will never go in there without a gift, so I huff off back to the escalators and the newsstand.

"Wait for me, Luna!"

"Come on, run."

"But it's forbidden to run in the hospital!"

"Why's that?"

"I don't know but it's forbidden. Maybe because the sick cannot run and therefore it's mean to let them see we can."

Sandro recoils into the room, slamming the door shut behind him. He'd been on his way out to smoke and now he's holding his freshly broken cigarette in his hand, tobacco crumbs between his fingers.

"Weren't you going out?" asks Rambo, seated beside the bed. Marino tries turning toward him too but his whole chest is covered with plaster. He looks like an upside-down turtle and all he can do is lift his head a little and remain stock-still, rigid, useless.

"I lost interest," says Sandro. But it's not true. The truth is that when he left the room he saw her, there in the hallway, the girl with the white hair who had been standing next to Serena at the funeral, Luca's little sister.

Had he at least been an only child, or had an older sister, an adult equipped for pain. But no, instead he had this tiny little white-all-over sister who was already missing a father—what a nasty, shitty situation. Sandro is dying of guilt and would like to do something for her, really do something, but now that he had bumped into her the best he could do was run. He had gone out to smoke and instead tore back into the room, out of breath.

Rambo stares at him, and Marino tries to stare at him, and fortunately the room is private, it's just the three of them. It costs a ton of money, and Marino with his fractured pelvis will have to be there for a long time, but sleeping in a room with other people is out of the question.

"What happened, Sandro?" he asks from the pillow. "You saw a doctor, didn't you? Did he tell you something? Something I don't know? Tell me, Sandro, you have to tell me!"

"Nothing happened. I wanted to go and now I'm not in the mood. I'm tired."

But it isn't true, he isn't tired, Sandro is simply a coward. She was right there. He could have gone to her, introduced himself, talked. Instead of agonizing about it day and night, he could have asked her how she was, if she could use anything, how school was going or if she needed help with her home-work or whether some classmate was giving her problems. He might even have apologized.

No smoother, more natural occasion would ever present itself. Sure, had he known before he could have braced himself, rather than being blindsided like this. Still, running away was pitiful. Yet it's normal: Sandro is a sad, miserable coward who deserves to go on like this, plagued with remorse by day and bad dreams by night, this sense of guilt crushing him the way he crushed his cigarette when he recoiled into the room.

Now he could really use a cigarette. Too much stress, too much anxiety. He fishes one from his pack and goes to leave the room when he hears footsteps growing louder out in the hall. He opens the door and something happens that, according to his father, never happens in this life: the occasion ambles up to him a second time.

The girl with white hair is coming back, alongside another, shorter kid. Sandro stands to face this new opportunity to be a decent man. He looks right at her, leans against the wall, and takes a breath, breathes poorly, stops breathing altogether . . . He dives back into Marino's room and slams the door even harder this time.

Rambo jumps to his feet. "What the fuck is with you?"

"Sandro, what's happening," says Marino. "You're acting strange. You know something. You have to tell me what it is, Sandro. What do you know? I'll be paralyzed forever, right, stuck in a wheelchair!"

Sandro doesn't answer, just stands there stiffly. He sweats, listening to the footsteps get closer, praying they'll do what footsteps ought to do—pass by quickly. Instead they stop. Right there. And two knocks at the door trip his nerves.

"Hello? Mr. Marino, may we?"

The thin, shaky voice could belong to either the girl or the boy, or to a robin dying slowly in the snow. "May we come in?"

Sandro looks around, stares into Rambo's gaping eyes, and then vaults into the bathroom. He steps inside and shuts the door. Perched on the can, he listens.

"It's us."

"Us who?" says Rambo.

"We're . . . two of Mr. Marino's disciples."

"Disciples? Okay, enter, disciples, your Messiah's in bed."

Sandro hears the soft patter of footsteps, greetings.

"Oh, children, my dear children," says Marino, the tone of his voice now a mix of suffering and wisdom, like a Zen master after a bar fight. "Have you come to see me? Why thank you. How are you? Hi Luna, hi Zot."

Luna, her name is Luna. And a thousand phrases dovetail in Sandro's mind: "Hello, Luna"; "I didn't mean to, Luna"; "Forgive me, Luna, please . . . "

"Excuse us, Mr. Marino," says the boy. "It disconcerts me to say we have come to you like this, empty-handed. The least we could do was bring you a newspaper, but we don't have two nickels to rub together."

"No cause for concern, Zot. And please, call me Marino."

"Oh no, you mustn't ask me to do such a thing, Mr. Marino. Especially now that I am mortified about not bringing you a present. But as you see, we came directly from school, and I cannot bring money to school."

"Why not?" says Rambo. "Against the rules?"

"No. But every day at recess I am subjected to a patdown by my peers. Carrying money on my person is as good as giving it to them."

"Bastards. I'll pop by school someday and scare 'em, eh?"

"Thank you, sir. Luna's mother used to, and it worked. But she doesn't leave the house anymore, so—"

Serena! Luna's mom! Sandro rises from the toilet, careful not to make a noise. He leans over and puts his eye to the keyhole, yet all he sees is a bright, static thing that may be the wall. Besides, there's nothing to see; it's not as though Serena is there. The boy said so himself: Serena doesn't leave the house anymore. She's not well and doesn't go anywhere anymore, not even to school. She's shut up at home and no one is around to defend these kids. All on account of him.

"Can I ask you something?" Now it's Luna speaking. "Did the car run right on top of you?"

"That's right, that's exactly what happened."

"But who was driving? Who did it?" she asks. Sandro squirms, for that's what she wants to know, that's what counts: whose *fault* it is, who's to blame.

"The Saturday evening crowd," Marino says with a sigh. "You know, it was late and we were out by the nightclubs."

"Scandalous," says the boy. "Two-bit punks. Lowlifes. Misfits with no moral compass. There ought to be a law against such bums!"

Rambo laughs. "Cool it, grandpa." There's the sound of scraping and crackling, which probably means Marino is trying to find a comfortable position, as if someone that banged-up could find a comfortable position.

"How long do you have to be in the hospital?" Luna asks.

"Oh, they're not sure exactly. A little while. Then there's rehabilitation, as long as nothing is damaged."

"Damaged?"

"That's right," says Marino, "there are a thousand possible scenarios. A fractured pelvis is like the lottery; how it'll turn out is anyone's guess. You need time, children, time and faith. We're in God's hands."

"Speaking of God," says the boy, "will you not be returning to catechism?"

"No, Zot. Not for a while at least."

"How long is a while?"

"Who knows? Like I said, we're in God's hands."

And then, after a moment of silence, it's Luna's turn to ask. Her voice is different, more pained, as if she hadn't really wanted to hear his answer. "But if you don't come, who will take your place at catechism?"

Marino doesn't answer right away. "I can't say for sure. But bear in mind that it won't be for long. You know, children, you won't even notice."

And the longer Marino dodges the question, the clearer his

answer becomes. In fact, after a moment of silence, Luna says, "Oh no. I knew it. It's Mother Greta, isn't it?"

"Children, what can I say? It's not up to me. And right now we have no choice. There are no other catechists."

"It's not fair," says Luna. "Can't we come here? We'll all come here on Saturday afternoon. We'll have catechism here at the hospital."

"That's right! We could do that!" says the boy excitedly. "Convent, hospital—what's the difference? The voice of God reaches everywhere. Otherwise it would be an injustice: those nightclub punks commit a crime and Luna and I suffer the consequences."

"Ahem," says Rambo, "the one really suffering the consequences is this bedridden, bent fender."

"Yes, it's true, please excuse me. I spoke rashly. Of course Mr. Marino has suffered more than all of us. Having a car run you over must really be a terrifying experience. And it must be even worse to have someone pee on you," says the boy. Silence.

A huge silence, so total that Sandro, sitting on the toilet, has the impression that the room on the other side of the door is no longer there. And perhaps it's his excitement or this very powerful disinfectant they use to clean the bathroom, but for a moment the thought really does cross his mind that everything has disappeared, his friends and the kids and the bed and the TV attached to the ceiling, and he almost reaches out his hand to open the door and see what's out there. But then comes the deafening laughter of Rambo, and amid the laughter, Marino's pitiful voice tries to rise above it and be heard: "It's not true! It's not true, children! Where did you—? Who told you that?"

"At school, Mr. Marino. Why?"

"Because it's not true! It's a lie, maliciousness spread by malicious people who take pleasure in other people's misfortunes! Don't believe them. It's not true. Tell everyone: it's not true!"

"All right, Mr. Marino," says Luna. "All right. But it wouldn't be that big a deal. I mean, it's not your fault if they peed on you."

"True," says the boy, "they spit on me every morning and wipe snot on my coat. I reckon pee would disgust me less than snot, since pee isn't as sticky. Is pee less sticky, Mr. Marino?"

"No, I . . . I don't know! Why are you asking me? I told you it isn't true, no one peed on me!"

Rambo chokes with laughter, the kids try to apologize in every way possible yet continue to bring up the story of his being peed on, and at a certain point Marino stops talking altogether. Soon all Sandro hears are bits of farewells, Luna telling Marino she'll see him at catechism soon, real soon, then the sound of the door closing and goodbye.

Sandro hangs back a minute. And another minute. Then opens the door a sliver and peers into the room where he finds Rambo, his eyes wet with tears, and Marino, who had forgotten all about Sandro in the bathroom, and who, upon seeing him, panics and screams.

Sandro rushes over and grabs his arm, and he probably shouldn't shake him so hard or shout so loud, but he can't help it if in the darkness of that crapper a light had come on.

"Listen, Marino. To hell with Mother Greta. I'm you're new catechist."

METAL DETECTOR

Today is Monday and no one comes to the beach on Mondays.

Just as no swallows appear in January, just as flowers don't bloom in the snow. Nature has its rhythms, and following those rhythms, every species on Earth dances to its tune. That's why upstanding, normal people come to the beach during the weekend. A pinch on Friday and all day Saturday through Sunday afternoon. Then they queue up on the turnpike and head back to Milan, Parma, Florence—wherever they have a job and a life with schedules and clear-cut responsibilities.

Summer is over, the holidays have come and gone, but it's still warm and only fair that on the weekend they soak up as much sun as they can before winter comes and it gets dark at five, when it's time to turn in as soon as you leave the office. So on Friday these upstanding people, men and women who work and may be married or living together and have kids—or dogs—haul their SUVs out of the garage and come to Forte dei Marmi for the weekend to lie in the sun, stroll on the shore, write their names in the sand with underneath the date of these feel-good days, which they photograph with their cell phones while awaiting sundown, the magic hour, which has happened every day since the beginning of time yet for the tourists remains a miracle with the power to stun, to compel them to snap an extra thousand photos of that overwhelming, fiery magnificence dominating the sky and pacifying the sea. All that appears on their cell phone screen is a bright little ball and yet they still rush to send the photo to relatives, friends, and acquaintances who have stayed home, so that they can feel as if they haven't stayed home, that they're in Forte dei Marmi, where every night the sun sets just for them.

Every night till Sunday. Then the upstanding people go home and the sun only sets for the crabs and the crows combing the shoreline, hunting for leftovers, and for Sandro and Rambo who, like the crabs and crows, also scrounge for leftovers, but with metal detectors.

"I don't think they work," huffs Sandro. They've been waving these clunkers over the sand for an hour to no avail.

"They work like gangbusters," says Rambo, "listen to this." Rambo lifts his metal detector to his stainless steel Navy SEAL watch and it gives a loud wavering beep. "See? Like gangbusters." And he goes back to swinging it this way and that over the sand, beaming with pride. Because he built these things himself. Three, to be exact, but now, with Marino in the hospital, for a while it'll be just the two of them hitting the beach every Monday.

It all began in the spring. One day Marino found some beach marbles with photos of cyclists inside, and they gushed about how fun it used to be to play on the beach, building racetracks with curves and ramps and sand traps. Gradually they began to grouse about how, at a certain point, life presents you with changes so big you quit playing. Then they wondered when that had happened to them, and what changes life had wrought for them, and they realized that it was perfectly fine for them to continue playing marbles. So they began squaring off on Monday afternoons at the empty beach, along with the Graziani brothers, one of whom had cooked his brain on ecstasy in the nineties and now receives disability benefits both brothers live off.

It was a kind of championship league, replete with a ranking system Marino would update every Monday evening and email to them. But on the third weekend, while they were dragging their butts over the sand to design the track, Marino let out a wail. Something had poked him. He started running around, clutching his thigh, hollering, "AIDS! AIDS! I got pricked by a syringe and now I've got AIDS!"

Turned out not to be a syringe but a brooch one of these upstanding citizens had lost in the sand during her golden weekend. The brooch was golden too. Literally, it was made of gold.

Marino kept it as compensation for the fear it put in him. He lit a candle for the Virgin Mary of Montenero, gave the brooch to his mother, and never spoke about it again. That is, until the week after, when playing had resumed and it was Sandro's turn to roll. When Sandro knelt down, he felt something hard and flat under his shin, which he discovered was a silver bracelet. He lifted it up and blew on it to take a closer look. Then he looked past it at Marino and Rambo, and that was it for marbles and the Graziani brothers. Now they spend their Mondays combing the beach with metal detectors.

Which Rambo built himself. He found instructions in a survival kit manual, assembled three broom handles, and attached an old pocket radio to the end of each along with a complimentary calculator from Esselunga. Absurd as it sounds, when there's something metal under the sand that radio goes off. Then they stop, set down their detectors, and start digging. It's easy, dirt cheap, and efficient.

Only the radio never goes off.

"Son of a bitch," cries Sandro. Holding this contraption makes his arm ache, his back too, and they haven't found shit. "All those people here yesterday and not one of them lost something? Son of a bitch, Jesus H—" he stops himself. Taking the Lord's name in vain would work wonders right now but he's got to start practicing restraint.

"Not even a catechist yet and already afraid to blaspheme?" ribs Rambo.

Sandro doesn't answer. He keeps swinging the broom and watching Rambo do the same, except more credibly and with greater oomph, thanks in part to his fatigues and combat boots.

"You know this catechist business is bullshit," says Rambo. "You know that, right?"

Sandro keeps his mouth shut. Maybe it is bullshit, but what else is he supposed to do? It's like that night when he was little and his dad took him gigging for garfish. From the pier Sandro pointed a super powerful flashlight down at the water, and soon the garfish arrived, all curious and circling around and around it, then his dad took aim and launched the gig with all his might. Except garfish are small, long, and skinny, like fingers, whereas the gig had a pointy end attached to a wooden handle—a log, really—so instead of skewering the fish, it split it in half, the head one way and the rest the other, and Sandro freaked out while shining a light on that silver thing, now two things, one slowly sinking into the dark water and the other, the tail, for some incredible reason still moving, thrashing this way and that. "Why is it doing that?" he asked his dad, trying not to drop the flashlight off the pier. His dad laughed. "What's he supposed to do, Sandro? You have a brighter idea?"

No, Sandro didn't have a brighter idea that night on the bridge, nor does he now. So it makes sense that the garfish tail would try every which way to escape and that he should become the new catechist for Luna, that little white-all-over girl.

He has to get to know her, talk to her, find out how she and her beautiful mom are faring. He hasn't a clue what he'll say or if he'll be capable of looking her in the face. All he knows is that he can't move on this way. Partly because for the past six months he hasn't moved at all.

His life has stalled. Ever since Luca died, the days come and go, and instead of building upon each other, they stack up into an empty heap of same old, same old.

Sandro had been swimming in the dark, confused, when a gig swung down and tore off his head, and now the only thing he can do is try every avenue of escape. Not because it will work or because there is somewhere to go, but because no better option exists. He simply has to become a catechist and see what comes of it.

"I don't think it's so hard," he says.

"What's that?" says Rambo, having paused in a place where the radio isn't beeping so much as making a noise like rain on a metal roof.

"Being a catechist. It can't be so hard. They're little kids, right? I might not know anything about that stuff, but they know even less. Plus if Marino can do it—"

"I wouldn't be so sure, eh. Marino's more equipped than you."

"Why's that?"

"For one, he goes to church."

"Whatever."

"For another, he believes in God."

"What's that got to do with anything? I believe in God."

"You do?"

"I do. I mean I could. Why not?"

Rambo answers with a laugh that makes him jiggle all over, then turns from their conversation as well as the spot setting the radio off and resumes swinging his metal detector around.

Toward the shore, where a colorful group of kids—clearly foreigners—have gathered. Germany, Holland, farther north, places so cold that on a day when the residents of Forte dei Marmi won't leave the house without an overcoat, these kids are diving in the water as if it were the middle of summer, returning to the shore and standing around in their swimsuits, laughing and running in the wind, sopping wet.

"What the fuck are they laughing about?" says Rambo.

"Why? What's the harm in being happy and laughing?"

"You don't think they're laughing at us, do you?"

"They couldn't care less about us. They're laughing because they're happy. That's normal, isn't it?" Sandro stops talking. In part because, as always, he thinks of Luca and the fact that he'll never laugh again, and in part because as he was talking his radio finally made a loud whistle.

Rambo stops what he's doing, runs over, dives on the ground, and begins digging, plunging his hands in the sand. He comes up with nothing but continues to dig; the radio whistles again, shouting to them to believe, that now is their time.

The sound attracts the attention of the Dutch kids, who clamber for a look, and, dripping wet, form a line to see what's going on. Sandro and Rambo keep digging. They try to play it cool but their desire to discover something overwhelms them, so they start screaming, cursing, egging each other on.

"Come on, Sandro, come on. It's huge. I can feel it. Fuck is it huge!"

Sandro nods. Sand lodges under his fingernails and they begin to hurt but he keeps at it while the radios continue to whistle and the foreign kids look on.

Finally Sandro feels something solid deep below, some treasure buried by the shore. He gets a hand on it and, out of breath, a smile trembling on his lips, pulls it up into the light of day.

But it's a nail, the large kind you'd find embedded in a beam or the hull of a ship. And it's completely covered in something soft, sticky, dark. Sandro sets it down on the sand, closes his eyes, rubs his hands together and lifts them to his nose.

Dog shit.

M e and the others are sitting on these low little chairs assembled in a circle, all filled except for the one normal chair, which is still empty. In fact Mother Melania just stuck her head in the room and told us to sit tight, that the catechist was on his way. But you can't lie to us. She might as well have said *her* way, since we all know that what would be appearing from behind that door was Mother Greta's mean mug. That's why I didn't want to come here.

I'd returned from school with Zot. It used to be that on Saturdays Mom would come home from work for five minutes, since the shop was open all day, make us each two grilled cheeses and a glass of milk, and then skedaddle. We'd eat then Luca would go surfing and I'd go to catechism. But that was then. It doesn't work like that anymore. Nothing works anymore.

Yet today I had stopped at Teresa's deli, picked up some white bread, ham, and Kraft Singles, and charged it to Grandpa's account. He might not be around any longer but his account at Teresa's is still active. Only Mom pays it. I mean she used to. Nowadays, beats me. And even though I was trying to concentrate on grilled cheeses, on how good they taste with two slices of Kraft and cooked right—dark on the outside so that it looks burnt but isn't—I couldn't get Mother Greta out of my head, her crossed eyes and that massive hairy jaw, and as I rode my bike, my legs shook from fear.

She says we're Satan's spawn and hates the lot of us, me

most of all after what happened the day of Luca's funeral. We'd come out of the dark church and started walking behind the coffin with my brother inside. There were a million people. The line was so long that halfway to the cemetery the caboose was still in the square outside the church. But Mother Greta shoved her way to the head of the line where Mom and I stood and told Miss Gemma to step aside so she could be next to us. What she really wanted was to be out front, for the whole town to see her as the one who prayed and consoled and loved everybody. She kept saying real loud: "What a golden boy. He'll be missed. But we have to stay strong. Life goes on." False as Judas. At one point I turned and saw her taking Mom by the shoulders and insisting she say the "Requiem Aeternam" even if she couldn't remember it—she didn't even know where she was—and Mother Greta was saying, "That's it, that's it, 'Eternal rest grant unto him, O Lord,' go on!" Then I felt something inside me that I'd never heard before, something hot, swelling, and really powerful reaching my lungs, clawing at my flesh and bones to get out, and in the end it found my mouth, shot past my teeth, and made me scream at Mother Greta to go away, that she wasn't wanted: "I hate you and Luca hated you and the whole world hates you! Go away! Go away!" I swear that's what I screamed, and everyone heard.

Miss Gemma put her arms around me, hugged me hard, and with her mouth to my ear said, "Luna, Luna, Luna, that's enough. Calm down. That's enough." But I wasn't listening. All I heard was Mother Greta looking around and telling people, "It's not her fault, the poor girl. She doesn't know what she's saying." Yet I'm positive that ever since that day she's been waiting for the right time to make me pay.

And that time is now, at catechism. You bet I didn't want to come. I had already devised a plan: I would tell Mom that I was coming here and instead I'd go to Zot's house. He'd skip catechism too and we would hide out in the woods of Ghost House. Sure it scares me, but not as much as Mother Greta.

Anyway, it's not like I really needed a plan. When I told her I was going to catechism, Mom looked at me weird for a minute, like she does in the morning when I tell her I'm going to school. To her, just my going out of the house seems ridiculous, so today I could have easily eaten my grilled cheese and stayed in my room without making up excuses, and I'd never have to go to catechism again.

That had been my dream. Had it happened last year I would have jumped for joy so high I would have hit my head on the ceiling. Yet today, well, dang it, today it's not fair. Ever since I was a baby they've forced me to come here on Saturday, memorize the Ten Commandments, the Seven Deadly Sins, the Three Theological Virtues, and a zillion other things to do and especially not do. I did baptism and first communion and every May I follow the Stations of the Cross. And of all years this is the year, the last year, after which I'm set for eternity, that no one cares if I go or not?

No way, Jesús. We've made it this far. Why stop now? It's like that joke Zot told me this morning. There's this crazy guy. One night he tries to break out of the insane asylum. But in order to escape he has to climb a hundred super tall fences, one by one. He climbs the first then the second. The whole night he's climbing fences. He grows more and more tired but he keeps going. And when he's climbed the ninety-ninth fence and arrives at the last one, he stares up at it breathlessly, shakes his head, and says, "No way, man, I can't go on." Then he turns around and climbs the others all over again.

Which is why I ate my grilled cheese, said goodbye to Mom and came here. And I'm quietly staring at the empty chair in front of me, waiting for Mother Greta's big butt to fill it. Because I'm at the ninety-ninth fence. Turning back now would be crazy-people stuff. And I'm not crazy, I don't think.

I nod yes, I nod no, and hug my knees harder and harder as I hear the footsteps approach from outside, someone enter the room, and a voice greet us. And once again everything suddenly changes.

"Good morning, children," says Sandro, entering the room. "Peace be with you."

He'd given it some thought and the phrase sounded right to him. That's what the priest used to say back when he attended mass, i.e., not since he was their age. But these kids fix their X-ray machines scanning him from his busted sneakers to his face, and while he tries to maintain a smile, Sandro senses a querulous tone in their voices as they answer in unison: "And also with you?"

There are about twenty of them sitting in a circle and staring. Blondes and brunettes and two with their hair hidden under hats. And off to his right Sandro lands on the only reason he threw himself into this absurd situation, a bright white reason staring at him from behind a huge pair of sunglasses with her mouth gaping open.

Luna. She's the reason Marino did him the favor of calling the parish priest and telling him that he was worried about the kids, that he had had a plan for their spiritual and human growth that was now at risk of being ruined because of his nasty accident. But he had a friend, a dear devoted friend, with whom he had spent many nights in Christian reflection. This friend doesn't attend the parish church often but he is a man of faith and it would ease Marino's pain to know the kids were in his hands. The hands of Sandro, that is.

Beautiful and moving as his words were, they're not the reason the priest said yes. Credit goes to the fact that ever since he was sixteen Sandro hasn't been able to sleep without the TV on. He flips to the documentary channel and falls asleep while specials about nature and history and science flicker on the screen. In his opinion, they function like those courses on tape they used to advertise in magazines: you put on your headphones and listen to them in your sleep and in the end, without even realizing it, you'd learned English, quantum physics, whatever your heart desired.

Thus Sandro often finds himself possessing random knowledge about parrots and giraffes or Hitler's passion for cars—he hasn't a clue where he first heard the stuff yet there it is, embedded in his brain. Like when he went to meet the parish priest. Things got off to a rough start, since the latter inquired as to why Sandro had never attended church, which was his favorite Gospel, which commandment he liked best. But when their talk turned to beavers, victory rose into view. Father Ermete said the Ten Commandments were fundamental, like the precious green wood with which beavers build their dams. The beavers are the children, see, and they have to build their dam to stop the flow of moral corruption.

"You must know that beavers are admirable animals," said Father Ermete, growing feverish. "They are strict monogamists, they mate for life. They have a faithful and loving spirit and they're devoted to their work."

And Sandro nodded in agreement, since, without understanding why, he knew those things too, and he added that beavers are larger than people think, can weigh up to forty pounds, and in prehistoric times there were beavers as big as bears, and . . .

And Father Ermete gazed at him, leaped to his feet in excitement, and the two continued to talk about beavers and their lives in the woods and by rivers, until somehow they arrived at the astonishing virtues of octopi, animals so intelligent they make fish look retarded.

Indeed, Sandro would make the perfect leader for the children; knowing the Gospel may be important but only a nutjob could ignore the presence of God in octopi, beavers, and

Nature's far-flung miracles. A nutjob like Mother Greta, for example, who had complained to the cardinal not once but twice about how Father Ermete dedicated his homilies almost exclusively to animals. "The mass is like a documentary film, Your Eminence, the faithful may as well stay on their couches in front of their television sets." Those were the exact words of that vile nun who knows nothing about religion and less about what makes the world turn. Case in point: the cardinal told Father Ermete all about it while unburdening him of two crates of exceptional white wine that Father Ermete's brother makes on his small vineyard in the hills of Candia, and the men laughed and raised a toast.

Sandro can raise a toast too, for he is officially the new catechist. And although it strikes him as ridiculous to be here teaching religion in this badly lit room papered with drawings of Jesus, Sandro looks around, takes a deep breath, and begins to usher the children toward Paradise. Or someplace nearby.

"All right. My name is Sandro. Don't bother telling me your name because I'll forget it immediately. How about I just point a finger when I'm speaking to one of you, okay?"

Everyone nods, and a hand shoots up beside Luna. It's the weirdly dressed kid who'd been at the hospital with her. He has on an extra large checked wool sweater and over that a checked vest.

"Excuse me, Mister Sandro, why's Mother Greta not here?"

And before he can get the last word out a kid twice his size sporting a beard of peach fuzz smacks him upside the head.

"That's easy. Mother Greta's not here because I'm here. Why? Would you guys rather have the Nazi nun?"

They all laugh and shake their heads. Sandro smiles back and crosses his legs, feeling as if he's already conquered them. Being a catechist isn't so hard. He might even have a talent for this. Of course that's the case; Sandro's sure of it. He lifts his eyes to the ceiling, to two water stains in the shape of Sardinia and Corsica, although he's really looking at the sky beyond. He resumes talking.

"Because if you like that old hag just say the word and I'll go get her." They laugh again, two girls hug each other, the big kid smacks Grandpa Kid on the back of the head again, to vent his joy. But most importantly there's Luna, who tries to hide her smile with her ghost-white hand. Sandro looks at her, and she quickly fixes her eyes on the ground. She tries to suppress her smile but it's no use.

"All right, kids, let's get started. Marino told me that last time you read a passage from the Gospel and analyzed it. Let's us do the same thing today, okay?"

They nod and pick up their Bibles. A blond boy in a Dolce & Gabbana T-shirt with a pair of sunglasses resting on his head says Marino already chose what to read for today.

"He did? All right, which one then?"

"Genesis 19."

Genesis 19. Where the hell is that? Couldn't they just say the page number? Plus his Bible is thousands of pages long, a tiny cube-shaped affair his mom has kept on her nightstand for her entire life and never once opened. The words Pocket Bible are written on the cover, and the text inside is so small that the lines look like layers of black streaks. Sandro looks up and peeks at the kids, who are open to the first page. Right, makes sense Genesis would be at the start of the story. There it is, and there's the number 16 in a slightly larger font, then 17, 18—here we go.

"O.K., guys, who'd like to read?"

The same blond boy informs him that last time the catechist read.

"O.K. then, pipe down and listen up, because afterward I'll ask you what happened and we'll analyze it, O.K.?" Sandro coughs, takes a breath, and begins:

Now the two angels came to Sodom in the evening as Lot was sitting in the gate of Sodom. When Lot saw them, he rose to meet them and bowed down with his face to the ground. And he said, "Now behold, my lords, please turn aside into your servant's house, and spend the night, and wash your feet; then you may rise early and go on your way." They said however, "No, but we shall spend the night in the square." Yet he urged them strongly, so they turned aside to him and entered his house; and he prepared a feast for them, and baked unleavened bread, and they ate.

Someone raises a hand and, despite having his head buried in that microscopic book, Sandro notices it. It's the same kid in the vest seated next to Luna.

"Excuse me, Mr. Sandro, what's 'unleavened bread'?"

"It's . . . well, it's simple. You should know the answer yourselves. Anyone know what it means?"

Silence. Everyone endeavors to disappear. Behind their Bible, behind their classmates. Even Luna becomes anxious; she stares at the ground and chews her lip. Sandro doesn't want to embarrass her, but the problem is that no one in this room knows what unleavened bread is, Sandro least of all. So he has to make something up.

"It's a grain, an ancient kind of grain they ate back then. Like beans."

"Aren't beans legumes?" asks the boy in the vest.

"I said *like* beans, *like*! No more interrupting. We're getting off track," says Sandro. Then the big kid with the beard smacks Grandpa Kid in the back of the head again, and Grandpa Kid apologizes and looks back down at his Bible.

"See, kids, the moral of this wonderful passage is to welcome people with open arms. Two strangers knock on the door and what does Lot do? He rushes to welcome them. He invites them into his home. What a wonderful gesture. Think about what you or your parents would do in that situation—would you have been that generous?"

"Things were different back then," says a little girl in a grown-up skirt and white button-down, by all appearances the world's worst enemy—a lawyer. "There are a lot of bad elements around nowadays. Our house got robbed three times in two months, even after my dad put bars in the windows. Besides, those two were angels. Of course he was kind to them. My dad would have invited two angels in too. I'd like to see Lot greet a couple of gypsies."

"Okay, thanks. Let's not lose sight of the gist of the story—the kind reception. Two angels arrive and Lot invites them into his home. What happens next?"

Before they lay down, the men of the city, the men of Sodom, surrounded the house, both young and old, all the people from every quarter; and they called to Lot and said to him, "Where are the men who came to you tonight? Bring them out to us that we may have relations with them."

Sandro breaks off. He goes back and rereads the passage. That's what it says. He stares at the words the way the kids stare at him—alert, dead silent. Everyone except for Grandpa Kid who, unsurprisingly, has his hand up again.

"Excuse me, Mr. Sandro, what do they mean 'relations'?"

"They don't mean anything. They wanted to have relations with the angels. That's all. But that doesn't matter, let's keep going."

"What does 'relations' mean?"

"Nothing. Like, bonding, you know, the way people bond over video games."

"But what does that mean then? Those men wanted to

play video games with the angels? How can you bond with an angel?"

"No, you can't bond with an angel, no—whatever, let's move on, I said no more interruptions!"

The one thing is to forge ahead, get past this story about the maniac neighbors and relations with angels and arrive at the moral of the story. There must be one and it must be good and religious—this is the Bible for fuck's sake.

But Lot went out to them at the doorway, and shut the door behind him, and said, "Please, my brothers, do not act wickedly. Now behold, I have two daughters who have not had relations with man; please let me bring them out to you, and do to them whatever you like."

Sandro stiffens once more. Who the hell wrote this? Is this really the holy book you have to read to go to heaven? Where are the loaves and fishes multiplied to feed the hungry? Where are the Samaritans helping their neighbors? Here the best neighbors can expect is rape and torture. How can you read this filth to minors?

Sandro draws a blank. He closes that tiny terrifying book and looks up at the wide-eyed stares of the kids. They too are stock-still, except for the blond kid who told him which passage to read. That little son of a whore is yukking it up.

The others start laughing too, hitting one another, shouting things like, "Let's have relations! Let's have relations!" The little girl dressed like a lawyer points straight at Luna and says, "Her! She's never had relations with a man. Give her to those people!" Luna looks at her. "What? And you have?" "More than you!" replies the girl. Luna sticks out her middle finger, and at that point Grandpa Kid gets between the girls, puts both hands out, and says, "Lord, please, let's not lose our cool. Let's not lapse into vulgarity. Remember, we must always maintain a certain—" then nothing, because in the general excitement he is struck by a wave of smacks, pinches, punches—everything human hands can think up to hurt someone.

"Shut up!" shouts Sandro. "Sit still and shut up or I'll call Mother Greta."

But no one falls for it. Or maybe they can't hear him amid the screams, the laughter, the falling chairs, the blond kid grabbing the hand of the girl next to him and trying to rub it against the crotch of his designer jeans. "Oh Monica, let's have relations together, let's have relations together!"

Sandro yells for them to be quiet and separates the kids, his teeth clenched and his hands making fists. The anger rises to his head and starts climbing up the few remaining hairs on his head. But they're fine and cut short, which may explain why the anger turns back, descends to his throat, and streams out by itself, and after a minute Sandro hears this cry escape his lips, bounce off the walls and the kids' heads and the magic marker drawings of Jesus, a cry that, returning to him, goes like this: "Enough, knock it off G—dammit!"

Just like that, plain and simple, during his very first catechism lesson Sandro has blasphemed in the convent. And afterward there's finally silence, a silence signaling the opposite of peace, like the silence after a gunshot, after thunder strikes overhead, and you keep quiet, not breathing, and check to see if you're still alive.

The kids look at each other, speechless. A shocked Grandpa Kid covers his ears with his hands as if the curse were still hovering in the air, waiting to ambush him.

It makes Sandro feel even dirtier, more revolting, more guilty. He'd like to say something, to try to make up for it, but at this point he can't trust what might escape his lips, so he keeps silent. He looks away, at the walls, at the window framing the sky strung with clouds, and Sandro thinks he'd like to be one of those clouds out there, shapeless, going where the wind takes him, and all it does is pass over and perhaps release lots of rain on the ground, and the drops of rain on the ground disappear without a trace, and . . .

"Amen."

Yes, "Amen." That's the word that breaks the deafening silence. "Amen." And it came from none other than Luna. She had taken off her sunglasses, her eyes were crystal clear, almost transparent, her expression serious but her lips quivering. In the end she gives in and smiles.

So who cares? He's not here to evangelize the youth. He doesn't give a shit about these kids. Let them join the Jehovah's Witnesses or the Manson Family. All that matters to him is that Luna is now beaming at him.

Sandro smiles back. He really smiles. For the first time in six months.

It's such an easy thing to do, when it's not impossible.

Memory Tsunami

I t was just your average Over-40 championship soccer match when the weather took center stage,
painting the field of Club Versilia 2000 white with
snow. A stunned referee Marchetti had to interrupt play.
"We were playing well," says Cantini, the top scorer for
VersilFungo-Ristorante Mamma Rosa. "We were outclass-
ing and outrunning Mastro Chiavaio, but with all the snow
we couldn't stay on our feet. It's too bad because in my
opinion . . . "

You turn the page. Clearly the star player is going to say that
if they hadn't stopped play his team would have won handily,
and below that the goalie for the other team will say the same
thing, only vice versa.

On the next page there's talk of the marble crisis in Carrara.
Once upon a time they made a killing selling it across the globe.
Then one day in addition to the marble they sold the equipment
to extract the stone from the mountains, and that was that.

You keep flipping through, already knowing which head-
lines you'll find, which photos, every word of every article in
your stack of newspapers. There are people who take pride in
reading a paper or two a day, but you, Serena, read fifteen. The
only difference is that every morning they go to the newsstand
to pick up the day's paper. You, on the other hand, stay shut
inside the house and flip through the same old papers from
March 23rd, the day time stopped.

Gemma rescued them from the library for you. The woman who works there gets her hair cut at the shop and just gave them to her, seeing as no one will ever come looking for them besides you. You said you wanted them for a keepsake. As if that were a day to remember, as if it were possible to forget.

You began reading them from the top down, every article, the classifieds and ads, and six months later you're still doing the same. By now you know all the pages by heart, which is a staggering undertaking but you don't care. What you're after is even more implausible: you want to know why on earth that day, that godforsaken day that should be ripped out of every calendar in the world and burned and have its ashes spit upon, Luca asked you to buy him the paper.

He'd never read the paper before, never even chanced to leaf through it. What was so important about that day? Did he want to know about the snow on the soccer field? The marble crisis? The hunting dog abandoned on the side of the highway that a month later found its way back home and bit its owner? You don't know, you can't know, maybe Luca simply wanted a copy of the paper printed on the same day he became an adult, and you're here chasing a thousand phantoms. Enough. You gather up the papers and throw them on the nightstand. Then you pick up your blue notebook.

In it you'd copied out the messages Luca had sent from Biarritz, that godforsaken place up north by the ocean. That way you kept them all together, and they became a memento for you, for him. Because memories are beautiful. To look back at what you used to be like makes you smile. Memories lend your life warmth. Yet then what happened happened, and now your life is over, and memories are all that's left. They have nothing to lend warmth to, so they catch fire, asphyxiate you, you no longer know where you are. And the more you try to escape them, the more they dog you.

We're headed back from catechism, and the air is weird. I ride behind Zot and the wind slithers inside my hood and runs through my hair. It's not cold but I feel it swirling around my glasses, riffling my eyebrows, tickling my neck. That must be why I'm laughing.

Or else it's because I'm kind of happy.

I had been expecting the massive jaw and evil eyes of Mother Greta, and instead she'd never showed. Not even afterward in the courtyard. In fact we walked out and the new catechist hung back with Zot and me. He asked us what kind of music we listened to. In his opinion, asking people's names and what they do and which sign they are is pointless. Finding out their favorite bands told you all you needed to know.

But I didn't answer, since I don't know much about music and I was afraid to say something stupid. Mr. Sandro kept insisting. "Go on, name a group you like, a singer, there's no wrong answer. It's like naming your favorite color. They're your tastes. That's all." And I was about to tell him that I love Michael Jackson when Zot fired off a bunch of super weird names of singers he likes and the only two I can remember now are Claudio Villa and Beniamino Gigli. Mr. Sandro looked at him and burst out laughing. Then he turned to me. "Sorry, Luna, but why do you hang around with your grandpa? You should leave him at home by the fireplace where he belongs."

I didn't want to but I laughed real hard. Zot kept on repeating that those guys were the foundation of Italian music, treasures that the Italians should be proud of rather than this new junk, that he'd like to see one of today's rappers try singing "Violino tzigano" or "Scapricciatiello."

But now we're arriving at my house and there's nothing left to laugh about. It's quiet and the shutters are closed as if it were night. Zot wants to walk me to the door. I tell him I can do it myself. When he insists, I remind him that just because I don't see well doesn't mean I'm an idiot. He nods, turns his bike around, and heads off to his house. I go inside.

The kitchen is dark and quiet and still, the only sounds are the noise of the fridge and the gurgle of the coffeemaker. Luca and I used to always tell Mom that the coffeemaker consumes a ton of electricity and the first thing she should do once the coffee was ready was turn it off. To which she'd reply that the first thing she did when the coffee was ready was drink it, and afterward she'd forget about it and go to work and the coffeemaker would be left on all day even if no one was home.

And now seems just like one of those times. And maybe it's true, maybe no one's home. I consider turning the coffeemaker off but wait a minute, listening to it continue to gurgle in the empty house, Mom having finally returned to work or at least left the house. Maybe she had put on her shoes, gotten dressed, even combed her hair before leaving.

Because she's not here. Not in bed, not in the bathroom. So maybe it really is true. I'd been good today. I could have stayed home and instead I went to catechism, and the Lord made me this present: while I was at the convent he gave Mom the strength to get out of bed, make herself a coffee, and leave the house, and now she could be at Gemma's shop or out running errands or wherever she wants.

Yet while I'm thinking of all the places she could be, above the noise of the fridge and the gurgle of the coffeemaker, I hear something else, a soft rustling from Luca's room. No one had touched it in six months. Even a sock he'd left behind still dangled from the radiator. His friends had been waiting outside in the van and they'd honked their horn and Luca had tossed it over his shoulder and it stayed there, dangling. Last month when Mom knocked it over she picked it up immediately and tried putting it back in place, but she couldn't remember exactly where it had been. She tried placing it this way and that, shaking her head and crying.

I go to Luca's room. The door is half shut and I'd rather leave it that way. I don't want to open it and look in, I want to remain in doubt a little longer before I find Mom sitting on the ground in the dark by the foot of the bed. Even if I can't see her well, I know what she's doing—flipping through her blue notebook.

The one with Luca's messages. Mom's always reading it. And she doesn't quit, even now as I enter the room and greet her. My voice sounds funny because my nose and my throat itch. Even my eyes itch some. I was right to be happy on the ride home, since that feeling's long gone now.

I call to her again, but Mom keeps her head buried in the book. Only after a while does she turn to me with a shudder. She says hi, then goes back to reading Luca's messages.

There aren't even that many of them—fifteen, twenty max, running five or six pages. She reads them first to last, last to first. Sometimes she smiles or laughs, as if the messages had just arrived, as if she'd never read them before. Then she starts over from the top and reads through to the end. Actually, there is no end.

"Hi, Mom. I was at catechism."

"That's nice, Luna. What time will you be back?"

"No, Mom, I went already. I'm back now."

"Ah, good." She returns to flipping through the five or six pages in the dark. It's so dark she probably can't even read them, but by now she knows the messages by heart and can recognize them by the order in which they appear, by their shape alone.

"We had a new catechist because our old one wound up in the hospital."

"Really?"

"Yeah. A car ran him over. Did you hear that, Mom? Are you listening?"

"Yes, I did. How old was your friend?"

"He's not my friend. He's the catechist. And he's not dead."

"Ah," she says, turning the page.

And now, after my eyes have stung a little, I feel the heat behind and inside them, but I don't want to cry. I try breathing deeply but I can't, the room becomes very narrow and if I think about the smile that had brought me joy on my bike, I feel like a total dummy.

"But then Mother Greta came," I add. I don't know why I say it, but that's all I say. Well, not exactly all. "She had a cane with her and she beat us."

"Really?" says Mom.

"Really. And afterward she told us to get naked."

"Really?"

"And then she took a bunch of photos of us that she plans to sell to perverts on the Internet."

Once upon a time, for a thing like that, or a fraction of a fraction of a thing like that, Mom would jump to her feet, reach the convent in a split second, crash through the gate, and set fire to Mother Greta. And she'd use the tires in the courtyard or the other nuns hanging around to stoke the flames. And that's not what I want. All I'm asking for is a look of anger, that's it, at least a look. Instead nothing. Mom keeps staring into the notebook—not listening to me, not caring.

I clench my teeth. I clench my fists real hard. I plant my nails into my palms. It hurts but not enough. I'd like to feel super strong pain, the kind that commands your complete attention, that erases your thoughts so that all you can think about is how badly it hurts. But nothing happens, not even a little blood spills, much as I'd like gallons of blood to gush from my hands like fountains, two fountains of blood that spray Mom, that fill the room and start floating around in it until the room is full and there's almost no air left, and Mom finally opens her eyes, looks at me desperately, and with her last breath says, "Luna, I'm begging you, no more, stop bleeding!"

But Mom sits there reading her blue notebook. She couldn't care less if her daughter had been caned by a nun, if they'd taken naked pictures of her and right now a million old pigs were eyeballing her on computers around the world. The thought of those old guys almost makes me believe the story I just made up, and I feel kind of nauseated, I feel puke rising in my throat. I open my mouth but no puke comes out. Words do. A lot of bitter, boiling words rolling around in my brain, my bones, my skin, piling up in my mouth and pushing and pushing and in the end they spew out, and I cry so hard the sound hurts my ears: "You don't care, Mom, do you? You don't care one bit!"

She stops reading, lifts her head, and in the dark I think I see her face, which is tired despite the fact that she never does anything.

"Listen, Luna, I'm sorry you didn't have a good time at catechism, but why go at all?"

"I—I went because—because it's Saturday. And on Saturday there's catechism. And this year we have confirmation."

"Confirmation?" Mom repeats back to me, as if it were a funny word she'd never heard before. She almost laughs, but doesn't. She opens her mouth and each word is like a kick in the face, and if you were to line up all these kicks in a row they'd sound like this:

"Confirmation? Catechism? What are you talking about, Luna? After everything that's happened, you still believe God exists?"

I swear that's what she says. Then she turns back to the notebook, as if I weren't there anymore.

And maybe that's the way it is: Mom tells me as much and I really do cease to exist. The floor caves in, the walls crumble, the ceiling collapses on my head and crushes me and I die and I don't go to Heaven. I don't even go to Hell. Because those are made-up places and everything ends when this ends. I breathe, or try to, but rather than enter my lungs this shoots out: "Fuck you, Mom, I hate you! Fuck you!"

I feel bad for saying so. I scare myself. But Mom doesn't react. She keeps flipping through that notebook, that shitty blue notebook. So then, just as I had spoken without knowing what I was saying, now I act without knowing what I'm doing. I bend over and tear the notebook away from her. I'd only wanted to take it from her to see if she'd wake up, if she'd listen to me for a second. But now that I have this small, fragile thing in my hands, I feel a huge desire to destroy it, to rip out the sheets and make it vanish from the world forever. I lift it up and start tugging. You can bet Mom looks at me after that. She jumps to her feet and shouts at me.

But I don't know what. My heart is beating so hard I don't hear her. I only hear shouting, her hands gripping me. I hear the paper, the sound of a page beginning to tear.

Followed immediately after by another sound, a hundred thousand times louder, right in my face. The notebook flies out of my hands, my sunglasses go flying.

A slap.

She'd slapped me, slapped me right on my cheek, and I didn't realize it immediately. For all I know it was a lightning bolt, a tsunami driving me to the ground. It takes me a while to understand what just happened, when the burning feeling crawls up my cheek and half my face, and my ears start to ring.

Mom may have slapped me, but she seems to have forgotten already. She's back on the floor holding her precious notebook, far from me. Or maybe not. Maybe I am the one taking leave, moving toward the door, out of Luca's room. I walk backwards, one hand on my cheek. I hardly know where the other one is. I bang my back against the edge of the kitchen table, fumble for the door, and walk out into the yard and the sun attacks me. Coming out of the dark without my glasses is like being stabbed in the brain. I almost fall but hang on to something. I should stay put for a moment but I can't. I put my hand out and find my bike. I hop on and pedal hard. And I don't know what's ahead of me, maybe nothing at all, nothing nowhere. I don't even know if cars are passing me on the road or if the noise I hear is a truck coming from far away or pieces of the world shattering and collapsing and dying forever. All I know is where I'm going.

Away.

Luna at the Bottom of the Sea

I ride so fast I don't feel it, but it's cold out. That weird wind has picked up, the one that comes out of nowhere and that Luca would sense immediately. He'd jump to his feet and say, "Here we go." Then he'd smile and run to get his surfboard. Because this wind is called the libeccio, and when the libeccio blows the sea churns and countless tall foam-filled waves mount along its spine.

The libeccio comes, the temperature drops, and the clouds shuttle across the sun, so that it's light/dark, light/dark, which for me is the absolute worst, since I can't see anything. I keep my eyes open just because I'm on my bike and that's what comes naturally, but riding with my eyes closed would amount to the same thing. On top of that, the trees shudder and the leaves fall. They scatter, making the ground slippery, and if I'm not careful I'll fall same as them.

I had run out of the house without my glasses on or my hat or sunscreen. It doesn't matter to me. I don't feel the cold or the sun. I only feel the wind against my cheek, just under my eye, where Mom slapped me.

Mom hit me. Not hard, not so badly that if I went on television and told my story the audience would scream she was a monster and show an ugly photo of her—although Mom always looks pretty in photos—and all the while she'd be crying on the phone saying she loves me, and the hostess would tell her, "Too late, lady."

No, she didn't hit me that hard, but she did lay a hand on

me. Nothing like that had ever happened in our house before. Were Luca there he'd have been speechless too. But that's just it. This would never have happened if Luca were still here.

Because when Luca was around everyone was happy. People were happy to run into him. They'd stop to say hi and listen to him with their jaws on the floor and their eyes wide so they could take in as much of him as they could. Mom would smile and I would too as I stood next to him. Occasionally they'd even ask me how I was doing. I'm good, I'd say, but they'd have already stopped listening, they'd have turned back to beaming at Luca.

And to be honest maybe I wasn't so good, but now I feel a hundred times worse, and while I ride all that flashes before my eyes is her hand, the blow, the nasty look on Mom's face afterward. And for what? Because I'd taken away her little blue notebook. Because I'd asked her to spend a second listening to my problems. My problems, which make no sense to her. My problems, which, like God, no longer exist.

The wind blows harder, the leaves on the road are slippery, at every bend my back wheel skids, going wherever it feels like going.

Same as always autumn arrives and the leaves fall. The bare tree stands and waits. Then winter ends. The leaves grow back fuller than before and brand new and start doing their job, absorbing the light and sending it all the way into the wood. But us, why is it that when we die we die and that's it? Isn't that absurd? It seems totally absurd to me. Wouldn't it be fairer if Luca were to come back in March? I'm not saying right away, just in March. That's it. The leaves would grow back and so would my brother. Or maybe it isn't absurd, maybe it's just as Mom says: God doesn't exist and there's no right or wrong. That things happen at random is normal.

Random, like the way I'm navigating the streets, which all intersect, narrow and identical. I only see the curbside hedges flitting by and a couple times I come close to crashing into them but then I swerve and go on pedaling. The wind rises and the light/dark makes my head spin, and here comes the third car horn to terrify me though I can't see the cars. I can't see whether I'm on the right or left side of the road or—more likely—zigzagging. Yet all the same I head straight toward the one thing that matters to me. I may not see it but I totally feel it. I head for the end, toward the sound of the sea.

I haven't been back since the day Luca died. I didn't even come this summer. I don't know why. Actually I do. Luca may have died far away yet he still died at sea, and the sea is the same everywhere. In a certain sense, it's kind of like he died right here.

Not coming here over the last few months hadn't felt weird. Maybe because so many weird things have happened that in the end I got used to not coming. Yet now that I've arrived at this broad, straight, shining road, and the whole sky has opened, and there's nothing to button it up down there, it seems impossible that I've stayed away from the sea for so long.

I still don't see it. A line of wooden cabanas conceals it though I catch the smell of sand and salt, hear the swish of water spreading along the shore and that slightly different sound of water raking the surface on its way back out to sea.

I squeeze through the narrow passage between the cabanas, then the shadows cease and I'm struck by the light from the sky, reflecting off the sea. I turn my head. My eyes burn. Yet even if I shut them tight, I feel the whole horizon opening out around me, the whole world laid bare before me. Suddenly there are no more obstacles no more trees no more billboards no more building walls. Here by the sea everything is open, all is mine.

Well, not just mine. I hear shouting and see something running down by the shore. People. Boys. From the sound of their voices, they must be my age or a little older, and there's no need to hear what language they're speaking to understand they're foreigners from way up north where it's always cold. Because despite the chilly wind and dark clouds and frozen water, they're horsing around, diving into the water as if it were mid-August.

They're a tougher breed, Grandpa used to say, they live in places where nature is merciless. As soon as they're born they're accustomed to suffering, therefore pain weighs less heavily on them. And Grandpa may have been thinking about the German pilot who'd shaken his hand rather than shot him, except that soldier never existed. Just as Grandpa no longer exists and Luca no longer exists and since that day God doesn't exist either. Nothing exists. Nothing.

And if that seems so awful to me, I'm to blame for being an egomaniac, for thinking only of myself. I shouldn't care one bit. I should stay in bed with Mom and let the days drift by— all the same, all meaningless. Instead here I am by the sea and the sea looks wonderful to me. I head toward the shore, toward these kids who are playing and laughing, and even if the world seems like it's over and doesn't make any sense, I want to be like them with all my heart.

Plus I look a little like them. They have pale skin and fair hair. Even their eyes are a lighter color. I'm much more like them than my classmates. So why am I shaking from the cold the closer I get to the shore? No, I have to resist. I take off my shoes and feel the water. It's so freezing I can't tell if it's cold or boiling hot, if I've stuck my foot in ice or in lava. I don't know and I shouldn't care.

Just as I shouldn't care about school, catechism, the nasty way my classmates treat me, God (who doesn't exist), these foreign kids laughing and having fun and completely ignoring me.

Except I do care, I dwell on it, because I'm an evil egomaniac. Mom was right to slap me. She's the good one, not me. I don't care about anything but me. Of course I have to; shucks, if I don't think about me, no one will. Sounds absurd, but when there was Luca, I existed a little. Now that my brother is gone it's as if he had been the only thing that existed. Thank God the icy water helps me not think about it or anything anymore. All it tells me is to enter, to keep going farther. A taller wave splashes my shirt and gets my stomach wet. A shiver travels up my spine to my ears. But that's just fine, I don't care, I stop thinking, all I do is walk straight. The water reaches my belly button. I can't breathe anymore. I can't see anything with all the little squares of light dancing over the surface and hitting my eyes. I just feel the cold rising all the way up to my chest, to the spot where many of my classmates already have boobs and I don't. Mom used to tell me it was too soon, that at my age she was flat as a board: "I didn't get them till high school and look at what great boobs I have now. Don't worry, Luna, it's too early, it's just too early." That's what Mom used to say before she stopped saying anything. First it was too soon, now it's too late.

The water reaches my neck, the sea overtakes me, buoys me, carries me where it will. I feel a piece of wood underfoot. A soft clump of seaweed drifts past and I don't know if I grab it or it grabs me. There's no more sand underfoot, it's all just water—in my hair, on my face. The cold burns every part of me, most of all where Mom slapped me. Maybe her handprint will stay there forever, even after I'm gone. Even if I sink to the bottom of the sea, where it keeps all of its beautiful and mysterious treasures, and every once in a while it would choose one to send to the shore as a gift to me. Now I'm the one traveling toward them. I sink. I feel like I'm falling asleep. Meanwhile I see all these things moving aside to make room for me, rolling about, to-ing and fro-ing, endlessly dancing at the bottom of the sea.

And me with them.

THE BOAR AND THE WHALE

You say, "Was it really necessary to put her with this old lady?" And the nurse says, "Quiet, Miss."

Quiet? Who gives a fig about being quiet? The old woman is stretched out over there with her face to the wall. You've been here for an hour and she hasn't moved once. She's probably dead. And if she is alive, she must be three hundred years old and knows perfectly well how old she is. But then you realize you're not keeping quiet for the old woman's sake but for Luna's. She's asleep too, and the doctors say that the more she sleeps the better. It will alleviate her fever and some other stuff you've never understood.

But you don't understand a thing. All the pills and drops you take must have made you mindless. The hospital called and it took you an eternity to figure out that they had your daughter, and then you hung up the phone and wandered around the house in circles trying to snap out of it. For six months you had been shut inside, and suddenly there you were performing a million absurd tasks. Like putting on your shoes, which were so pinched and uncomfy it was almost impossible to wedge your feet inside. Then you staggered out of the house and down the walkway, and the grass underfoot felt soft and slippery, navigating it was difficult, your legs trembled, as did your back all the way up to your head and the tips of your hair, all disheveled and shaken about by something even more absurd, the wind, which blew wildly and stank of leaves, rotten wood, mushrooms maybe.

You reached the car, plopped down in the seat, and shut the door. For a minute you felt better.

Then you realized the keys might be of use.

You searched your pockets, your tracksuit bottoms, your pajama top, your winter coat. You checked the dashboard, the dusty mats, the seat under your butt and the one next to you. Nothing. As anyone would, you tried to remember where you put the keys the last time you'd driven the car. Only for you the last time was six months ago, the same day you'd picked up Luna at church on your way home and found Gemma out front with the carabinieri and the ambulance. That had been the last day for a lot of things. You stopped looking for the keys, gripped the wheel, leaned your head against it, and started to cry.

And what with all your crying, you hit the horn with your forehead. It went off like a bomb. You startled and your eyes fell on the key still in the ignition, just waiting to be turned. You'd had no idea, hadn't even checked there.

You turned the key but nothing happened. It just made a sound like a small animal dying. You tried again and again got nothing but that sound. The car had sat too long and the battery had died, or something else was wrong with that mysterious thing they call an engine. You couldn't check under the hood because you didn't know what to look for, so once again you clasped the key and turned, as if you were twisting some brat's ear. And the car realized it had better obey: it came alive.

Street signs, traffic lights, pedestrians crossing, old women tottering on bikes, dogs, badly parked cars. Life went on, people got out of bed, left the house, insisted on doing things. All of it ridiculous, all of it crazy. Meanwhile you kept wondering why in the world Luna had gone to the beach, how had she wound up in the water, had she had fallen in or really wanted to swim.

But you had no idea. You don't know what Luna did today

or for the last six months for that matter. There had been no more lunches, no more Tuesday pizzas by the sea, no more racing to the gate in the morning (with serious kicking and shoving). You had stopped ad-libbing the words of the presenters on the Moroccan TV shows that, for some mysterious reason, you get at home. You had stopped playing the game at night where whoever could stay awake longer than the other got to yell in that person's ear, "Wake up!!!" You hadn't even given her a hug, a kiss, a caress. Nothing.

Actually, worse than nothing: you had slapped her. At the last red light, just as you glimpsed that boxy white hospital beyond the pines, you remembered. You sat staring at it over there. When the light turned green the car behind you honked its horn. You told it to fuck off, first with your finger and then in your head.

You slapped your daughter. You slapped her and she ran off, dove into the sea, and now was at the hospital. What did you do, Serena? What the fuck did you do?

In the parking lot you flew out of the car without locking it.

You walked through the revolving door and into the gigantic lobby, and the voices on the loudspeaker, the voices of the people scattered about and brushing past you, the coughs, the variety of faces, the horrible haircuts, the stink of sweat old age mold smoke food—all this stuff you'd forgotten—assaulted your senses and made you feel sick, as did the thought of slapping your child, which memory you had tried to suppress yet now comes back clear, precise, frightening.

And now as you stand by her bed in this room you keep thinking about it, and you clench your fists and your teeth.

She's still sleeping, her sheet tucked under her chin, white as her hair and the pillow underneath, white as her skin, which, however, now has dark streaks from the cold she suffered in the water. There's a strange halo on her cheek and, impossible as it seems, you think it might be the mark from where you hit her, so you lower your gaze and close your eyes. You feel anger mixed with guilt, remorse, and a hundred other things that make it hard to breathe. If you don't smoke a cigarette you'll suffocate to death.

You take one, put it in your mouth, and start to leave, but before you go you look back at Luna a moment and wave to her even though she's asleep. If your daughter doesn't hurry and wake up soon, you'll wake her up yourself, because you want to hug her and tell her how much you love her, that and a million other things that for now you carry with you as you go.

Sandro climbs the stairs, running his fingers over this flat, smooth, bright white object in his grip. It's a bone, a wild boar bone. It had once been inside that animal and allowed it to function well for years, yet to look at it now you'd think it were completely unrelated to that dark, wiry-coated wild animal.

Death's like that. It takes everything away. Actually, no, that's not true, not everything. Death always leaves something behind, only what it leaves behind no longer has anything to do with what came before. And yet it's all that remains, so you cling to it.

Sandro is in fact clinging to the bone as he climbs to the third floor to visit Luna, hoping his present will make her smile the way she had at catechism.

He'd gotten it from Rambo, who belongs to a group called the Friends of the Wild Boar, a coterie of men perpetually sporting fatigues who demonstrate their friendship with the animal by climbing the Apuan Alps and shooting at it every time they cross its path. Then they haul its carcass to the valley and hack it up into equal parts. And seeing as Rambo doesn't have a wife or children or any friends besides Sandro and Marino, his freezer is always packed with cuts of wild boar.

To get rid of it, occasionally he invites his two friends over, and his mother prepares boar crostini, pappardelle with boar ragu, boar stew, and, to top it off, chocolate-covered boar, a famous dish that might sound nasty but one taste and you'll discover for yourself just how nasty it really is.

At the end of such a dinner, Rambo was regarding the bones on his plate when he found one that, in his opinion, was shaped like a shark's tooth. And maybe it was the wine or that their blood, busy digesting, had evacuated their brains, but the three men hit upon a genius idea to make some money in the "indigenous artisan" trade: foreign tourists would totally flip for these hand-carved bones—engraved, say, with seafaring sayings in Latin or drawings of ships and fish. So what if none of them knew how to engrave? Bully for them: the shoddier the drawings, the more primitive they'd appear. They'd string up broken nets by the pier and, barefoot and dressed in rags, sell them as shark and whale bones. "The tourists will kill each other to get their hands on them—kill each other!"

They each took a few home to get started on. And Sandro can't remember now whether it proved too challenging or someone cut himself, but whatever the reason, nothing came of it, and they had put it out of mind.

Until one morning at school it all came back to him when Luca asked, "Teach, you think I'll find a whalebone up there?"

"Huh?"

"A whalebone in Biarritz, think I'll find one?"

"Beats me. Maybe. I don't know. Why do you ask?"

He asked beacuse every day, several times a day, his sister would ask him for one: "Please, would you bring me a whalebone?" She'd read somewhere that Biarritz had once been an important port of departure for whaling fleets and now she was obsessed. "A humpback whalebone. No, wait, a spermwhale bone. No, wait, humpback. Or whatever you can find. What difference does it make?"

Luca had told her he would. But whaling fleets, that's century-old stuff, nowadays it'd be easier to kill a person, and whale-

218 · FABIO GENOVESI

bones must be in short supply, or maybe, who knows, maybe even banned.

So Sandro told him, "Don't worry, go have fun in Biarritz and keep your eye out. If none turns up, I'll take care of it. I've got this fantastic bone to give you, white and smooth. It belongs to a wild boar but it could easily pass for a humpback or sperm whale or what have you."

And now Sandro is about to meet Luna and preparing to tell her that the bone in his hands belongs to a whale. He knew that she'd wanted a whalebone and that Luca hadn't been able to get one for her, so he'd taken it upon himself to bring her this gift and wish her a speedy recovery.

In the hall Sandro passes patients and relatives and feels almost happy to have a nice speech, a beautiful gift, no troubles in sight. Well, besides one, which is why his legs tremble when the number on the door comes into view. Would he bump into Serena in there? They hadn't spoken since the day at the newsstand that spring. So much had happened in the meantime, including the awful event that had robbed her of everything and for which he was to blame.

But wait a second. It's also true that some tragedies unfortunately happen and there's nothing anyone can do about them. Serena's smart. She knows that. She has no intention of making judgments or allocating blame. There's no place for accusations in a situation this serious, no point in hatred. All that the survivors can do is hug one another and give each other strength. Yes, that's it, that's how it must be. Sandro reaches the door, takes one last breath as if rather than entering the room he were plunging into deep water, and then plunges.

But no one is in the room.

No one, that is, besides an old woman in the corner sleeping on her side with her face to the wall, wrapped in at least three blankets. And Luna, also asleep, in the bed just in front of him.

Sandro approaches and takes her in. All the whiteness—of her, the bed, the walls around them—make a strange impression on him. She's like a ghost, or a dream with a ghost in it. He gets scared. About what he couldn't say. Ghosts, maybe. Or something more realistic, like the noise coming from the hall that could be the footsteps of someone entering, that could be Serena, and Sandro hopes it both is and isn't her.

Because the white of this room and the smell of disinfectant and the neon light make him gag, and if there is one place not to see her again, this is it. Now watch: she'll walk in and find him holding this bone and the girl asleep looking like she's dead, and it will all turn out sad and anguished, and sayonara.

So Sandro tiptoes over to Luna, sets the bone on the blanket next to the pillow, and turns to leave. They can catch up at the next catechism. She'll thank him for the gift and perhaps tell her mother what a kind and swell guy the new catechist is. Yeah, sure, but now is not the time to dwell. Now is the time to get out of here. He looks at Luna for another second and then hears footsteps coming from outside, voices, *her* voice. Here she comes. What will Sandro do? Why did he come here? Why the fuck did he come here?

Rather than move he remains standing next to Luna, thinking, facing the door, totally frozen, as if he were waiting for fate to take his photo.

"No, not like that. You have to go from the root to the tip, from the root to the tip. You'll see. It's another thing altogether," you say. The nurse thanks you and keeps walking.

You'd bumped into her smoking downstairs, and she'd wasted no time asking for advice about her hair. Which you gave her, surprised by how much you still remembered. Then she offered you a coffee at the café, and now you're returning to the room with a greater craving to smoke than when you'd left. And you realize that you could have bought your daughter something, a snack, cookies, anything would do, anything would be better than the nothing you got her, the nothing you've given her for months. Maybe you've unlearned what being a mother entails, as if maternity were a battery that ran out of juice and died, and there was nothing you could do about it. You enter the room with this combination of anxiety, anger, guilt, and shame clinging to your skin like a cobweb, and you're about to grab one of the hundred sheets covering the old woman to wipe your face with.

But there's someone in the room, right beside Luna, and you stiffen when you see him. The two of you freeze.

He looks at you and you at him, and it all comes rushing back: school, the parent-teacher conference, Luca's nonstop talk about Mr. Mancini, the English sub you'd liked too. He's to blame if you were about to break your record of zero dates in ten years. He's to blame for your sending Luca to Biarritz. He'd been so insistent about that Wile E. Coyote story, the umbrella, the boulder plummeting toward you.

In actuality you're not sure how much he's to blame but you'd rather not think about it. At first you'd dwelled on it, you were in a fury, then you stopped caring about him along with everything else. You'd let it go. But here he is, the asshole who'd taught English to Luca, and now Luca is gone and he's here at the hospital hovering over your daughter. And you have no idea what the hell he wants or what he's up to, you just go flying. You fly across the room, land on top of him, and throw him against the wall.

You smack him, lift him to his feet, smack him again. He looks at you bug-eyed and opens his mouth to say something, but the only time you let go of his throat is to hit him and then you go back to cutting off his airflow. And even if by some miracle he were able to get a word in, it would be drowned out by your deep raspy cry, which before escaping your mouth passes through your flesh, your guts, your blood—those places inside that ignite you and pump you full of life. It doesn't sound like your voice, Serena, it sounds as if all of your anger at the world balled up inside your body were exploding in the sky. "Do you want to kill both of them, you son of a bitch? Do you want to kill both of them?" You say it again and again, and after every cry you shove him against the wall, harder each time. You have no intention of stopping.

But a minute later everything comes to a halt. The fury of cries is checked by just one word, so faint and faraway who knows how you managed to hear it. It comes from the bed across from you. "Mom," it says, and it has Luna's voice.

She's awake. She looks at you, holding something in her hand.

"Who brought this, Mom? I—did you bring it?"

"Sweetheart! How are you?" You let go of that idiot teacher hanging from the wall like a crooked painting.

"Did you bring it, Mom?" Luna rattles this white thing, white like her, like her beautiful hair in which it's caught.

"No, Luna. What is it?"

You take her in your arms and squeeze her tightly. She looks over your shoulder at the teacher.

"It's a bone. A whalebone. Did you bring it?" Your daughter's question is directed at the moron leaning against the wall. You turn and find him covering his nose to stop the bleeding. He doesn't answer right away.

"Hey, asshole," you say, "was it you brought this thing?"

For another minute he does nothing, then he shakes his head.

And you're shaking your head too as you look at your daughter staring at the bone. She untangles it from her hair, lies back down and holds it—and you—tightly to her chest. "I knew it, I knew it!" she says, her voice muffled because she's prone, because she's laughing and crying at the same time.

She's laughing and crying, your Luna, and repeating, "Yes, I knew it, thank you, I knew it!"

Bully for her, Serena, since you haven't a goddamn clue what's going on.

Save Our Ship

The doctors finally said I could go home and home is where we're going, me and Mom and the raindrops hitting the windows and splattering across the road, and as the wheels roll over them they make a noise like tape being torn.

"I'm going to get some money and we can go shopping, Luna. Or would you rather stay home while I went? What would make you happier?"

My only answer is to smile. I'm happy this way, in general. After six months my zombielike Mom is out of the house and asking me what I would prefer and her voice is no longer flat-lined but alive. It travels up and down while she talks. Heck no I'm staying home while she goes shopping.

But we still have to stop there a minute. Mom leaves the engine running and gets out. She asks me if I need to go to the bathroom but I don't, so I sit here alone, with the idle engine just barely rattling me. Merged with the patter of the rain, the sound makes me sleepy. I close my eyes, stick my hand in my sweatshirt pocket, and run my fingers over this wonderful bone again. It's very smooth with every once in a while some rougher spots, like little close-knit holes, which may be the sea's doing or else that's the way it was made and nature knows what these little holes are for. Rubbing this whalebone puts me at ease, really soothes me. When I think about how I came to find it, I start shaking and my heart begins to pound.

I asked Mom. I asked the nurses in the ER. No one had seen it. Of course they hadn't. I'd fainted and they'd wasted no time. They said that I was strung with seaweed, twigs stuck to my shirt, but who would have noticed a bone this white in my white hair? My big brother, who'd promised it to me, had kept it well hidden.

The night he died I sat in a chair with Mom and Miss Gemma. Sometimes I'd drift off and sometimes I wouldn't, and amid all those awful thoughts about Luca swirling in my head—if he'd been aware what was happening, if he'd suffered, where he was, if he was somewhere at all—amid all those things I suddenly remembered the last words I'd said to him as he was running out of the house with his backpack on and his friends waiting for him in the van. He'd stopped, turned around, kissed Mom on the cheek and me on the forehead. To Mom he'd said thanks and to me he'd said he loved me. And I'm so ashamed I didn't answer him: "I do too, I love you so much, Luca." No, all I'd said (referring to the whalebone) was: "Will you really get me one?" He laughed. "Of course I'll get you one. Look, Luna, I won't come home until I've found one for you, understand?"

In fact he never did come home. Yet he'd gotten the bone and made sure it found its way to me. How did he do it? What happened? How . . .

I don't know. I'm totally in the dark. Except I know that when I rub this wonderful bone it feels like when Luca used to hug me and I'd yell, "Stop it! Stop it!" even though I didn't really want him to stop. And his skin was kind of smooth yet rough in places on account of his beard, exactly like this bone. I run my finger over it and it's like picking up his scent, seeing him again for a second, hearing his voice.

Then, once that second's up, I hear nothing but Mom cursing, soupy from the rain.

She enters the car. Raindrops splash my hands and face.

"What happened, Mom? Did something happen?"

She doesn't answer right away. She opens a soaking wet piece of paper, irons it out on her chest, and reads it again.

"Mom, what happened? Did something happen to the house?"

"No, Luna. I don't know. No . . . It's locked. I didn't go in." And her voice has gone flat and robotic again. She sounds like those machines you put money into that say, "Have a nice day."

"What do you mean locked? You don't have the keys?"

"I do but they don't work . . . " Her back begins to shake weirdly, as if she had the hiccups. But it's not hiccups, I don't think. It's that she's really crying.

I look at her and run my finger along the bone. I so badly want to do something, or say something, the right thing, whatever will make her feel better. But it's hard when you don't know what's the matter, when you understand zippo. Still, I try telling her not to worry if she doesn't feel like going shopping, that maybe I really am tired and we can go lie down in the house for a while. But that makes Mom cry harder, so I sit still and say and do nothing.

Till a minute later I jump from fright when from outside in the pounding rain comes a knock on the window and a scream, a voice almost drowning, crying for help.

Mom grabs the handle and rolls down the window, and in comes the rain and the face of Zot.

"What's up, kid? What is it?"

"For the love of God, help! SOS! SOS!"

"Zot, calm down, what happened? Catch your breath and tell me what happened."

"SOS! SOS!"

"What does SOS mean?" I ask.

Zot clutches his chest and, with what little breath he has left, replies: "SOS . . . it's the inter . . . international . . . distress . . . signal . . . it means Save Our Souls . . . or Save Our Ship . . . in Morse code . . . it's three dits . . . three dahs . . . and—"

I'm about to ask what a Morse code is when Mom grabs him by the arm. "Cut the crap. What happened?"

"Grandfather . . . Grandfather . . . SOS."

"Ferro?" I ask, and Zot nods.

"Grandfather . . . Dry Death . . . help!"

"What the hell are you two talking about?" says Mom.

Zot doesn't answer. He just stands there in the rain, clutching his chest. Mom steps out of the car, picks him up, and tosses him in the backseat like he was junk mail. Then we speed off toward his house. But I'm wondering, if this is such an emergency, why didn't he call a neighbor instead of coming all the way over here? I take a minute to think about it, about the houses between here and Ghost House. One belongs to a Milanese, one to a man from Parma, and three to Russians. Who the others belong to is anyone's guess. They're always empty. The windows are open just one month during the year, in August, the rest of the time they're sealed shut. So, even if there are two streets crammed with mansions and mini-mansions between our house and Ghost House, Zot's real neighbors are Mom and me.

Who drive all the way to his house; jump out of the car, and cut through the forest, where the rain has lifted a little and there's the powerful smell of a thousand things balled together. We enter the house and everything is just the same as it was the other day, except Ferro is lying facedown on the floor, not moving, one arm twisted like it were fake. And next to him a rifle.

DRY DEATH

Grandfather! Dearly beloved Granddaddy!"
Zot drops to his knees next to Mr. Ferro, makes the sign of the cross, and tries to hug him, but it's not so easy with him laid out on the floor like that. "Talk to me, Grandfather! I implore you, Granddaddy!"

Ferro has on two gigantic wooden clogs and no socks, and the arm near his rifle is droopy and whitish like a dead octopus tentacle at the fish market.

I don't know what happens next, since Mom shields my eyes with her hands.

"It's not fair!" screams Zot, his voice trembling. "He was so good. He didn't seem good but he was. He had a heart of gold. Grandfather, sweet Granddaddy, why? O Lord up in Heaven, o Saint Felix, o Saint Catherine of Siena . . . ."

Mom takes her hands off my eyes, because she needs them to shove aside Zot and lean over Ferro. She removes the rifle, takes the old man by his droopy dead arm, and, tugging hard, manages to turn him over on his backside. She places two fingers on his neck and her ear to his heart. But maybe she can't hear him too well, since she moves her head up and down endlessly until this booming voice full of phlegm emerges from the afterlife: "Oh yeah, that's a good girl, keep going, the grand prize is right down there."

Mom bolts to her feet and Zot throws himself on top of Mr. Ferro.

"Grandfather! You're alive! Jesus of love aflame, thank you! Thank you, Lord! Sweet Granddaddy!"

"Get lost, blue-baller, leave me and this pretty piece of tail alone!"

Ferro tries to get up but doesn't have the strength, so he turns on his side instead. His white shirt is hiked up and you can see his gut, which is so big it hides his underwear, mercifully, and below that two bony legs that don't seem to belong to him, like two sticks jammed on at the end.

"Who are you supposed to be, good-looking, my nurse?"

"Me? I'm nobody. Zot called me—"

"Ah, you're his friend, huh? You Russians sure are little devils. Your friend likes to pretend he's an orphan from Chernobyl. What about you? You a nurse or street meat?"

"Neither. I only came here to see if you were dead. Unfortunately it appears you're not."

Ferro makes a noise I can't interpret. I don't even know where it comes from. It sounds like a cross between a coughing fit and a pebble caught in a lawnmower.

"Don't bullshit me. You're an infiltrator same as him. They put him in my house and told him he was a radioactive orphan. Who'd ever buy that? You hear him speak Italian? Christ, kid talks better than me."

"But it's a simple language, Grandfather. Besides, I like it. I learned it by listening to your greatest singers: Claudio Villa, the Quartetto Cetra, Gino Latilla . . . Sister Anna was Italian. We used to sing those songs together all the time."

"Sure, you bet, an Italian nun in Chernobyl. A spy is what I call her. First comes this rotten kid and now you with your nurse/street meat routine. You pretend to minister to me meanwhile you're slowly poisoning me to death. That's your plan, isn't it? But I don't care. Go back to Russia and tell them Ferruccio Marrai isn't going anywhere. This is my house and I won't budge."

No one says anything. So I do: "Mr. Ferro, Mom's not Russian. She's my mom."

"Is that right? Then how come Snow White's mother isn't all white too?"

"Listen up, asshole," says Mom, walking over to the sink and snatching two rags that may not be clean but at least aren't filthy. She passes one to me and we start drying off. "You can say whatever you want about Zot. Touch my daughter and I'll kick you so hard in the balls you'll turn blond. We came here to see if you were alive, but as far as I'm concerned you can drop dead. I'll hand your keys over to the Russians myself. Better them than an asshole like you."

It's silent for a minute. Mr. Ferruccio looks at her and coughs again. "So, kid, you're Italian after all."

"No, I'm not Italian. I'm from Forte dei Marmi."

"Maremma Cane." That's all Ferro says. Then he tries to hoist himself up by latching onto the oven. He falls to the floor again. "Give me a hand!"

Mom takes one arm, Zot and I the other. But Zot can barely lift him. There's not a muscle in his body. Practically all he does is keep his hand on mine. Yet Ferruccio finally stands, turns toward the sink, and spits in it. He points to his rifle and Zot picks it up and hands it to him. Ferro leans on it like it was a cane.

"You really from Forte dei Marmi or you yanking my chain?"

"I'm from Forte. And don't ask me again. Your bullshit is getting tired."

Ferro thinks for a minute, then: "That's the style all right. Whose daughter are you anyway?"

"I'm the daughter of Lari."

"You mean Stelio Lari? Pinhead?"

Mom nods just once.

"I've known your dad a lifetime. We grew up together. Crawled off the deep end in his dotage, right?"

"Yeah, sort of."

"No offense, kid, but he was always kind of stupid. Otherwise he'd never have married your mom. What a nag that woman was, always complaining, with that little voice of hers that just wore you to pieces. No wonder he lost his mind. How did your daddy put up with her?

"You said it yourself, he was kind of stupid."

"Whoa there, kid," Ferro says to Mom, suddenly very serious. "Don't you dare insult Stelio, hear me? You better rinse your mouth before saying anything about Pinhead. He may have been set in his ways but next to you all he was a champ. Now us, we were a whole other generation, we really lived life. You all find your food in the fridge or run to the supermarket or go to a restaurant. We toiled away, busted our asses, and set this country in motion. Then you went and sold it for chickenfeed."

"Honestly, I always saw you at the beach doing dick all," says Mom. "You used to lie under an umbrella and sleep."

"I wasn't sleeping. I had my eye on the sea. That's what a lifeguard does: keeps alert, never takes his eyes off the sea."

"Clearly. So alert you were snoring."

"Me, snore? Occasionally I'd lie down to relax, sure; lifeguarding is grueling work. But I was always vigilant and kept an eye on the sea."

"Is that why you were on the floor earlier, Grandfather?" asks Zot. "Were you relaxing?"

Ferro leans on his rifle, shakes his head. "Nope. I was sound asleep earlier. That a crime?"

"You were asleep on the ground?"

"Yeah, and it felt heavenly."

"But did you lie down or—"

"Or?"

"Or did you fall like last time?"

"No, I lay down. I took one look at the floor and said Sweet Mary that looks comfy. Then I stretched out. Is that okay by you?"

"Actually it's not, Grandfather."

"Why not?"

"Because I can smell it, Grandfather. It was the Dry Death again."

I turn to Zot but there's no need to ask; he points down at something. "Under the table," he says. I bend over. Under the table is a huge dark glass pitcher, a jug filled with something that looks like water but isn't water. Even with the cap on, the smell makes my eyes water and my throat burn.

"Is it poison?" I ask, standing up. My head spins a little.

"Poison?" says Ferro. "Nonsense." He starts laughing and his tummy jiggles underneath his T-shirt. "That's the best grappa on the planet."

"It's called Dry Death," Zot says gravely, as if he were introducing me to somebody he really didn't like.

"At first it was just called 'Dry,'" says Ferro. "Because we wanted it to be real dry, real strong. We set up shop back of Gino's place so you couldn't see what we were doing from the street. Because making grappa yourself is illegal. Did you know that? What kind of country doesn't allow you to make home-made grappa? How's that a crime?"

"So why did you call it Dry *Death*?" I ask.

"Because people died making it."

"They died?"

"Yeah, two people. We spent a week there, made enough for an army. We had rotten fruit, wine dregs, potato skins. Anything works for grappa, kids, long as it's got juice inside, long as it's good and potent. Even fertilizer will do. During the war they used sludge from the cesspools. They say that was special. Choice stuff. But we used rotten fruit. And as always Gino acted like he was an expert, the only one who knew what he was doing. 'Out of the way,' he said, 'I'll handle it, out of the way . . . ' In the end he handled it all right; the gas tank blew up and he and poor Mauro bit it. May their souls rest in peace.

Goodbye still and goodbye gas tank—everything was ruined forever. But we'd already brewed tons of Dry Death, so each of us took a bottle home. Amen to that."

He shuffles to the table, leans his rifle against the wall, and slowly sits down with an "Aaahhh," which sounds like a cross between a sigh and a burp.

"So what are you doing with a demijohn if you all brought back bottles?" asks Mom. She crouches next to the black barrel, unscrews the cap, and stands back up with her eyes half-mast.

"Whoever dies leaves his share of Dry Death to his friends. We go to the funeral, take the bottle off the corpse, and divvy it up. That's the way it's always been. And now . . . " Ferro pauses. "Now I'm the only one left and it's all here with me. It's just me and Dry Death."

For a while everyone's silent except Zot. A faint sound comes from his mouth. "Hey," it seems to say, "I'm here, I live in this house too." But he doesn't actually talk. Mom does. "Ferro, can I taste this Dry Death?"

"Maremma Cane!" he says with glee, and he leans against the rifle to stand up, but the gun slips out of his hand and falls on the ground. The barrel is pointing straight at me.

Mom picks it up. "Maybe we ought to put this away."

But Zot explains that it's useless, there's another one in the bathroom.

"Really? What are you doing with two rifles?"

"Two, shmoo. I've got eleven thank you very much."

"Eleven rifles?"

"Yep. Same rules as Dry Death. Whoever dies leaves his friends his grappa and his guns. I have a rifle for every window in the house and a supply of grappa that'll last me a hundred years. Tell the Russians to bring it. Tell those sons of bitches from the agency to come here and tell me I have no choice but to sell. I may be alone but my friends are still here and ready to fight by my side." He gestures to the haunted kitchen with a sweep of his arm. "We're here and we're not going anywhere."

He sits there staring into the emptiness and nodding his head while Mom pours Dry Death into a glass and sits down beside him. I almost sit myself. My legs hurt. The doctors told me I should rest, that I should take it easy for a while, but there hasn't been any taking it easy on our trip back from the hospital.

Mom lifts the glass to her lips, takes a breath, and downs her drink. She coughs, exhales, coughs again.

When she looks like she's started to breathe again, I ask her if we're going to go shopping. It's late and I'm tired.

"We're not going, Luna. I don't think we're going to make it."

"But there's nothing to eat at home. What'll we do?"

Mom doesn't answer right away. Maybe it's the Dry Death rising back up her throat. Or maybe what she has to say to me is the kind of thing that comes out of your mouth with difficulty.

"Luna, listen, there is no more home, we don't have one anymore."

FLEEING THE FUTURE

H uman life counts for fuck all nowadays," says Rambo. "How can you treat a person like a dog? I'm speechless, Sandro, speechless."

He says he's speechless but the words keep coming. Sandro listens and nods, and Rambo talks so loudly that the two old guys on the bench, Pino and Topo, can hear him too. Those two have been on the pier forever, holding their fishing rods, scanning the water to see if anything's bit, hoping nothing has so they won't have to get up and do something.

Even Mojito, the dog Rambo occasionally walks for his neighbors, can hear him. Today the dog is tied to the wheelchair of a stiff, unmoving old lady wrapped in three plaid blankets, like an Egyptian mummy yet highly sensitive to the cold.

"What's the world coming to when a dog and a person are counted equal? I said it myself: 'Have you lost your minds? Do you have a conscience? I wouldn't take that old lady for under ten euros.'"

He's referring to her but the lady smothered in plaid doesn't realize it. She is and isn't here. Above the cocoon of blankets, her face is set in an eternal grimace, half surprised and half frightened, one eye permanently shut and the other staring out at nothing, her mouth drawn and tilting to the left. She's been this way since her stroke, and the more Sandro looks at her, the more he's reminded of those poor souls from Pompei engulfed by the lava of Vesuvius in the middle of the night while they were sleeping and turned into statues, just as scared and bewildered today as they were when the lava woke them one night two thousand years ago.

Same goes for the old lady, and if she looks like she's shaking it's only because every so often Mojito yanks on the leash and rattles her wheelchair.

Mojito is a husky beagle that pants nonstop. Rambo usually walks him with Rimmel, a younger dog that doesn't look as much like a garbage can with paws. Only today the owner's daughter had come back from Milan and they'd all gone out for a stroll, dragging the fitter dog behind them.

"So, seeing as I have to keep an eye on just one dog, they said I could take the old lady out too. Same price. Can you believe that? 'Fuck no,' I told them, 'for the old lady I want ten euros minimum.'"

"Why? What do you usually get?"

"Seven euros. But that's for two dogs. A person isn't a dog. You know what they said? They said the old lady was worth *less* than a dog. She doesn't talk or run and does her business in a diaper. 'We should be paying you less,' they said, 'not more . . .' What dicks. Can you believe that, Sandro? Can you believe that?"

Sandro nods, half listening. "So what did you settle on?"

"I stood my ground. It was a question of principle. I said, 'Fuck no. At a minimum you should be paying me the usual rate.'" He rests his hand on Mojito's head. The dog closes his eyes and lifts his muzzle to absorb the full weight of Rambo's touch. "What kind of dirty animal cuts corners on his own mother? And let's be clear here: They live off this woman. The day she dies, the party's over for all of them, you know?"

Sandro nods but neglects to ask what will kill the party. Because he has other things on his mind and doesn't care. Because the north wind is picking up, and it may not be strong but it's enough to make his nose ache, his nose that is still swollen and warmer than the rest of his face. Besides, there's no point in asking; Rambo will go on to explain why with or without his asking.

"You'll see. She's never done squat and he works at a marble sawing mill, but now with the marble crisis he's almost always at home, and they have this bitch of a daughter studying in Milan, but if you ask me all she's boning up on is cock. And you know where they went today? They're taking a break at the spa in Montecatini—a break from what? They don't do shit! And who do you think's footing the bill?" Rambo points his finger at the old woman, only right in her face, his index finger is almost touching her eye, which is still open and still bewildered. "This lady's husband worked for the coast guard. His monthly retirement check was solid gold. But the minute this old lady dies, bye-bye money, bye-bye spa, bye-bye everything. This right here is their wealth, this old lady is their future, and they're haggling over two or three euros. The world is fucked." Rambo makes a disgusted sound with his throat. He adjusts his camouflage hunting hat, turns to the sea, spits in it, and then loses himself for a while musing on that shining immensity which captures men's attention and grants them the gift of confusion, a yearning to do nothing, and a dangerous habit of turning philosophical.

In fact, when Rambo addresses Sandro again, his voice is different, wise and deep. "Look here, Sandrino, look closely," he says, pointing at the old lady, his finger still a millimeter from her frozen grimace. "Gruesome sight, right? But you know what the real problem is? It's that we say, 'That's life, we all must resign ourselves to fate.' But it's not true. It's not a question of resignation. This here is hardly the worst. This here is the *best* that can happen. We tiptoe forward all careful about what we do and what we eat, praying we don't get sick or wind up crushed by a truck, and for what? To hope we might one day turn out like this. Shit, this here is our finish line. Don't you see? If we're lucky, this old lady is our future. Our best possible future. You getting this or not?"

Sandro nods just once. He feels short of breath. His nose aches, his head aches. He's felt this way since Saturday, since the woman he loves bashed him against the wall like an octopus against a rock. His head was still spinning when he'd left the room, so he'd thought maybe he should get a CAT scan. It was hardly a ridiculous idea. After all, he was already at the hospital; it would cost him little effort. He went down to radiology and asked for a brain CAT scan. The nurse told him he needed to make an appointment, that it would take up to three months. Three months? Aren't these for emergencies? "Yes, of course," she said, "when they're emergencies." "And how do you know if they're emergencies?" She told him that emergencies arrive on their backs. Then she looked at his nose, opened a drawer, and handed him a bag of dry ice.

Sandro left the hospital holding the ice partly to his nose and partly to his head, and the cold calmed him down. Of course, on the road back every so often he had checked the mirror to see if his pupils were dilated, if one were larger than the other, if his eyes could follow his finger. But it was hard to keep an eye on the road and look at your finger and check to see if your pupils were following along. After a while he felt nauseated, and nausea is another symptom of brain trauma, and so he really was about to turn around and head back to the hospital, but then he'd already arrived home, and the sight of the walls, the door, the plastic and iron roof his father had welded and hammered on by himself, gave him a sense of reality, resilience, manliness, and he chucked the idea.

All that grit, that energy to build things—Sandro must have it lying around somewhere too. This manly spirit that takes stuff by force and alters it to build other stuff, to make the world the way you want it with the swing of a hammer. It must be in his blood. It's called DNA. It's science. There's no disputing science.

Enough, he said. No more catechism, no more boar bones, no more trying to score with someone who'd rather beat your head against a hospital wall till you were dead. He'd tried, he'd held out hope, but all he'd gotten for his efforts were insults, a (nearly) broken nose, a classroom of pesky religious kids, and brain trauma (or thereabouts). Enough. For real. Sandro had once read something a sports star said—he can neither remember who nor what sport the guy played—but it went something like "a true champion is the one who makes the simplest move at the right time." Beautiful words to live by. From now on he too would act like a champion, and the simplest move to make was to quit trying, and the right time was immediately. He nodded at the door in front of him, lifted his arms, and shouted, "Champion of the world! Champion of the world!"

But the door opened abruptly and his mother found him like that, his arms in the air and his nose swollen, and she began to whimper. "Jesus, Joseph, and Mary, what happened, Sandro? Oh my Lord, what happened, Sandrino?" And he told her what he's told her since he was in elementary school, i.e., he had fallen down while playing with his friends, and he looked on while she, now as then, ran to fetch cotton swabs and peroxide. He heard his mother's voice in ultrasounds, and he felt the slight burning of the disinfectant on his nose. Its smell entered his nose and pained him, and he let himself be carried off by both her voice and the smell.

He'd like the same thing to happen now, with the breeze and the scent of the sea, only he can't stop staring at the old lady and her eternally terrified grimace.

Because unfortunately Rambo is right: Misery is the most we can expect, the finish line for those who are prudent and take care of themselves and aspire to live for a thousand years. That's the most divine future awaiting us. So no, goddammit, he's not having it. If this is the best he can hope for the future, Sandro at least wants to fight for a less miserable present.

If he lets a few punches, a swollen nose, and slight brain trauma stop him, well then, Sandro can't claim to have tried. He tried a little, but a little doesn't amount to dick. Did he take a beating? He has to take double that. He has to welcome every scuffle and every smackdown coming to him as if it were a push in the direction he desires. Without asking himself what he wants, without always kowtowing to his damn brain, which is only good at coming up with excuses to do nothing.

And if Sandro drops dead from one of these beatings, well, that would be fair, sort of: that's what happened to Luca and he's to blame, so, worse comes to worst, Sandro pays for what he did.

He clenches his teeth and regards the old lady. For a moment she seems to smile, to twist that drawn, fixed mouth of hers and say, "Right on, young man, right on. Rock out, run free, burn!"

But it's just a trick of the light. Or perhaps Mojito is yanking the leash and shaking her. Perhaps it's a hallucination brought on by Sandro's very real brain trauma that, without a CAT scan, won't be discovered and will pretty soon carry him off to heaven or hell, if such places exist. They exist all right. Of course they exist. He's a catechist now, a believer. He has to believe. Because Sandro is a fighter, Sandro doesn't cave, and if the future sucks so much, then shit, we're better off diving headfirst into all the present we can find.

TU SEI ROMANTICA

Bambina bellaa
sono l'ultimo poeta che si ispira ad una stellaaa.
Bambina miaaa
sono l'ultimo inguaribile malato di poesiaaa.
E voglio bene a te, perché sei come mee
romanticaaa . . .

That's what I wake up to, after a night of deep dreaming. Tages and I were at the beach. The dream lasted all night but we didn't speak, not once. All we did was swim. Then suddenly these words come crashing into my ear, accompanied by a kind of busted accordion.

I sit up, scared, and bump my head against Mom's. She'd also jumped in fright. Then we both fall back in bed, Mom smothers herself with a pillow, and I can hear her saying underneath it, "I'll kill him, I'll kill him." It's one thing to wake up in the morning, but Zot's singing and that accordion blaring is pure murder, and I'd rather be stuck in a horrible nightmare where werewolves eat you bit by bit than hear this stuff, and if his pathetic notes were to come barging in on your nightmare, you'd turn to the wolves and beg, "Eat my ears first, please, my ears first!"

This has been our alarm clock since Monday, when we came to stay at Ghost House. I'd been scared of hearing chains rattling, doors creaking, spirits moaning, but Zot's morning serenades are much, much worse.

The first night, when we found Mr. Ferro passed out from Dry Death, I had had no clue we'd be staying here. We went to get groceries at Teresa's and bought a bunch of stuff, then we came back to Ghost House and Mom made tordelli. They're like tortelli except spelled with a *d* rather than a *t* and filled with meat instead of anything else.

Around here tordelli is food for the holidays—Christmas, Easter, and, unfortunately, Ferragosto, when the lifeguards gather on the beach and eat a pot per person. You heard me right, Ferragosto, when the beach gets so crowded you worry the water will spill over the edge, like in a bathtub, and flood town. During Ferragosto the tourists feel compelled to go cliff-diving even if they swim as well as cinder blocks. The life-guards know it but they eat their pots of tordelli anyway because that's the tradition, then wash it down with a bottle of black wine and afterward stare at the sea and pant for air, and if they see an arm waving for help, it takes a few minutes for them to remember what they're supposed to do.

In fact someone always dies on Ferragosto. There's a saying that goes, "Holy Mary, every year you carry one away." It has scared me ever since I was a little girl and would picture the Virgin coming down from Heaven, looking at all those happy people in their bathing suits—ladies and daddies and chil-dren—and picking the person to carry away that year. Then I thought about it some more and realized it was just an excuse, a way of laying the blame on the Virgin, when really it's the fault of the lifeguards struggling to digest their tordelli.

Which were awesome the other night. I didn't even know Mom could cook them. Her most complicated meal was fish sticks with melted cheese on top, and even those she managed to burn from time to time. The tordelli were delicious. Mr. Ferro had three helpings and afterward he practically fell asleep in his chair. He held his stomach and finally burped so loud I could hear it inside my stomach. Then he turned to Zot.

"Where are your manners, kid? You should be ashamed of yourself!"

And Zot said, "Calumny! I did nothing of the sort. Luna, you know it wasn't me, right?"

Mr. Ferro stood up and went to the bathroom. Then he stopped at the door, close to where Mom was clearing our plates.

"So, you sold your place just like everyone else, huh?"

"I didn't sell anything. My mother's asshole siblings did."

"Aren't they in Milan? What the hell do they want?"

"Money. They waited for my dad to die and it was either sell or pay them their share."

"Sons of bitches."

"Exactly. To think that after my mom died they had the temerity to ask for rent every month."

"What shits. How much did you give them?"

"I never game them a cent, but it was a ton of money that they're now claiming I owe them, and they're going to take it out of my share of the sale, so I'll get practically nothing."

Although it was the first time I ever heard such things, I understood immediately they weren't good. I stood up, took the empty plastic soup bowl that a moment ago had been full of tordelli, and carried it to the sink. Zot did the same with the glasses, then said, "But that's highway robbery. Is there nothing we can do? You must be protected under the law."

Ferro started to say something but Mom beat him to it: "What law, kid? Laws are written by lowlifes to protect lowlifes."

Mom rinsed a plate and handed it to him along with that tart truth. Zot took it and dried it off then handed it to me to put away. But how was I to know where the plates went? I mean, I didn't even know where I was supposed to go. This wasn't our home. Nor, so it seemed, did we have a home anymore.

Mom had tried calling Miss Gemma, and she'd picked up, but her daughter was crying hard in the background over a fight she'd had with her boyfriend and had come home to spend the night, so Mom didn't ask Miss Gemma for anything. Maybe we would go sleep on the street or in one of the big yards belonging to an empty villa. Who knew?

"Impossible," said Zot, "the law has to help you. The point of the law is to punish wrongdoers."

"Sure, kid, the law punishes wrongdoers," said Mom. "The problem is that according to the law they're not wrongdoers. The law lets them do their shady business. Actually it protects them. But if I were to take a shovel and stab them in the brain, the law would be quick to identify its wrongdoer, and I'd go straight to jail. You happy, mister friend of the law?"

"That's the straight stuff," said Mr. Ferro, still standing by the door. Then he said it again with all his heart, "That there's the straight stuff."

Zot said nothing. Or rather, he dried a plate and handed it to me, and something escaped his lips that sounded like, "No. I'm not happy. Not one bit."

"All right, I'm off to bed," Ferro finally said. "Don't make a racket and don't clog the crapper. Your room's over there. Sheets are in the closet. Rifle's by the window."

I turned abruptly to Mom. Up until that moment I honestly had no idea we were going to stay here at Ghost House. There was barely any light and I couldn't see if she was happy or not. She just washed the plastic soup bowl and—maybe—nodded. Then I looked at Zot. He wore a smile so wide I could see the white of his small, crooked teeth randomly tossed together in his mouth.

And I see them again now as he sings his morning serenade at the top of his lungs.

Tu sei romanticaaa
amarti è un po' rivivereee
nella semplicità, nell'irrealtà
di un'altra etààà.
Tu sei romantica
amica delle nuvoleee
che cercano lassù
un po' di sol, come fai tuuu

The most I'd been able to tell him was that maybe he could just sing instead, without the accordion, but he took it badly. He says he taught himself how to play with the talent he inherited from his dad, a violinist who used to roam around Russia playing for spare change. What with all his roaming around, his dad met a beautiful young baroness. They spent one night together and Zot was born. But Zot never met either of them. He'd heard the story from a nun, Mother Anna, the only kind person in the orphanage. She told him that his mom and dad never saw each other again, that his dad left for another town the day after, and having a son out of the blue would have been a scandal for his mom, so her super-conniving family gave him to the nuns. His dad didn't even know he had a son, had never had the chance to play with him, had never taught him the facts of life. But according to Zot he'd left him this great gift for music.

The whole thing seems so unfair to me. How could the son of a baroness wind up in an orphanage? "But can't he at least find her?" I asked Mom and Ferro while Zot was in the bathroom. "Is that so hard? How many baronesses could there be in Chernobyl?"

"None, Luna," said Mom. "None."

"What do you mean 'none'? Then who did the violin player make Zot with?"

Mom didn't answer. Neither did Ferro. Sometimes when

you want someone to really understand something the best thing to do is not answer. That way the person sits there in silence thinking about her question and slowly arrives at the answer on her own. I was beginning to get it, in fact. But I didn't want to. I want the baroness to spend every night thinking about her child off somewhere God only knows. I want there to be an extra bit of sadness in his dad's violin playing for the son he doesn't know he has.

But what I want counts for nothing, so I stay in bed and force myself to listen to Zot sing from start to finish, even when Mom rips the pillow off her head and huffs off to the bathroom, and he stops playing a minute to let her pass the narrow labyrinth of boxes our room is buried in.

We brought them from home. Practically everything in them belongs to Luca. We packed up everything in his room and left the rest behind. We pretended as though we were putting it in the attic, that our stuff was back there waiting for us, when really the van would be coming by to cart everything off to the dump.

On our first night I walked out of the bathroom and found Mom gazing at the boxes. She was sitting on the bed, staring at them in the dark. When she noticed me, she said, "Maybe being away from home is a good thing, you know?"

"You really think so, Mom?" And she said, "Yes, I do," all shaking, then she started to cry. I know why she was crying. Because she was surrounded by Luca's things but not by the walls of his room, not the kitchen where we used to eat together, not the yard where he kept his surfboard. After Luca all we had left were bits and pieces, and of those bits and pieces we could only fit smaller bits and pieces into boxes. If things continued this way, pretty soon we'd have nothing. As I see it, that's what Mom was thinking about that night. Or at least I was.

When I think back on it, I feel the urge to cry a little too.

But whenever that happens, I know what I have to do: I turn to the big box beside the bed, now a nightstand, reach out, and rub my whalebone. That way I remember this one crazy fact: I may be losing many of my brother's things, but a new and wonderful one made its way to me.

I had asked for it so much that, even if he himself never returned from Biarritz, he still managed to bring this back. I had passed out in the sea and he'd hidden it in my hair. So today, a Saturday, maybe I'll stop by the beach before catechism and take a walk and feel the sand under my feet, in part because I have this ridiculous and top-secret idea in my head that maybe my brother has another present for me.

Tu sei la musica
che ispira l'anima
sei tu il mio angelo di Paradiso,
per meee.
Ed io che accanto a te
sono ritornato a vivere
a te racconterò, affideròòò
i sogni miei.
Perché romanticaaa
tu sss—

Zot's song is cut short, as is his voice, when Mr. Ferro charges in, grabs the accordion, and hurls it out the window. Then he spots it there in the grass, picks up his rifle, and shoots.

Mom comes out of the bathroom but realizes it's just the usual round of accordion fire practice and disappears again. This is the daily routine. The room immediately fills with the smell of smoke and Ferro sets down his rifle and says, "Next time it won't be the accordion." Then he walks off.

But it isn't true. He said the same thing yesterday. And the day before that. Zot goes to retrieve it, covers the holes with insulating tape, and everything is back to the way it was. Worse, actually, because the accordion sounds more and more dreadful and warped yet Zot doesn't quit.

Not even now, with the last bit of song stuck in his throat. He takes a breath, extends his arms, and draws the curtain on his performance:

"Perché romanticaaa, tu seeeiii . . . "

I stay where I am, my head against the pillow, and watch him. But there's not much light and the only thing I can make out is Zot's wide smile, so broad it covers up everything else, like a gigantic billboard commanding you to be happy. Only the billboard is planted in a nuclear wasteland strewn with broken things—rubble, ashes, bare trees—a place happiness is unheard of. And yet the colorful billboard stands its ground, there in front of you, so that it really does bring you a bit of joy.

"Did you like today's song, Luna?"

I don't answer right away. I try to come up with something to say that's kind of true but won't hurt Zot's feelings. I come up with nothing, so I keep quiet. I just nod my head.

"All right! I couldn't decide between that and '*Sapore di sale*.' But '*Sapore di sale*' is a sea shanty. It would be more appropriate if I sang it to you at the beach this afternoon."

"But today's Saturday. We have catechism."

"Yes, of course. But first we're going to the beach. To see if your brother has brought you another present."

THE MEANING OF A PAN

I s it really a sail?" asks Zot. Yes, I tell him. A transparent sail on their back. That's why they're called by-the-wind sailors.

"They're like itty-bitty jellyfish, flat and blue. They look like contact lenses. They ride the skin of the water and this delicate part on top acts like a sail. The breeze blows them all over the place. Eventually the waves strand them on the beach. And on those days the whole shore turns blue, a long blue road paved with by-the-wind sailors," I say, and I point it out, even though Zot and I are the only ones here.

"Where do these prodigious creatures come from?"

"I don't know."

"But how do they all arrive in the same place at the same time if they've been sailing around at random?"

"I don't know. All I know is that they have this sail and they go with the wind. My brother told me so."

Suddenly Zot shouts, "Red alert!" and tries to pull me away from the shore at the sight of a bigger wave. It's the third time he's shouted, "Red alert!" when the water is already nipping at our ankles.

Not that the water bothers me. Actually I like it. I've taken off my shoes and go barefoot. But he insists on wearing his leather boots, which are sopping wet, and every step he takes sounds like a duck being crushed to death at the bottom of a well.

On our way to the beach Zot had ridden in front of me and

wouldn't stop crying, "Bump alert!" "Dangerous curve alert!" "Extremely grainy asphalt alert!"

It's my fault. I'd told him about the time that I'd seen a lamppost and wanted to tie my bike to it. I'd been riding fast and it had looked far away but turned out to be real close. I slammed into it and fell over. Ever since then Zot rides ahead of me and makes a running commentary of our route. I tell him to be quiet and he promises to, even raises his hand and apologizes, but a minute later he's back at it again.

Like now with the big waves on the shore.

"Watch out! You'll get wet, Luna!"

"But I'm barefoot. It's no big deal. I like it."

"Cold water at this time of year is not salubrious. Your joints are going to be in serious pain after."

"Pain, shmain."

"Look here, kid, laugh all you want at your age. The day you get arthritis you'll lift your eyes to heaven and say, 'Ah, how right my poor Zot was, may his soul rest in peace.'"

"How do you know you'll die before me?"

"It's natural. One generation makes way for the next."

"We're the same age, Zot. I might even die before you."

"Oh no, Luna, don't even joke about that. Aside from the fact that they explained to me several times at the orphanage that because I was born in a nuclear fallout zone I won't live very long, if you die, I'll die of heartache right after. At most it'll be a draw."

I keep my mouth shut because this nuclear fallout business makes me sad. Even though I'd like to tell Zot that you can't die from heartache. That much I know. Otherwise I'd already be dead, and Mom would be super dead. You can't die from heartache. Period.

Zot stops because he can't walk straight, and I take the chance to adjust my sunglasses and hoodie even though there isn't much you can do to stop a little light getting through. Meanwhile he removes one of his boots and turns it upside down. Water and seaweed fall out onto the shore. He slips it back on, but his wet sock is caked in sand and slippery. He loses his footing. I try to catch his arm but miss and grab a handful of air, while Zot falls face-first. He finishes putting on his boot like that, tugging and sort of shouting. Then he stands up again, adjusts his dead-mouse-colored raincoat, and we continue walking along the water's edge with our eyes on the ground.

We take a few steps before he stops again. "Impossible!" He picks up this round silver object from the sand. "It's another pan, Luna! I can't believe it!"

We must have walked ten minutes on the water's edge hoping to see if the waves had brought anything interesting, and this is the fifth pan we've found. Zot turns it over. The metal is still sort of shiny, despite being corroded by salt and covered with dandelions.

"What do you think?" he asks, and I press my face to it. I inhale the bittersweet smell of algae. "Any interest?"

I try to look at it but the sun hits the water and shatters into a thousand tiny darting pieces surrounding me on all sides. I can't keep my eyes open, can't even see the pan. All I see are flashes from my headache.

"No, it's trash."

"Sure? Get a good look. Touch it."

"What's the point? It's a pan. Do you think Luca would send me a pan? What would I do with one?"

"I don't know. But we've found five pans and three lids already . . . Maybe he's sending you a full set."

"Right, that must be it. My brother is sending me a set of pans from the afterlife. What could that possibly mean?"

Zot doesn't answer right away. He looks down at the sand. "I don't know. Maybe he wants you to learn how to cook. It's an important skill for housewives," he says. Thank God another gust from the libeccio arrives and blows his stupid words away. It blows hard and gets under my windbreaker. The jacket balloons and almost lifts me off the ground. It used to belong to Luca and is huge on me.

I had rummaged through the boxes looking for my own jacket this morning. I was running late for catechism and Mom told me, "Take this." She threw it on me and zipped it up in front and the draft of air smelled like my brother. Then and there I thought that maybe it was all in my head, that it couldn't be true. But Mom just stood there, like me not moving, zipper in hand. We hugged, squeezed each other hard. I felt my eyes sting, but Mom said, "No crying, Luna, deal? Let's not cry, okay? It's a beautiful jacket and it looks good on you and we're not going to cry."

But now I can't smell Luca anymore. Instead I suddenly catch a whiff of this bitter smell, like rotten wood. I turn around and find Zot waving this dark thing in my face. Turns out it's rotten wood.

"What about this, Luna? Look at it. This might be interesting, don't you think?"

"It's a piece of wood. Lose it."

"Give it a good look. See how weird it's shaped?"

"It's just a piece of wood. Lose it."

"Give it a good look. Don't you see—"

"No, I can't see it, Zot! I can't see anything with the sun today! You've been asking me to look at stuff for three hours now but you're the only one who can see them. I can't see anything!"

For a moment all we can hear are the waves spreading out along the sand, nibbling our feet. I feel bad for shouting. But it's true, I can hardly see anything, and sometimes it really makes me mad.

"Sorry, Luna, I didn't want you to. I mean I don't want you to look at it. I want you to feel it."

"All I can smell is the stink of rotten wood."

"Don't smell it. I said feel it, feel it with your powers."

"Powers?"

Zot takes another step forward, crushing another duck to death. Then we stop. "Yes," he says. "You have powers, Luna. It's clear. Like your friend Tages."

That's what he says. I lift my head up and look at him. I can't see anything—what with the sun and the sea behind him—but somehow I still manage to hold his gaze.

"Did he appear in your dreams again?"

I stand there and don't say anything, not yes and not no.

"He did, didn't he?"

"Twice."

"All right. And what happened?"

"I can't remember one of the times. But last night we were at the beach together."

"Ah!" says Zot, his eyes so big I can see them, two white circles pointing straight at me like ping-pong balls, bouncing around at random. "That's how you tell me?"

"How should I tell you?"

"It's incredible! The beach of all places! Can't you see I'm right?"

"Right about what?" I ask. Even if I think I know the answer. I know everything. "You think Tages is trying to tell me something, right?"

"No, Luna. I think you're Tages."

Me, Tages? What a dumb idea. Total garbage. Only Zot could think up something like that. Only Zot. And me. It had crossed my mind, but I didn't want to wind up in the insane asylum so I never told anyone. Actually, I never even admitted it to myself. But now, hearing it from someone else's lips, it doesn't sound so crazy.

"Think about it, Luna. You have white hair just like him. You're two kids with white hair."

"I'm not a kid. I'm a young lady."

"Of course, a beautiful young lady, the most beautiful. But more importantly you have white hair and you were born here, which means you have Etruscan blood in your veins."

"What does that matter?"

"It matters because they used to communicate with lightning, with the flight of birds, that kind of stuff, right? And you, well, you communicate with the things in the sea."

"You're loony," I say. But the problem is we're both loony, since I would like him to quit saying such ridiculous stuff and at the same time I'm counting on him to continue saying what I already know myself.

"Think about it. Why did you collect all this stuff from the beach? Because it was pretty?"

"Yes, exactly, it was pretty."

"I hate to contradict you, but come on, sticks? Empty cans? Broken toys? That's your definition of pretty?"

"They're particular."

"Exactly. To you they're particular! To me they all look like the same stuff scattered on the beach, but you feel certain things are special, am I right or wrong?"

Wrong. I want to say wrong. But he's right. So I stand here and say nothing. Zot speaks for both of us anyways.

"What about the whalebone—don't you think that's a sign?"

"No. Yes. I don't know. But I had nothing to do with that. I had it on me when I woke up. What's that got to do with me?"

"Everything! Weren't you the one who came to the beach that day, after all those months away?"

I nod.

"It was cold and windy yet you still dove in. Right?"

I nod again.

"How come?"

I think about it and shake my head. I don't know. I mean, I kind of thought I did, but it turns out I don't.

"Of course you don't know. Because you didn't want to. You only did it because you *felt* you had to. And if you hadn't come to the beach, if you hadn't dived in, you would never have found your brother's bone. But you had to find it. So you dove in. And in my opinion you're supposed to find something else today."

"You're saying I have to dive in again?"

"No. Let's look for it on the beach. And don't worry if you don't see it, I'll be your eyes, I'll see for you. You just need to concentrate and feel. Unless you feel like you have to dive in the water. In that case, dive immediately!"

I shake my head and look at the water, the little bits of light dancing on the surface. I look at the sand and want to say that it's all nonsense, that none of it's true, that I don't believe such things or even think about them, since I'm a normal person who only believes in normal stuff.

Except, see, nothing's been normal around here. Not for a long time. And that's exactly what normal things should be: stuff that happens all the time. Instead here everything's crazy. So I look out at the beach, at the sticks and pans that the sea has left there. I look at Zot covered in sand and I look at myself. What could you possibly call normal around here?

For sure not us.

The Smell of Home

Y ou walk slowly, glancing about. You reach the inter-section and think briefly before taking a left onto Via Donati. You're just lucky no one's around: the houses empty and shuttered, the lawns hushed, nothing on the streets but leaves noiselessly falling. Lucky because otherwise you might ask someone, "Excuse me, can you tell me where I am? I'm lost." And anyone in this neighborhood in which you've spent your entire life would think you were winding them up.

But it's not your fault. You know where Ghost House is and how to get there. The problem is that it feels strange to come back after spending the afternoon at your own house. Not that it's yours anymore. You had to call the woman from the agency in order to get in because they'd changed the locks and your keys no longer work. You had told her that you'd left some-thing in the house. Any chance it's still there? Yes, she'd said, "They'll be by on Monday for your things," by which she meant the men from the dump would be by on Monday to carry everything off and your life's memories would become a matter for the municipality to dispose of.

Yet you didn't go back home to save your stuff. You went back is all, needing to see it one last time. You had promised yourself you'd resist going, then you figured that in a little while they would gut the place, tear it down, there would be nothing to go back to, and at that point resisting would be easy.

So you went with the lady from the company and asked her to let you have an hour, giving her God knows what kind of a look, but it worked. The woman raised her hands and disappeared, leaving you alone with your house.

You entered, and in the dark rooms, surrounded by the silent walls, what struck you most was the smell. Every house has its own smell. But yours even more so.

It's the product of many years, various lives, all the things people carried inside themselves. Her great-grandparents, who built it with their bare hands at the far end of a backwater belonging to no one, with money they'd earned from the powder factory located a little farther on. It supplied the entire Italian army, that factory. They were constantly hiring, since a couple of times a year there'd be an explosion and workers would die and need to be replaced. Meanwhile the economy marched on. How people could die so easily in that factory was a mystery, since the explosives coming out of that place never hurt anyone. The German kind, the American kind—they did real damage. Italian grenades, on the other hand, Grandpa used to say that as long as you had on a coat nothing would happen if one landed near you. That's why the war was always in the winter.

In any case, the smell of your home contains your great-grandparents' gunpowder, and your grandparents' manure and cut grass, and the hides of wild animals that once provided this place with food. Now the place is crowded with country homes and country mansions but once upon a time it was a jungle. Even your father would carry a rifle out of the house at night or—if his brothers needed the rifle—a club with a nail poking out of the top. Then the trees came down, the walls came down, many lives passed through and added their own something to this smell. Pine resin, boiled potatoes, oakum, motor oil, olive oil, stuff you don't recognize belonging to lives you hardly brushed past that nevertheless stick in your nose, as well as the wax Luca used to coat his surfboard with, and Luna's sunscreen, and what you added to this smell—whatever it was, you could smell it along with everything else as you stood there breathing in the hallway of your home.

But soon the smell would be gone, along with the kitchen, the bathroom, Luca's room, your and Luna's room. The bulldozer will tear everything down, piece by piece, until there's nothing but broken bricks and plaster. The smell will vanish forever, mingled with the fumes of the bulldozer, the workers' cigarettes, the ground ripped up as they dismantle the driveway and carve out a swimming pool.

It couldn't—shouldn't—happen like that. So you went to each and every window, opened the shutters and the glass and let the light and air in, then returned to the hallway, lay down on the floor, stared up at the ceiling, and lit a cigarette as the current of air began to sweep through the rooms.

Because if the smell really had to disappear, then you wanted to be the one to make it disappear—no mess, no falling objects—drifting calmly in the air. That way when the bulldozers showed up they'd find nothing left to destroy, only bricks and beams and tiles, nothing of value, nothing of yours.

You lay on the ground thinking and smoking. The smoke would rise for a moment and then the air would pick it up and send it flying in all directions, carrying it off, out of sight. The wind happily swept through the windows, splintered off into separate rooms, reconvened in the middle, and carried off the smell of home, your smell, joining it to the rest of the world, so that in the end it became nothing, or maybe, who knows, maybe it became everything.

No, no. It became nothing.

Anyways now you're back in the dark, amid the knotty branches of trees that cross like fingers and block out the light and keep the rest of the world from reaching the woods around Ghost House.

Walking, you keep your eyes on the sky, on the tops of these crooked, gnarled, bent trees. It's as if they couldn't grow normally, as if weirdness were the law of the land. And it works, actually. The woods grow. The wind thrashes them about but the crooked trees lean on one another and remain standing through the late-summer storms and tornadoes that tear up the neighboring lawns and bring down the carefully pruned, straight-backed pine trees and holm oaks.

And now you take your last steps, looking up, grimacing every time a bit of sun breaks through or a drop of resin touches your skin, and these gnarled trees almost make you feel good. Maybe good is an overstatement. Not bad—that's it. At least not as bad as before, which is saying something.

"Hands up! Who goes there?" From the other end of the woods comes the booming voice of Ferro, standing in front of the house.

"Easy, Ferro, it's just me."

"Me who?"

"Me Serena."

"Ah, we've known each other all of two minutes and you answer 'It's me'? We're off to a good start." Ferro doesn't say anything else, but you hear a click that must be the rifle being disarmed, his way of saying welcome.

The woods end and you approach the house. Ferro is standing next to an old rusty boiler split in two, a giant hammer in his hand. He studies the boiler on the lawn, turns it over, picks a spot, and starts hammering away.

"What are you doing?" you ask. Or try to ask. Only on the third try do you manage to slip your question past the hammer blows and make yourself heard. Ferro straightens up and looks at you, breathless.

"I'm building a barbywho," he says, then drops the hammer again.

"A what?"

"A barbygue . . . barbochoo . . . a grill for making meat. Whatever the hell you call it!"

"Ah, a barbecue grill!"

"Yep, exactly, one of those." The hammer drops again.

You stare at this dented hunk, its rusted bits spilled on the ground, and struggle to picture a grill emerging from it. Especially if Ferro's one solution is to pound it with a hammer.

"I've got a craving for grilled meat. Said so last night and the kids went nuts. 'Let's grill out! Let's buy a grill and grill out!' That's the problem these days: People want something and their first thought is that they need money to buy it. They don't think they can make it themself. But wait and see what I'm about to make. A barbeshoe grill better than store-bought. That's Ferrucio's word." He gets up and dries his head with the sleeve of his shirt, a white shirt with the words IL FAGIANO—ROTISSERIE PIZZERIA—LUNCH 'N' STUFF emblazoned on the front.

You nod and think about what he'd just said: Ferruccio's word. So fitting you almost smile.

"What are you laughing about? You think I'm not up to the challenge?"

"No, no, it's just . . . I was thinking what a beautiful name Ferruccio is."

"No shit. Most beautiful name in the world. My mom gave it to me. And when my brother was born, she called him the same thing."

"What? You both had the same name? That must have been confusing."

"It wasn't. For six years Mom called us Ferro and Ferrino."

"Ferrino's nice," you say, and start to smile again. "But why only six years?"

"Ferrino died."

"He died?"

"Yep. Liked tractors too much. He'd always be hanging around them, climbing up on them. Ultimately, one of them ran him over," he says. He goes back to hammering. You feel the hammering in your head, your bones. For a minute you stop asking questions.

Then: "And the others?"

"What others?"

"I don't know, your mother? What did she do when Ferrino died?"

"Nothing. She called me Ferro. That's all."

"You mean she didn't do anything—"

"Wasn't any time for that, kid. There was corn to plant. We had to move on. She still had me. And my sisters. Then another was born, during the grape harvest. Mother left the vineyard and went into the house a minute, had the baby, then went back to picking grapes. Those were different times. People were serious. Not like now, where women go to the hospital to give birth like it were a sickness. The first thing you see when you're born is a hospital room, those beds, the stink of medicine. Shit, we already have to die in hospitals. The least we could do is come into this world somewhere nice. Am I right?" He makes a phlegmy noise with his throat. "Life goes on, kid, what happens happens. It keeps going on. And it couldn't care less if you want to leave off or stick around. Life takes you where it wants to take you."

Ferro looks at you for a moment, stares at you, narrows his eyes in an expression of dead seriousness. Or maybe they sting from his sweat.

Then he raises his hammer again and starts pounding away. This time it's clear he won't stop until he's done, until that rusty tank has been fashioned into a barbecue grill. You look at the boiler. You still don't see how it could possibly turn into one. But with each blow its shape changes. Every time Ferro hammers it, the boiler becomes something different. So who knows, maybe at some point it really will become a barbecue grill.

The only thing to do is keep going and see what happens.

Wood pigeon?" I say, twisting my mouth in disgust. "I'm not eating wood pigeon."

"Why not?" asks Ferro.

"Because I don't like it."

"Have you ever eaten it?"

I look at him. We're sitting close to each other. He's at the head of the table with some kind of green blanket for a napkin slung across his belly. Then I turn to my Mom standing over the stove. In the neon light, I can't see her very well, but it looks to me like she's shaking her head.

"No," I say, "I've never eaten it before, so? I've never eaten a . . . a porcupine before, but that doesn't mean I'd ever eat a porcupine."

"Come again? For your information, porcupine is real tasty," says Ferro. "What I wouldn't give for a nice porcupine right now. But wood pigeon's good too. You don't know what you're missing."

I shake my head, cross my arms, and shut my mouth tight, meaning I'm done talking and I'm not letting one bit of dead bird pass my lips. Partly because before sitting down I walked by the stove and caught a glimpse of that scrawny animal, its chest out and its legs shriveled, drowning in a pan of boiling tomato sauce. I may not know how to cook very well, but if there's one thing I do know, it's that the darker the food, the bitterer it is, so that wood pigeon must be real bitter.

"All right, your loss," says Ferro. "That means more for us, right, kid?" He looks at Zot sitting next to me.

"Zot, are you really going to eat that poor bird?" I ask, and only then do I realize why he's kept silent until now, not butting into the conversation the way he always does.

In fact he remains frozen, fork and knife in hand, his face over his plate. Then he says softly: "Luna, once upon a time wild pigeon was the food of kings."

"Hear that?" says Ferro. "Kings used to eat them. And you won't even taste it. You know what you could use, kid? You could use a little wartime. Or else being born in a shithole like him. Then you'd see. You'd be doing cartwheels if you caught a whiff of this scent."

I close my mouth again and try not to think about it, about this scent, which isn't a scent at all and that's the biggest problem. Because with an ugly thing you can close your eyes and not see it, you can keep far away and not touch it. But smells don't ask permission. Smells turn up and creep into your nose and there's nothing you can do about it. And this smell is filling the kitchen and climbing down my throat—bitter as that stiff black bird.

"I'm not eating it," I say. "I'll eat a piece of bread if there's any, but wood pigeon, no way."

"That's fine, Luna," Mom says. "I bought fish sticks. I'll heat up the oven and they'll be ready in a second."

"Fish sticks? What the hell are fish sticks?" asks Ferro.

"Good stuff," I say. And I picture the crunchy, golden crust that you lift with your fork and underneath is the fish, so soft, so white.

"Where did they come from?"

"Teresa's," says Mom. "I went shopping. Do you want some, Zot?"

Zot sits there, dumbfounded, still gripping his silverware tight. He looks at Mom all excited, then looks at Ferro, who replies: "No, not him! You'll spoil him and he won't eat what's in the house anymore."

"Grandfather, I'm begging you, just this once, just tonight!"

"Out of the question."

"I swear I won't get spoiled. As God is my witness."

"I don't give a holler. Tonight we're having wood pigeon. Did I shoot that thing for nothing?"

"You *shot* it?" I ask.

"You bet I did. I tried to coax it down from the tree but it wouldn't listen."

I sit there, not saying another word. No one says another word. Then Mom: "Come on, Ferro, just tonight, this once and that's it."

Ferro remains motionless for a minute, then makes a noise with his throat, a cross between a cough and a burp, which is his way of saying, "What do I care? Do what you want." And while Zot's crying "All right!" he fills his glass to the brim with wine, swallows it in one gulp, and his face turns weird, like someone who's thinking a thought so huge it makes him sick. Then he opens his mouth and burps for real.

"Fish sticks, what a load of crap. Where'd you get the money to buy them anyhow?"

"Don't fret, Ferruccio," says Mom, "I paid for them with my own money." She checks the pigeon again, and every time she lifts the lid a mushroom cloud of smoke springs up, a steaming mushroom that rises in the air like the Hiroshima bomb our history teacher at school brought us a photo of and had us pass around our desks while she explained the perils of nuclear energy. She'd talked about the bomb and told us about Chernobyl too, where there had been an accident so serious that even in Tuscany people didn't eat lettuce for months.

At that point everyone looked at Zot. Maicol Silvestri said, "Thanks for poisoning our food, half-blood," and then people threw a book, two pens, and a calculator at him, so that amid all the chaos someone managed to doodle a penis on the photo.

"Well, paying for it with your own money seems like the least you could do," says Ferro. "But where did you get the money if you don't work?"

"We still have some set aside."

"Ah, then you can find a nice little house to rent, no?"

"No. We've got money for fish sticks, not rent."

"My point exactly. Know what a person does when she doesn't have any money? She looks for a job!"

"But Mom already has a job," I say. "She's a hairdresser."

"Is that right? Then I guess hairdressers have changed since my day too. They used to go to a store to cut hair far as I remember. I guess nowadays they stay home and don't do shit, huh?"

Mom puts the lid back on the pan. She wipes her hands on her army pants. "It's been a while since I've been back," she says, not turning around.

You haven't been back since March, Serena. There are many things you haven't done since March, and regardless of the fact that you've begun to get out of the house a little, you still can't go to the shop. You know too many people there, and even those whom you barely know stop you in the street. Those who before wouldn't even wave to you feel the need to say, "Chin up," or worse, they look at you with those pained smiles, as if someone in a wheelchair had just passed by, some three-legged dog.

But today was even worse. Today you left Ferro banging on the boiler to grind out his barbecue, went to Teresa's to buy fish sticks, and walked straight into the jaws of Vera, a woman whose daughter waitressed one summer in a seafood restaurant on the promenade. The night of Ferragosto she'd been working late, and Vera was waiting up for her at home when she began to feel somewhat uneasy at the thought of her daughter returning home so late on her scooter. So she asked her son to go pick her up in his car, and he was pissed off, he was already in bed watching TV, and he made a stink about it but in the end he went to fetch his sister. They had almost made it home when, at an intersection, a jeep failed to stop at a red light. The driver was so drunk he hadn't even seen the signal. So long, Vera's kids. Ever since, Vera wanders the streets of town, and people keep a wide berth, because if she catches you, you can expect an earful of her usual complaints: that they shouldn't sell jeeps—or alcohol for that matter—and how is it possible that restaurants stay open until one in the morning? Who eats dinner at one in the morning?

As soon as she saw you enter the grocer's, puffy-eyed Vera walked right up to you and hugged you hard, like a massive rock chained to your neck and dragging you to the bottom of the sea. When she finally let go, she looked at you with her permanently bloodshot eyes and said, "Brave, we need to be brave. It's tough right now, I know, but it'll get worse with time. Much, much worse." That's what she said to you, smiling bizarrely. Then she went back to staring at the cheese and ham in the display case while you snatched the fish sticks and took off, all the air trapped somewhere between your stomach and throat.

And if you return to work, Serena, you know that every minute will be just like that. Hugs, long looks, assurances. And you can't take it. Not now. One day maybe. Though you can't be sure. All you know is: not now.

Thank God Gemma hired that girl on a trial basis, that girl who just finished that totally bullshit beauty academy and who may not know how to do anything yet still gives it her all, working for next to nothing in the hopes that one day Gemma will officially hire her, even though in reality Gemma's just waiting for you to return to the shop, and then she'll bid her goodbye and send her back out onto the street, in search of the next illusion.

In the meantime you open the freezer, and after the scalding steam from the pan, the cool breeze on your face carries you back to the here and now, to the kitchen, to Ghost House. You pick up the fish sticks, reseal them, and go back to listening to Ferro. "And that's how I fed him. I'd chew it up good, then he'd stick his head in my mouth and eat."

You don't understand. You missed part of the conversation. You ask who was eating from his mouth, and the kids with their excited cries tear you away from the last bit of elsewhere you'd drifted off to.

"Checco, Mom! He ate right from inside his mouth!"

"Who's Checco?" Mom asks.

"Checco was Mr. Ferro's wood pigeon!"

"A live wood pigeon?"

I nod yes and so does Zot, harder and harder and over and over.

"He lived with Grandfather, right, Grandfather? Tell her!"

Ferro grunts. "All right, I'll start over from the beginning, seeing as dinner's never coming. But I'll stick to the short version cause I don't feel like telling it again." He makes himself comfy, leaning back in the chair and removing the napkin/blanket from his belly. His shirt underneath is so full of stains I don't know what good a napkin would do.

"So, one day I go outside to hit the crapper."

"Ah," Mom says. "You had an outhouse?"

"Of course. It was a shed, it was big, and it suited me just fine. Then that dimwit daughter of mine started in complaining and I had to install it inside. I spent a ton of money and then she up and took off. And she left me with that cramped toilet and this boy wonder in the house," he says. (There's no need for him to indicate Zot.) "Anyway, I go out to the crapper, and I find this little hairball on the ground. A wood pigeon had fallen from its nest. I picked it up, thinking I'd smash it against a tree to put it out of its misery. But I saw it was pretty much alive, raising its head, sizing me up . . ."

"So Grandfather brought it into the house!" exclaims Zot.

"Yep, I brought it into the house. I wanted to raise it. But that's no small chore. Wood pigeon aren't like other birds. Blackbirds, finches—they open their beaks, they're there with their beaks open waiting for their mother to toss them their food. In fact, if you want to raise them, all you need to do is spread some mash on a stick, put it in its mouth, and they knock it back. But not wood pigeon. It's a tough bird. It's proud. Soon as it's born it wants to eat all on its own. The mother stands there with food in her mouth, and he stretches his neck out, sticks his beak in, and grabs it himself. So what could I do? I'd eat lunch and dinner like normal. Then I'd chew up the last bite and stick it in my mouth. I'd go to Checco and he'd stretch out his head and eat. Just like that."

"Just like that, Grandfather? From your mouth?" Zot asks, and he attempts to put a finger in his mouth as if it were Checco's beak. Except he still has the fork in his hand and almost takes out an eye.

"Yep, like that, for a month and a half. And in the meantime Checco grew up, fledged, started flying. He trailed me everywhere, always stayed close. It was incredible. I'd go to the kitchen and he'd follow. I'd sit down on the sofa and he'd perch on the arm. Even when I went to the crapper he'd stand there in front of the bowl. Birds don't smell anything, after all. At least I don't think they do. Cause if they do I don't know how he was able to stand it in there sometimes. Anyways, always underfoot, like a dog. Then one day we were in the garden hunting for mushrooms and another wood pigeon arrived. Perched right on top of a pine tree. Checco noticed her, looked up, then flew over to the tree for a bit. He came back to me, rubbed his little head against my leg like always, and then flew away with that other one. So long, Checco," says Ferro. He looks at us a moment, then down at his empty plate.

"What happened after that?" Zot asks.

"After that nothing. He left. And that's how it ought to be. That's nature. But you know what happened?"

We quickly shake our heads, happy just to know something else happened. Anything is better than Checco going away and never coming back.

"A month went by. I was in the garden sawing wood. I remember it like it was right now. I hear a sound and recognize Checco's call. *Glu gluuu, glu gluuu.* I look up and there he is on that same branch with the other wood pigeon and two little ones. He'd come to show me his family, get it? He flew down for a moment and rested his head against my leg, all the while keeping an eye on his family up there. I pet him, told him he was a good wood pigeon, and then they all flew off."

"And after that?" I ask, my voice so weak it almost dies before leaving my mouth.

"After what?"

"After that he never came back again?"

He shakes his head.

"I'm very sorry, Mr. Ferro."

Ferro doesn't answer immediately. He picks up his glass and rests it on his lips, even though it's empty. He coughs. "What the hell are you sorry about, kid? That's nature, that's the way it goes. He was born with wings, he was meant to fly. Besides, ever since then, tons of wood pigeons have taken up residence in these parts." Ferro raises his hand and flaps it in the air, as if the kitchen were full of flying wood pigeons.

"Are they Checco's kids?" I ask.

"You bet. And grandkids."

I turn to Mom and the pan puffing smoke while one of Checco's kids or grandkids cooks inside. Now I'm positive I won't eat it. I think of Ferro chewing his dinner and leaning over for the bird to pick food from his mouth. Then I think of Ferro loading his rifle, aiming between the branches, and bringing down that same bird, picking it up off the ground, plucking it, tossing it into a sauce. Same person, same birds—does that change anything? I don't know. But I'm not the only one who doesn't know, since Mom stops stirring, kneels to turn the fish sticks in the oven, and says, "Wait a second, Ferro, you saved Checco and cared for him like he was a person. Then you turn around and shoot his grandkids and eat them?"

"Why not? What's so strange about that?" Ferro pours himself more wine and takes another drink. His voice keeps getting louder and drowsier, and more and more often the words out of his mouth are curse words. "That's life, boys and girls. The faster you learn that, the better. Life's a storm. A squall. It's a flurry of beatings, and every once and while, by accident, there comes a caress. But that caress is one out of a hundred thousand. The rest is just beatings delivered good and hard. In fact, I helped Checco, in the sense that I took him in, raised him myself, and placed him back among the living. But this here is life. I cared for him, but at the same time that was his own goddamn business. And his kids' goddamn business, and his grandkids' . . . one day someone gives you something to eat, the next he shoots you and cooks you for dinner. These things happen, they happen all the time. They're beatings, kids, beatings every day: the sooner you learn to take them, the better."

That's all Ferro says before sliding his chair out, turning to Mom, and asking when we're going to eat—he's dying of hunger.

"Yes, Grandfather, but . . ." Zot says. "But in my opinion the important thing is never to get used to those beatings. To not reach the point that our face becomes accustomed to them, because when that marvelous caress finally comes, we have to feel the full force of it, we have to relish it deep down," he says, smiling broadly, staring down at his plate. Even Mom turns around to look at him, and for a moment in the kitchen there's only a great big silence that no one wants to break.

Then comes Ferro's voice, shattering everything. "I can't believe my ears, kid. Did you really just say that crap? You're not normal, dammit. Life has given you nothing but beatings and you talk about caresses with a straight face . . . Hey there, wake up! You were born in Chernobyl, *Maremma Cane!* They locked you up in an orphanage. They shipped you off here and never came back for you. What does life have to do to you for you to wake up? I don't know how the hell you do it. I don't know how this kid here can even stand being your girlfriend."

I open my mouth, ready to snap at him for the thousandth time that no, I'm not Zot's girlfriend. But there's Zot with his head down by his plate, his fork still in his hand, something quivering across his face, and I'm pretty sure it's not a smile. So I say nothing and keep still.

Leave it to Mom to lift the siege. She turns off the flame under the wood pigeon, which probably isn't quite done cooking, but who cares, it's time to bring it to the table and fill Ferro's stomach with something other than wine.

She puts the lid back on, picks the pan off the stove by its handle, carries it to the table, and says, "There. We're ready. Careful not to bu—"

The last word catches in her throat as the pan flips over and falls on the floor. Or rather, not on the floor but on Mom. Wood pigeon, steaming sauce, everything. Over her army pants, her bare feet. And the sauce drips down and whatever it touches it burns, and Mom screams.

I jump up and run over to her. So does Zot. I look for a dish towel, Zot passes it to me, I place it on her ankle, and Mom screams louder.

"Sorry, Mom, sorry, sorry, sorry!"

"Cold water," says Ferro, trying to extract himself from his chair. "Pour cold water over her foot!"

Zot runs to the sink, grabs a pot, and fills it with water,

which he proceeds to pour over Mom's leg. Somehow he manages to soak everything but her foot—her pants, her shirt, even me.

"What the hell are you doing!" cries Ferro. "Pour it on her foot, don't drop a water bomb on her!"

"It's fine, Ferro," Mom says. "It's fine this way."

She snatches the dish towel out of my hands and dabs her foot. She makes a noise through her teeth like she's sucking air.

"Goddammit, kid," says Ferro. "Be careful with hot stuff, it's dangerous."

"Careful?!" she says, waving something black in her hand. "The handle broke. You and your shitty pans!"

Ferro doesn't say anything, just makes a noise with his throat, and he stays that way while Mom lifts the dish towel a little to examine underneath. I don't look. I can't. I look at Zot, and Zot looks at me. Our eyes wide, our mouths open. We don't say a word, but there's no need, we both have the same thoughts banging around in our heads, scattered and broken and shining in places, like the pans, handles, and lids that the sea washed ashore today.

The sea had warned me to be careful. It tried to. And seeing as I did not understand, it screamed its warning with a hundred thousand pans and lids scattered across the beach. I can see them again now, even when I close my eyes and squeeze them tight. And the harder I squeeze, the brighter the pans shine in the dark, and I don't know how long I can stand to keep them closed.

Gucci is a toy poodle the size of a sewer rat, with two giant bug eyes with which she gives the world dirty looks as she trolls the shops downtown in her owner's purse. Mummy and Daddy are nuts about her, but splitting their time between London, New York, and the Côte d'Azur, they only get to enjoy her a month out of the year, at their villa in Forte dei Marmi, where they have her shipped over from Saint Petersburg on a private jet.

Gucci travels with diamond collars, two Louis Vuitton handbags stuffed with toys and tailor-made coats, and her nanny, a Filipina whose name nobody knows. Gucci hates her nanny, just as she hates everything else in the world that isn't Mummy and Daddy. The one way she expresses her disdain for the totality of existence? Gucci barks. Nonstop. She opens her microscopic mouth and spits out this sharp yet gruff noise, a jarful of nails that stabs you in the brain.

Gucci barks at this miserable, mediocre, inferior world that insists on assaulting her long-suffering gaze with what it thinks is a fine figure. She barks when she does her business. She barks when she eats her chicken bonbons with tuna hearts. Even in her sleep Gucci barks. She barks at her Filipina nanny, the pilot, the hostess, and, upon landing in Pisa, the airport personnel. She barks at the driver who chauffeurs her to Forte dei Marmi and at every single stoplight they encounter on the road. No one in her vicinity is spared, and every morning her Filipina nanny wakes up to find thicker and thicker clumps of hair in her hands.

But for Rambo, her bark is a blessing. If Gucci and family are arriving, he can hear her from a mile away, just in time to jump out of the pool, climb the hedge, and disappear. Altough in two years of training in the Russians' pool that's only happened once. The villa is always empty and locked, the pool his for the taking. It merely requires he pause every five laps, pull his head out of the water, and prick up his ears: if all he hears are the mingled songs of blackbirds and finches, Rambo can go on swimming.

Which has worked wonders for him. Ever since he started coming here he's felt his abdomen tighten, his legs grow stronger, who knows what a stud he'll shape up to be if those fools don't order the workers to drain the pool this fall.

Once he's done his laps, he'll dry off, throw on his fatigues, and head to the hospital to see Marino, who asked him for the crossword, a phone card, and a box of crackers. Shit his mom should handle, but the old woman is slipping. She forgets everything. The thought of her pisses Rambo off and he drives his arms into the water as if he were slapping her senseless. Life's shit. You're born and you grow up to be strong and agile. Then one day something changes, you've reached the top and begun your descent down a muddy road full of potholes. At every pothole you lose a little something, and in no time you've become an old clunker scrambling to keep up. That's how it goes. Nature cheats you. Nature and society. One makes you old and the other chokes you to death with its bullshit rules and conventions. But Rambo won't stand for it. Rambo's a fighter. He'll stay fit and answer the assault blow for blow, kicking nature in the ass and knocking society in the jaw. In fact he trains every day now, only stopping to hear if that asshole dog is coming before launching forward again.

Things have actually been looking up in the last few days, now that Sandro's accompanying him to the house. While Rambo swims, Sandro stands by the towering hedge that separates the street from the yard. He practically acts as his lookout. Perfect, even if the reason for his friend being here is so sad and pathetic that, in theory, Rambo should be pissed off and spit in his face.

But he doesn't have time for that. Right now the only thing that exists for him is swimming. His lungs bellow out the air, his big commanding muscles labor, and the water around him makes a sound like a smote enemy surrendering. Rambo plows forward, feeling a pleasure inside his body that couldn't possibly be topped. He probably shouldn't say so, seeing as he's never had sex before, but there's no way sleeping with a woman can be more pleasurable than this.

The laurel hedge is towering, nine or ten feet high, and thick as a wall. But laurel is made of leaves and branches, and if you squint you can manage to see to the other side. In fact that's what Sandro's doing here; if he buries his head in the leaves he can catch a glimpse of the street and the little wall out front, he can catch a glimpse of Serena.

Every day around 3 o'clock she comes to the cemetery. He found out thanks to Zot, who can't help but run his mouth at catechism. The only time he stops talking is when the other kids slap him or kick him in the backside. After which he launches into yet another discourse apropos of nothing. The discourses themselves drift like sand but run a metal detector over the whole expanse and every so often you might unearth something interesting. It's how Sandro discovered Serena now leaves the house and walks to the cemetery every day around 3 o'clock.

You can only get to the cemetery from the street on the other side of the hedge, a narrow stretched deserted and called, not incidentally, Paradise Road, which is why every day Sandro comes here and waits for her. Rambo swims and counts laps aloud while Sandro keeps watch, his head stuck between the dark pointy branches.

Sometimes he hears footsteps and his heart starts racing, but it turns out to be just an old lady carrying flowers or a dog on a leash. But when Serena actually turns up, there's no way you can mistake her: one day she's in running shoes and the next in combat boots, yet her movements are always quick and graceful, they become attuned to his heartbeat while his throat begins to constrict and his eyes open wide to take all of her in, to smear her across his retinas as much as possible while her footsteps set her long soft hair dancing. Her hair moves in one long wave from her shoulder to her back, and at the same time in many different waves, both placid and relentless, stealing the air around her, sucking it all into a whirlpool. Sandro watches her, breathless. He clasps the laurel branches and squeezes them till they pierce his skin, more and more tempted to climb this hedge, fling himself at Serena, and—so much for the romance of wave-like hair and fairy-tale footsteps—put his arms around her, push her up against the little wall on Paradise Road and wear down his dick to a nub inside her.

That's it, like that, just like that, thinks Sandro. But he knows he won't do it, that it's just some phony notion risen up from the depths of whatever male pride he has left, like some last-ditch effort to make himself forget the reality of this pathetic situation: a man all alone, a world of opportunity spread out before him, peeping on a deserted street and praying that sooner or later she'll turn up. Not that he'll ever go out to meet her or fling himself at her. He'll just spy on her from a distance for a few seconds, a total loser, a sleaze for the record books, worthy of being crowned Biggest Failure with the Ladies, an honor Sandro had hitherto bestowed on the poet of poets Dante Alighieri.

Dante's love for Beatrice drove him berserk, but instead of telling her, "Look, Beatrice, I'm getting good vibes from you, let me take you out one night and show you what's what," Dante stood back and admired her from afar, in churches, squares, on the street. He pined away, dedicated a thousand poems to her soul yet said nothing to her in person. Actually, even worse: in order not to raise any suspicions and put her in an uncomfortable position in town, Dante invented some bullshit "screen lady." He picked a chick he didn't give a crap about and pretended to love her so as to further shield Beatrice from humiliating rumors. And what did Dante do with those killer words of love, words with which he could have slept with all of Florence and Tuscany? He committed them to paper, and afterward they became masterpieces of world literature, but in his own day they lured exactly nobody to bed. And by the time Dante became the poet of poets he was already dead and buried, his ever-new dick reduced to a moldy pile of dust.

Total loser, thought Sandro when he'd studied his life. But Sandro was in high school then and could never have suspected that one day he would find himself in the same situation. Or worse. At least Dante had chosen a real woman to be his screen lady. Sandro's screen is a laurel hedge.

It would be so easy to wait on the street and stop her when she comes. Sandro knows as much. But he also knows that the last time at the hospital Serena nearly put him in the ER. At the cemetery she's likely to dig him a grave.

Besides, beyond the kicks and punches he might have to endure, Sandro is scared of something else: he doesn't know what to do or say, and every word, every wrong move could alienate this wonderful woman, who may be the last hope for his life to have meaning. Therefore it would be wise to think hard before meeting her, it would be wise to stand on this side of the hedge and do the one thing Sandro does best: take his time and do nothing.

"Forty! Hey, Sandro! Forty!" shouts Rambo from the pool, one arm pumping the air and the other leaning against the white marble edge. "Forty laps! It's a record! A record!"

Sandro turns around and gives him a thumbs-up before signaling with his whole hand not to shout. Better yet, to keep his mouth shut. Serena could arrive at any minute.

"Come on, man, take a dip yourself! What are you doing over there? Take a dip! Live a little for Christ's sake! They're going to drain this thing soon, jump in while there's still time!"

"I don't have a bathing suit," says Sandro in a muffled, distorted voice, trying to keep the volume down yet still reach Rambo.

"What?"

"I don't have a bathing suit."

"Who cares? Go in your undies!"

"Oh right, then I can go to the hospital in wet undies."

"What?"

"I'll get my undies wet."

"I didn't catch that. Speak up. What's the matter?"

"And get my undies wet!" shouts Sandro, this time real loud and bristling with anger. Anger at this gigantic lawn where you need to shout to be understood; at Rambo, who can't hear because his ears are clogged with water; at his back, which aches from crouching behind the hedge and waiting for a woman who despises him and has yet to show her face. "My undies wet! My undies wet!" he shouts as loud as he can.

Then everything goes silent. Even the birds stop singing. The wind stops rustling the leaves, and making that sound like a thousand small clusters of applause in the air.

Sandro turns back to the hedge, braced to see the same little street again, the same wall topped with dingy grass. But before he can adjust his focus, Sandro realizes he'll not see them again, because between the view and viewer stand two legs, a bust, a face with two amazing eyes staring back at him. Of course. It had to happen now, at the absolute worst time it could have happened, Serena had to pass by. She had been walking quietly alone on her way to the cemetery to see her son when she heard a voice shouting behind the hedge, "My undies wet! My undies wet!"

Puny as a plastic bag in the rain, Sandro tries to smile but only succeeds in lifting one side of his mouth, as if he'd had a stroke. Then he raises his hand. Not high, about shoulder height. He opens it, waves it around three or four times. But Serena doesn't wave back. She stands there staring at him from the other side and in her warm lyrical voice says: "What the fuck are you doing?"

"Serena! Hi—I—nothing. Just relaxing in this here yard."

"And getting your undies wet."

"No, no, not a chance. We were just goufing around. They're totally dry."

"Is this your house?"

"Yes—no—I mean it belongs to friends. I was here by the pool and . . . and if you'd like to take a dip, hey, be my guest. Even now, or whenever you feel like it, but a dip now would be good." Sandro keeps talking, unaware of what he's saying, merely listening, like Serena, to the words coming out of his mouth. Actually, scratch that, Serena isn't listening. "Do whatever you want," she interrupts, then backs away from the hedge and starts to leave.

"No! Serena, wait!"

And perhaps because he can't let her go like this, perhaps because he can't reach the other side of the hedge with his hands and has to try to stop her with his voice, Sandro opens his mouth and expels everything he can think of: "Serena, listen to me, give me a second. There's something I have to tell you. I have to tell you that I'm just an idiot."

"I already knew that."

"Yeah, right, but the important thing is that I'm *just* an idiot. I'm not an asshole, not some presumptuous teacher who thinks he knows everything in life and makes the kids do his bidding. I don't pretend to know everything in life. Actually, I don't know shit. I'm not even a real teacher. If I told Luca to leave this place, it's only because I never did and I regretted it. It's only because I wanted to make an impression on him. And on you. Because I'm an idiot, Serena. I'm just stupid, real stupid. That's all."

Sandro leaves his mouth open, hoping to go. But just as he hadn't elected to talk, neither had he elected to quit talking. The words came of their own accord, from first to last, and now they'd left him quiet and drained, praying Serena wouldn't leave.

And she doesn't. She actually walks back over to the edge, bends over, and glares at him through the leaves, so hard she might burn them, the hedge might actually catch fire and someone need to call the firemen.

"Look, teacher. Or catechist. Or whatever you are. I don't think you're an asshole. I don't even blame you for—I don't blame you for anything. If only. If only I could blame you, at least then you'd serve a purpose. But no. I'm the one who sent him. I'd wanted to say no to him, I *should* have said no, like any good mother in the world would have. But who could say no to Luca? It was impossible. Luca was always in the right. Always. Except that one time. I was right that time. And in fact I should have said no. All Luca needed was a mother who'd have said no. I actually felt it. I felt it in my bones. But instead I let him go. I listened to you tell me the same things that I'd already been thinking. 'Sure,' I said, 'what's the big deal? Go ahead.' And now Luca's gone. I know you're not mean or cruel. You're not anything at all. Like you said, you're just an idiot. But that's even worse, because it makes me realize just how stupid I was to listen to an idiot like you. The stupider you are, the more I'm to blame. Is this getting through to you?"

Sandro doesn't answer. He just stands there, crouching behind the hedge. What would be the point? Serena has already stopped talking, turned, and gone, and now he's faced with the view of a deserted street and a little wall, and the uncomfortable sensation of having really wet his underwear.

While from the far end of the yard, Rambo comes back to life. "Fifty! Fifty laps! Can you believe it? Can you believe it, Sandro?"

Honestly, I pictured it more crowded," says Zot as we step off the bus and into the parking lot, a stretch of cement with several spaces for cars. But aside from us, there's no one here.

Today we've come on a field trip to Luni, an ancient city in Liguria, just above Tuscany, and I'm happy even if I sat for the entire ride next to Zot, who kept trying to talk to me, and I didn't want to because I knew exactly what he wanted to talk about.

"Those pans on the beach were a sign, Luna, a message."

"Leave me alone, Zot. They meant nothing."

"How can you say they meant nothing? After that handle broke, come on, we absolutely have to believe."

No, actually, I didn't have to believe. If I did they'd put me in a straitjacket and lock me up in an insane asylum for real. Just when Mom is getting better and we have a house, sort of. No, I don't want to.

It's true that there were tons of pans on the beach. But it could be a ship carrying kitchen supplies had sunk and maybe in a couple of days we'd come across silverware, glasses, and trays as well. It was a coincidence, like the whalebone ending up in my hair. Whales live in the sea, where else would their bones be? Had I found a whalebone in my hair after hiking in the mountains, well, that would be weird. This wasn't.

I'm sick of weird stuff. I want normal things, lots of normal things that happen to people who are normal—the way I want to be. And I don't want to believe in that stuff anymore. I want it all to be nonsense. I want to laugh and think that we'd have to be total fools to believe something like that. Fools like Zot, who was born in an orphanage and might find himself at home in an insane asylum. But not me. I only believe what I see. And now I see the entrance to Luni and I'm happy to be visiting someplace ancient, where they'll tell us dates and numbers, there'll be stones and bits of stuff from long ago, stuff that's real and practical, like stuff should be.

But the entrance to the site isn't exactly a stunner. It's a kind of small run-down building with three poles on the roof: one with a tattered Italian flag, another with a faded and dirty European flag, and the third with nothing at all. The entrance is at the top of a set of steps, the first of which is broken. The Pheasant skips over it and climbs all the way up to the door, but it's locked and no one is there.

The Pheasant is our Italian and history sub and she's the one responsible for organizing the trip. She's young and I like her a lot. Her real name is Miss Binelli but we call her the Pheasant because on the first day of class she wore a really long dress with dozens of pheasants drawn on it: pheasants walking, pheasants flying, pheasants sitting still and staring at you. Even the custodian calls her that. One time she came into the class and said, "The principal is making an announcement, Miss Pheasant." Everyone laughed. The teacher told her that her name wasn't Miss Pheasant, that she shouldn't call her that. "I apologize, my mistake" said the custodian, then as she was leaving she looked at us and flapped her arms and made a call that sounded more like a crow than a pheasant. We laughed anyway.

Everyone's laughing now, too, because Settembrini has found a used condom on the ground, picked it up with a stick, and is dangling it near Zot's face.

"Check it out, Chernobyl, a yummy snack for you. Open wide!"

Zot shoots up the stairs and in a girly voice screams, "Settembrini, are you crazy? We're in AIDS territory here. We're in sexually transmitted disease territory."

Our gym teacher Mr. Venturi does nothing to stop Settembrini. Actually he joins in the laughter. Only the Pheasant shouts at Settembrini to quit it but no one listens to her.

The door suddenly swings open and this really large woman goes, "Hey! What's all the commotion? This is a museum for freak's sake."

"I apologize, Miss," says the Pheasant. "Good morning. We're here on the field trip."

"How many are you?" she asks, mop in hand.

"Two classes. Sixty kids," says the Pheasant. "Wait, make that sixty-two."

"Did you at least call ahead?"

"Yes, naturally, last week we sent an email."

"E-mail? I don't know nothing about that. Anyway, in you come, the dig's that way."

"Great, thank you. Is the guide already out there?"

"Guide? There's no guide here."

"What do you mean? Your website says 'Guided tours.'"

"Website?"

In the back, Mr. Venturi laughs and shakes his head.

"*Your* website," says the Pheasant. "It says 'Guided tours Monday through Friday, for groups and . . . ' Look, I'll show you." She takes her phone out of her purse.

"Don't bother. You can show me all you want but it's still just me here. The place is open, go on in. Happy hunting." The woman throws a rag on the ground, drags it across the floor, and disappears inside.

"Excuse me, Miss, but do you at least have a pamphlet or, I don't know, an introduction or, I don't know, a catalogue or, I don't know, a brochure," asks the Pheasant. Her confidence wanes a little after every "I don't know". By the time she gets to the bit about the brochure, she says it under her breath and almost fails to get the whole thing out. The woman continues mopping and doesn't answer. Mr. Venturi lets out another laugh before leading the kids inside.

Me, I stick by our teacher and smile at her, cause I'm sorry that the trip is going badly. I want to tell her the others may be fools but I'm happy we've come to this place that almost has the same name as me. But I get embarrassed and keep my mouth shut.

Out by the site the sun is beating down. I can't see anything for a bit and have to stop. "Luna, please put your sunscreen on," says the teacher. Says Zot too. He'd said the same thing outside of school before hopping on the minibus. And Mom said it this morning. I nod, take out the little tube, and spread it over my face and arms, even if I put some on five minutes ago. That's how things go: everyone always tells me what to do, and if I say I did it already, I'll never hear the end of it. It's easier to lather it on and amen.

But we have to get a move on, Venturi and the others have already reached the start of the site, screened by blockades and topped with sheet iron. If you ask me, we don't really have to catch up with them. After all, we're two separate, remote groups totally different—On one hand there's Venturi with everyone else; they hardly glance at the first dig and stop in a clearing, where, by the noise they're making my guess is they've already fished out the soccer ball. Then there's my group, with the Pheasant, Zot, and two kids the teachers call "special." One is Allegria. He's cross-eyed and always staring at the sky. He laughs constantly and drools, as if someone were performing an endless stand-up routine in his head. The other is a girl with really long red hair. I always see her during recess crouching in the corner of the hallway or kneeling in the courtyard with her eyes on the ground.

She never talks, is always super serious, and I swear while we were climbing onto the bus I heard her mom whisper to the Pheasant, "Please don't let her eat too many ants." I swear I heard her say that.

And, well, I know we're not supposed to judge people, especially by their appearance, but look, if this is special-people group, being special doesn't seem so hot. I'd rather be normal, totally normal.

"How exciting, Miss Binelli," says Zot, "if I'm not mistaken, this first dig is the ancient forum of Luni."

At the word "forum" Allegria bursts out laughing. Then he goes back to regular laughing. The Pheasant looks down at the square of dirt and stones lined up behind the blockades, trying to read what the sign says, but it's way down there, all washed-out, so old the ancient Romans themselves may have put it there when they built the forum walls. Were it a forum.

"Actually, Zot," says the Pheasant, "this is the famous House of Mosaics differently."

Zot studies the row of stones and says, "Sorry, Miss, but are you sure? Honestly, I had picture the House of Mosaics differently."

"What were you expecting?"

"I don't know, a mosaic or two?"

"Oh, they were there once upon a time. Magnificent mosaics. They were probably there, and down at the far end, all around that area. But, let's get one thing straight, kids. If you want to see things here, you have to use your imagination. Otherwise you won't see anything." The Pheasant smiles. And I smile back at her, because I do that all the time, I see what I can see and then go with imagination.

"And yes, Zot, I *am* sure. I know a thing or two about Luni. I would remind you I'm the History teacher *and* I have a degree in Archaeology."

"You do?" I say. "Then why aren't you an archaeologist?"

"Easier said than done. I tried, but I had to find another job."

"Is that when you began teaching?"

"No. For a while I worked at Decathlon, the sporting goods store. Then the school came calling."

"Teaching is better, right?"

"Not exactly. I earned more at Decathlon."

"Sure," says Zot, "but it must be so satisfying to be called 'teacher'!"

"Oh, Zot, I'm not sure I'd call it satisfying. Besides, so far all anyone calls me is the Pheasant."

After she's done speaking, we sit in silence for a moment. I fix my eyes on the ground, ashamed, but then the Pheasant laughs, takes a breath, and, a different tone of voice, rich and stagy, begins: "Well then, in the absence of official guides, I will act as your guide today. I'd like to welcome you children to Luni, especially you, Luna—welcome home!"

I smile. I actually laugh. I feel like covering my mouth with my hand.

"This city is the only place in the world dedicated exclusively to the goddess Luna. The biggest temple was the goddess's, and it faced the sea from the highest point in town. So it's an honor to be here with you, Luna," says the Pheasant, giving a little curtsy. I laugh and curtsy back.

Meanwhile Ant Girl stands there and says nothing, and Allegria continues laughing to himself. Neither listens. But when we leave the House of Mosaics they follow behind, which is something.

Past the roof covering this part of the site, we finally find the city spread out before us: you can make out the streets, the foundations of buildings, and a round piazza with a few broken columns. The Pheasant tells us that Luni was an important and very wealthy city, that before the Romans there were many other inhabitants: Italics, Ligurians, Etruscans . . .

The Etruscans! I try to hide my excitement at the news.

But with Zot there's no hiding anything. He grabs my arm and shouts, "The Etruscans, Luna! The Etruscans were here!" And he looks at me with his great big bulging eyes. I try to smile but it comes out crooked and I nod just once.

"Of course there were Etruscans," continues the Pheasant. "First there were the local tribes, then the Etruscans, then the Romans came and took control. In the Roman Empire, all of the priests were Etruscans. They were great experts in certain things; only they knew magic. If strange phenomena occurred—say a statue wept, or a bolt of lightning split a tree apart, or a sheep was born with six hooves—then the only thing the Romans could do, despite all their might, was seek out an Etruscan and ask him what it meant. The Etruscans were always in demand. Not least in Luna, which was a magic city where strange things happened every day."

"Luna?" I ask. "Wasn't this place called Luni?"

"Later, yes, but the real name was Luna, like the goddess. Like you." She smiles. "Speaking of goddesses, follow me, I want to show you something really cool."

We pass by a gravelly clearing where the rest of the group has gathered. The boys are playing soccer and the girls are sitting around taking photos with their phones. The Pheasant tells Venturi that we're going on ahead. He says they'll catch up as soon as the game's over, but then the boys scream something and he says, "All right, all right. We'll finish this one, play a rematch, and then we'll catch up with them."

While the Pheasant takes us down a path in the middle of a field, she explains that everyone came to Luni because it was a splendid natural-made port, perfect for ships. There was an inlet on the coast where the sea was always calm. "Can you guess what that inlet was shaped like?"

Zot elbows me. A pan, he says. The Pheasant laughs and shakes her head. I guess something else. I say that the port was shaped like a moon, and the teacher says, "Brava." She explains that the coast here is like a huge crescent moon curving inwards from the sea to the heart of the city.

Next we walk as far as the point on the path where the walls and roofs terminate. The Pheasant stops and I stop behind her, wondering why she's not walking and talking anymore. But when I squint and look around, I understand immediately. Right in front of us, on the top of a hill, is this large dazzling thing, taller than everything else: amid the rocks, ruts, and pieces of wall there stands a building, still erect. It's too far away and the sun's too bright to make it out clearly, but it's white and gigantic and surrounded by all these houses and squares you can only imagine. That thing in front of us is serious business.

"There it is. That's the temple of the goddess Luna," says the Pheasant, placing a hand on my shoulder.

I stand still for a second. There are so many things I'd like to ask her but don't. Instead I start walking toward the temple. But, after a few steps I notice it's fenced off, and at the end of the path there's a sign hanging from the gate that says NO TRESPASSING.

I turn around to look for the Pheasant and ask her if we can still go in, but my answer comes immediately in the form of my teacher kicking the iron gate. The gate swings open.

"But . . . is that allowed?" asks Zot.

The Pheasant waves me in, takes Allegria and Ant Girl by the hand. "There should be guides, guardians, and researchers here," she tells Zot, "to conduct studies and show us around." Instead there's no one. But look on the bright side: there's no one around to give us a hard time either.

The grass is tall here, and occasionally it yields large stones I can't see well. I slip, almost fall, but manage to stay on my feet and keep moving forward, and the closer I get, the higher the temple rises toward the sky and covers everything and seems to sprout up around me. The grass comes to an end and under my feet I feel a hard, flat thing, the first marble step leading up to the temple. I stop and turn toward the Pheasant, who gives me a light push and signals for me to climb up.

The boiling sun beats down on the white marble. I feel as though I'm moving inside one never-ending flash, as if this light were bearing me up and propelling me forward. I arrive at the top of the stairs and look down at the town, and even though everything is white and shining I can feel that I am at the highest point of Luni, or Luna, as it was really called. I take off my sunglasses. The light forms a wall around me, yet I seem to see just fine. I see the city as it once was, flourishing, when its people were rich and had jobs and soaked in the thermal baths and waited for ships to haul in precious goods from unknown lands. I see the harbor and the square—it, too, shaped like a crescent moon—then a long avenue dotted with columns cutting a path from the town to the temple, and all the people climbing up from the street and the sea to the foot of the steps, and standing down there to worship the goddess Luna up here. What they asked her I don't know, since there were a lot of gods and each specialized in something. So when the Pheasant asks me if everything's all right, I ask her what the goddess Luna did exactly.

"What do you mean?"

"What was she the goddess of?"

"Luna was the goddess of the night and the afterlife. She was the god who brought our world into contact with the world of the dead."

Word for word, I swear, and Zot, who had stopped halfway up to catch his breath, shouts up at me all freaked out, "Hear that, Luna? In contact with the world of the dead! With the world of the dead!"

Me on the other hand, I'm totally cool. Because maybe I really am crazy. Crazy and cool. I put a hand in my jeans and feel my whalebone there, safe, smooth, rough in places. I feel like smiling. I do smile.

Meanwhile the Pheasant continues telling us about the founding of Luni and its downfall, about a Viking king who attacked the city with ships, thinking it was Rome . . . But I've stopped listening. Too many things are spinning around in my head, like the thoughts that send the waves rolling toward me, and they dance this way and that and they're all I see.

Zot on the other hand, he does listen. He asks lots of questions, too, finally forcing the Pheasant to finally tell him she doesn't have all the answers. "But that's not because I don't know the answers. No one knows; they're still mysteries."

"Mysteries?" says Zot.

"That's right, this place is full of mysteries. Lots of ancient and unknown magical rituals, undoubtedly linked to the people of Luna, no doubt."

"The people of Luna?" I ask. I'd never heard of them before but I sure liked the sound of them.

"Yes, they were a prehistoric people that lived in the woods of Lunigiana thousands of years ago. We know next to nothing about them. They didn't even have a name. All they left behind are stele statues, stone sculptures that they left in the middle of the woods, human bodies with heads in the shape of the moon. There are tons in Pontremoli. Clearly the cult of Luna gave way to the Etruscans and Romans . . . "

The teacher goes on, but I can't manage to follow her because there's too much stuff to keep straight. Mysterious people from prehistory, statues with moon-shaped heads, magic rituals—they bounce around inside me and I stop listening for a while. When I came back to earth, the Pheasant has switched to talking about another sculpture called the Holy Face. She said it was in Lucca and it was a wooden Jesus, strange and dark and very old. For thousands of years pilgrims from all over Europe have traveled to look at it, because it's miraculous. It comes from faraway lands, where Jesus was born. The man who sculpted it wasn't a sculptor. He was a normal guy who happened to be the last person alive to have known Jesus, and so he felt compelled to carve his face. Only he wasn't a sculptor, so it wasn't coming out how he wanted. But for some reason he kept at it day and night, night and day.

I listen and keep my mouth shut, though I can guess why. It's the same with me and Mom collecting photos of Luca. The photos pile yet we continue to go around asking his friends if they have others. Because this strange thing happens that the longer you go without seeing a person, the more you love him, the more you forget what he was like. You even forget his face, his appearance. It's strange, but that's the way it is. Maybe because, while you try to call it up, so many other things come to mind: his voice, things he'd say and how he'd say them, his smell, the way he walked. And yet his face you forget. That's why we want all of those photos of Luca and why we're always looking for more and why we ask for them from people who knew him. That's why I can picture this man loving Jesus so much and forgetting his face and despite not being a sculptor chiseling away at the wood with his hammer or scalpel or whatever he had. It's not like there were photos back then.

Poor guy. I think about him and feel sad. But luckily the Pheasant keeps talking and tells us about this incredible thing that happened one day. What with all his working and not eating or sleeping, at some point the man collapsed. He drops like a pear from a branch and sleeps for a whole day and night. And when he wakes up, he lifts his eyes to that piece of wood and there's the Holy Face, identical to the face of Jesus.

"Incredible!" says Zot. "Isn't that incredible, Luna? Isn't it?"

Yes, it is, totally incredible. But there's one thing I don't get. "If they sculpted the Holy Face in Palestine and now it's in Lucca, what does that have to do with Luni?"

"Well," says the teacher, "they didn't bring it to Lucca till later. It landed here first."

"Really? How did it get here? Who brought it?"

The Pheasant answers, and even if her voice is the same as before, even if she answers me while bending over Ant Girl, who is threatening to fall, each word she says sticks deep into my brain and bones and every place in my body where my beating heart can be felt. "No one, Luna. It was brought by the sea."

I'm speechless. The thing is so incredible that even Zot can't speak. And the teacher explains that back then a lot of people were against sacred sculptures. Said they were a mortal sin, seized them, burned them. And so our friend put the Holy Face in a boat and let it go. Nobody on board, no oars, no sail. Set adrift. The boat crossed the entire Mediterranean before landing here. It entered the harbor by itself, washed up on shore.

Zot and I stare at one another the same way Allegria stares at the sky and Ant Girl looks at the ground. And my guess is, seen from afar, we hardly look more normal than them.

But what the freak, it's not our fault. Does the Pheasant's story sound normal? This thing that's exactly like the whalebone? Like the pans on the beach? No way. These kinds of things are totally absurd and unbelievable, and maybe a person refuses to think about or believe them, yet they keep happening, in every age, continuously. They happen so often that at this point I don't know anymore why they shouldn't be normal.

So I stand here and Zot keeps walking up but not all the way to the top. He stops at the last step and doesn't speak. Besides, we both know there'd be no point. In silence we look down at the city spread beneath the temple of the goddess Luna, at all its mysteries, and at that sea down there which bears them.

And I pray to God that the rooms they place us in will be

decent and have windows, if barred so be it, at least so you can see the sky outside, and that the straitjackets are comfy enough and clean.

Because at this point no one can save us from the insane asylum.

This Candy Is for God

EE-sgusting. Can you believe that? Can you believe the world we live in?"

Sandro nods. He's been nodding for at least a minute, ever since he found himself standing next to Rambo facing Marino's house inside one of two ten-story apartment buildings called the Querceta Skyscrapers.

Marino's apartment is on the ninth floor, almost the penthouse. As kids, Sandro and Rambo would come here to look down at Versilia, which from up there seemed to lay down its arms and surrender to them. They'd devise thousands of ways at their disposal to dominate that land one day, from the hills behind them to the burnished blue sea below. But until that day came they were content to stick their heads out the window and spit on the heads of passersby.

Eventually they stopped coming over because Marino's mom, though always a ballbuster, had gotten worse with age, and at some point making them remove their shoes wasn't good enough for her, they had to wear disposable slippers and leave their coats outside to keep from tracking germs and toxins into the house. After all those years, Sandro and Rambo are once again climbing up to the ninth floor. Climbing the stairs, that is; Rambo doesn't take elevators.

"This is a seismic zone, riding an elevator is suicide," he says. Not that walking up nine flights of stairs in one go is any better. At least for Sandro. Rambo climbs them quickly and painlessly, with enough breath to keep repeating how disgusting it is, how the world has stooped so low it's spinning round in the gutter of the universe and pretty soon it'll be all-out war, every man for himself.

It's his usual spiel, but today there's a chance Rambo is right. Because they're climbing the stairs to get Marino's insurance card, which the hospital expects you to have the day you check in. Soon he'll be released and they can't wait any longer.

"Your mother still hasn't brought it?" Rambo asked while Sandro was at catechism. Marino replied that his mom wasn't right in the head anymore, she kept forgetting. And this time Rambo really lost his cool. He told Marino to call his mother immediately and make her pack his insurance card while they were on the phone. Marino shook his head and kept saying it was better if he didn't, and Rambo insisted, until finally Marino, in this thin wire of a voice, muffled by the pillow where he'd planted his face in shame, confessed to something crazy: His mother never visits him. She couldn't care less because she has a partner and spends all her time with him. In short, she's a slave to love. Marino's mom.

"Do you realize how disgusting that is? I feel like puking," says Rambo. Sandro doesn't answer. He, too, feels like he might puke a little. Especially after the exertion of keeping up with Rambo, but also at the thought of Marino's mom in someone's embrace, sweaty and bedraggled, her wrinkled skin rubbing up against other wrinkled skin.

"Plus, you know, whatever," says Rambo, "it's awful enough that at her age she'd still be thinking about that stuff, but the fact that she's neglected her son? Shit, that's taking it too far. You ever see that slut come to the hospital?"

Sandro continues not to respond. He's out of breath. When they finally reach the right floor, he leans against the wall, bends over, and tries to catch his breath, while Rambo stabs the doorbell and lets it ring good and long. No one answers.

Rambo rings the bell again and again silence. He pounds the door with his fists. Nothing.

"The whore isn't in," he says. "Must be out getting plugged." He starts searching his pockets for Marino's keys. For any normal person it would be a quick operation, but Rambo has pants pockets, coat pockets, tactical assault vest pockets; it takes a bit to rifle through each one, plenty of time for him to reiterate how disgusting it is that at five in the afternoon this bitch is out there doing her disgusting business while her son is in the hospital, and how his parents are fundamentally no better, how every Saturday night they go out dancing at the Silver Fox, the nonagenarian version of a velvet rope club, and the only reason they don't erupt into post-dance orgies is because their legs'll give out and—

"Motherfucker. I left the keys in the jeep."

Rambo drives a jeep, a 1980s Defender, practically military issue. He paid nothing for it because it's ancient and riddled with bullet holes, a castoff from the Civil Defense that he found through a friend of a friend, with a ladder in back, a shovel, thousands of spotlights, and a muffler that runs all the way up to the roof like a kind of chimney, so that he can drive it into a cresting African river and travel with the water up to the windows no sweat. In fact Rambo greets every fair-weather day and dry road with regret, eagerly awaiting the fall and its massive floods that never fail to hit the Tuscan and Ligurian Riviera. Catastrophic conditions are his idea of fun: he slaps on his knee-highs and blasts off in his jeep to lend a hand in disaster areas.

And though the jeep may run great in floods and rising rivers, on a sunny Saturday like today it's stopped working. So Rambo left it at home. With Marino's keys inside.

"How the hell did you get here then?"

"By bike," says Rambo, eyes down.

"Now what are we going to do?"

"Go get the keys is what."

"Fuck that. I'll wait for you here."

"Come on, keep me company."

"Fuck that," Sandro repeats, leaning his back against the wall and sliding to the floor. He crosses his arms and stays that way.

Rambo starts cursing again. He throws his army coat on and heads for the stairs. First he disappears and then, slowly, so does the sound of his combat boots on the stairs. The echo carries, as if it were coming from a narrowing tube. Finally there's just the silence of the walls, of the three doors on the landing and the three carpets in front of them, two of which have nothing to say while the other, a fat liar, bids you WELCOME.

Sandro is by himself in the shadows, which smell like a thousand lunches and dinners lumped together and topped with detergent. He's sorry for treating Rambo poorly. He hadn't done anything to deserve it. All he did was forget the keys in his car. It happens. Sandro forgets things all the time too. But Sandro couldn't accompany him home, he didn't have it in him and he didn't feel like explaining why. Didn't feel like telling him that his Vespa doesn't work either, that after catechism he'd had to push it from Forte dei Marmi to Querceta, that the road stank of exhaust from the trucks going back and forth from the hills to the sea, that he sweated like a pig on the overpass. No, he hadn't felt like telling Rambo that. He himself doesn't want to think about it. All Sandro wants is for things not to be the way they are.

For their cars, those rusty traitors, to not be stuck or defective or caked with dust or low on gas all the time. He'd like brilliant, powerful cars that also happen to be clean, like the ones bearing the rest of Europe and the civilized world forward. Fast cars with the latest technology that never break down, and if every once in a while they make a sound that's just a tad off, they're immediately swept into shops that look like clinics, where serious and honest mechanics in white lab coats replace a single part, and then they're off again, actually everything continues running without ever having stopped, and the mechanics don't pretend to have changed two parts if they only changed one or ask you to pay them under the table or leave you sitting here in front of a closed door wondering why the Vespa conked out, why the jeep died, why you're always left to push and sweat and swear and get oil and sludge on your hands and try to switch them on again, hoping that maybe now, by some miracle, they'll start, and you can go on for a little longer, just a little, just enough to give some meaning to the day.

Sandro sits in silence, a silence that seems to be pressing in on him more and more and more and more. To keep from gagging he latches onto the one thing he has with him, the papers folded in his jacket pocket, and tries to read.

It's the paper Zot turned in at catechism. Last week Sandro had assigned them a paper for homework so that at least today they'd have something to talk about and he could fill up the hour and half, which was otherwise interminable. The topic was "The Best Day of My Summer"—sunny, clean, perfect. Except it wasn't. No, actually Sandro is an idiot, because afterward Luna came up to him and regretfully asked him if she could make one up, since she hadn't seen one good day that summer. Bravo, Sandro, genius topic. Why not ask an orphan to write about his latest adventure with Daddy? Or a kid in a wheelchair about his last soccer match?

"Of course you can make it up!" he'd told her. "Actually, you know what? Come to think of it, it's a totally dumb topic for a take-home essay. Don't bother, scratch it. Use that time to do something you like, okay?"

Luna smiled her slightly sneaky smile and didn't do the paper. But neither did any of the other kids. Except for Zot, who had handed him these pages—twenty minimum—saying he was sorry but he had gotten carried away.

And now Sandro is attacking those pages to distract himself. He pulls them out and finds a weird bulge in one corner. He flips to the last page. Underneath Zot's signature is a candy stuck on with a piece of tape, milk-and-honey flavor. Sandro tears off the tape, unwraps the candy and pops it in his mouth. For a moment the sound of it between his teeth fills the silence while his eyes run over the crooked lines and he begins to read Zot's paper.

An entire page is taken up with apologies for not writing about the summer, but he'd spent the summer taking turns guarding the house with his grandfather, and the shifts are longer in the high season because there are more Russians around. Instead his paper is about last Tuesday, a really beautiful and important day, a sunny day for a nice field trip, though their destination could have been better kept, could have been better looked after, the signs more legible, and maybe a network of tour guides hired and . . . and Sandro, already bored, is about to skip ahead. But a few lines down he sees Luna's name. He stops and goes back. Rather than how nice the day was, says Zot, he really wants to talk about the mysterious stuff that happened there.

Because lately some very weird things have been happening to us, to me and Luna, and maybe I should keep them secret, but I think that if I tell them to you, our catechist, it's like going to confession, right, Mister Sandro? So I'm confessing these things to you because I trust in the sacramental seal and that your eyes will only be a conduit and my words are reserved for the Lord. But not the milk and honey candy at the end. That's for you.

I digress; please accept my apologies. What I feel compelled to tell you is that some very peculiar things have been happening to us of late, and by us I mean Luna and me, and to keep attributing them to coincidence or chance is out of the question. Luna still tries to, but after last Tuesday it is all too clear. Because, and this must stay between you and me, Mister Sandro, or between the Lord and me, actually . . .

And Zot launches—literally has liftoff—into pages and pages of stories about the city of Luni, about the goddess Luna who used to bring the living into contact with the dead, about the Romans and Etruscans, about a boy with white hair named Tages, about priests who studied lightning and bird flight. About the sea and waves bearing things to the shore, pans and lids and Serena burning her foot, about whalebones in Luna's hair and about Luca, how he is the one who sent these things, God knows wherefrom, God knows why.

In short, Mister Sandro, they're signs, occurrences we cannot not believe in. Because when Jesus rose from the grave and went to find his friends, Saint Thomas didn't believe it was him until Jesus said, "Come, feel my hands, put your finger into my wounds." And Thomas did and then he believed, but Jesus wasn't happy about it, and he said that if someone needs proof to believe then he isn't a true believer. Who knows how angry he'd be with Luna and me, after all the proof we've had, if we still didn't believe!

Therefore they believe, and if they haven't done anything about it that's only because they're too young. Had they a car, they'd immediately take off for Pontremoli to find statues with heads in the shape of crescent moons. Everything is connected. Miss Pheasant said so. They just don't know how they're connected, since they haven't gone yet.

We asked Grandfather to take us, and I can't write down the words he used because it would be like writing them for the Lord, and Grandfather insulted the Lord about a hundred thousand times.

We asked Miss Pheasant too, but she's a substitute, so she doesn't count for anything. Then we asked the gym teacher, Mister Venturi, but while I was explaining our reasons for going to Pontremoli, two kids grabbed my arms while another pulled down my pants and wrote something on my backside. I asked them what he wrote but they wouldn't tell me, all they did was laugh. When I asked Mr. Venturi, he laughed too.

And do you know what hurts the most, Mister Sandro? That once upon a time I was convinced that all kids are mean and stupid and like to treat others like dirt, but I just had to be patient and suck it up because that's how kids are, and when they grow up they quit it and become kind and intelligent. I really believed that. And instead Mister Venturi and people like him make me think that won't happen, that it will always be the same, that grown-ups can be cruel and do awful mean things too.

I'll stop there. Thank you for being the Lord's conduit.
Sincerely,

Zot

Sandro rereads the last few sentences then folds the paper in two and returns to looking out at the dark landing again. But he doesn't really see it. Instead he sees a kind of gigantic aquarium, and in that turbid water, walled with seaweed, little shiny fish are moving around aimlessly—Luna, Luca, Serena, the whalebone, the Etruscans, Pontremoli. They swim hither and thither but all end up getting snared by the soft ranks of seaweed merging together to form this one thing that keeps getting bigger and denser. It's dark, slimy, gross, and Sandro is almost ashamed to look at it, since that thing is the diabolical idea taking shape in his head. It keeps expanding, covering everything, and now stands there before him.

Zot said so himself: adults can do awful things. And that kid can't even begin to appreciate how right he is.

LIVES ON ICE

I f one day they actually find a way to shrink a submarine, like in that sixties-era film, and instead of launching it on a mission into a human body they sent it to plumb the depths of an ashtray in a dive bar at the end of a Saturday night, well, the stink couldn't be much worse than the one that assaults Sandro and Rambo upon entering Marino's house.

His mom smokes four packs a day, four, except in May, the month of the Virgin, when she cuts back to three in honor of the Blessed Virgin Mary of Montenero. And everything in this house is enveloped by that sick acrid smell, like a coat of bad varnish poisoning the walls the furniture the sofa the lace pillowcases and lace curtains and in a matter of seconds it clings to Sandro and Rambo's clothes as they wander around the living room trying to inhale as little as possible.

Marino's dad has been dead a long time, felled by a smoker's affliction. The doctors took X-rays and told him he had to quite smoking immediately, only he'd never touched a cigarette in his life. Marino didn't smoke either but by dint of living with his mom one day he'll meet the same fate as his dad, while she goes on sucking down her four packs a day and feeling fine. Around the room there are thousands of flyers for organized trips to sanctuaries, forgotten cities in Umbria, thermal spas, one- or two-day bus trips she permits herself every month, only to spend the next week complaining in her tarry voice how uncomfortable the seats were, what invasive bores her fellow passengers were, how she ate poorly and slept worse. And while she grumbles she scans more flyers for the next trip, and the room is full of these colorful slips of paper with photos of a cross, an olive tree fronting a wall, Padre Pio with his hand raised.

But Marino's insurance card is nowhere to be found.

Marino hadn't, in fact, been able to remember if it was in one of the drawers in the living room or in his bedroom, where Sandro and Rambo now stand stiff, like two people who have just exited a time machine and are trying to figure out what era they've landed in. Because Marino's room is identical to when he was in middle school: the same white furniture with the same stickers, the headboard painted with roses and a nightingale on top, on the wall above his bed a painting of Jesus made by his uncle Terzo, who owned a hardware store but loved to paint landscapes of the sea and mountains. But no one wanted the landscapes; all his relatives asked for were paintings of Jesus to hang above their children's beds for communion or confirmation. It made Terzo livid, and he would vent his anger by saddling Jesus with a giant black cross and smearing the canvas with rivers of blood that dripped from the crown of thorns down his face and neck to his chest, a splatter scene that helped him stay sane yet without fail chewed through his little tube of red paint.

On the opposite wall there are still posters of Bon Jovi and Kelly LeBrock in *Weird Science*, the movie where two kids use a computer to create this up-for-anything superhottie, clearly a complicated enterprise but more probable than the classic alternative, i.e., finding a real woman who'll date you for who you are.

While Rambo opens the dresser drawer to look for the insurance card, Sandro continues to ponder all this stuff, this room just the same as it was thirty years ago when they would come over for playdates. Seeing it like this feels funny yet somehow seems perfectly normal.

He leaves Rambo there and goes to the kitchen for a glass of water. He drinks. It tastes rusty but it's better than the stink of smoke that has stuck to his palate. He coughs. He looks out the window with a view of Versilia below and tries to empty his mind.

Then he puts the glass in the sink and is about to return to Rambo when he passes in front of a gigantic freezer by the door. He stops, suddenly grabs the handle, opens it, and looks inside.

Just like that, not looking for anything, not apprehending anything, not even intuiting anything. He'd overlooked the dirty plates in the sink, the moldy red sauce, hadn't detected the basil plant dead of thirst next to it, its leaves scattered around the pot. Not even the gigantic freezer struck him as odd; it had been there since they were little and they would use it to make popsicles by stirring water, sugar, and lemon juice in plastic cups. Their popsicles always turned out gross yet they ate them all summer anyway. Sandro is thinking of those popsicles, of popsicles and nothing else, when he opens the freezer and the icy smoke drifts up to the ceiling and disappears, leaving him to look inside.

Two frozen pizzas, Tupperware filled with homemade ragout, a small carton of mozzarella sticks, and finally this huge hard thing crowding everything out and touching the top.

Marino's mom, wrapped in plaid.

Marino cries, his face hidden underneath the covers. He makes a low, continuous sound that is chilling enough on its own, but even worse for Sandro, since it's the same sound that damn freezer made. It enters his ears and climbs up to his brain, where it will stick forever alongside the vision of Marino's mom, her hard blue face encrusted with ice.

As soon as he and Rambo had walked into the hospital room, Marino asked them with a nervous smile if they'd found his insurance card. They didn't answer, but they must have looked at him in such a way as to make everything crystal clear, because he threw the blanket over his head and began making this continuous moaning sound, which has been going on for ten minutes now and may never let up.

Yet it does, suddenly, as soon as Rambo asks, "Well, did you kill her?"

For a minute nothing, then Marino tears the sheet away to reveal two bulging eyes. "What? Are you crazy? You guys are my best friends, my brothers, do you really think . . . that I . . . you're both insane! Totally insane!"

"Whoa," says Rambo. "We were just at your house and found your mom in the freezer and you're calling us insane?"

Marino stares at him, then at Sandro, then raises his eyes to a spot just above them. His eyes narrow to slits and stay that way. His mouth stops trembling, his arms lie at his sides, and when he speaks his tone is flat and faraway, like in those films with séances where guys slip into a trance.

"It wasn't me," he says. "I swear. It was this summer, when we went to the pine grove in Versiliana to study the pine trees."

Sandro nods. He knows it doesn't matter what happened, he could never think ill of Marino, of someone who could stuff his dead mom into the freezer yet talks about studying pine trees because he's too ashamed to admit that they had been steal pine nuts to sell to restaurants.

"Afterward I went back home. I was filthy with resin. I said hi to my mom who was on the couch smoking and watching TV. She'd already laid out vegetable minestrone on the table. It's what we start every meal with. It's good for you and expands your stomach. I was starving. We'd really worked up a sweat that day at the pine grove."

"Yeah, and we hardly even turned up any pine nuts," says Rambo. Sandro glares at him and signals for him to shut up, but Marino appears not to have heard.

"I said hi to her and went to take a shower, a good long one, because the resin wouldn't wash off. Then I went back to the living room and my mom was still there. She wasn't smoking anymore but there was a weird smell. Something burning. She had the butt between her fingers. It was all black. And her fingers were all black too. The cigarette had burned down to the filter and singed her hand, but she kept clutching it, her eyes glued to the TV. I shouted at her and tried to wring the butt from her hand. But it took a while since she kept clutching it, her hand was hard as a rock, it felt fake. I shouted, 'Put it down, Mom! You're burning yourself! Let it go, Mommy!' And I pulled hard, but she wouldn't let go. I was tugging and sweating, pulling on her hand, no idea what was happening. I mean, maybe I knew, but I didn't want to admit it. I didn't want to call an ambulance or the police. I didn't want to call anyone. I didn't want them to answer. I didn't want to have to tell them what had happened. If I didn't know what had happened, how could I explain it to them? What had happened was, everything had come crashing down, that's what had happened," he says. Then he stops. He keeps staring at that same vague spot, and sneers with his mouth closed.

"What did you do after that?" asks Sandro. Marino takes a deep breath. They can see his skinny, prone body rising under the sheet. Then with the same breath he responds: "After that I sat down at the table and ate the minestrone."

"Wait a sec," says Rambo. "Your mom was lying dead on the couch and you ate dinner?"

Marino nods once, his eyes still fixed on the ceiling.

"Shit, you must have been starving."

For a while no one says anything. Only the sound of the freezer rises up from Marino's throat, once again giving Sandro goose bumps.

"I ate my bowl. And hers. And while I was eating I told her

about Versiliana. What a beautiful place it was. How I'd take
her one day. I kept it up all night, and I think . . . yes, I think
that was the moment. I mean, had I called somebody right
away, even you guys, maybe things would have turned out differently. Had I cried and screamed maybe. Instead I sat down
at the table, ate my minestrone, and started talking to my mom.
Meanwhile I kept thinking about what would happen. Now
they would come and carry her out of the house. Forever. I
would never see her again. And the same thing would happen
to me. Not that they would carry me out of the house but that
I'd be forced to leave—without Mom's retirement money, who
was going to pay the rent? And where would I go then? For
her it was simple: they'd put her in a wood box and that would
be the end of it. But me?"

"So you put her on ice," concludes Rambo.

Marino doesn't say anything. There's no point. He only
answers Sandro when asked about the plaid.

"What?"

"The plaid blanket. She was wrapped in plaid."

"Ah, yeah, that was me. So she doesn't catch cold," he says
ingenuously.

Rambo and Sandro look at one another. They don't speak.
What would they say if they could? Some time passes before
they manage to ask him how it's possible no one has come
looking for her yet.

"Who would? Mom never had visitors and never went out.
I took care of the shopping, bought her her cigarettes, withdrew the retirement checks. I mean, withdraw them."

Marino stops talking. He keeps his eyes on the ceiling, lies
back down same as before, and yet it's as if something is missing, as if the line between him and the world got disconnected
and goodnight, Marino.

Rambo motions to Sandro and the two walk over to the
window, out of earshot.

"Can you believe it?" he whispers. "I mean, can you believe it, Sandro?"

Sandro doesn't know what to believe but nods anyway.

"Can you believe what a bastard he is? He's had the house to himself for two months and didn't say shit to us about it." Rambo shakes his head in disgust.

Sandro turns away, toward the window, and looks down at the meadow outside the hospital, at the doctors and nurses trampling it, smoking and talking on their cell phones, and the people coming and going, visiting family, friends, acquaintances, bringing them cookies or chocolates or flowers or magazines, telling them, 'There you go, there you go, you're looking well," and staying for a while talking and listening to the sick. And even if they don't show it, they're in a hurry to bid them farewell and get back out of there as soon as possible, past the pine trees in the park, past the walls and the gates, out where they have things to do and days to fill and lives to get on with, all pretty much the same yet each absurd in his own way.

Like Marino, whom Sandro has known since elementary school, the kindest person in the world who nevertheless wrapped his mom in plaid and stuck her in the freezer. Like Rambo, who only finds the situation scandalous because no one invited him to take advantage of it. Like himself, who when faced with this mess watches the sun setting out the window and wonders whether the stores are still open, because he has to buy a scalpel for reasons he can't disclose.

We're all normal, until you get to know us better.

DIRTY AND HAPPY

Oh, today I see real well. Because the sky is all one cloud draped over the sun, the sea below is dark and lackluster and the same color as the sky, and the two hook up at the horizon to form a single gray wall. That's how it always is: I see fine when there's nothing to see.

Anyway, today I walk on the shore and can pick out the wood washed up on the sand, which forms the border of the waves that brought it there, the clumps of seaweed that look like slimy wigs and beached jellyfish that are like huge contact lenses lined with purple. But I'm not happy. I prefer my days sunny. With the sun I see worse but feel better.

Zot doesn't get it.

"The sun is bad for you, Luna, really bad. How can you possibly like it?"

"Listen, the sun's pretty, way prettier than the clouds. So it's bad for me, what does that have to do with anything? Those tragic people who can't eat sweets? They suffer in silence. It's not like they go around saying that chocolate is nasty. If they did they'd be tragic and foolish."

"You're not tragic, Luna."

"No. But maybe I'm foolish."

Zot nods at first. Then he shakes his head. Then he fixes his eyes on the sand and returns to studying the wood, the bits of toys and mysterious soda cans that the sea has carried to the shore. I try to do the same but have absolutely no desire to keep quiet.

"Long live the sun, Zot! Long live the blue sky and the light and sunburns. I want to lie under the sun and get so burned I catch fire. How awesome would that be? One of these days I'm really going to do it!"

"Joke all you want. Jokes always end in tears. You kids these days are all the same: you want to be rebels. You don't do the things you're supposed to do, and the things you're not supposed to do you love to death. Reckless reprobates!"

"We're the same age, Zot, the same age."

"You can't say that Luna. You don't know that," says Zot, picking up the pace. I don't say anything because no one actually knows when he was born. Not exactly. First he told me his birthday was October 23rd, but that was only because the 23rd is the Day of Saint Ignatius, for whom the orphanage was named, and some well-dressed women would come by with candy and clothes, and for Zot that was the closest thing to a birthday he knew.

"Whatever," I say, "you're more or less my age, so cut the old man speak."

"Exactly, *more or less*. Perfunctoriness is one of the great afflictions of your generation. What is the world coming to, dear Luna, what is it coming to . . . "

I shut my mouth and stare at the sand along the water's edge, where the waves flatten out for a second then retreat. I don't know what it's coming to, but maybe I don't care much either. First I'd like to know what's coming next. And I have no idea. So I walk straight ahead with my eyes fixed on the beach, hoping the sea will clue me in. Because I don't think anyone on land can help me.

Of course there was Luca; my big brother used to know lots of things and now he knows even more. When you die, you suddenly know lots of new and super important things. For one, you discover what happens when you die. And after taking a look around, you also figure out whether aliens exist.

Because, you know, if you die and all you find on the other side are souls from earth, that means that UFOs are make-believe. Or else aliens are pure evil and they all live in Hell, meaning Luca can't see them, because he's in Heaven. I wonder if, surrounded by all that splendid stuff, every once in a while he thinks about me.

But suddenly, as I'm delving further and further into my nonsense thoughts, pain brings me back to the shore: a sting, a tingling sensation, a splinter on the bottom of my foot. I've stepped on a piece of wood. Flat, like a thin slice of bark. I pick it up, blow the sand off, hold it up to the sky, and notice something dark on it. I pull it toward my face till it's almost touching my eye, then Zot arrives and we examine it cheek-to-cheek, so close our breathing becomes a single breath, if we're able to breathe.

No, we're not. We're breathless because what we're looking at is totally out of this world. Yet there it is, right in front of us. Here I'd been walking and wondering if maybe Luca ever thought of me, and the whole time my brother was talking to me from the sea.

"Yes, goddammit, yes!" thinks Sandro. Or thinks aloud. He punches the cabana. Why not? No one can see or hear him. He stands hidden behind the cabanas at the far end of the beach. From here he can spy the two kids down by the shore. They stop at the right spot, Luna picks something up off the ground, and they bend over to examine it, just as he'd hoped they would. "Bravo! kids, fucking A!" He punches the cabana again. He'd keep punching it had his fingers not been aching since the other night. Could be his right pinky is broken.

Stone carving is no walk in the park. It's actually pretty dangerous. Sandro had discovered that for himself Saturday night. After the hospital he'd gone to the hardware store. At the back of the store, past the rigging and chainsaws and hedge trimmers and other no-shit stuff, there's a box of more refined tools, like brushes and paint, labeled FOR WOMEN. He bought a kind of chisel, went to the river and took the biggest stone he could carry back home, scoured the Internet for those stone statues with moon-shaped heads from Pontremoli, and spent the night carving one.

Meaning he spent the night maiming himself. While trying to turn the head of that mutant freak into a moon, he hammered his pinky so hard he cried. It's still swollen, he can hardly bend it. It looks like a useless appendage produced by accident at the end of his hand.

Like Van Gogh his ear, Sandro sacrificed a finger to art, and that sacrifice didn't even serve a purpose. He has to admit that those primitives weren't primitive at all. Stele statues may look simple, like stone plates with round heads, hands, a knife carved into their chests, tits sometimes, yet after one night of work his opus still resembled a stone someone found by a river and batted around for a few hours. In the morning he flew into a rage, quit smashing it, and dumped it along with his master plan, which had failed miserably before ever getting off the ground.

But there was no point in his getting upset. Actually, it turned out for the best. Marino explained it to him that afternoon from his sickbed. Sandro had been complaining about how he couldn't feel his pinky anymore and told him how he'd broken it and while he was at it revealed his plan to his friends, and for half an hour Marino kept telling him how horrific and awful and morally reprehensible his idea was, and how egotistical he was, how for his own vulgar self-interest he was willing to deceive two innocent dreamers who were still reeling from the major loss they'd suffered. How could he even think of doing such a thing, how could he have made up his mind to—

Marino would have gone on like that for who knows how long had Sandro not reminded him that he, Marino, had locked his dead mother in a freezer so that he could collect her retirement checks. Marino stopped talking for a moment, lifted his eyes to the ceiling, and then broke into that absent, far-off séance voice from the day before. And rather than criticize his friend's sordid plan, he began to dispense very useful advice about how to execute it.

"A stone makes no sense. Firstly, it is extremely difficult to carve a stone. Secondly, how could a stone that heavy be carried by the waves? And the inscription on it? Who do you suppose carved that? Luca in Heaven? Please, don't give me that nonsense. Those two may be young but they're not stupid."

Sandro stood there silently absorbing the lesson from this new Marino, cool and pragmatic as a KGB agent, before stammering out a question: "So what should I do?"

"Simple. Switch to a piece of wood, a flat board, they're easier to carve. Sculpt it to look like a stele statue, then throw some dirt on top of it, smash it up so that it looks old, then cover it with bits of moss and woodchips, like it had been dragged up from the bottom of the sea. Then you go to the kiosk by the merry-go-round. Go see that dickhead who sells leather bracelets with names on them. Ask him to make one for Sandro and one for—what's Luna's mom's name? Serena, right? Okay. Then make them look beat-up too. A grater would work. Or sandpaper. Then stick the bracelets onto the wood, as if it had all gotten tangled together at the bottom of the sea. Voila."

Thus spoke Marino. And the quick and forceful way he said voila left no room for argument. Sandro, in a daze, tried to remember the instructions, then thanked him and ran off to fetch a wood board and the bracelets.

Only carving wood isn't so easy either. He tried cutting it but it came out horrible. Even with the bracelets tacked on, it looked cheap. Rambo confirmed his suspicions. He took one look and said, "What is this shit?" Then he threw it in the back

314 · FABIO GENOVESI

of his jeep and told him if he brought him two more bracelets and a replacement board, he'd handle it himself.

In all honesty, Rambo's work is a hundred times better. The names are legible, the shape of the statue recognizable. Sandro couldn't stop admiring it on the beach. Then he saw the kids coming on their bicycles. He ran downshore, set the wood in the sand—first upright, then, for plausibility's sake, laid flat—hid behind the cabanas, and turned back to witness his triumph.

And now he's watching the kids study this incredible thing that the sea brought them, this miraculous, crystal-clear message delivered by Luca himself: they must go to Pontremoli to see the statues with moon-shaped heads. And they must take their mom and him—their catechist, Mr. Sandro—along with them.

So long as there isn't another Sandro in their lives, an uncle maybe, or maybe a friend. He'd thought of writing MISTER SANDRO on the bracelet just in case. Except that might arouse suspicions, so he figured no, better not. Better to trust the kids. They have such lively imaginations and believe in things. And Luna and Zot, man, they believe in everything. Such innocents, lambs ready to roast in Hell, two fawns crossing the highway, stopping to smile at the truck heading straight for them, mistaking the headlights for benevolent stars.

In fact, Sandro, who's helming that truck and pounding the gas, feels partly exultant and partly like an asshole: it was one thing to not speak up when Luna mistook the boar bone for a whalebone sent by her brother; it's quite another to make stuff up out of thin air in order to get them to do his bidding.

That's why he'd sat on his plan for so long. Well, not that long. He'd sat on it for a solid few minutes, while he was writing up the list of things he needed. But he's not to blame. The fact is he has to see Serena again, spend time with her, talk to her, make her understand what, at the moment, he himself doesn't even understand.

Because now is the time he has to do something. Anything. Sandro is forty years old, goddammit, forty. As a boy he'd think of the year 2000 and picture himself taking his kids to school in a spaceship and leaving them with robots for teachers. Instead we passed 2000 a ways back and we're still stuck with cars that spit oil and toxins, and the most robots can do is whisk your fruit and switch on the sprinklers in your yard. Besides, Sandro doesn't have any kids to take to school. He doesn't even have a real job. Nothing real has ever happened in his life. No big break, no major decision. The few things that have changed changed because they disappeared: love run its course, hangouts closed or burned down, open fields transformed into shopping centers, people gone elsewhere to live or who quit living altogether. Sandro's life isn't about following a path; it's about losing parts along the way and still trying to go on.

So fuck it. No matter what, doing something, deciding to make a move, feels novel and right. Exploiting the innocence and pain of a little girl and her gullible friend may be cruel, but if Sandro wants to become someone who makes things happen, someone who leaves a mark on the world, he has to accept the fact that that is how the world works. It's full of potholes and puddles, and getting your hands dirty is part of the game.

Right now, in fact, from behind the cabanas, Sandro watches the kids swallow the bait and feels very dirty and very happy.

A re you asleep, Mom?"

"No. You?"

"Not really."

"How come?"

"I don't know. Why aren't you?"

"Beats me. But you need to get some sleep."

"And you don't?"

"I do, but you have school tomorrow."

"True. In fact I'm going to sleep now. But can I ask you something first?"

"Shoot."

"Actually, two things, Mom."

"Okay," you say, "shoot." But Luna doesn't speak right away. You hear your child breathing on your neck, the soft noise she makes chewing the skin around her nails.

Then: "Have you ever been to Pontremoli?"

"Pontremoli? No, I don't think so. I passed it on a train once. It's in the mountains on the road to Parma. Why do you ask?"

"Cause. Would you like to go?"

"No."

"What do you mean *No*?"

"I don't know. Of all the pretty places in the world Pontremoli is the last place I'd go."

"Yeah but you don't go anywhere."

"Fair enough. But if I were to go somewhere it wouldn't be Pontremoli."

"Why not?"

"How should I know? Why do you suddenly care so much about Pontremoli?"

"No reason. But i bet is it's a nice place. We should see it."

"Okay. And I bet is it's not. Glad that's settled."

You turn on your side and slam your knee against one of the boxes stacked beside the bed. You need to organize them better. Tomorrow you can take care of it. Tomorrow you can open them, take everything out and put things in order. It won't take much: stick the clothes in the drawers, throw away some of the boxes. But just thinking about it makes you anxious, makes it hard to breathe. Spending an entire afternoon going through, piece by piece—you can't handle it. Not now. Maybe tomorrow or the day after tomorrow. Maybe—

"And the stele statues?"

"Huh?"

"The stele statues. Wouldn't you like to see them?"

"What on earth are the stele statues?" you ask, although you've heard of them before, maybe you read about them somewhere, maybe saw them on TV.

"They're these beautiful sculptures built years ago, three thousand years ago, maybe more. They're in Pontremoli and I'd really really like to go see them."

"Oh God, Luna, look at you, a girl your age, of all the places in the world, that's what you're thinking about? You're not drawn to Paris? New York makes you gag?"

"No, but right now I'd like to go to Pontremoli."

"Good for you, Luna, good for you. Now go to sleep."

"Okay, but can we?"

"Can we what?"

"Can we go or not?"

"I don't know. Maybe one day. Now go to sleep."

For a moment the nighttime silence descends over the room, as do the thousands of noises night brings with it: the owl with its steady and unvarying whistle, something moving among the junk piled up in the yard, probably a mouse. Ignore it.

"But I haven't asked you the second question yet."

"The statues were the second question."

"No, the statues were the second part of the first question. The real second question is, in your opinion, what happens when you die?"

That's what Luna asks, point-blank, then silence again. The owl, creatures roaming the yard, pieces of metal stirring in the wind. Nothing is sleeping tonight, everything tosses and turns, you included. Nights are the worst. At least during the day things occasionally happen to distract you for a second or two. At night Luca is all there is, so much so you can't resist him, you feel your mind laboring and your thoughts become increasingly tangled, stitched together, until finally, rather than thoughts they're just images, fragments of phrases, smells, colors that remind you of your son. You keep staring at them with your eyes closed, in a state that only looks like sleep from the outside.

That's what your nights are like, revolving around Luca, clinging to someone who's not there. Never mind when Luna asks you that sort of question.

"What sort of a question is that? Why are you thinking about that at this time of night?"

"I mean, in your opinion, Mom, what happens when you die? In your opinion, is it possible that we're still around, that we can see what's going on in the world . . . I mean, when you die do you die? Or are you maybe always partly alive?"

"I don't know, Luna, how would I know? I don't know, you don't know, no one knows. We only know when we're dead," you say.

"True. I feel the same way. When we die we know a lot of things. At least I think so. I'm not sure. But if I were dead I'd know for sure."

"Right, well, there's no need to rush to find out. Remember, if you die you won't be able to go to Pontremoli."

"Exactly! But we're alive, Mom, so shouldn't we go while we're alive? There are statues there with heads shaped like crescent moons. No one knows who made them or even why. They're a mystery. How cool is that? Can we go see them?"

Now that she mentions crescent moon heads you realize you know what they are, these statues. You're not sure where you first heard of them, but recently they'd rediscovered one. A farmer had been plowing his field for corn when he drove his tractor into it head-on and split it in two. Later it was pieced together and put in a museum. Maybe you heard about it or dreamed it, you don't know. All you know is you don't want to go to Pontremoli now, you can't go, and you should respond to Luna's "Can we go, Mom? Can we?" by saying, "Enough. Go to bed. It's late."

"But we have to go. We have to. Can we? Come on, tell me we'll go."

"One of these days."

"Oh, Mom, I know when you say 'one of these days' you mean never. Well, why not? We'll take a little trip, see some nice places—why don't you want to?"

"It's not that I don't want to, Luna, it's that . . . " You pause for a moment, and as the words funnel out, they collide with something lodged in your throat that throws your voice. "It's that I can't. I can't right now. Let the school take you. See if they'll organize a trip. I can't come."

"But I want to go with you, Mom, what would that cost you? I'm asking you for a favor."

"No, Luna, I said no. Don't nag. Don't push me. Have I ever pushed you?"

Luna doesn't speak, but you can tell by her hair brushing your arm that she's shaking her head.

"There. Now go to sleep, tomorrow you have school. And

if you don't want to go to school, I won't force you to go. Say the word and I'll turn the alarm off. Do you want to stay home?"

Again that brush of her hair that means *No*.

"All right then. Now go to sleep. Tomorrow you have to be up early."

For a while it really seems as if she's through. Silence returns, the owl, the mouse, night. But Luna isn't through, you can tell by the way she's breathing against your chest.

"But why, Mom? I don't want to nag or force you, but tell me why. Because of Luca?"

His name. You think about Luca constantly. He's always on your mind, burning under your skin. Your life is a blur behind him. And yet hearing his name still catches you by surprise. Whoever utters it drives you mad, as if they were using it up, ruining it, even Luna. You'd rather it were otherwise but that's how it is.

"What's this got to do with Luca?"

"Nothing. I mean, in my opinion Luca wouldn't be happy about your always being here either, Mom. He liked doing lots of things. Do you remember the time he was at the newsstand and a truck bound for Germany braked and he hopped on board and hid in the back because he wanted to see what Germany was like?"

"Of course. I remember that clearly," you say. The word "clearly" comes out sounding slightly bitter. Since what you mean is you're the only one who remembers. Luna can't, she was too young. She only knows because you told her. He made it all the way to Bolzano on that truck. He'd gotten off at a rest stop because of the cold. He asked a family headed to Bologna for a lift, a truck driver took him to Florence, and you went to pick him up there, after a day of panic and fear. You even tried to say something to him when he got in the car, to give him a talking-to for the length of the trip. But he went to hug you, and when he saw how angry you were, this look of surprise came over his face. He really didn't get it. He flashed you a smile, sat back in his seat, and began telling you about the places up there, how cool they were, about the spotless rest stops in the middle of the woods, about the music that sounded a bit like Romagnol folk music except more aggressive, and, and—your anger didn't stand a chance.

But now he's not here and your anger is stronger than ever. Despite yourself, you feel it at the back of your throat tonight as you ask your daughter what the hell that truck has to do with anything.

"It has to do with his being happy if you got out sometimes, Mom. Luca doesn't want you shut inside the house. Luca wants you to go to Pontremoli."

"What on earth are you talking about, Luna? What are you talking about?"

"He told me himself, Mom. I swear. I didn't believe it but it's true. Luca talks to me. It sounds crazy but I swear it's true."

"Are you crazy? Have you lost it? When does he talk to you? How?"

Your anger fuses into a kind of evil and desperate laugh, and perhaps what you'd really like to ask her is, "Why doesn't he talk to me?"

"He doesn't actually talk to me. He sends me things. He sends things to the seashore and I interpret what he's trying to tell me. Did you see the whalebone in my hair? That was a present from him. He was supposed to bring it to me from France. He also told me about the pan that broke and burnt your foot. Now he's telling me you have to go to Pontremoli. And I'm coming with you. And Zot too. And Mr. Sandro, our catechist, has to come too, and . . . "

Luna carries on like that, raining down words, each more unbelievable than the last. She unleashes them on you. You try to shield yourself but you're overwhelmed. You bristle. Just as you do whenever someone wants to talk to you about Luca. Like your mother's old friend—and like your mother, a total bitch—who waylaid you at the funeral, saying, "Don't cry, Serena, don't cry. Luca is a little angel now looking down on you from heaven." And you told her to go fuck herself. What the hell did she know? Garbage, empty sentiments meant to make her feel good and wise, which she had simply tossed out there before turning around and putting it out of mind, which she offered to you, who think about him every second, every moment of your life.

Luna drives you mad too. Her words drive you mad, reaching your ears aslant now that she's gotten out of bed and gone to fetch something. She moves ably in the dark, goes, comes back. "Look," she says, "look what I found today." But you don't know what you're supposed to look at because all you see is darkness, darkness broken by those ridiculous words, until by dint of thwacking your box-cum-nightstand you find the light switch, and in that suddenly illuminated room is your disheveled daughter, rushing to cover her eyes with one hand while in the other holding up a grimy piece of wood.

Flat. Shaped like a mushroom. A round head and two eyes. Whatever this thing is, it really shoddily put together, something a preschooler might make, with two dark strips tacked on made of something like rubber or leather. Luna holds one up to your face and says, "Read this, Mom. Read it." You take it. It says SANDRO. "Wait, no, sorry. Read the other one." The other says SERENA.

Big deal. What the hell did that prove, that you're not the only one who has to endure the name Serena? What does Luca have to do with junk like this? Luca only made wonderful things. What does this piece of shit have to do with your son? The thought makes your hands tremble with anger. You tighten your grip on the wood, you squeeze it harder, you hear it creaking as if it were about to break. "No," screams Luna.

But you persist. You grit your teeth and tighten your grip around the wood. Not that you have anything against this junk, or against your daughter; your anger is blind and aimless and has nowhere to escape, so it spills out everywhere, trying to pounce and tug and break and destroy until there's nothing left, not a thing.

Not even your daughter, who's still here. She grabs onto the wood and tries to pull it away but is blinded by the glare of the lamp. She loses her footing, slips off the bed, and falls backward, and as she falls she opens her eyes to see what's happening, yet she continues to see nothing, she tries to latch onto something but there's only air around her, then the hard *thunk* of her head hitting the floor. You hear it too, while Luna disappears for what feels like forever, far longer than this miserable night.

You dive on top of her. Your child's eyes are closed. You hold her head up and hug her with all your strength. You hug her and ask for forgiveness. You hug her and cry.

"I'm sorry, Lunetta, I'm sorry. Your mother's a cretin. Your mother is a stupid dumb idiot. How on earth a mother this stupid and dumb and idiotic could have two such amazing kids I don't know. I swear I don't. We're going to go to Pontremoli, okay? We're going to go together and look at the statues and do whatever you feel like. And we'll bring blankets from the house and picnic in a park. Did you hear that, Luna? Would that make you happy? Tell me it would. Answer me. Tell me you're happy. Say it, Luna. Say it!"

Then you stop talking. You try to stop crying, too, since all you want is to hear your daughter. But she doesn't move. She doesn't open her eyes and she doesn't talk. The silence of the night has subsided into real silence, no more owls and mice and things moving in the dark. Everything has stopped to listen.

Finally there comes the voice of Luna, held tightly in your arms, saying, "Yes, Mom, I'm happy, very happy. But if the catechist comes, would you please not beat him up this time?"

CAIN'S DOG

Sandro and Rambo hoof it to the ninth floor of the sky-scraper, bowed by shopping bags. They'd stopped by Eurospin and picked up frozen pizza, potato chips, generic beer, a square of ham big as a shoebox, cartons of milk, peeled tomatoes and beans and anchovies and four different kinds of cheese, cornflakes and chocolate cookies and a five-liter plastic bottle of white wine.

They'd fished out a ton of money from the common pot, savings for moving in together they weren't supposed to touch, but Marino was about to be discharged from the hospital, and he can't stay here by himself, so they're all moving into his apartment together. The money had to be spent, no harm done.

Aside from Marino's mom's cold dead body in the freezer.

"I'm serious. This thing doesn't make the slightest impression on me," Rambo says, entering the house. "Do you know how much those sons of bitches at funeral parlors make? They exploit people's pain and take them for a ride. The coffin, transportation, flowers, a whole song and dance just to slide you down a hole. Besides, what's the big difference between being underground or in a freezer?"

Sandro nods.

"There was this story in last week's *Tirreno*. A guy from Poggibonsi electrocuted himself in his house. They found out a month later cause he hadn't paid his rent. They went in and he was dead in the bathtub, and in the freezer was his old man, a disabled vet."

"Figures, given the cost of funerals. Plus, yo, you know how much money a disabled vet makes a month? Once you're dead they turn off that tap, you know, goodbye and god bless. Nah, Sandro, nowadays if someone dies on you, you're better off keeping him in the house. I know it still feels weird to us, but it'll become the norm. This recession changed how we live, don't think it won't change how we die."

Sandro nods and places his bags on the living room table. Rambo drops his on the couch. For now neither has any desire to carry them into the kitchen.

"So, where we going to put the frozen pizzas?"

"Beats me," says Rambo. "In the fridge. There must be a freezer in the fridge, right?"

"I hope so, cause I'm not putting them in the freezer with Marino's mom."

"Obviously not! That freezer is sacred. We've got to treat it like a tomb. No way we're putting pizzas on top of Marino's mom. See now that would be wrong. That'd be like going from perfectly rational to twisted."

Sandro looks at Rambo, Rambo looks at Sandro, and they both nod as if to convince each other that, as long as they find another space for the pizzas, all will be well.

But that isn't even what's bothering Sandro. Marino's mom is dead, packed in ice in the kitchen with a blanket wrapped around her—that's life. What's really weighing on him is this business of the statuette that he left for the kids to find on the beach; the more he thinks about his master plan, the shittier he feels. First he helped Luca, a wonderful kid with a bright future, squander that future in one fell swoop. Now he's exploiting his death to dupe two little kids and get close to the woman he likes. In short: first I kill you, then I come find you beyond the grave and use you to sleep with your mom. That's the truth, no excuses this time, no ifs, ands, or buts about it. The situation is cold, stiff, irreversible—like Marino's mom inside the freezer.

Thinking about it sets Sandro on edge. His throat tightens and his heart beats faster than when he was climbing nine flights of stairs. Even if deep down he knows perfectly well that his real problem isn't that he duped those two kids. His real problem is that Zot and Luna haven't called him yet.

Perhaps they're not so gullible after all and figured out his piece of wood was junk. Or maybe they know another Sandro—an uncle, a neighbor, worse yet some idiot courting Serena—and hadn't thought of him. Writing SANDRO on the bracelet wasn't explicit enough. He should have written SAN-DRO THE CATECHIST. He'd mulled that over but it had seemed excessive. So he asked for a cross after his name, but that moron who makes the bracelets told him it was impossible, best he could do was put an X at the end. Yep, that there is the root of the problem: disorganization plus perfunctoriness plus a lack of means. It's the story of Italy, the story of Sandro's life. Poor motherland. Poor me.

"Poor motherland," he says aloud, trying to buck himself up and heading for the kitchen to find a place to store the pizzas.

Rambo trails him. "You said it," he adds, "the motherland's really taking it in the ass."

And for some reason, actually for no logical reason at all, Sandro and Rambo briefly exchange glances then burst out laughing. A lot. And loudly. They can't stop. They stand in the kitchen, holding their frozen pizzas, laughing. They take down two glasses to get a drink. The tap makes a weird noise and the water comes out all brown, and there are only two or three things in the fridge which haven't gone bad, and what keeps best is a dead lady in the freezer, and Sandro and Rambo do the one thing they can: keep laughing. They laugh so hard they cry. They could carry on like this all day, all night, until the neighbors come complain about the racket, but were they to enter, they would immediately start laughing and crying for no reason and every reason in the world, and never stop.

But Sandro and Rambo, they do stop, they stop on a dime at the sound of the doorbell.

The noise is hysterical and jarring, like a bomb going off in the empty afternoon. Rambo ducks behind the wall and signals to Sandro to keep quiet. They both stop breathing.

A moment later the bell rings again. And again. It's not a bomb; it's a bombardment. And when they hope that it's all over, that this pain in the ass at the door has finally given up, there comes the only sound more terrible than the doorbell: the sound of a human voice shouting, "I know you're in there! I heard you laughing! I know you're in there!"

It's a man's voice. He begins knocking harder. At a certain point they can no longer tell whether he's knocking or trying to break down the door.

They have to come up with something fast before this idiot attracts the attention of the whole building. They run to the living room. Rambo points toward the door, stations himself in the middle of the room with his fists up, and whispers, "Go on. Open it. I've got your back."

Sandro tries to look through the peephole but can't see anything. He opens the door a crack, plugs it with his foot, and sticks his head through the chink. And there, a speck on the dark landing, is a short, skinny, seventy-something wearing a striped apron, bug-eyed, with a wispy comb-over.

"Hello," he says.

"Hello," replies the man.

"May I help you?"

"I—I don't—sorry, who are you?"

"Who are you?"

"I'm Franco. From the veggie mart downstairs. I'm looking for Ms. Lidia."

"Sorry, the lady isn't in."

"Where is she?"

"Not in. She's gone on a trip."

"She's been gone two months for crying Cain's dog. Just how long is this trip?"

At first Sandro nods, then he shakes his head, still peeking from the chink. Rambo comes up from behind him, shoves the door open, and puffs out his chest. "We don't need any produce. We just got back from Eurospin. Thanks anyway."

Franco looks at him then at Sandro then hangs his head. With a hand he smooths down his hair from his temple across his skull. Then his hand drops to his face and shields his eyes. All Franco manages to say is, "I see," before bursting into tears, stifled tears that sound more like coughs and make his apron jiggle.

"Please don't take it so hard," says Sandro. "We just happened to be at Eurospin and figured while we were there we'd pick up some produce too."

"It was convenient," says Rambo, "plus they've got deep discounts."

"I know," Franco says between hiccups. "It's a question of quantity. They . . . they're a big operation, they make big orders, they can afford to charge those prices. Not me. I can't, for the love of Cain's dog. I'm—all—alone." An even bigger flood of tears drowns out his voice.

"We're alone too," says Sandro. "Next time we'll get our produce from you. Rambo eats a ton of fruit."

"Bet your ass I do," says Rambo. "Fruit and vegetables are the bricks that form the foundation of a healthy body. Next time we'll go to your place. So will the lady of the house, when she's back."

Franco shakes his head. "No, she never comes. She always sends her son."

"Marino?"

"Yeah. But I haven't seen him in a while either."

"Of course not. He's in the hospital."

"What? Cain's dog! What happened?"

"Hit and run. But he's fine. He comes back home the day after tomorrow," says Sandro.

"Ah," says Franco. He takes his eyes off the ground and looks at them again. "He'll be back the day after tomorrow?"

Sandro nods and, without knowing why exactly, senses he'd have been better off not doing so.

"I take it Ms. Lidia is looking after him at the hospital."

"Yeah, sure, yeah."

"So the day after tomorrow she'll be back too."

"No, her no," intervenes Rambo, "she was at the hospital with Marino, but then she had an emergency to attend to." For a moment it's silent.

"How can she go out of town when her son's in the hospital?"

"It was an emergency. She has an aunt who isn't well, an aunt in Milan."

"I see. But, in the name of Cain's dog, her son gets run over by a car and she goes to Milan?"

"Exactly. Besides, we're here to help," says Rambo. "This aunt on the other hand, she's alone, and Ms. Lidia really cares about her. This aunt saved her life. Back in World War II. The SS were aiming to shoot and rape her, but her aunt hid her in the back of a closet and they never found her."

"Why would they have wanted to shoot her?"

"Because . . . because she was with the Resistance. Ms. Lidia was a partisan. They used to call her the Wolf of Versilia. She's mentioned in a bunch of books. History books." Rambo stops there. He sneaks a look at Sandro but Sandro is a horror show, so he goes back to looking at Franco, who's now staring at him more intently.

"Listen, boys, you're not selling me a bill of goods, are you?"

"What?" says Sandro. "What bill of goods, Mr. Franco? The Resistance is nothing to joke about."

"You sure? Because Lidia was born in '46. Cain's dog, at most her mother could have been the Wolf of Versilia!"

Nothing. Just silence. Sandro looks at Rambo, Rambo looks at Sandro. Then a couple of grunts: yes, of course, the Wolf was her mother.

"Right, obviously the aunt didn't save her; she saved her mom. But Lidia was still indebted to her. I mean, it's not like Lidia would have been born had her mom died. She may as well have saved her is what I mean."

Franco studies them, his head tilted forward, his eyes dead serious under eyebrows so bushy they look as if two hairy caterpillars were ambling across his forehead.

"Boys, please, tell me what's really going on."

"We told you. That's the truth."

"Please, boys, cut the crap. Humping Cain's dog, I've a right to know what's going on."

"Look," says Rambo, "enough. We told you what's going on. What right do you have anyway? What's it to you? A woman goes away for a couple of days and she's supposed to alert her grocer?"

Franco doesn't answer right away. First he fixes his comb-over and takes a few breaths, then the words tumble out as though they'd been pushing at the back of his teeth for too long, trying to emerge into the light. "I'm not just her grocer; Lidia and I are lovers."

His absurd words bounce off the landing like berserk rubber balls. Rambo and Sandro turn their heads this way and that, trying to follow their trajectory or at least avoid getting hit in the face.

"Boys, that's the truth. There's nothing wrong with it. We met and we liked each other. We took it to a physical level. No strings, just good times. This is the 2000s. It's normal. Lidia and I are fuck buddies."

Rambo and Sandro don't say anything. They don't move. They stand there clinging to the door. At first they'd been keeping the door from opening all the way. Now the door is keeping them from falling.

"But we haven't seen each other for two months. No message, no nothing. I waited a bit. I didn't want to come here and bump into her son. But after a while I got worried maybe she was sick or something happened, so I mustered the courage to come here, but no one was ever home. Cain's dog knows I know we agreed no strings attached, but we were happy together, she was happy too, or at least she seemed that way. People don't up and disappear like that, do they?"

"Women are wired weird, man," says Rambo. He extends his arm and almost props it on his shoulder but hesitates and winds up leaning it against the wall.

Franco nods, his eyes on the ground, and wipes the sweat running from his forehead to his eyebrows. "It's true, boys, they really are. Cain's dog, they're huge sluts. No offense, eh? You're not related, are you?" They shake their heads. "Can I level with you?" They nod, even though they'd rather he didn't. "Well, you've got to understand, that lady was a crazy whore, a pony without a bit."

"Are you talking about Ms. Lidia?" says Rambo, emitting a whimper.

"The very one. In the name of Cain's dog, she'd come to my shop, pull down the shutters, and showtime."

"I thought Marino was the one who did the shopping," says Sandro.

"Yeah, yeah. He'd fetch the stuff in the morning and she'd come in the afternoon to complain about how it was rotten. You tell me, wouldn't it have been easier if she came down herself, without sending her son first?"

In all honesty, Rambo and Sandro hadn't thought of that. They can't think of anything. They just stand there quietly listening.

"No way in Cain's dog. She'd send her son cause it turned her on. She'd come in the afternoon wielding that sack. 'Look, Franco,' she'd say, 'what kind of nasty fruit did you give that dumbass son of mine?' And afterward, while I was harpooning her, she'd scream, 'Yes, yes, you take advantage of that dumbass, huh, you really take advantage of him, don't you?'"

Franco's words pierce Sandro and Rambo's ears and cut a path to their brains, despite all their effort to shut them out, now and forever.

"Can you believe that?" Franco casts his eyes on the floor again, his hand covering his face. "But for all Cain's dogs I can't get her out of my head."

Sandro would like to say something to console him, but he doesn't know what. He tries to hug him but after having pictured him and Lidia naked, the whole idea of physical contact makes him want to throw up, so he stands with his arms extended toward this desperate runt of a man, like a mummy in an old horror movie. But few movies are as gory as this one.

"Apologies, boys, apologies," says Franco, his voice cracking. "These are my problems and I shouldn't—I shouldn't—"

"Don't worry about it. Actually, we feel really bad. If we can be of any help . . . "

Franco tries to smile, shakes his head. "Thanks, I don't need anything, boys." Then he coughs, once, twice. "Actually, could I get a glass of water?"

He motions for the door but Rambo slides in front of him and spreads out his arms.

Franco looks at him and coughs again.

"A glass of water and I'll be on my way." He tries to get by Rambo but Rambo blocks him. "No," he says.

In hindsight, even a second's worth of hindsight, he could have said, "Sure, Franco, go on in, make yourself comfy." He could've shown him a seat in the living room, brought him a nice big glass of water or beer they'd just bought. Patted him on the back after offering various manly consolations about how women are all sluts, especially those who don't put out, then goodbye and good riddance.

Life would be just like that, simple and fair, if you could have that extra second. Except that extra second is an eternity, and its errors crushing, its bad decisions, its poor choices of words: they're the treacherous animals that live in the wrinkles of now, that slip through and wreak havoc. A second later is too late. By the time a second later arrives one's life is in serious need of repair.

Sandro tries to repair things by going to the kitchen to fetch a glass of water while Rambo blocks the door. The water is brown and rusty. So what? He fills the glass and returns to find the two men mutely staring each other down. He passes the glass to Franco, who takes it but doesn't drink.

"Everything's okay in the house then?"

"Yeah, just swell. We're cleaning up before Marino gets back."

"Ah. Good to hear. But Lidia's not in there, is she?"

"Nope. Like we told you, she's at her sister's in Milan."

"I thought she was at her aunt's?"

"Her aunt's. Of course."

"I see," says Franco. "And when is Ferdinando coming to see his nephew?"

"Ferdinando who?"

"Come on, boys, Ferdinando Cosci, Marino's uncle. You must know him. He's the chief of police in Forte dei Marmi. Happens to be a close friend," says Franco, all the kindness gone out of his eyes, replaced by a glint far different from the light in his eyes when he was talking about fuck buddies and harpoons. Colder, more cutting, it continues to shine while he walks backward toward the elevator, presses the button, and the doors open immediately, as if the elevator had been waiting for him the whole time. Franco gets in and the doors close on him, on his comb-over, on his fixed and pointed stare.

Sandro and Rambo stand there, alone and terrified, like a pair of thrushes locked in a cage the night before the hunt.

Cain's dog.

The road is dusty and full of potholes but leads straight to glory.

Finally Luna and Zot had gone to the hospital to see Marino and ask for Sandro's phone number. They'd called him and told him about a trip they felt they needed to take, a formative and religious journey that required his presence as their spiritual guide. So here comes Sandro, their spiritual guide guiding this killer jeep, gripping the wheel tightly with both hands while the hood swallows up the pavement in front of him, his eyes point straight toward the horizon, the power of the four-wheel drive sinks its teeth into the road, the engine thumps like a helicopter terrorizing a village and an earth-shattering feeling of power shimmies down his spine.

Even with Rambo sitting next to him busting his balls.

"Firmer with the stick. Slam the clutch nice and hard. Don't waste your time signaling. When this beast wants to turn everyone knows it. There's no point in switching on those gay lights."

And Sandro, who would usually tell him to go fuck himself, listens to him today. He even asks random questions about useless information, because Rambo is a lifesaver for loaning him his beloved jeep; it's not as if he could have taken everybody to Pontremoli on his Vespa, or worse, asked Serena if they could take her car. No, that would have signaled the end before they'd even hit the road.

A man can have the most chilling defects in the world without there being a problem. Men who don't wash, men who don't listen or look right through you and only open their mouths to say what they think and what life is like and what you should do better: women, with their taste for suffering, always find a way to put up with them. But the one thing a woman cannot accept is a guy who doesn't act like a man. For that you get a cringe of sympathy, and the slightest whiff hormones is strangled in its cradle. Sandro doesn't want to end up like that. Sandro wants to be a man in Serena's eyes, and a real man shows up in a real car. That's why this jeep is perfect and why his friend Rambo is letting him borrow it.

And to show his gratitude, Sandro is leaving his friend to his own devices. Today of all days, when Marino is being discharged from the hospital and they have to take him home and keep an eye on him and an eye out for Franco, who could show up at any moment, perhaps with his friend the chief of police.

In short, Sandro should be staying today. Yet he can't. Therefore neither can he go hard on Rambo, who has spent the last half hour saying he's abandoning him in the trenches, that at the start of the battle he's leaving him to face the enemy just so he, Sandro, can screw some chick.

Rambo has a point. Especially about abandoning him in the trenches. About sleeping with Serena, however, he's way off. Some men aim to sleep with a woman on the first night out and others aspire to snag a kiss and a second date; Sandro would settle for not getting punched in the nose.

That might sound desperate to some, but as he grips the wheel and feels the tires hugging the road the tenements and the large plazas and the sheet-metal warehouses behind him, Sandro may not know exactly where they'll end up or what will happen, but, Christ, today he has the road ahead of him and direction in his heart. And a man seeking hope needs nothing else.

"Hurray! Hurray!"
Zot is already on the curb, jumping and shouting. He has an

Italian flag in his hand, a blue bag over his shoulder, a hand-kerchief around his neck, and a gigantic straw hat on his head. When he sees the jeep he leaps to his feet. The first time he jumps he loses his hat, and with every subsequent jump, something goes flying out of his bag, falls to the ground, and makes a noise like something breaking, yet if you close your eyes it sounds a lot like the clatter of happiness.

"Hurray! Luna! Luna! Come see this amazing car! It's a military jeep! A military jeep! Lord almighty what a fantastic day! Lord, what a wonderful day this is! Blessed Jesus, my heart's beating fast!"

Sandro and Rambo climb down and Zot is immediately at their side. First he shakes their hands, but a handshake is too trivial for what he has inside of him, so he hugs them tightly, even though Rambo is so big that hugging all of him proves difficult.

Then Luna passes through the gate. She, too, stops to admire the jeep, and Zot runs over to her.

"Yo," says Rambo, "I'm taking the bike and getting out of here."

Sandro doesn't answer. He hadn't even heard Rambo. He stands there staring at the gate, his hands now in his pockets, now behind his back, like they were trash he'd picked up off the road but didn't know what to do with. And he waits to catch a glimpse of Serena.

Meanwhile he feels ants mounting his feet and climbing up his legs under his pants, running up his sides to his chest, where they begin patiently sucking the breath out of him.

But here she comes. A shadow from the dense brush of the yard stretches past the gate and across the road, spreading longer and longer, and that's enough for Sandro to recognize her. Rather, than he recognize her, he simply knows it's her. That gait, that way she cocks her head to one side a little— Sandro doesn't know whether to gape or squint, since there's no right way to prepare himself for looking at someone that stunning.

Only it isn't her. Nor is it close to stunning. Out strolls this old guy in slippers, pajama bottoms, and a stained camouflage top, and when you can discern stains on a camouflage tee, you know those stains are serious. He has on a red beret too, with something written across it that Sandro can't quite make out yet isn't all that interested in either, since the matter of most importance right now is that this old guy is pointing a rifle at him.

"What the hell's going on here? What the hell do you want?"

Rambo sees the gun and dives behind the Defender. "Get down, Sandro! Get down! Fire in the hole! Fire in the hole!"

Sandro turns to look at him but remains standing, his arms hanging limply. First he had been worried about Serena's fists, now he was going to be gunned down by an old fart in PJs. Life is one never-ending surprise.

"This is private property. Hands up!" says the old man, his voice sandpaper rubbed against sandpaper. He comes closer, and Sandro raises his hands as high as he can, and the last words to cross his mind before he dies will be the ones written on the old man's beret which he can now read clearly: PARIDE GIANNOTTI'S PAINT 'N' PROVISIONS. If there are worse ways to die, he can't think of any now.

Yet the whole time Zot and Luna are totally cool. They keep loading bags and rucksacks into the back of the jeep, taking care not to step on Rambo.

"This is my house," says the old man. "Go back where you came from. Go back to Russia."

"We're not Russians," Sandro manages.

"Ah, mercenaries on the Russian payroll, eh? Even worse."

"No, frankly we're—"

"Doesn't matter, you can't come in. The yard's mined."

Luna freezes, her blue bag half inside the jeep. "What do you mean the yard is mined?"

"Nothing to worry about," says Zot. "Just a little bit, in a part we never go."

"Clamp it, spy! The whole yard's mined. One step and the crows will be picking up the pieces," he shouts, and the more he shouts, the more agitated he becomes and the more the mouth of his rifle wavers up and down—and, up or down, it's still pointing at Sandro, who keeps his hands raised, waiting for the shot to drill a hole in his stomach, his chest, his neck, down between his legs, back up to his stomach.

Following the up-down of the gun sends Sandro into a trance, paralyzed as he is by fear and the dark narrow metal barrel's dance that could, at any moment, definitively cut his path short, just when it appeared he'd finally found one.

But he doesn't really believe he's going to die. Look, the old man may be berserk but not to the point of shooting somebody, and the kids continue to smile happily beside the jeep, and even Rambo has risen to his feet and is coming out from behind the car. Because we're all calm, sane people. Moreover, we're all Italian. Maybe in America things would end badly; the Americans like going out with a bang or two hundred. Or maybe in Germany. When the Germans get started on something they plow ahead with their heads down, neither speeding up nor slowing down, they just get to the bottom of the thing. But not in our house, nope, not here. Here they eyeball the pavement job. Here only half the houses are put up with a permit. Here you might cry, you might even fall on the ground, but when you get up you check to see if you got your shirt dirty, and afterward you go to the beach or out for a glass of wine and everything morphs into a pretty story for the bar scene, long and teeming with details but with no real ending, with no—

And then, out of nowhere, the gun goes off for real.

The deafening shot ricochets off the tops of the trees and even causes a few leaves to fall, leaves that fall slowly in the air and by the time they touch the ground Sandro is lying on the pavement.

"What the fuck are you doing, kid!" shouts the old man.

Sandro's ears are ringing but he can hear the man's gravelly voice answered by another, softer voice: "Your hands were shaking so much they scared me, Ferro."

If he can hear these words, that means he's not dead. He opens his eyes and sees the old man up there on his feet, and next to him the rifle aimed at the sky, in the firm grasp of Serena, beautiful and savage. And to see her this way, from the ground, without a laurel hedge between them, he feels the urge to jump up and squeeze her and kiss her and carry her into the house and make love to her until their bodies are worn through from rubbing against one another and all that's left of them are two puddles of sweat and pleasure and the smell of happiness.

But for now Sandro should settle for getting back up; that alone proves difficult given how much his legs are shaking.

The old man takes back his rifle, holds it against his side, and continues to glare at him. "Okay, but tell me what the hell is going on already."

"Of course, Grandfather!" says Zot, running to his side, Serena goes to Luna, and Rambo starts loading the bags into the jeep. All of a sudden nobody cares about Sandro anymore and he almost wishes they could go back to a minute before, when he might have been staring down the barrel of a gun but at least he'd had people's attention.

"I'll explain everything, Grandfather! Luna and I are going on a great adventure! Great mysteries await us, secrets buried for thousands of years, ancient legends in places where magic reigns, where maybe we'll find an answer to all—"

"Would somebody give me the abridged version?"

"We're going to Pontremoli, Ferro," says Serena.

"Pontremoli? What the hell are you going to Pontremoli for?"

"The kids are dead set on going and I'm taking them." Next to her, Luna smiles so widely her sunglasses pop off her cheeks and almost slide down her nose. She holds them as she turns to Sandro, and now her beautiful smile falls on him. She has her mother's smile, and Sandro stands there staring at it.

"Thanks for the spiritual guidance, Mr. Sandro, I'm glad you found the time to come with us."

He smiles, and he would like to say something beautiful and intelligent in response but he hasn't pulled himself together yet.

Plus the old man is fleeter of foot. "Got it, but what the hell are you going to do in Pontremoli?"

"We're taking an excursion." says Serena. The kids want to go. They found a piece of wood at the sea and they got it into their heads that, well, it's a long story. But they keep insisting and it's best I take them so that at least they can put it to rest."

Ferro nods. Rather than open his mouth he just nods all serious. Then he turns to the jeep, bangs on the side, kicks the tires a couple of times, looks in the window, smirks, and nods again, as if giving the car his blessing. He walks back to Serena, looks at her, looks up at the treetops, and continues nodding. It takes a while until he finally speaks, and when he does he barely mutters two words, like someone responding curtly to a question no one asked. "Okay, off we go," he says.

After that, silence. Maybe they didn't understand him. Maybe they don't want to understand. The silence lasts a moment, then Zot starts jumping around again and loses his hat and cheers, "Granddaddy! Is my beloved grandfather coming too?" His eyes get so wide his eyebrows touch his hair. "Would you do us this great honor?"

"Of course. I've got custody of you. You hurt yourself or you get lost, I'm the one they come harrass. No way I'm leaving you in the care of this fag." He points to Sandro.

Who tries to respond: "Ah, look, seeing as I was called for this express purpose, I'm honestly not sure it's necessary that you come along," he says. He had already pictured himself alone with Serena, the two of them, two adults taking a trip with two kids, practically man and wife. Now this old lunatic was threatening to ruin everything. "There are already four of us plus luggage. There's no room."

"What are you, an idiot? At least six people could fit in there. There's plenty of room."

"Okay, but, aside from how much room there is, we're going up into the mountains. There'll be steep ascents, rocks, rough terrain. With all due respect, it seems a little risky for someone your age."

"Risky, my ass! Who the hell do you think you're talking to, kid? Me, in those mountains, I used to massacre so many boars I'd be giving meat away on the road back." Ferro shakes his head and looks at Serena. "I'm coming, end of story. And if I don't go, neither does the boy. I've got custody." He drops a hand on Zot's shoulder so hard he almost drives him into the ground. "Besides, I can't take being stuck here anymore. I want to see a bit of the world again. Even a tiny dump will do."

"Hurray! Hurray!" shouts Zot, hugging his grandfather and racing to join Luna in the jeep. They stick their faces out the window and watch as the adults waste time below.

"Only problem is the house," says Ferro. "It's not like I can leave it unprotected. That's all they're waiting for. The Russian flag will be flying from my roof in five minutes flat."

"Good point," Sandro chimes in, "that's a good point. I think you're running that risk too. Maybe you ought to stay back and stand guard."

"Are you still talking? Look here, if I don't go that boy doesn't go either, got it? So we have to find a solution that makes everybody happy. I just need a friend I can trust to look after it for a bit. But they're all dead, the bastards. It would have to be a real man, one with balls, a warrior who—"

"Roger that, Mr. Ferro, I'll stay." The voice is firm, commanding, so deep and hardscrabble Sandro doesn't recognize it at first. It comes from the back of the jeep, where a minute later an army jacket comes into view. Rambo.

"Who are you supposed to be?" asks Ferro, but in a different tone of voice, one that bears no trace of the tone he levels at Sandro.

"People call me Rambo."

"Perfect, that's all we needed," says Serena. She turns toward the gate and disappears into the woods again, leaving the men to sniff each other over.

"Rambo, eh?" says Ferro. "Nice name, long dong. Tell me Rambo, what's in it for you?"

"I'm in a bind at the moment, sir. A friend of mine, a reliable guy, gets out of the hospital today, and it's best we hole up in your house till dark, so no one can find him."

"There someone bothering you?"

"Everybody, sir, since the day I was born. But they don't know who they're messing with, because I'm the kind of guy who answers fire with fire. Scratch that. With a flamethrower."

Rambo speaks in all seriousness and Ferro nods, his jaw jutting forward. "You know how to defend a house?"

"Yessir. And I'm still carrying around the anger inside me from when they robbed me of mine." Rambo looks up at the plane trees and starts talking, his mouth twisted in agony. "I was born in Forte dei Marmi same as you, sir, but my folks sold their house. 'We could use the money, we're getting a good price for it.' That was that, sayonara to the house I was born in. I watched them tear it down with my own eyes. Now there's this butt-ugly villa with columns and mosaics. And there was nothing I could do about it, sir, I was too young at the time. I—"

344 · FABIO GENOVESI

"At the time you were thirty-five," says Sandro. But despite the fact that he's standing right beside them, they take no notice.

"It was my house, sir, my land. And do you know what we did with that money? We bought a house in Massarosa. Do you know where Massarosa is, sir?"

"Yes, son, I do," says Ferro, clearly aggrieved.

"Right, well, the sun never shines on that backwater, not ever. I was born by the sea. Jesus Christ himself wanted it that way. But for a couple bucks I now have to live in that black hole. And the people are different. And the customs are different. And the climate, and the language—"

"Massarosa is fifteen minutes from here," says Sandro, who keeps talking even though it's as if he had ceased to exist.

"I'm an outsider, sir, a stranger in a strange land, always searching for home. Which is ridiculous cause, shit, I know where home is. Home is right here, in this town where I was born and where I can't live. So if you ask me if I'm ready to defend your house, Mr. Ferro, I'm telling you I'm ready to give my life for your house! I'd set fire to it and burn to death inside before I handed it over to the enemy!"

Ferro listens to him with bated breath. He nods so briskly his beret flies off. Then he holds out his arm and grabs Rambo's hand and shakes it with such passion that the only reason they don't embrace is because they're real men, and men don't hug. But the energy, the look, the gooseflesh they share is the equivalent of a long and intense hug, and maybe a little tongue action too, dripping as they are with admiration for one another and hatred for everything else.

Serena returns carrying two bottles of water, just in time to witness the end of this amorous handshake.

"Come on, Rambo," says Ferro. "Courage, man. This is the perimeter you have to defend."

Rambo takes a look and signals he understand before walking behind the jeep to retrieve his bike. Then he hears someone banging on the window. He looks up to find the little bright white girl staring at him from behind the glass and gesturing for him to come closer.

"Mr. Rambo? Um, look, I don't see anything wrong with it. Actually, I think it's totally fine. But Ferro is very old and there are certain things he can't understand, so I think you're better off not telling him that you like men."

Rambo stiffens. He stands there holding his bike in the air, at a loss for words. Well, except one word, a short one, which he keeps repeating, "But, but . . . "

"I know it's a totally normal thing but he's old, that's just the way he is. We'd be happy to have you stay with us, and that's totally cool if your boyfriend comes here from the hospital. Just don't tell Ferro, otherwise he might get mad and not leave you with the house and not let Zot come."

"But I—but look that's not true, I—who told you that, huh? Did Sandro tell you that? What the hell do you talk about in catechism?"

"No, no one told me, Mr. Rambo. I figured it out myself."

"Like hell you figured it out. It's totally untrue. Do I look to you like somebody who likes men? Look me in the eye and say so. Do I look like I'm into men?"

"I, um, I think so."

"What? What do you mean you think so?"

"Don't get mad, Mr. Rambo," says Zot beside her, smiling calmly. "There's nothing wrong with liking men. I think I might like them too. What's the big fuss?"

Luna whips around. "I thought you were in love with me, Zot."

"Yes, of course I am. You're the most beautiful of them all, Luna. But I don't typically like women. I only like you because you're an extraordinary creature. But who can say what happens when you grow up? Who can say whether I'll like men or women or both?"

For a moment Luna frowns as she considers what Zot just said. Then she smiles and the two of them go back to staring at Rambo. He takes a step backward, his eyes wide, holding his bike in front of him like a shield and shaking his head. "You kids are mistaken, you know that? Real mistaken. Super mistaken. What do you know? You're just kids. You don't know anything. You're totally off the mark. You don't—you—"

Ferro hollers from the gate. "Rambo! Rambo! Come here, I want to show you the arsenal!"

Rambo twists around. "On my way," he shouts, with more grit than is natural. He looks back at those two goddamn kids then carries his bike off. But Zot climbs down and runs to embrace Ferro with all his strength.

"What the hell are you doing? Are you dumb?"

"Grandfather—Granddaddy—let me hug you!"

"What the hell do you want? Hands off, tick!"

"Let me hug you a little, Grandfather. I'm going to miss you so much, you know."

"You haven't understood a thing, have you? I'm coming with you."

"I know, and it's wonderful. It's very touching and a great favor to us. But look, this is a real adventure, an important quest, and none of us is ignoring what happens when a group of people embarks upon a major quest. Like the explorers who climbed Everest or the guys who discovered the North Pole. We're going on an adventure, and adventures come at a price, and that price is always the death of someone. Everyone else completes the quest, and they're both happy and a little sad when they consider their companion who didn't make it. And, well, given your age, Grandfather, unfortunately it's clear that the companion who doesn't make it back is you. So let me hug you, Granddaddy, before it's too late."

"What the hell do you want, dickhead!" says Ferro, flinging

the boy off and grabbing his balls with both hands. "Fuck off, you goddamn hex!"

Ferro finally collects himself and hands Rambo the keys to the house, salutes him military style, then returns to the jeep, opens the passenger-side door, and gets in. Just like that, in nothing but pajama bottoms, a stained tee, and a beret.

"Wait," says Sandro. "Let Serena sit up front. She'll be more comfortable."

He knows it's pointless but says it all the same. Because, well, it's not fair. He'd envisioned spending this trip with her beside him, the sun gleaming in her hair, every once in a while their eyes meeting by chance, their legs touching . . . But those are dreams, they belong to dreamland, and if you try to smuggle your dreams across that hazardous bridge connecting paradise to reality, well, you can see for yourself what happens: they turn into an old man in PJs who hops into the front seat and says, "Get a move on, I sit too long and my hemorrhoids will burst."

PART 3

And if you think that you can tell a bigger tale
I swear to God you'd have to tell a lie
—TOM WAITS

CHIMNEY SWEEP

Some guys get girls just by saying, "I'll take you to Côte d'Azur, I know it well, it's practically my second home." And if it's not Côte d'Azur then it's the Costa Smeralda or Lake Como or Venice or one of those places where the name alone makes a guy sound like a pimp, and if he knows them well that means he leads *la bella vita*, and if you get your hooks into him maybe your life will become *bella* too: one day on the lake, one day on the Riviera, one day somewhere you can't even imagine yet must be even dreamier than the others.

As for Sandro, the only place he knows well is the highway.

Which isn't a place but a straight and tedious line that separates places. But that's the way he is, ever since he was a little boy: the time that he went to Madonna di Campiglio with his mom and dad, to Piacenza to visit his aunt Gina in the hospital, to the zoo in Pistoia to see the polar bears stare desperately into your eyes while they melted. His adventure would begin when they hit the highway and end as soon as they arrived at their destination. The others would get out of the car and straighten their clothes, excited for the start of their trip, while for him the best part would already be over. The wheels ceased to spin, the houses and trees and people ceased to whizz by, and Sandro could see they weren't as beautiful or interesting as they'd been before, when they'd flitted past the glass and lingered in his head like a long and colorful contrail.

Then Sandro finally turned eighteen. He got his license and could hop on the highway whenever he felt like it. How beautiful it is to pull up to the tollbooth, take a ticket, and enter this remarkable world. Italians all bitch about how paying tolls is a scandal, how in more developed countries the highway's free because it's paid for with tax money. But he doesn't feel that way. In Holland, in Sweden, in all those civilized and by-the-book places where the people's money is used for construction projects for the people, the highway may be free but it doesn't have the same magic. In our country there's one booth when you enter and one when you exit, and the highway really is another world, an amazing show set far apart from everything else, and it's only fair you buy a ticket for a show like that. You pay for movies, you pay for concerts—and Sandro can't remember a film or a band that gave him more of a thrill than driving for hours, crossing plains and hummocks and the various wonky bends in this screwed-up nation.

Sandro has spent the best nights of his life that way. And perhaps that says more about his social life, but what's the point in pretending otherwise? The best Saturday nights in his twenties were when he would jump in his car, enter at Versilia, and decide north or south. Once, on a night when he couldn't buck the need to disappear someplace, Sandro took the highway for Florence, then for Bologna, and from there drove all the way to Rimini. Coast to coast, from the Tyrrhenian to the Adriatic. By the time he got back home the sun was up. His mom had been worried but his dad couldn't stop smiling. He patted him on the back and winked at him, pleased his son was spending his nights doing what he no longer could. And Sandro grinned back, slyly, knowingly, because it was better that way, better to make his dad think that he had blown his money on a fancy dinner and condoms to chasten the chick he'd taken out. Instead it had gone to pay for tolls, gas to get nowhere, and a sandwich and beer consumed alone at an Autogrill in Rimini, where Sandro had felt good to be that far away.

And he's feeling good now, in Rambo's jeep, even if he's
not alone. As a matter of fact it's crowded and chaotic. He
checks the side-view mirrors and sees these two tiny hands,
one here and one there, one hand belonging to Zot and the
other blindingly white hand belonging to Luna, minuscule
hands dangling from the open windows and flapping in the
wind, like birds with their wings out. Sandro would like to be
that weightless, that free, the wind blowing him about and
carrying him off. But for the time being it's enough to see the
kids' hands in the mirror, and every so often he looks up and
finds Serena's face. He doesn't want to look at her too long
but his eyes won't listen to reason. He commands them to
look at the road but they spring back up every chance they
get. If there's a better place than this one, with his hand on the
wheel and the open road in front of him and all the wonders
to marvel at back there, well, you'll have to tell Sandro yourself, because he's never heard of it.

Come to think of it, don't waste your breath. He doesn't care.

The others chatter and study their maps after every town
we pass, and that fool Sandro at the wheel spends most of the
time looking at you in the mirror. Not you, Serena, you fix your
eyes on the seat in front of you and try not to notice the cars
overtaking you, the campers overtaking you, even trucks bearing huge loads and old men in hats overtake you. Everything is
going faster than this jeep, which rocks back and forth and rattles like fifty broken washing machines trying to clean a stone.
But really you're practically stopped.

And that's just fine. Actually, you'd prefer it if he did stop
or better yet shifted into reverse and brought you back to
Forte dei Marmi.

It's the first time you've traveled this far from home. The
first time in your life post-Luca, that is. Hardly a life but you
don't know what else to call it, so that's what we say, and even

the word home doesn't make much sense, seeing as you don't have one anymore. Not even you know what it is you're afraid of leaving behind, Serena. Maybe the streets that take you back to Luca, the pain that sits on your chest whenever you see something that reminds you of him; hearing, smelling, touching—all five senses gang up to make sure you don't get a moment's peace, to reinflict the pain you've pushed away, and yet for some frightening reason, having it around calms you down, since it has become the one thing you can count on every day. Maybe that's why you don't want to travel far; you don't want to leave your pain alone and unguarded. Even if no one would ever want to take that from you, and besides there's no way you can leave it behind: this pain follows you everywhere, it clings to you even on the highway in the middle of the Apennines, surrounded by woods and valleys and villages built who knows how many centuries ago on mountaintops to get away from a world that may never have been very good. You've lost sight of the sea. You try to get your bearings, to figure out what side it's on, but you can't tell where Forte dei Marmi is nor your street nor the cemetery.

By now that's your center. Actually, it's not even a center—it's the only piece of the world where you somehow manage to stay on your feet. It's like when the amusement parks and circuses used to pitch tents for the summer. On the one hand you were sad because the cats in town began disappearing. Your mother blamed the gypsies, said they stole them to feed to the lions and tigers, which had always sounded like bullshit to you and you never believed her but, honestly, the cats *were* disappearing. And yet you were happy, too, because in addition to the circus came the amusement parks and their rides. In a corner by the sea was your favorite, the Tagada, which was practically just a platform balanced on a pole where kids sat in a circle while the platform spun around and around and you had to stay seated and tough it out. But there was always this little punk in a vest and jeans rocking El Camperos and a shark-tooth necklace, his hair short in front and long in back. As soon as the ride started up, he'd go stand in the middle of the Tagada, stick his hands in his pockets, and whistle to show he could take it in stride. And he'd move his feet in such a way that the whole ride spun in circles while he stood still in the center. You have no idea who that tamarro was. You wouldn't see him all year but when the Tagada arrived he'd materialize in the middle of the ride. And now that the amusement park has stopped coming, who can say what happened to him, whether he's still alive, what he does, if he found another axis to stand on and play cool. You don't know, Serena, all you know is how much you've come to resemble that boy; the world spins around you warped and at warp speed while you try to stay on your feet in the center, which is made up of a bed, a street, and a cemetery, and if you move even just a foot you're sure you will fall and hit the ground and the world will spit you out into nothing.

In fact you should be there right now, in bed, the shutters closed and your head on the pillow. Instead the road runs on and the villages go by, and Sandro calls the kids' attention to a sign that says WELCOME TO LUNIGIANA, with a drawing of a moon and a photo of those stone statues your little girl was telling you about. Luna and Zot look at one another and shout, "Yeeeeee!" They really believe this business about Luca sending messages, but you don't, you can't let yourself believe. Luna is young and has time to adjust. You on the other hand have reached an age when the damage is beyond repair, when all that's left are dents and scratches that add up to one big wreck answering to your name. You mustn't give in, Serena, you must hold fast to something solid, true. Except nothing in this jeep fits that description; everything wobbles and totters as you officially enter Lunigiana. So you try to hang on to the kids' joyful "Yeeeee!" after every little village and to Luna's eyes; even behind her dark shades you can see them. You don't need to see them to know what your daughter's eyes look like. They're happy, wide open and full of excitement as they take in everything passing by outside. Happy, too, is her voice as she touches your arm and asks you something.

Only you didn't hear what. You look, you take a breath. "Sorry, Luna, I didn't catch that," you say, and you try to smile at your daughter, you try to stay strong for her.

"Sorry, Luna, I didn't catch that," Mom says.

So I ask her again if there's any chance she brought a tape to listen to.

"Tapes? Who listens to tapes anymore?"

In the front Mr. Sandro raises his hand. There's no car radio but he brought a tape player and three cassettes he made specially for this trip. But Zot brought some too, a whole bagful Ferro is rummaging through. He handles it so roughly the plastic sounds like it'll tear. He holds the bag up and examines what's inside. "Gino Latilla, Giorgio Consolini, Nilla Pizzi, the Quartetto Cetra . . . "

"Anything recorded after World War II?" Mom asks.

Immediately Mr. Sandro says that he has something, that his tapes are more modern, or modern enough. But Mom ignores him. Besides, there's nothing left to discuss; Ferro drops the bag of tapes and holds one up in the air.

"Here we go! Bow to the king!"

I can't see what it is, then Ferro removes the tape and hands me the case. I hold it to my face. The words *Claudio Villa, Emperor of the Italian Songbook* appear above a photo of a man dressed as a matador, with that little hat matadors wear, like an upside-down flowerpot.

"Oh no, not Claudio Villa," says Mom all desperate.

"But Villa is one of the greats," says Zot. "His vocals will break your heart."

"Don't count on it," says Mom. And Mr. Sandro immediately sides with her and says Villa is unlistenable, that his tapes are better, that he made them specially for this nice trip and—

"Save it for your fag stags," says Ferro. "Now quit insulting the great Claudio. Pipe down and brace yourselves for a trip to melody heaven."

He rams the cassette into the tape player and out comes this screech of violins and a voice that screeches even louder and makes my head spin.

> When winter comes to town
> and snow coats the ground
> I hug my bundle of pain
> and hum my refrain
> heading out for far lands

"Oh, hell yes!" says Ferro. He lifts his hand and twirls it around in the chaotic air. Next to me Zot does the same. "'Chimney Sweep'—now this is a song. How do we pump up the volume on this contraption?"

Mom points out to him that her ears are already ringing, and Mr. Sandro says it's already as loud as it will go. So Ferro adds his own crackly voice to Mr. Villa's.

> I fly like a swift,
> not knowing what I'll find,
> without a ray of sunshine,
> without a cozy nest.
> Chimney Sweep's the only name I know,
> never felt my mom's caress,
> never got from her a kiss,
> the only mother I ever had was the snow

He turns back to look at Zot, the only one to give him

satisfaction. But Zot has stopped twirling his hand in the air. Actually his hands are busy covering his face.

"You okay, Zot?" he asks.

No answer.

"Yo, kid. What's up?"

"Nothing, sorry." His voice is trembling so much you can hardly understand him. "It's just this bit, this part with the mom . . . fast forward, Grandfather, please." Then he stops talking and tries to shake it off with a few heaves that might be coughs. But Zot's not coughing; he's crying. It seems so unlikely. Zot always smiles. The only times he isn't smiling are when he's laughing. Now he's all hunched and bent over the seat because of the story of a boy who sweeps chimneys and doesn't have a mom.

I don't know what to say or do but I try. I put my arm around his shoulder and squeeze. "Oh, Zot, it's just a song."

So it's Christmas, Chimney Sweep,
put it out of mind,
so every child's got his fireside,
his toys beside him in a heap,

when you ask if you can play
you're treated awful meanly:
"Don't touch," he says, "go away,
run along and sweep the chimney."

"Son of a bitch," says Ferro. "That spoiled little shit with his toys and his warm fire. Chimney Sweep ought to kick his ass."

No one comments. Or I do, actually. "You said it, Mr. Ferro," I tell him. I didn't mean to but that's what came out, since, well, that rich kid really bothered me. And I know it's a song and that kid doesn't actually exist, but in the real world there are a lot of people meaner than him, and no one ever does anything to them and they continue to be as mean as they feel like. So if this kid in the song got what's coming to him that would be music to my ears. But nope, nothing, all poor Chimney Sweep does is sing.

The violins grow louder, as does the voice of Mr. Villa, and they give it one more shot, planting the song deep down in your skull. Then the song is over.

Mom says, "Hallelujah" and sigh. Zot dries his eyes and Ferro does too before asking how to rewind the tape.

"Why?" we all ask, terrorized to guess what he wants. Unfortunately, we guess right: "Because we've got to hear it again. Suck it up."

But nobody offers to help, so he tries doing it himself, smacking and punching the machine, and all he succeeds in doing is turning the radio off for a while.

"It's not fair," I say. And I don't just think it. I actually say it out loud. Because, sheesh, it's not the littlest bit fair.

"What's not fair, Luna?"

"That they treat that poor guy so mean."

"Who?"

"Chimney Sweep. Why do they treat him like that?"

"Because he's black," says Ferro. "What with working in the chimneys he's all black, so people steer clear of him."

"I get that. But people steer clear of me because I'm all white. What do you have to be for people to like you?"

For a moment no one answers me, in part, I think, because there is no answer. But then Mr. Sandro goes, "You know, Luna, I think that in this world, if you want people to like you, you have to be as gray as they are. We're not gray, and they make us pay for that fact every day."

I don't think he even realizes how beautiful what he said is. But he must when he sees all of us in the backseat staring at him, speechless. He turns around for a minute to see what's going on and I smile nice and big, and Zot most definitely does too, and Mom turns the other way but not immediately. For a minute she looks back at him too, and this silence is really beautiful and could last all the way to Pontremoli.

Instead it lasts a few seconds, until Ferro gets back to hitting the tape player and somehow manages to rewind the song and Claudio Villa starts singing about poor Chimney Sweep again, only not from the beginning.

"Listen to those golden pipes. Shit, Villa's the greatest, hands down; other singers are shit under his shoe."

"You're right, Grandfather, he was great. Although I prefer it when Robertino sings this song."

Ferro whips around, his hands gripping the seat. "What the hell did you say? Robertino?"

"Yes, in my opinion, his version of 'Chimney Sweep' is more intense."

"Hold it a minute, you're comparing that half-pint Robertino to King Claudio Villa? Watch what you say or I'll toss you out of this car."

"Excuse me," I say, "who is Robertino?"

"What you need to know, Luna, is that Robertino was very famous in the glorious sixties," says Zot. "He was a boy with a heavenly voice."

"Listen to him. *Heavenly*." Ferro spits a laugh. "No one in Italy's ever heard of Robertino. He was big in Denmark, Germany, those countries up north."

"He was very popular in Russia too."

"My point exactly. What the hell would you know? He was export-quality, like mozzarella with dioxins, like hazelnut oil. Claudio Villa on the other hand was an artist. You know what's written on his tombstone? No little angels, no bullshit from the Gospel your friend the catechist here pushes. There's just something the great Claudio said: 'Life, you're beautiful. Death, you suck.' Period. What a maestro. What a poet. And what a voice he had, listen to that—how do you raise the volume on this thing?"

"It's all the way up! It's all the way up!"

Ferro leans back into his seat and listens to King Villa once again arriving at that sad finale of this super sad song.

Only, like all artists, Mr. Claudio Villa is an unpredictable person and this time decides to do the finale totally different. His voice begins climbing toward that high note and screeching like before but all of a sudden it dips, his voice sinks, trembles, and crumples up into a low, twisted note, and then, along with the music, drops dead.

"Whoa, what's going on?" screams Ferro. He'd had his hand on his heart, braced to sing along to the finale, and now he uses both to strangle the tape player.

"Easy," says Sandro. "It must be the batteries. The batteries must be dead."

"Then put some new ones in pronto!"

"I don't have any."

"Goddammit! What about you all?"

We shake our heads.

"Well then, we'll have to hit the next Autogrill. There's one before Pontremoli."

"No way," goes Mom, "we'll pick them up in Pontremoli. We can survive without music for a while. In fact we'll be just fine."

Ferro turns around, sneers, rattles the tape player again, but it only makes a noise like bits slamming against other bits.

And then, out of nowhere, Zot shouts, "Aha!" He springs into the back of the jeep and starts rummaging through the stuff we packed. Ferro watches him, praying he's brought batteries. Mom looks on, baffled. And me, I don't even bother to look, because unfortunately I already know what he's up to.

No one else gets it until Zot returns clutching his accordion, broken and stitched together, with pieces of scotch tape dangling off it.

"Surprise! We don't need to be without music!"

"I can't believe you brought that shit!"

"Well, I did, Granddaddy! And it doesn't need batteries. All it needs is enthusiasm!"

He places his hands on the keys and readies himself. "All right, I'd like to begin with an original track. I composed this song last night and I'm dedicating it to this adventure of ours. It's called 'A Promise to Grandpa.' And a one, and a two, and a one-two-three-four." And all revved-up Zot starts squeezing the accordion. It just huffs at first. Then that huff gives way to something more like a coughing fit, then out come these whelps that remind me of little dogs fighting. And into the fray enters Zot's voice, singing:

Happiness is this trip we're onnnnn.
Luna, Serena, Sandro and Zot.
It's each other we looovvvvve.
But I'm making a promise
with the voice of a doooovvvve.
Grandpa, I'll place a flower
on top of your tombstonnnne.

"Zip it for Christ's sake!" shouts Ferro, giving him the sign of the horns, and with his free hand he tugs at what's between his legs. "If I die I'm taking you with me you little shit. I'm taking you with me!"

"Yes, Grandfather, that way we can be together in Heaven!"

Zot returns to playing. Ferro reaches out and tries to nab him, and Mr. Sandro tries to intervene. "Behave yourselves!" But all that gets him is an elbow in the shoulder. "Shut up and drive, queen." The car swerves to one side and everything jostles. I press close to Mom and Mom screams real loud, "Enough! Quit it! We'll stop at the Autogrill—happy?

Now enough. I swear the next one to act up gets clocked in the teeth."

No one moves. No one says anything anymore. We just stare at the road in front of us and steer straight ahead without ever stopping. Till we get to the Autogrill, that is.

The house belongs to the old man."

"What old man?"

"The old man I was telling you about, the one who left with Sandro."

"Oh right, sorry," says Marino, and goes back to staring at the space between him and the damp-stained walls half hidden behind piles of junk. "It's true, you did tell me that."

Of course Rambo had told him. He'd also explained what they were doing there, how it wasn't prudent to show up at Marino's house in the ambulance. There were too many nosy folks hanging around; it was better to have them drop him off here. And tonight when Sandro gets back from his little field trip, they'll take him to the apartment under cover of night, without the risk of someone coming to bust his balls.

"But who'd ever do that."

"I don't know. Your uncle, for example, the chief of police."

"Not a chance. He's my dad's—rest his soul—brother. He doesn't even talk to Mom. There's no risk of his coming. Please let's go to my house."

"We can't, Marino. Don't push it."

"Please, Rambo, Ghost House scares me. Don't you remember the story about the partisans being hanged? They strung them up from those trees outside. Do you realize that? From those trees there. Let's go to my house. I'm asking you nicely."

No, said Rambo. And Marino said yes. Rambo said no. And Marino, yes. So Rambo was obliged to tell him everything. About the guy from the veggie mart who had come looking for his mother and why he was looking for her. And Marino sat there for five minutes, silent and motionless, looking up at the ceiling in this little dark room. Then he asked Rambo where they were again, as if his brain were trying to erase all that unpleasantness and reset the clock. Except every time it was the same shit all over again.

Worse, actually, since Marino keeps recalling new details, and details are what do you in. Ugly things, accidents, defeats, people you love who leave you—over time the great pains burn a little less, once you manage to put them in perspective, regard them as general facts in a larger context that justifies and softens them so that they become formative experiences or instances of growing up, because deep down they're not such tragic events, no, instead they're necessary steps in life and everybody has to take them. They concern the universe and not just you. Come to think of it, they don't concern you at all . . . And that line of reasoning almost works, the survival instinct befuddles you into believing it. But then come the details, and they're what really screw you, those minor details hiding in the folds of your brain, and when you try to lead a tidy and peaceful and happy life, they turn up to pitch you into the darkest depths of reality: the whiff of ragout filling the hallway when she bid you goodbye, the thick pants you were wearing that made your legs itch, the cutting look she gave you as she was leaving and you asked if she was already seeing somebody else . . . Details are tiny, pointy shards of reality embedded in your brain that remind you that such moments aren't everybody's, aren't just life or a universal experience, that this shitty thing happened in one place at one time, it happened to you, and the details of it will stick to your soul forever.

That is what is happening right now to Marino, his head on

the pillow and his eyes roaming at random. He should stay nice and quiet, stare at the ceiling and think as little as possible. Instead he's still laboring to deny it and continuing to hurt himself. "I'm sorry, it doesn't add up," he says, suddenly turning to Rambo. "How come she always sent me to the store? Couldn't she have gone herself?"

"Beats me. Maybe she didn't want to see him in the morning," Rambo improvises. "Maybe all she wanted in the morning was fresh fruit and she'd send you to pick it up."

"No, Mom never ate fruit. She made me eat it because it's good for me. Then she'd get mad when Franco sold me the crappy stuff. And I used to tell her, 'Mom, you're never happy with Franco's fruit. Tomorrow I'll go get it somewhere else.' And she: 'That's not happening. Not ever.' She always sent me to him and there was always something wrong with the fruit and every day she would bring it back to him and . . . "

Marino goes no further. Or maybe he does, but only to himself, and there he sees things that will make you lose your voice. Things Rambo knows, and Sandro too, but they had decided not to disclose them to their friend. What was the point of telling him the truth when it didn't help anything, when it is so shitty that there is no way it could be of any benefit to you. So Rambo looks at Marino and says nothing, then goes to the window and checks outside. The silence is oppressive.

But it's even worse when Marino breaks the silence to ask for his pan.

The nurses had left it for him. They call it a pan but it looks more like a plastic white scooper. Rambo had asked them what he was supposed to do with it and they had told him that he'd understand as soon as the time came. Now that time has come, and Rambo understands he has to slip it between Marino's legs, wait until what needs to be drained is drained, throw everything away, and rinse the pan, and everything would be in order.

Fat chance it would be in order.

"Look, Marino, I'll close my eyes and hold it under your butt. You have to do the rest on your own. Got it?"

"Sure, if I'm able to, sure."

"You have to be able to. Then I'll hand you a towel and you can wipe yourself off and we're good. Good?"

"I don't know if I can do that."

"Of course you can. Because if you can't, you'll make do. Sorry, I don't mean to be a dick and it's not that I'm not a true friend. Actually it's on account of our being friends. Because if I have to pick up your shit and wipe your ass when you're done, well, forget friendship, after that I couldn't even look you in the face. You understand, right?"

Marino frowns, nods. Rambo lifts the sheet and spies Marino's prone legs slightly spread apart. He sets the pan down by his feet and slowly slides it upward, reaches Marino's knees, and closes his eyes. With just two fingers he slides it farther up, and when he feels it bump into something, he stops.

"Let it rip, Marino."

"Hold on, you stuck it under my thigh," he says, tugging the sheet.

Rambo opens his right eye a tiny bit, gets Marino's naked body in focus, and spots the white pan that had snagged under his leg—oddly in shape for a guy who doesn't play sports and spends most of his time in bed. Not muscular but, you know, nicely made. But Rambo can't think about that right now.

He sticks out the same two fingers that have already been contaminated, frees the pan, and this time, without closing his eyes, tries to guide it straight up to where it has to be inserted. But the pan won't budge. It gets stuck just below and lodges there, obliging Rambo to sacrifice another finger. He joins it to the others and pushes. Nothing. He takes the plastic with his whole hand and feels something warm that may be the naked skin of Marino's thigh, so with a flash of energy he slides the pan farther up, really hard, and lodges it so deep Marino yelps and sticks his hands between his legs, over his naked junk, which he now squeezes himself yet a moment before, for just a second, Rambo had held it in his hand.

"Agh! That's too far! Too far up!" cries Marino, who manages to push it away.

Rather than apologize, Rambo springs back against the wall, his eyes bulging, and his hand a mile away from the rest of his body, on the end of his arm which he holds out in front of him. Like in that film he'd seen as a boy where the guy loses his hand and they sew on another one, only it belongs to this real psychopath who'd been executed the night before, and at first it works great and everything's dandy, but later the hand starts to kill people again and in the end even tries to murder its new owner, who looks at it just as Rambo is looking at his hand now, there at the end of his arm: his since birth yet suddenly unrecognizable.

"Rambo, please. I can't go if you're here."

Without even answering he runs out of the room and slams the door behind him.

He runs down the hall and into the kitchen, where the walls aren't as black, and a large window lets the afternoon light in. And underneath the window is another rifle waiting for him.

But Rambo doesn't pick it up right away. He can't. First he turns the tap as far it will go and sticks his hand under the jet of water, palm up, palm down. Then he pours half a bottle of dish soap over it and rubs it in till it vanishes into a cloud of lemon foam. Next he picks up the sink sponge and begins scrubbing his hand with the coarse side, hard, so hard it hurts. But Rambo doesn't stop. Because the germs may have died a while back, and gone, too, is any trace of disgust at his having touched Marino there, at his having felt something clammy rub against his palm. Yet something else won't be rubbed out.

Something resistant to water, soap, and his will to tear the skin off his hand. It remains behind. Much as Rambo scrubs, he can still feel it making every muscle in his body shiver. An absurd, frightening sensation that feels a lot like pleasure.

That's right, the sick pleasure of having touched that naked skin, along with the even sicker desire to touch it again and again.

No way. Impossible. It can't be true. Those two kids are to blame. It was they who had come up with that story about his liking men. That's what they'd said to Rambo. Who the hell were those two to talk? A girl pale as a ghost and a spastic, radioactive boy—what the fuck do two freak shows like that know about men and women, or life, or normal stuff? Two of nature's gags rely on other people being sick and queer as them. Pure rubbish. Utter madness. Him like men? He's not even attracted to women. He doesn't look at them when they pass by nor has he ever touched one in his life. And if he's not into women, the idea of his being into men is a joke.

The truth is that Rambo is a fighter. He's against everybody. Love plays no part in his life. There's only war. There's only battling the world that keeps him down. For him there's no woman, no soul mate. He's a real rebel. Not like those phonies who act cool, whom all the girls go mad for. And if every once in a while he feels this strange sensation, when he's watching the TV, when he's passing by a shop downtown, when he used to go to the public pool and get changed with other dudes, that's normal. It happens. They're mind games. Society seeping into Rambo's thick skin. The trick is to avoid it, keep your distance, and scrub it off like he's doing now.

He turns the tap off, gazes out the window, and sighs. He's finally ready to pick up that rifle.

A double-barrel Benelli that has seen better days yet will get the job done. Just like Rambo, if the old man is to be believed and someone really has his sights on capturing this house. The Russians, the Chinese, heck even the Americans, the Germans, the Arabs or Italians—powerful millionaires run rampant the world over. Morals, on the other hand, are nowhere to be found.

That's where men like him come in, men who dig in and won't abandon the trenches, even if this isn't his house, even if this is a pretty hard perimeter to defend. Walled with thick trees, like a forest. Or rather a jungle where your only chance of winning is to employ guerrilla tactics. The place is practically Vietnam, and Rambo knows all about Vietnam. He may never have been, but he's seen a barrage of movies about that spectacularly bloody conflict. So what if almost all of them were shot in some Hollywood studio? Or that the Italian versions were made in the middle of the Apennines? That doesn't mean anything. In fact it's better that way, because it shows you that Vietnam doesn't only exist in Vietnam. It exists everywhere. Vietnam is a messy situation where people ambush you and slit your throat and unfortunately that description fits the entire planet. Enemies and dangers are everywhere, ready to destroy you. On the road, in front of Marino's apartment, amid the tangled branches of this jungle, but even here at home, even in your own hands, under your skin, in your head.

Every place is Vietnam. And Rambo knows it. His life is war.

FIRST STEPS

Go on, Sandro, now's your shot.

The kids asked for ten euros for a guide to Lunigiana and between the two of them it will take an hour to decide what to get. The old man went to the bathroom and before going asked for a sheet of paper and a pen—you'd rather not know what for.

And now you and Serena are alone amid the aisles of the Autogrill.

She has paused in one corner where there's a mirror and products like lipstick, eye shadow, random makeup, stuff women make themselves pretty with; a good sign, perhaps. She bends over and pokes around the boxes, and Sandro watches her from the other end of the aisle, trying to figure out what makes this woman so mesmerizing, how her beauty can withstand Serena's abuse, her boys' clothes, her hair in disarray, those combat boots on her feet that would ruin the thighs of every other woman on the planet. Everyone's but hers, that is; her brand of beauty refuses to be mortified. On the contrary, it attacks with greater ferocity, like a wild boar, and if you're going to shoot a boar, you'd better lay it out flat with the first shot, because if you merely graze it, it'll go berserk, overpower you, toss you in the air, and pummel you into the earth, while you turn around and around and if you have an arm left to wave you start waving it wildly, bidding the world goodbye.

That's what Serena's beauty is like. Now, Sandro probably shouldn't explain to her that she reminds him of a wounded boar, but he at least ought to make something up and go tell her right away.

Go on, Sandro, now is your shot.

And Sandro needs to strike quick, since under normal circumstances, he might not do anything. No, Sandro would spend another hour spying on her and contemplating her mysterious beauty, telling himself oh well, they're spending an afternoon together, and they may never have spoken but at least she didn't beat him up, so you might say things hadn't gone so badly. That it was a first step. Which is exactly what always burns Sandro, this first step business. Because he could easily go home right now and be happy to cling to that first step—not a big one but real nonetheless—and use it to sleep tight and hold out hope for tomorrow, then for the day after tomorrow, then for the following week, then for the spring to melt their hearts in just five or six months and ignite Serena's passion . . . and he'd go on that way until it was too late and all he could do was resent his hard luck while trying to cancel Serena from his thoughts.

But not this time, if things don't go smoothly this time it's his fault, his and this first step nonsense, which only means something if afterward there's a second step and a third and so on, and all those steps point in a specific direction, which in the end leads to where you want to go. Or in the ballpark. If the second and third don't exist, however, then taking the first step is like putting one foot in front of the other—what the hell are you doing then? Nothing, that's what you're doing, and in fact that is the story of Sandro's life, one step to the right, one step to the left, one foot forward, one back . . . it's like a dance you make up, and, dancing, you sway and skip, and you might even break a sweat but by the end of it you're still in the same spot.

At first that was fine. The party was full of beautiful girls, interesting people, killer songs. The dance floor was crowded and everyone was dancing and grinding. Then, gradually, people started edging away, couples withdrew into the dark corners of the club, sucking face on love seats, screwing in the stalls, fogging their car windows outside, and then they were off, on the road, speeding toward the future. And Sandro? Look at Sandro, still here, all by himself in the middle of an empty dance floor, one foot forward, one foot back, left-right, forward-back, shake them hips, hands in the air . . . the colorful lights go out, the music fades, and the floor is so empty that one step won't change a thing, no matter the direction, you will always be a fool stranded alone in the middle of nothing. Well then, shit, enough already. It's time Sandro took the plunge, lived his life, tried doing what he'd told Luca to do, yes, and if it works, yahoo, and if it fails whogivesashit, he deserved it. Fuck first steps, Sandro will take twelve in a row, as many as it takes to cross the aisle, walk past the salamis and cheeses and gardening tools, and reach this wonderful woman with her skin the color of June year-round, leaning over, looking for God knows what but it doesn't matter now, because Serena may not know it yet, but what she's really looking for is him.

"Can I give you a hand?" he says, his voice not too high, his tone convincing, the trace of a smile across his lips. In other words, nothing is wanting. Except for a reply from Serena, who doesn't even look his way.

"They stock the most ridiculous stuff at the Autogrill, don't they?"

"   . . .   "

"I mean, what the hell would somebody traveling on the highway want with a whole leg of prosciutto, for example? Or a huge wedge of Parmesan? Or a satellite dish or a baton—Do you think anybody buys this stuff?"

Serena doesn't answer but for a second she looks at him with her mesmerizing eyes and lifts the corners of her lips into something that, if you wanted to think positively, you might take for a smile. And we have to shoot for maximum positivity, on par with his friend Marino that time he came the closest he ever would to being with a girl, i.e., the night he ran into one he liked at a club and to everyone's surprise worked up the courage to go and talk to her. Hi, he said, and immediately she asked him if he was alone. When he told her he'd come with friends, she said, "Good, then you have someone to go back to." And he did go back to them yet came back happy. He told them what happened and they asked him what the hell he had to be happy about and he said, "It's sweet, she was worried I was by myself."

Well, there you go, in order for Sandro to take Serena's wince for a smile, he has to arrive at that level of positivity, a positivity that will lead you to a life of happiness in a brightly lit, rose-colored world. Sure, over the years, the slings and arrows of real life poke holes in that world till you find yourself sticking your mother in the freezer, but that's another story Sandro needn't think about right now. Right now Sandro must persevere. Step by step, Sandrino, step by step . . .

"If you're looking for batteries, they're at the register," he says. "But don't bother, the tape player's mine and I'll buy them. If you're hungry there's pizza over there. If you're thirsty drinks are in the fridge down there. Or—"

"Listen, catechist, thanks but I don't need anything. The one thing I needed was for you to tell the kids no, but it's too late for that now."

Sandro looks at her. He'd like to say something but the lines he'd rehearsed had to do with other retail items at the Autogrill and perhaps no longer bear much relevance.

"Do you even know why they want to go to Pontremoli? Did they tell you about that piece of wood they found with some bracelets stuck on?"

"Yeah. I mean, actually, not really."

"Well, see, I was forced to say yes; Luna's my daughter. What choice did I have? But you? I had hoped that you would have said no, that it was absurd, that you had to work. I mean forty years old and taking a trip on a Wednesday on the spur of the moment no problem—don't you have a job? Commitments? What the fuck do you do in this life?"

"I—I mean, I don't—" Sandro chews crumbs of words until there are no crumbs left to chew. He just shakes his head and nods and makes a strange movement with his neck, like those bobblehead dogs his dad used to line up on his dashboard. But he can stop worrying about which way his head's moving because Serena has stopped looking at him. Actually he'd be better off backing up a bit—three, four steps—and disappearing. Maybe go buy batteries; that way they can return to the car and play the tapes he stayed up all night recording. Three ninety-minute tapes with a wisely chosen mix of songs that would penetrate Serena's ears and flood her heart and make her understand that love cannot be stopped, that if it comes knocking you cannot tell it to take a hike as if it were some Sunday morning Jehovah's Witness.

Right, just like that, that is all Sandro need do now: leave Serena, trust in the power of music, and wait, and wait . . . Only before leaving he looks at her one last second as she takes a rubber band from her wrist and carelessly ties her hair back in a sloppy ponytail. And something happens, something he doesn't even have a say in. What happens is, as she cinches her hair into a sloppy ponytail, Sandro's mouth opens and speaks of its own accord. It says: "Quit it, Serena, quit it."

Like that. And she whips around, her eyes wide. She can't believe her ears and neither can Sandro. Yet he goes on: "Treat me badly, tell me I'm a fool and that I don't do dick in life, punch me again or kick me or whatever you feel will make you feel good. But quit tying your hair that way. And quit dressing like crap. The baggy clothes and that military gear and those combat boots—have you seen yourself? When was the last time you looked in the mirror? There's a mirror right there, look at yourself, do you know what you look like, Serena?"

Serena keeps staring at him, not moving, aside from shaking her head once to signal that, no, she doesn't know.

"Christ, you're beautiful. You're the most beautiful woman in the world, or at least what I've seen of the world, and I may not have traveled much but so what, I've never seen a knockout like you anywhere. Other women make themselves up, try to look nice, put some thought into their hair and clothes, while you do nothing and you still come out looking beautiful. Actually, you know what really pisses me off? Now you're more beautiful than before. Every time I see you, you're more beautiful, for fuck's sake, and you don't deserve to be, Serena, you don't deserve it. But that's how it is and there's nothing you can do about it. So at least do me a favor: stop tying your hair like you don't care and stop dressing this way. Quit wasting your time denigrating yourself and trying to make yourself look ugly. It won't work. It only makes you look ridiculous and pathetic. And totally beautiful."

Sandro said it. Incredible as it is, he said all of it. It flew out of his mouth word by word, one word after another, so powerfully that for a moment the words hang suspended in the air between him and Serena. And he wishes they would vanish, the way he used to wish his dad's gigantic undies would vanish when he was a little boy and his buddies would come over to play, and his mom would leave those undies hanging up in front of the house, wide as tablecloths, and Sandro would see them and die of shame. The same goes for the words that have just escaped his mouth and hang there, silently staring back at them, embarrassing Sandro to death.

Luckily Zot and Luna return, running and shouting, to shake the air out and fill it with other words.

"Mom, Mom, we need a few more euros."

Serena doesn't answer right away. She looks at Luna for a moment, then manages to say: "More? How much does that guide cost?"

"No, we got the guide, but we have to get antivenom."

"What the heck do we need antivenom for?"

"Ha," says Zot, pointing his index finger in the air, "those are the famous last words that are running through your head when the poison stops your heart."

"Listen, kids, we're going to a museum. Even if it is in the middle of the woods, I'm pretty sure there are no snakes creeping around inside the museum. Okay? Besides, if a snake were to bite you, all we'd need to do is keep calm and call a doctor. No one's at risk of dying from a snakebite."

"Not us," says Zot, "but . . . "

"But?"

"Nothing. I feel apprehensive about . . . " Zot nods toward Luna a few times.

"Apprehensive about what? I don't follow."

"Well, you see, Luna is frail. I'm not sure she could withstand poison the way we—"

"Fuck you, Zot!" says Luna, and what with her mouth, her wispy voice that always labors to emerge, that "fuck you" seems completely out of place, like a starfish on Mont Blanc. "I am not frail. Besides, look who's talking. You have to put a sweater on to go to the bathroom."

"That's because bathrooms are often quite damp! Is that my fault? Mr. Sandro, Ms. Serena, please explain to Luna that at a certain age rheumatism sets in and you can no longer joke around about the damp."

Serena looks at him, starts to say something, then shuts her mouth, shakes her head, sighs.

Once again Sandro feels that now is his shot. He searches inside himself for a confident, firm voice befitting a man who can fix the situation, then explains to the kids that they won't find antivenom at the Autogrill. Only pharmacies carry it.

"Is that true? Are there pharmacies in Pontremoli?"

"Yes. I mean, there must be a pharmacy."

"Very well then, we can procure some at our destination," says Zot. "Happy, Luna? You don't have to feel anxious about it anymore."

"But I wasn't anxious," Luna shoots back. Then out of the blue she says it's late and heads for the exit. Zot follows her and puts a hand on her arm to guide her, but she wiggles away and shoos him like a fly.

Sandro watches them for a moment and fails to see that Serena is backing away from the shelves and walking off too. He only hears her as she brushes past him: "Nice work. Now we're stopping at the pharmacy too."

But there's no spite in her voice. Less than before anyway. Or maybe Sandro would just like to think so, to feel better as they leave the Autogrill and get back in the jeep, where Ferro has already returned and is grousing about how everything in the bathroom is automatic, how the tap only runs when it feels like it and the toilet flushes by itself the minute you move and almost gives you a heart attack. Also, the skanks have stopped leaving their phone numbers on the wall. As a matter of fact, there are no more walls; now there are these smooth dark wood panels only the homos write on, and Ferro is revolted because once upon a time they weren't there, or at least they didn't mention they were homos. All they said was that they were seeking a man and there was the number to call. And maybe afterward if you called them they'd try to convince you otherwise, but at least while reading the messages you could picture a hot piece of ass. Men used to be allowed to dream. Now they come right out and say it: "Gay seeks company," "Boy seeks dick for hot night." What kind of world are we living in? What kind of nasty world are we living in? Then he places a sheet of paper on the dashboard on which he'd jotted down the numbers of a couple trannies.

"Put the music back on, would you? I need a little soul," he says while the jeep lurches back onto the highway. Silence rather than music, fills the car. Ferro turns around, and everyone's eyes search everyone else's eyes, but no one speaks. No one remembered to buy batteries.

On cue, the old man looses a barrage of insults at God and the Virgin and several saints, some of who may not even exist, coupling them with various disease-carrying animals that slither in the mud.

Serena doesn't even attempt to tell him to shut up, and the kids sit there with their eyes wide open, absorbing these new and terrifying blasphemies. Sandro is the only one, after a certain point, to say enough. (If anyone should be scandalized, Sandro should. He's the catechist after all.) He asks Ferro to stop and points his finger at something above them, at the roof of the jeep, beyond which there's also heaven.

"What the hell do you want? I'm blowing off steam."

"I'm asking you to blow off steam in some other fashion besides blaspheming."

"Why? So God doesn't get offended? Do you really think there's a guy up there with a white beard who minds if I tell him to get fucked? Do you really believe there's someone like that up there?"

Sandro doesn't answer right away. For a while he only hears the noise of the tires on the road and feels everyone's eyes on him. "I mean, look, I believe there's something superior out there."

"Big whoop," says Ferro. "Superior to you? Imagine that."

Three Cheers for Camping

ttention, all passengers, we have an important
announcement to make," says Mr. Sandro when we
pull up to the tollbooth. He pays with the change in
the ashtray even though Mom's back here waving a five-euro
bill, then we take off again and there are signs and behind the
signs there's a huge curve and behind that there's a river and
old houses made of stone. And in this strange voice like he's
talking on the radio, Sandro says: "Ladies and gentlemen, the
important announcement is that we have arrived in the lovely
city of . . . Pontremoli!"

And that's when Zot and I look at each other and raise our
arms and shout, "Yaaay!"

I turn to Mom, put my hand on her leg, and squeeze. And
she squeezes me back, hard, the whole enchilada of me.
Meanwhile Ferro says, "What are you all so happy about? It
took us half a day to reach the world's butthole."

To be fair, we were supposed to be here after lunch and
instead we're passing by the town's streets and houses and the
sun is disappearing behind it all, since it's almost six o'clock. But
that isn't our fault. After the Autogrill we got back on the highway and within five minutes there were all these cars stopped in
front of us, so we stopped too and sat there for three hours.

Sandro switched off the engine, Ferro cursed, Mom kept
quiet but I could feel her getting antsy and she had her hands on
her legs and was wiping them up and down like she was drying
them off though they weren't the least bit wet. Zot on the other

hand asked Sandro if we could use this time to go over the ten commandments, the seven cardinal sins, the three theological virtues, and other questions the bishop might ask us before confirmation. And when no one answered him he launched into the commandments himself, saying them straight through and all stuck together so that it seemed like there weren't ten of them but just one long and impossible to obey commandment: "IamtheLordthyGodthoushalthavenootherGodsbeforemethus hallnottakethenameoftheLordthyGodinvain . . . "

At that point Ferro grabbed the door handle and said the name of the Lord a dozen times, almost always in vain, then got out of the car and went to talk with a man leaning against a truck in front of us. And after a little, while Zot was listing off the sins and virtues, one by one we got out of the car too, then got back in, then got out once more, and finally ran back to the jeep because the cars were starting to move again. Slowly, we moved too.

We were hungry and thirsty and I had to go pee, but I forgot about everything when we passed the point where that never-ending line had begun. The metal thing that splits the highway in two was all cracked, there was even a hole, and the truck driver from before had explained to Ferro that a car going the other direction had knocked into something, flown into our lane, and hit another car head-on. There were still millions of pieces of glass and broken junk on the side of the road, and the police were on the pavement with men dressed in orange and big, strange, dark stripes. We passed the scene slowly and Zot said, "Saint Christopher, Protector of Motorists, is anybody injured?" And Ferro said probably not. More likely they were all dead.

Then the road opened up and we began driving fast, and Ferro said, "Oh, finally. Three hours wasted in line. If we hadn't stopped at the Autogrill, we'd have missed the accident and been in Pontremoli ages ago."

So then Mom told him that he was the one who wanted to stop at the Autogrill, and he replied, "Yeah, but all we had to do was get batteries and go, and instead you wandered around looking at other junk and even forgot the batteries. Had we left earlier, the accident would have been at our backs and we'd already be in Pontremoli."

"Yeah," I said, "or else that car in the other lane would have flown into us."

Well, that's what I thought anyway, and I think I may have been right, since for a while no one spoke. I stuck my hand in my jeans pocket and touched the bone Luca gave me. I thanked it and ran my finger along it, and even if that accident was totally awful and I feel really bad about it, touching the bone always makes me smile.

And my smile's grown now that we're leaving the jeep in a wide square piazza and all getting out to finally see the famous Pontremoli. And it could be that the piazza is big and all I see around me is a gray blur but it looks emptier than Forte dei Marmi in winter. No matter, I didn't come here to make friends. All I want is to see the statues of the people of Luna and pretty soon I will. I want to climb the street where the sign says at the top is the Castle of Piagnaro with the museum inside. I want to enter and I want those ancient statues to explain why Luca made us come here, and I want their answer to be something beautiful that helps us understand many other things that are so beautiful that everything becomes clear, even the darkest stuff that has happened, and Mom and I hug each other hard and cry a little, just for a minute though cause then we laugh and we're happy and she goes back to work and Tuesdays we eat pizza by the sea and I get confirmed. I finish middle school and grow boobs and I wear dresses where you can sort of see the boobs, and afterward people might look at me on account of them instead of on account of my white hair and transparent eyes, and they stop being faraway and actually want to get close to me and we talk and play and it's like what it should be like when you feel good.

There. That's what I want.

Instead of what really happens, which is us stopping in front of the castle door. The door is closed and there's a piece of washed-out paper on it. Sandro reads it for me and says that the museum isn't even there. It's under construction. So they moved it to the village, to the town hall downtown.

Where exactly downtown we don't know, not even where approximately, and there's no one around to ask. We go back to the piazza where we find a man reading the obituary notices. He doesn't know where the statues are but he knows where the town hall is; it's in another smaller piazza and to get there we pass under what for me is only a dark roof but turns out to be a row of arches, cause while we're passing under them Zot says these arches are beautiful. And after them there's the town hall building and there is a big door with a woman leaning up against it. We ask her about the statues and she tells us they are there but she doesn't know where because it's not her job. So we go into a café next door that doesn't have a sign which we would never have noticed without Ferro, who knew there was one cause he says that next to every town hall there's always a café, otherwise the municipality's employees wouldn't know where to go all day.

As a matter of fact there is a café, but the only person inside is a lady behind the counter washing glasses, and the place is so empty I wonder who could have gotten those glasses dirty. But I'm more interested to know where the statues are, and the lady knows, they're the town hall right next door. "It's a cellar, sort of. Past the main building you'll find stairs that lead underground. But you'll have to hurry because in a little while it closes. You better run."

We say thanks and run for it but stop a second in the doorway because outside a guy rides by on a tricked-out Vespa making mutiny, and he honks the horn and sails off, and the woman at the counter yells, "Ciao, Silvano!" and tells us we needn't rush, we can get comfy and have a drink: Silvano is the museum guard; if he's headed home that means it's closed.

So we all quit smiling and thanking her and just stand there. Then I ask if I can pee and go to the bathroom. The bathroom smells like rose petals and medicine, and when I go back outside they are all standing quietly in the street. No one says anything. And if you ask me they haven't said anything, not even while I was in the bathroom, they've just been listening to the wind blowing in the trees and the river running over the rocks.

"I'm sorry, kids," Mom says after a bit. She makes a gesture with her hand I can't see but that may be a signal to go to her, and she takes me in her arms and hugs me. "I'm so sorry, Luna, really and truly."

"Don't worry, Mom—"

"I'm so awfully sorry. We came to Pontremoli, see, we tried. I'm so, so sorry."

"Me too," says Mr. Sandro behind me. "It's disappointing, kids, but sometimes things don't work out the way we want them to."

"I know," I say. "But it's really not a problem for me. To be honest, I'm happier this way."

And it seems like the most normal thing in the world but maybe it's only normal for me, cause Mom stops hugging me and keeps holding my arms but pulls away a little and looks at me. "What do you mean you're happier this way?"

"A lot happier, Mom. So is Zot. Right, Zot?"

Zot doesn't respond. He always agrees with me, but not this time. I mean, he tries to, he tries nodding but all I see is his hair tossing this way and that with no rhyme or reason.

Ferro goes: "You knock your noggin, kid?"

"No, no," says Sandro, "don't you get it? This is the perfect example of Christian acceptance. Sometimes earthly life presents us with setbacks and disappointments, but the Christian soul knows how to accept them with serenity and regard them as tests of faith. I'm impressed, Luna, and pretty proud of the work we've done together."

"Thanks, Mr. Sandro, but I don't understand. I mean, obviously I'm happy. If anything I thought it would be a problem for you guys."

"Us, no way," says Mom. "You won't hear any complaints from us!"

"Well then, awesome!" I say. "We'll go to the museum tomorrow morning, and I'll be super happy to spend the night here. It'll be way cool."

I almost jump for joy. But everyone else stands there quietly, so I do too.

Mom goes: "Hold it a sec, Luna. Hold it . . . We're not spending the night here. We're going home now."

"Huh? How can we do that, Mom, we haven't seen the statues yet."

"I know, but we'll come back some other time. We'll be back one day."

"Sure, that means we're never coming back!"

"Don't push it, Luna, one of these days we'll be back. End of story."

"But we're here now. And think about how beautiful it'll be to sleep in the mountains. It's like . . . like going camping!"

"Three cheers for camping!" says Zot.

"We've never been, Mom. We always said we would with Luca but then we never did. Even when he went to France we told him that it wasn't fair that we always stayed home. And do you remember what he said? He said that we'd all go camping together this summer. Remember that, Mom? Remember that?"

"Yes but not now, now we . . . with Luca, we were going to go camping with Luca."

"But Luca's not around to take us camping anymore, Mom, so we need to take ourselves. You and me will do the camping. Come on, Mom, you and me."

"And me!" says Zot. "It just so happens I brought a tent in the event of an emergency"

He talks and I raise my hands in the air. He joins me and together we start jumping, and while we're jumping we get close, and I don't know if I'm the one to make the last move or he is, but our arms cross and we end up hugging each other. And Zot immediately stops jumping. He whispers two or three words in my ear but I don't catch them. One may be my name but I can't be sure. Because after a second I let go of him and go hug Mom, and she doesn't move either, which is fine by me. I jump for both of us, for all three of us, and for Mr. Sandro and Ferro too. Now that I think about it, we didn't even ask them how they feel. Not that it matters. There are things so wonderful in the world it doesn't make sense to ask questions. All that makes sense is jumping.

I'm Not a Cook

The nine flights of stairs to reach Marino's house are too few; Rambo climbs them and wishes there were ninety, or nine hundred, wishes they'd never end. Because in spite of his killing himself doing targeted exercises, his quadriceps are barely chiseled. On the contrary, for some inexplicable reason Marino's thighs are more toned. Marino, who considers billiards a sport and has been lying in bed for almost a month.

Those thin but strong legs, the heat of that smooth skin he touched without wanting to and can still feel on his fingers—it's like when you accidentally brush against poison ivy and it continues to burn, and the more you scratch the worse it gets.

Rambo reaches the ninth floor, looks over his shoulder, and scans the darker corners of the landing. The coast is clear. He pulls out the keys, opens the door, and enters Marino's house, where there is all the stuff he and Sandro had bought to eat, back when they'd thought they would come live here together. Hardly a day has gone by yet it feels like another era, a happy and peaceful era. Well, happy may be an overstatement, but it was definitely a happier time than now, what with the goddamn veggie mart man watching over them, and it was even better before he and Sandro discovered Marino's mom in the freezer. That's life; every day brings one boot in the ass and another in the teeth, and the most painful blows are the ones that come when you start to relax and figure everything's cool.

Small wonder Rambo doesn't turn the light on when he enters, silently creeping along the wall, crouching and skittish.

He's ready to answer fire with fire, and if there's a special outfit of cops working for Marino's uncle behind the curtains or the couch, Rambo feels sorry for them and the poor families back home pointlessly waiting up for them.

But there is no one in the living room. Or the kitchen for that matter. There's only the stale smell of cigarettes and the sound of the freezer, and maybe it's just him but it seems to be ringing really loudly in his ears. No call for heroics, Rambo just has to fetch a few things to eat, throw them in a bag, and head back to Ghost House. Not that he's happy about it. Right now he could use a good ambush, some mole who would force him to drop everything and sharpen his body and mind into arrows aimed at the enemy, leaving no room for other thoughts that were sick and pointless as the image of a man's bare legs, his skin, the hair covering them.

No, it's all nonsense circling his head like a carousel he'd rather not get off of. Rambo doesn't desire other men. Don't be daft. He only wants to be like them. Muscular, toned—with all his exercising he's earned it. It's a question of justice, of hard work and the rewards you reap for hard work, and he is a man who still believes in certain values, that's all. So when he thinks of these naked bodies, of bulging muscles and the heat those muscles give off, well, Rambo thinks of justice.

Justice occupies his entire mind; he can't think of anything else and, because of that, can't find a good reason as to why the bodies that have the greatest effect on him, the kind that really attract him, are slender and pale and delicate. It shouldn't be that way—it can't be that way—Rambo mustn't think about it. Anything else would be better.

So it's no surprise that on his way out with the bag full of food, Rambo is kind of pleased to look up and find a black figure in the doorframe, motionless in the dark, staring back at him. He drops the bag, slaps the light switch on, and sees the crooked smile of the goddamn veggie mart man trying to get in.

Rambo switches off the light again, picks up his bag, and goes to face the man, chest to chest, propelling the man back, and this body-on-body contact has no effect on him, doesn't give him the shivers, only a sense of the primitive clash between human beings. Nothing wrong with that.

"Let me in, for Cain's dog, let me in!"

Rambo propels him out to the landing, closes the door, behind him and turns the key.

"Enough," he says. "Nobody's home. You've nudged me too far this time."

"Why? I . . . "

"Enough, Franco. I'm sorry but I can't help you."

"Cain's dog, you can't. Let me in the house. Just for a minute."

"But the lady of the house isn't in, I swear, she's not in!"

Franco looks at him then at the door behind him. "Let me check the place out. It'll ease my nerves."

"Look, there's nothing to check out. There's no—"

"Listen, boy, let's talk openly," he says, and trains his eyes on Rambo's again. "Look, I get what's going on in there, okay?"

Rambo stands there for a moment. He grips the bag firmly but shakes so much the plastic starts to rattle. "What's there to get?"

"Why hide it?" asks Franco.

Rambo wants to say Marino is to blame; he's the dumbass who hid her. Rambo didn't know anything. He had nothing to do with this.

"Look, boy, there's nothing wrong with it."

"There isn't?"

"Of course not! I may look like an old bigot to you, but this is the twenty-first century, do you know how many guys like other guys and move in together? I've got a nephew like you, lives in Milan with a cook. What am I supposed to do about it?"

"But I'm—but—but—what the fuck are you saying? Are you calling me a fag?"

"No, of course not. I wouldn't dare. Homosexual is what you say, right? Or queer."

"I'll pop you in the nose, dickhead. What the fuck do you want from me!"

"There's nothing wrong with it. You can tell by looking at you. There's no point in hiding it."

"What the fuck can you tell?" says Rambo, bristling, waving his arms so wildly things begin falling out of the bag. "This is legit paratrooper camo, battle-issue. And combat boots. And my head's shaved to the bone. What the fuck can you tell? What the fuck are you trying to say!"

"Hey, my nephew's boyfriend dresses that way, spitting image."

"Yeah but that guy's a cook, a faggy cook! I'm not a fag. Cooking makes me puke. I couldn't cook a bowl of spaghetti!"

"Sure about that? You sure you didn't come here to live with your playmate?"

"No! That's disgusting! I live at home with my parents!"

"Ah. So the groceries aren't for you guys."

"No! No they're not for us."

"Fine then," says Franco, "fine, fine, fine, fine, fine." And the more he says it the less it sounds like things are actually fine. "But I mean, if you don't live here and Lidia's son is in the hospital, who are you guys always carrying around groceries for?"

Rambo hesitates for a moment. Looks at the bag. Looks at the provolone and hunk of prosciutto on the ground. "Well, all right, they're for me. But I didn't bring it here. It's stuff I picked up here to take away."

"But of course, it's all clear now. You do your shopping in other people's houses."

"Yes. I mean no. It's Marino's stuff. They're discharging him soon and . . . "

"Sure, they're discharging him from the hospital and his mom doesn't care. She's gone to do her own thing and adios, right? I'm not buying that bullshit. Let me in so I can have a look around."

"No," says Rambo. And he plants himself in front of the door.

"What's it to you if everything's kosher? I go in and take a good look around, two minutes tops, so I can put my heart at ease and stop busting your balls."

"No. I'm sorry but I can't let you. This is private property. When you were at the door earlier it was almost trespassing, got that?"

"Oh, I get it," says Franco. "Guess I'll have to wait for my friend Ferdinando to get off work. I can enter with the police chief, can't I?"

"Nope! You cannot. Mussolini isn't in charge anymore. There are laws. Private property is private, and . . . "

Rambo stops talking. He stares at Franco, his eyes two slits, his teeth clenched. Something ought to be done here and pronto. But he doesn't know what.

"Listen, I've got to get going. I've got stuff to do."

"Me too. I've got a store to run," says Franco, and starts smiling again. He walks to the elevator, pushes the button, the doors open immediately, and he signals to Rambo to get in first.

"No thanks, I prefer to take the stairs."

"Ah, right," says Franco, raising his hands. He enters the elevator and the doors begin to close. "My nephew always takes the stairs too. Strengthens the glutes."

Panda Italia '90

Rambo handles the wheel as if it were a neck he were breaking, but after a right-hand turn he has to loosen his grip because the plastic cracks and he realizes he really is breaking it. Even if the damage were minor, he has enough problems as it is; now's not the time to create more for himself. He has to scope out his surroundings, especially in the rear, make sure no one is following him, and get to Ghost House in one piece. Tonight of all nights, when he'd lent Sandro his jeep, all hell had to break loose, and he has to get through it in this busted tuna-fish can.

A Fiat Panda specially manufactured for the 1990 World Cup in Italy, white with a thin Tricolore running along the exterior, plastic hubcaps with black and white diamonds made to resemble soccer balls, and on the door a decal of the '90 Italia mascot, this stick figure with red, white, and green squares called Ciao that sucked serious shlong. The whole car sucks shlong. The twisted designers who cooked it up were champs at capturing the spirit of that shitty World Cup, which was finally being played in Italy again and that meant we had to win, but like always when everything is organized and all that's called for is a little order and fair play and no fuck-ups, Italy cut a sorry-ass figure. Because we're only good at pulling off miracles, at scoring the desperation goal, when there's no hope left to do and a final flash of wickedly grandiose inspiration is unleashed. On the other hand, when all is going swimmingly and winning merely calls for not messing up, we revert to our devastating incapacity to be decent, to be consistent, to be average.

And that fact has always pissed Rambo off. But not tonight. Tonight he is clinging to that very moment-of-desperation genius, because if ever there were a desperate moment, this is it, him driving a tin can that stinks of smoke, and floating in the air are the ashes from years and years of cigarettes sucked down by Marino's mom, wrapped in two blankets in the backseat.

Rambo knows it's crazy. He thinks about it and feels a cold shiver down his spine, partly because of fear and partly because Marino's frozen mom is in fact expelling cold air like those plastic thingamajigs you put in your cooler when you go on trips. But those things expire quickly; you open the cooler and get ready to drink a cold Coke and find yourself sipping broth, and that's what'll happen to Lady Lidia, who was rock solid when Rambo took her—she wouldn't come loose on account of her butt being stuck to the bottom of the freezer—but is slowly melting now and threatening to make a much bigger mess.

But what can he do? He'd called Sandro, he'd called Marino, the telephone kept ringing but neither friend came to his aid. Rambo kept calling and getting dead air. Sandro is busy playing the fool with some girl and couldn't care less. Marino is stuck in bed or maybe sound asleep after the medicine Rambo had given him before leaving; by accident he'd given him too much, but hell, better too much than too little, at least he won't feel the pain and can rest. That's just how Rambo is. He cares for other people. On the battlefield he has his friends' backs. But when he's the one who could use some help, there's no one to turn to.

He'd gone back upstairs and entered the apartment not knowing what to do. All he'd known was that he needed to act; time was running out and any minute the police chief could get off work and ride up there with Franco, and then it would be all over. For Marino as well as for him and Sandro, accomplices in this stinker, up to their necks in shit. Just as things seemed to be getting better, when they'd had a house and a stable pension to forge ahead. Rambo had thought about it while wandering through the rooms of the apartment—not huge but comfortable—perfect for the three of them. And every noise, every blip of the elevator, had made him twitch. Then he'd walked through the living room and seen the keys to the car with the original cloth Fiat keychain still attached and another one with the face of Padre Pio and above that the words DON'T RUN, THINK OF ME. And rather than think of Padre Pio, he had thought of Marino's mom's Fiat Panda Italia '90 still parked down below with those hideous soccer-ball hubcaps. Then he'd taken the keys, grabbed the old woman, gone down the stairs with his legs shaking at every step, hopped inside the car, turned the key, and taken off.

And now he's pumping the gas, slamming it against the floor. The whole car is vibrating and hot air—not the cool he needs—is entering through the vents and making the old lady thaw more quickly. Maybe it's just his impression but Rambo thinks he smells something rotting. He rolls down the window and spits and speeds along the narrow roads toward Ghost House, fleeing danger and death. Too bad both are along for the ride tonight—and have made themselves much more comfortable than Rambo.

How Come There Are Still Monkeys

"But here is all rock," Ferro says to Sandro now that the jeep pulls off the road and slows in a clearing. The gravel makes a crunching sound under the wheels. "Hey genius, you plan on pitching tent on a pile of rocks?"

"No, Ferro, no. We're stopping to get something to eat. That's all. It might be nice to eat something before going to sleep, don't you think?"

"Ah, that's for sure. Were you planning on sending me to bed without supper, genius?"

"I know where I'd send you," says Sandro, his voice half suppressed by the engine, which he switches off in the middle of this stone white lot facing a church that's also made of stones, only bigger ones set on top of one another and running all the way to the roof—it, too, made of stone—and the closer I get the older it appears, built by people who didn't have time to waste on finishing touches. All they needed was a church to pray in and a square hole to enter through and above that another hole more or less in the shape of a cross to let the light in.

Beside the church is a road, which if you ask me wasn't there when they built it, and there definitely wasn't that light at the end of the road that to me just looks like blurry streak in the dark. Yet the others read something into it, because Mr. Sandro crosses the road then stops in the middle and asks us how we take our sandwiches.

I say cheese. Ditto Zot. Then he says, "Make that cheese and ham." Ferro wants cheese and anchovies, heavy on the anchovies, so Zot says he's changed his mind and would like ham and cheese and anchovies. Anything's cool by Mom as long as the bread isn't whole wheat. Sandro meanwhile is standing in the middle of the road in the dark and says that it's late and they'll have to settle for what's left, so Mom goes, "Fine, get whatever you want, I already know you'll screw the order up." And Sandro, serious: "Good point, Serena, I'll definitely screw it up seeing as I've already forgotten everybody's order. Why don't you come give me a hand?" She doesn't answer right away. When she does she says in that case she can go alone, and he says no, they're going together, and he heads in the direction of the one light in the dark.

Mom doesn't move and I tell her it would be nice if she went because she knows what kind of cheese I like, seeing as it's not like I like every every kind. Plus while they're at the store I'd like to go see inside the church.

"Your choice, Mom. You can go get sandwiches or else come with me to see the church," I say. "Maybe there are paintings inside, sacred images. We can study the columns and symbols—"

And before I have the chance to finish, Mom takes off, crosses the road, and finally disappears behind Mr. Sandro.

Zot and I enter the church. I take one step, two, and what happens next is what always happens when I enter a closed and dim place: in seconds I'm totally cool. There's no light forcing me to shut my eyes, my skin doesn't burn, I can see well, or at least better than usual. I enter this very old dark church with a couple of lit candles along the walls and a damp smell that slows your breathing, and I feel that this is the place for me. The whole business really ticks me off.

Why should I be happy? I want to be in the sun and the light with the breeze whipping my clothes. I want the smell of the sea and the sound of the waves and seagulls flying by me making their weird caw. I want to go barefoot and have the water soak my feet and retreat, soak them and retreat. I want to feel as if the place for me is that place rather than this dark hole.

In here I can relax and keep my eyes open, my head doesn't hurt, I don't burn up, the light doesn't blind me—but whoever said feeling good means feeling nothing? It's like saying that having fun is not being tired, that being happy is having nothing bad happen. And I know a lot of people think that way, but that just means those people are fools. The more at home I feel in here, the angrier I become. In fact I turn around immediately and head for the door. But as soon as I turn around I see this gray boxy shape in the back corner, and I forget everything. I go and stand in front of this gigantic, rude cut of stone. I look at her and she looks back at me with her round eyes, and I turn to stone just like her. Because the plaque next to her is written in tiny print I can't read, but I don't need to. No one needs to tell me I'm standing in front of a statue of the people of Luna.

Right here, leaning against the wall of the church. I stick out my hand and touch it. It's cold and real hard. I run my finger along it like the whalebone Luca gave me. It's rough and smooth. I look into its eyes—two deep circles—and I swear that it looks back at me. In fact even if I feel foolish I open my mouth and under my breath say, "Hello." That she doesn't answer makes me upset.

Then come Zot's footsteps as he runs over and stops beside me.

"Is that her?"

I nod.

"What's it doing here?"

I point to the plaque below, he bends over, studies it, and begins reading aloud that this statue is a very ancient warrior sculpted by the mysterious people of Luna three thousand years ago. It was discovered in this church; actually it was a piece of the church itself and had been used with the stones to erect the church walls.

I look at it and picture this place three thousand years ago, the woods where these mysterious people lived who left nothing behind, not even the side of a house or a piece of writing, since they didn't have time to learn how to write or give themselves a name. They would spend their days at work on these gigantic stones, flattening them, smoothing them down, carving them into shapes to resemble men and women like them, like us, and planting them upright in specific spots in the woods for reasons we don't know but for sure involve magic. And I wonder how the people who built this church could ever have treated it like some rock or brick. It's unbelievable. I can't fathom it. You see this statue—you feel it—and immediately want to respect it, admire it with all your—

"What is that shit?" says Ferro, coming closer.

"It's a stele statue," I reply, curt as I can.

"Hmph. Looks like a spaz to me."

"But Grandfather," says Zot, "you're standing in front of an ancient warrior of the extinct people of Luna, men of valor and strength and—"

"Of course they went extinct—if they were protected by a spaz like that."

Zot tries to find another answer for him but I don't. All I want is for Ferro to wander off elsewhere, someplace that interests him more. Instead he keeps poking fun of the statue, saying it's identical to a kid from Florence who used to come to the beach when Ferro was a lifeguard, and the parents would insist he was normal when what he was was retarded, and every time he tried to take a swim Ferro had to dive in and save him because he'd immediately sink like this hunk of stone here. I tell him it's not a hunk of stone, and he says of course it's a hunk of stone, then starts banging it with his fist like he were trying to knock it over.

So I'm relieved to see Mom and Sandro walk through the church door carrying a bag of sandwiches and another bag with what I guess is stuff to drink. And with them enters something else, something strange and incredible: Mom's laughter. Strange because everything in the church echoes and also because I haven't heard that sound in forever.

"But there was no light in that store," says Sandro, "it looked like Pecorino."

And she: "Keep telling yourself that!"

"What? It was dark in that frigging store. You couldn't see anything."

"Nice try. Anyone could tell that was a piece of lard. So now you get to eat a sandwich stuffed with it."

"But lard makes me sick!"

Mom laughs louder. When they reach us they lower their voices and then go dead silent, the only sound the shuffling of plastic bags. I'm happy that Mom's laughing and that Ferro has stopped saying nasty things about the statue. But it doesn't last long, the time it takes them to adjust to the shade. "What's the statue?" asks Sandro. "It looks just like Panizzi!"

"Who's Panizzi?" I ask. But I'm not sure I want to know.

"He was the principal at the high school I went to. Guy from Carrara. He'd always come to school in a black leather jacket that dragged on the ground. Looked like Dracula."

Mom goes: "Yeah, I know him! Panizzi was my principal too!"

"Um, obviously. We went to the same high school."

"Huh?"

"That's right, Serena. Same year. I was in section B and you were in C."

"How did you know I was in C?"

"Because I was there! We went to school together for five years. We even went on a field trip to Recanati together, to Leopardi's house."

"I remember that," says Mom, and she steps back for a second to scrutinize at Sandro as if she were looking at him for the first time. "But I don't remember you at all."

"I realize that. How kind of you. That makes me so happy. Five years together. Five."

"That was a long time ago. Maybe you've changed and I don't recognize you."

"No, no, no, no. I haven't changed at all. It's just that we were in two different worlds. You were way up top, the prettiest girl in school, while I, unfortunately, was on the minor slopes of dorkdom. But jeezus. You'd think looking at me, now that I've told you at least . . . jeezus."

"Don't take it so hard, Mr. Sandro, and don't worry about it," says Zot. "You're among friends here; Luna and I are the dorks at school, too."

"Speak for yourself," I say. "I'm not a dork. I'm a loner."

"Me too," says Sandro, "that's what I was: a rebel, different, zero interest in being lumped together with winners like your mom."

"Nah," she says, "you wish. You were a total dork. Period."

"You don't even remember me."

"Exactly. I would have noticed a rebel. Rebels are hot. You on the other hand were definitely nothing but a dork."

For a little while Mr. Sandro says nothing, just nods. Then he says, "You're right, Serena, you're right. Strange to think that you did this thing at school one day that I still remember as being one of the most beautiful things in my life. How about that," he says, and that's all. He goes to study the statue.

"And what was it I did? When? What did I do?"

"Nothing, nothing, I'm too much of a dork to talk to you. I might as well keep it to myself."

"Come on, tell me."

Mr. Sandro shakes his head, sticks his hands in his pockets, and leans over to look at the stone, the pattern made from stone hammering stone, then the feet, the hands, the round eyes returning his stare.

"This thing really does look like Panizzi."

"Would you tell me what I did? When was it? At school? On a field trip?"

"It's identical to Panizzi. I'm sorry I don't have a photo to show you, kids, because that's him all right."

And then Ferro, who in the meantime had found a seat on a bench and kept his mouth shut, chimes in too. "You ask me, he looks like a kid from Florence from back in my lifeguarding days. Very same scrawny legs."

"But think about it, Grandfather, this intrepid warrior is three thousand years old. Don't you find that incredible?"

"Sure do. In fact that thing they say about the giraffe is utter bullshit."

"What thing about the giraffe?"

"That thing they say on television, that giraffes got those long necks because the ones with longer necks could hack it better, so afterward they were all born that way."

"Evolution, Grandfather. Evolution, theorized by Professor Charles Darwin."

"I don't know his name. All I know is, it's a crock. How could people believe that? Once upon a time people would believe anything you told them."

"But they still believe it, Grandfather! I mean it's true, it's one of the most important discoveries in the history of the universe."

"Cut the crap. Open your eyes and you see immediately it's not true. Take that statue there. How old is it?"

"Three thousand years old."

"Right, and it looks like a kid who used to come to my beach. And it looks like their principal. In three thousand years we haven't changed a smidge. And why's that?"

"What do you mean?" asks Mr. Sandro.

"I mean that at a certain point we descended from monkeys, right? That's how the story goes: there were monkeys and then they began to lose their hair and straighten their backs and then came men, no? So how is it we stopped there? Christ, that guy looks exactly like us. We haven't changed a bit."

"Fair enough, Ferro. But it takes time to change."

"Time? Didn't you hear the kid? That thing is three thousand years old. And what about the giraffes? Why did the giraffe's neck not keep getting longer? At what point did it decide to stop?"

"Well," says Sandro, "it's not like it can go on for infinity—"

"It's a fairy tale, a stupid fairy tale people believe because they don't want to dwell on it, so they say sure, who cares, must be true. And instead it's a crock. Get off it. First there were fish, then fish suddenly come out of the water and crawl to the shore since their fins have turned into arms, and they stop breathing water and start breathing air instead; they grow legs and lollygag around . . . Get off it, people, does that really sound possible to you?"

Sandro looks at Zot, Zot I guess looks at me, but Mom and me haven't said anything from the start, so don't count on us finding our voices now. Ferro alone is left to explain how life functions in the universe, and his voice keeps rising and echoing off the church walls. That must be the reason he seems so serious.

"And how come if dinosaurs were so tough they aren't around anymore, while fleas, cockroaches, ticks, and sewer rats still abound? And look at these two," he says, waving his arms at Zot and me. I figured he would come around to us. I didn't want to have any part in this story. All I wanted was to look at the statue of the people of Luna in peace. But no.

"If that thing about selection were true, these two would have lasted five minutes. Six, tops. Instead here they are, wandering around, and tonight they'll sleep in a tent and enjoy themselves too, and maybe someone might poke fun of them, sure, but you'll see, they'll shrug it off and stay their course. Because everything operates according to destiny. Evolution is a crock. Strong or weak, right or wrong, everything happens the way it happens because it has to happen that way."

"Okay," I say, "does that make Zot and me fleas and ticks?"

"Exactly," says Ferro. "Hit the nail on the head. See? The girl gets it. Now that's enough talking. My throat's sore. Did you get me my wine?"

Mr. Sandro looks at Mom, Mom I guess looks at him, and they take out two big bottles of water. Ferro raises his arms and you can see he's about to offend some saint, then he remembers where he is and steps out of the church first.

He hurries over to the door, then stops abruptly and turns around. And with the evening light behind him, he becomes a dark upright figure staring at us.

"And another thing: if we come from monkeys, how come there are still monkeys?"

If there were a horror movie on at night, Marino's mom had to watch it, and because they only had one TV there were no other options. Well, except one: Marino could stay in his room, crank up Bon Jovi, and keep doing his homework. Sometimes, however, his mom wanted company, and she'd tell him, "Turn off those girly-haired queers." Bon Jovi aren't queer, he'd say. On the contrary, every time they left the house they had to run for it because thousands of women were waiting to throw themselves at them, and she'd say, "Of course they'd run, they're queers. Quit dreaming, Marino. Come watch a little reality with me." Marino would do as told and go sit beside her and they'd watch these tales of haunted castles and zombies and vampires and Egyptian mummies who'd come back to avenge themselves on random people. In the dark of the living room the cigarette smoke mounted like the ghostly clouds in those movies.

Everything scared him, even when nothing was happening, even during the happy scenes. They were the worst, actually, since Marino knew that those happy people were headed for the gory bit, then the gory bit came and he would cover his eyes but it was no use because the freaky music would make him even more terrified.

When the movies ended, Marino's nightmares began. Lying in bed in the dark, he'd watch the objects around him suddenly turn sinister and frightening: a white shirt on his chair flickered like a ghost, the collection of Smurfs on his bookshelf transformed into small blue malevolent monsters, even Bon Jovi stared at him from the poster hanging in his closet, demons with teased hair.

So you can imagine how he feels right now, all alone in the dark, lying on a moldy bed in Ghost House. He hadn't wanted to stay here. He'd wanted to go back to his place with Rambo, and instead Rambo had gone alone and left him here; he'd given him one pill for the pain and one to sleep and sayonara. What's more, at the hospital they administered half a pill each, but Rambo told him that didn't make sense, that if half a pill were enough then why didn't they come like that in the box, halved. So he'd made him swallow them, and now Marino doesn't feel any pain; he doesn't feel anything besides a heavy sleep closing his eyes and a terrible fear keeping them open. And in the battle between the two he lies there motionless staring at the shadows of the woods outside entering through the little window, cast by the light of the full moon.

Long and strange, they stretch from the dirty floor to the walls then taper and climb to the ceiling, sharp and menacing and black. Marino turns to look at them, dark shadows faintly shifting in the evening wind; as he watches them he feels his eyes closing, sliding downward into the sands of sleep. But then something rouses him, a whisper or a glimmer. He looks around and a lump forms in his throat.

Standing at he foot of the bed are five malicious figures. Five men armed with rifles, dressed in rags, and pointing their narrow, twinkling eyes at him.

"Yo," says the tallest, and his deep and distant voice comes from the deep of night, from the center of the mysterious spiral of fate. "Hey there, doofus."

"Who are you?" asks Marino, his voice trembling. "Please don't hurt me, I'm begging you."

"You know exactly who we are."

"No, I—I really don't. Are you the owners? I didn't want to come here, I swear. Rambo's to blame. I wanted to go to my place. I own an apartment in the Querceta Skyscrapers. Not to brag, but it's the penthouse."

"Skyscrapers? In Querceta?" asks another shadow, a white kerchief around his neck. "I'm from Querceta and I've never heard of them before."

"Really? They're famous. They've been around since the sixties."

"Ah, that explains it. We died in '44."

Silence. Or a kind of silence disrupted by Marino's heart, which is now beating in his ears so loudly it nearly knocks him out of bed.

"Come on, Marino, you still don't know who we are?"

"No, I'm afraid I don't. Are you Mom's friends? Friends of Franco from the veggie mart?"

"No. We're not anybody's friends. We're the five partisans," says the tallest one, coolly. And he looks at Marino with one eye protruding from its socket.

"What do you mean? Which partisans?"

"The five partisans murdered tragically."

"Eh? In what sense?"

"What do they call this place?"

"Ghost House!"

"Attaboy. This is the house and we're the ghosts. Got it?"

Marino nods unconvincingly. "The partisans they hanged?"

They all nod once, slowly.

"But . . . but I'd heard they were four men and a woman. You're all men."

"I'm a woman!" says the one with the white kerchief.

Marino looks at her, examines her closely. "Really?"

"Really, asshole."

"Sorry. Maybe standards have changed. And what with the war, the suffering . . . okay, I'll take your word for it."

The ghost with the kerchief springs forward but is held back by the one next to her.

"Would you listen to this asshole? We come to save him and this is how he treats us."

"Save me?"

"That's right. Although you don't deserve it."

"Save me from what? Oh God, what's happening?"

"Calm down and listen. You know how we died, right?"

"Sure, strung up from those trees outside."

"Exactly. We were hiding out here. We'd gotten wind that German command was looking for us and we needed to leave. But it was raining hard, so we decided to stay another night. We'd get some rest and leave for the mountains by sunup. Only the Germans came that night and we never lived to see sunup."

The supposedly female ghost with the kerchief finishes her story and all five hang their heads and stand silently with the light of the moon casting a chilly glare over them, like morning frost on the grass in winter. Then the tall one speaks again: "Anyway, you don't have to make the same mistake. We stayed another night but there was no such night for us. There's no such night for you either, Marino."

"Huh? What do you mean? Pardon me but what do the Germans want from me?"

"Germans? You wish! The war's over, the Germans have other fish to fry. They're working hard and kicking our keisters—what would the Germans want with you?"

"Right, my point exactly. So what's the problem?"

"The problem is time's up, Marino, you have to hustle. Tomorrow it will be too late."

"But what can I do? Can't you see the state I'm in?"

"Enough with the excuses. For forty years you were just fine, and what did you do? Zilch. So now that you're in a bind you have to use your head. Drop the dead weight, Marino, or it'll sink you. Whatever's dead doesn't exist anymore. Dump it, Marino, throw it away."

"Look who's talking, you died in '44 and you're still here."

"Listen, dickhead," says the one who claims to be a woman, "we died for your sake. We sacrificed ourselves so that future generations could be free. And frankly, seeing what you've done with all that freedom, I don't think I'd do it again."

The others look at each other and nod. "We sacrificed ourselves for you and you spend your days zoning out with your cell phones and computers and televisions. We should have fucked off into a hole and waited out the end of the war there."

Marino looks at them, but they've stopped looking at him. They stare at the floor and sigh. They don't want to talk anymore. They don't want anything.

"Listen, I'm sorry. We didn't do it on purpose. It's not our fault. When you were young, there was no such thing as the Internet. There were no cell phones, no videogames, none of that stuff. Had there been, maybe you would have used it the same as young people today."

"Young people? Marino, you're not young anymore. You ought to be a man and you're not even that. You're nothing. You're forty years old and you still haven't begun living. But if you don't get a move on tonight, you'll run out of road before you've even launched. Understand?"

"Yes. I mean, no. I mean, I don't know. But—"

"But nothing, Marino. We warned you. Now it's up to you. Just remember there's no time to lose. It's now or never. Now or never."

The last words echo as if they were coming from far away. The trembling light of the moon fades and the five profiles blur and bleed into the wall behind them until all Marino can see is that wall. As a matter of fact, Marino can see nothing, because his eyes are closed.

He only opens them now as he feels a powerful grip shaking him. Above him, right on top of him, stands another ghost, as white as the others, same eyes spilling out of their sockets, same words spilling out of his mouth: "Marino, wake up, there's no time to lose, we've got to get a move on!"

Marino pulls himself up as best he can, smiles, and tries to bring his friend Rambo into focus. "I know, they told me already."

"Huh? When?"

"Just now. They've been telling me for the last three hours."

"Okaay . . . Anyhow, listen carefully. Something bad happened. I called you and you didn't pick up. I called Sandro and he didn't pick up. So I had to make a decision. I had to, Marino. I brought your Mom here."

"Really? That's fantastic, Rambo, where is she? Why hasn't she come to say hi?"

Rambo looks at him and frowns. "Isn't she dead, Marino?"

"Yes, of course, I just thought that . . . seeing as the partisans were here, see—"

"She's in the kitchen. I'm sorry but I had no other option. We couldn't keep her in your house. And she can't stay here either. We've got to get going immediately. I'm sorry, pal, but we have to."

"I know we have to, Rambo, and right away. We owe it to the partisans."

Rambo pulls backs but continues to stare at his friend. His face, the expression written on it.

Sometimes nothing is more unsettling than a smile.

THE MUSHROOMS OF TRANSYLVANIA

Georg keeps walking in the dark. He looks around but sees nothing. He's desperate. He doesn't know what to do. He's given up looking for mushrooms. All he wants is to reach the road back and find his friends, but he doesn't know which way to go, so he stops for a minute. And that's when he hears it. It sounds like a sigh, although maybe someone was whispering. But who? And what could they be saying? George doesn't know and doesn't want to know. All he wants is to get out of there. He starts to run, but he's traveling in circles in this really intricate forest, and he's getting tired, and that evil sigh keeps getting closer and closer . . . "

Mr. Sandro makes these really weird scary faces while he tells this story, the flashlight pointed under his chin. It's completely dark except for the lone light contorting his face and this huge shadow on the side of the tent behind him, all the scarier given that the tent should be taut and firm but instead it sags and looks like it could collapse on top of us at any moment.

Ferro's tent is real old. It's not even really his. Some German tourists ditched it years ago. They'd tried to camp out on the beach at night but that's illegal, and Ferro had gone to tell them to leave. And seeing as you never know who you might come across in the dark, he'd gone out there armed with a paddle. He woke them by thwacking the tent a couple times and they ran off as they were and were never seen again. What can still be seen are the holes the paddle made, two or three on one side. Mice have made some smaller holes.

So what if it's saggy and bitten-through? The tent's still stand-ing and we're here sitting in a circle while Mr. Sandro tells us this story about poor George who had gone looking for mushrooms with his friends and instead got lost in a freaky forest.

"And all of a sudden, from up in a chestnut tree, he hears a different sound, a sinister sound. He looks up and sees a large bat flying in circles above him, diving toward him, poised to strike. So George throws his basket of mushrooms at it—it was empty anyways—and runs toward the trees, and each step brings him farther into the mysterious dark, and George is des-perate because he knows that the Apennines are unpre-dictable, dangerous mountains and who knows what's hiding around every corner in that—"

"The Apennines?" says Zot, his voice trembling. "Excuse me, Mr. Sandro, I thought this was in Transylvania?"

"Right, sorry, did I say the Apennines? I meant Transylvania. Moving along—"

And like George, we hear this weird noise come out of nowhere, like when something nasty gets caught in the sink and the water goes up and down. But it's not a sink; it's Ferro, lying in the back of the tent, trying to speak.

"You can find . . . porcini there . . . thick as table legs."

"Where, Grandfather? In Transylvania?"

"No, no, in the Apennines."

"But we're not in the Apennines. We're in Transylvania."

Ferro doesn't say anything else. He lifts his arm and waves it around at random. Then it flops back down at his side. He snorts, maybe falls asleep, and the tent fills with his poisonous breath. Since they hadn't bought him wine and he and water don't mix, he'd eaten his cheese and anchovy sandwich with half a bottle of Dry Death he'd brought along for the trip. Now his breath is making my head spin.

"Anyways, George is running in the haunted forest in Transylvania. The trees coil together right in front of his eyes, and the branches look like skeletons' arms reaching out to grab him, and behind him the bat continues its pursuit, and around him he hears moaning and the rattling of chains getting closer and closer. But just when he thinks his time is up, George reaches a place where the trees thin out. He sees the sky and the moon shining above. The moon is gigantic and full, just like the moon tonight, kids. So George stops and feels this force burning underneath his skin. He feels these hairs shooting up from his body, mounds of wiry hair. He feels his face warping and stretching. He feels his nails fall out and in their place spring these long sharp claws. He raises his head to the moon and out comes a frightening howl: Owooooo!"

"So it's a werewolf story!" says Zot with what little breath he has left. "At first it had all the makings of a ghost story."

"Or a vampire story," I say. "What with the huge bat."

"Phooey," says Ferro, splayed out behind us, "more like a shitty story."

Mr. Sandro doesn't answer, just goes: "Fine. Then I won't tell you how it ends." He removes the flashlight from under his chin and switches it off. Suddenly the tent goes real dark. Zot and I would like him to switch it back on and continue so we can find out what happens, but maybe it's better this way. It could be too scary. So we keep quiet, and Mom gets the final word: "More like not the kind of story you tell kids who are about to spend the night in the woods." She gets up. "Well, I'm tired. I'm going to sleep. Are you sure you kids still want to sleep in this stinky contraption?"

We don't answer immediately but as soon as I say I'm sure Zot seconds me. Just the two of us sleep here, and the grown ups go sleep in the back of the jeep, since there's room enough for them to be almost comfy. I'd liked this idea of sleeping in the tent, I still like it, but in the dark I'm slowly beginning to see the shadows of trees moving across the tent, and they sort of scare me.

And anyhow the forest is still wonderful. We totally lucked out coming here. We left the little square by the church and there was a sign indicating SELVA DI FILETTO—PICNIC AREA. And maybe we didn't come here to picnic, but we did have the sandwiches, and wherever there's a picnic area there's space. So we came here. And on the way Zot opened the guide to Lunigiana, flipped to the page about these woods, and cried, "Saint Catherine of Siena!" He grabbed my arm and squeezed it so hard my skin stung. Then he read it to me:

"The Filetto Forest is a goldmine of stele statues. Many have been rediscovered in this ancient forest. Some are still standing in their original spots. They may have been placed here by the people of Luna to protect this thousand-year-old forest, which was considered magical even in prehistoric times, when tribes would gather in the night for pagan rituals."

That's what the guide said and no one had anything else to add. Even Mom quit complaining. Clearly we were supposed to spend the night here.

Only now, after Mr. Sandro's story, this forest is beginning to scare me, and while he and Mom get up to leave us, it makes me happy to hear Ferro snoring heavily. Even if we wanted to wake him up, it would be impossible to drag him out of the tent.

"So you're staying, kids?" asks Mom.

"Yeah, we'll hold each other a little."

"Luna, do you want me to stay here too?"

"No, really, Mom, Ferro's here. We're good."

"Okay. But I'm right next door, all right? Should anything happen, I'm right here."

"Okay. I'm good."

"And tomorrow we'll visit the museum with the Luna statues, okay?"

"Yeah, Mom, we're psyched. Can you believe practically all of them were here? The people of Luna planted them all right where we are."

"Precisely," says Zot, "and who knows how many have yet to be discovered." I had been about to say the same thing. I turn toward him and we nod at each other for a bit, and we don't stop till Mom leans over and kisses me, then goes to kiss Zot, who flinches at first because he doesn't know what Mom wants, whether she intends to slap him or spit on him. When she kisses him on the cheek, Zot lets out this jittery, excited laugh. Then he gets real quiet.

"Goodnight, kids," says Sandro, "may the Lord be with you."

"Goodnight," I say. "Tomorrow you'll tell us how George's story ends, right?"

Sandro chuckles and nods, then zips the tent shut and he and Mom become two real long shadows headed for the jeep. And we lie here in silence.

Well, sort of silence. Ferro's snoring and every so often mumbles what could be words but sound more like broken stuff rattling inside a large box. I lie tummy up with Zot next to me and we watch the light of the moon turn red across the deflated, torn tent. I pull the blanket up and it feels much better to be under here, lying on the ground, on top of us the blanket, above us the tent and the trees of the forest that stretch out right in front of us and finally the moon, way up there, fuller than full.

"How do you think it'll end, Zot?" I whisper.

"How will what end? George's story or ours in Lunigiana?"

"George's."

"Ah, unfortunately I don't know the answer to that. Maybe now that he's a wolf he can get away faster or his instincts give him the passion he needs to fight back or . . . I couldn't say. The possibilities are endless."

"And ours? How does ours end?"

"Oh boy, who knows how ours ends, Luna, who knows."

And we lie there, in the silence of the night, while the crickets play their song to make the females fall in love with them. How can the female figure out who plays best inside all that music? It's one unchanging noise on all sides, and if you ask me, the female cricket must tire of listening at some point and pick one at random, must latch onto the first cricket she finds, fine by her.

And Ferro piles onto the crickets' song, snoring and drowning everything out, only stopping occasionally, and when he does stop, he makes these noises with his mouth that sometimes seem like words.

But at a certain point they become actual words. I understand them and Zot must understand them too since he squeezes my arm under the blanket. And we listen breathlessly to this warped voice that doesn't even sound like his. It's deeper, as if it were coming from far away, rising and falling real weird. Weirder yet is what he says: "The chestnut . . . under the chestnut . . . hurry . . . I'm waiting for you under the V-shaped chestnut tree."

I swear that's what he says.

A faint garbled noise has persisted since they left Ghost House. For a minute Rambo had imagined it was coming from inside the bag on the seat next to him. Moaning, maybe, or maybe the nails of Marino's mom had thawed out and were starting to move again and scratching the plastic to get free. That's not it. Clearly that's not it. To entertain the thought for even a second is ridiculous. But hell, when you're driving beside a dead woman it's hard to remain sharp and lucid.

Anyhow, the noise has a simple explanation: the wheels of the Panda are scraping the frame under the weight of their load. Marino explains it to him, half prone in the backseat, his voice pained but rational. He's been like this since Rambo arrived at Ghost House with the old lady. On the way there he had thought of a thousand ways of clarifying the situation to his friend, ways of getting it through to him that they had to move out, that they had no alternative and there was no time and they had to do something quick. But Marino was already convinced they needed to do something. He'd even come up with a killer plan.

He'd sent Rambo to pick up black garbage bags, rope, and the cinder blocks outside Ice Dream Gelato.

"What cinder blocks?"

"The ones used for umbrella stands."

"What are we going to do with them?"

"We need weight and Ice Dream has the heaviest blocks.

The ones outside the bar in front of the newsstand are heavy too, but that's too far downtown and someone could see you. Ice Dream is the perfect weight-to-risk compromise. Get four."

"Heck, I'll get five."

"Overkill. Four will do. Now get going."

And Rambo had gone, and sure enough it was a desert outside the gelato shop and the cinder blocks were seriously heavy. He'd loaded them into the trunk of the Panda and returned to Ghost House, broke his back for good carrying Marino and then Marino's mom to the Panda, and they were off. Then came this godawful sound, but it's not her scratching the bag, it's the wheels abrading the fender of this shitty car in this shitty night and how things will turn out Rambo hasn't a clue. Luckily Marino knows everything. His degree of pragmatism and clear-headedness is frightening, apart from the occasional mention of partisans that Rambo doesn't understand, but now is not the time for understanding.

"We're going to Bagno Italia. It has access to the sea. We'll run to the beach and snag the paddleboat closest to the water.

"Okay. Let's hope we find a paddleboat with oars."

"Now that squid season has begun, it'll be full of paddleboats. We'll find as many as we want and pick the one closest to shore."

They ride on, all the way to the coastal road, which during the summer is noisy and lit up at night, with cars zipping by, so many that if you drank in the thousand headlights passing by they'd turn into a shimmering river carrying you toward life, toward possibility, toward the future. Now, a month later, there's nothing but a Panda Italia '90 struggling to cross it, and on this long stretch of asphalt flanked by closed beach clubs and closed restaurants and closed discos, it's just the two of them. Or three, if Marino's mom counts. But maybe she doesn't count.

"You sure the sea is our best option?"

"Yes," says Marino.

"It wouldn't be better if, for example . . . don't take this the wrong way, but wouldn't it be better if we burned her?"

"No. That's overkill. Mom has to disappear but with the utmost dignity. Setting her on fire is out of the question."

"You've got a point. But say there's a storm and she washes back up."

"With the cinder blocks that would be impossible. She'll sink to the bottom and the sand will gradually cover her. If you think about it, it's the burial of a lifetime, at the bottom of the blue sea instead of underground with the worms. See, Mom loved two things: going to the beach and keeping me out of trouble." As he speaks, Marino smiles and points upward. "You know, Rambo, I feel like at this moment Mom's happy up there. I am too. And so are the partisans."

JELLYFISH SEX

If you want to sleep alone, you can take the car and I'll sleep outside. Really, it's not a problem," says Sandro, opening the rear hatch of the jeep.

This magic hole they call a mouth continues to surprise him. Like a magician's hat, out come rabbits, flowers, doves. Anything can escape your mouth, except what you're really thinking.

Yet Serena doesn't answer him, just enters the jeep, so he climbs in and removes the seats, which were designed to make room for shovels, pitchforks, submachine guns, ammunition chests, and whatever other paraphernalia could come in handy for the owner of a tank like that. Or for the two of them to lie down, if this amazing woman, her hair dancing in the moonlight, should say that no, she doesn't mind if he sleeps there. But no such luck; she just spreads a towel out and sits down and her eyes wander over the metal body of the car and the large side windows and the small windows on the roof framing the stars. Finally Serena's eyes land on him, and even if eyes that magnificent tell you a million things all at once, each frighteningly profound, in reality Serena says nothing. So Sandro tries to smile, waves his hand, climbs down from the jeep, and starts to close the hatch.

"Where the hell are you going?"

"Um, outside. Or in the tent with the kids."

"There's no room in the tent."

"True. On the ground then. It's not a problem. It's not that cold out."

"Right, sure it isn't," says Serena. She lies back, crosses her arms behind her head, and looks at him from down there in all her beauty. "Where do you think you're going? Come here."

Sandro swallows deeply a few times, nods, and tries to keep from smiling too much. Go on, Sandro, go on, Sandrino, tonight's your night. She told you she'll sleep with you. She said "Come here," in a voice as steamy as the radiators in Aunt Gilda and Uncle Athos's house. Athos had fought in Russia and endured such cold weather that he never wanted to endure it again, so they blasted the radiators year-round. Five minutes at their place and fruit would rot. One time they got a goldfish that practically died on arrival, slowly boiled in its bowl. That's the effect this insanely hot woman's voice has on him—clearly she's the woman for him—and she's lying there in the moonlight asking him to come to her. A woman who the day before only wanted to punch and kick him, and now she's agreeing to sleep together. Well, not exactly together, but pretty damn close. And Sandro needs to remain calm and navigate this smoothly. Step by step, Sandrino, step by step.

He gets in the car and closes the hatch behind him as if he were shutting out the rest of the world. Beat it, universe, go screw things up elsewhere. Leave us alone tonight.

Sandro lies down next to Serena and would like to hurry up and say something intelligent but nothing comes to him. So he racks his brain for something perhaps not so intelligent that will at least fill up the silence, but not even that comes to him. Luckily she thinks of something.

"Look, now you have to tell me."

"Tell you what, sorry?"

"The story from before. You can't start to say something like that and just stop; tell me what happened."

"Oh, nothing. Actually I was making it up as I went along. Maybe it ends with him turning into a werewolf and killing the bat. Or maybe he finds his way back to the road and is saved. Or maybe—"

"Who cares about that story? I meant the thing at school."

" . . . "

"Come on, that thing before in the church, what I did at high school that you said was one of the most beautiful moments in your life. What did I do? I don't remember."

"Of course you don't. You don't even remember that I went to school with you."

"It's not that I don't remember you; I'm convinced you weren't there."

"What?" Sandro tries to sound offended but can't help laughing. "Not only do you not remember me, now you want to erase five years of my life."

"It's just I really don't—"

"Go ahead. Erase them. You'd actually be doing me a favor. Five shitty years."

"Really?"

"Really. Nothing went the way I wanted. I wanted the girls to throw themselves at me and clearly none of you even noticed I was there, and as if to make up for that, all the guys threw themselves at me—to kick my ass."

"Kick your ass? Why would they do that?"

"Because I wasn't like them. I was a rebel. I was punk."

"Wait a second, were you that guy with the red mohawk and the pin in his car?"

"No, that was Bindi."

"There, see, him I remember. He was hot. Did you have a mohawk?"

"No, I was—I had long hair. I mean, longish. And I wore this leather jacket with pins."

"Huh. I don't think you were a rebel. If you were I'd have noticed you. I've always been into rebels, unfortunately."

"Hold up. You were into posers, like your fiancé Fiori. It's easy to rock ratty clothes and play the guitar on the road when daddy's a notary and you go home and there's a housemaid to heat your supper. You know what happened to Fiori? Same thing that happened to all of his kind: he wears a coat and tie to breakfast and dinners he organizes at the Lions Club. Some rebel your friend turned out to be."

Sandro unravels; it's a subject that pisses him off and he's even raised his voice. Serena remains silent for a minute, long enough to make him worry. Fool, all he had to do was talk and let her talk, crack two simpatico jokes, smile, and gradually snuggle up to her. Instead he got carried away thinking about that asshole Fiori who had once snatched a Dead Kennedys button from his backpack, spat on it, and placed it back. "There," he'd said, "Tomorrow I'll wash another for you." Even today, more than twenty years later, that dick continues to ruin his life, putting poisonous words in his mouth to repel Serena.

Only they don't. Fortunately after another moment she starts talking again. "I know he's rich and sad, but do you know what's really sad? That I was with him for a year and I left him right after discovering he was rich. Tell me I'm not a fool."

"No, Serena, you're not a fool. You were right to leave him. He may have been loaded, but imagine how depressing your life would have been."

"Hah. And look at me now—sheer joy." She pulls herself up, leans toward the window, and looks out at the dark and the tent surrounded by the dark. It must be peaceful out there, because a minute later she turns back and lies down next to him again. And maybe it's just him, but he senses Serena's a little closer now, her hand on the carpet almost touching him.

"All right, time's up. Tell me what I did in high school that you liked so much."

"Okay. I mean, it's no big deal, you probably didn't think twice about it."

"Probably not, but now I want to know." She turns on her side and draws about an inch closer, which may not be much but Sandro can feel her all over his skin.

And that may explain why he doesn't know where to start. He takes a deep breath, so deep his lungs hurt, but along with the air he inhales Serena's scent, which helps him launch into the story.

"It was the end-of-year senior dance, at that club on the coastal road that's now been converted into apartments."

"La Caravella."

"Right, that's it. You were out in the middle of the dance floor circled by a bunch of guys who were trying to dance with you."

"Ah," says Serena briskly. She looks at him quietly for a moment, then: "And one of those losers was you."

"No, I was in a corner with my friends, by the bathroom."

"What were you doing?"

"What I was doing doesn't matter. I don't remember. Most likely we were talking shit about everyone who passed by and the commercial music they were playing."

"Sounds fun."

"There wasn't anything else to do. Besides, no one was paying any attention to us. Anyways, you were off dancing and every guy in school was standing around you trying to catch your eye. The saddest people imaginable. And at one point . . . at one point someone on the dance floor fainted, just dropped to the ground."

"What? I didn't see that. I wasn't aware."

"Of course you were, you were the first person to run over there. You went and—"

"No I didn't. Look, I may be an idiot but I would have remembered that. If someone fainted in front of me there's no way I'd forget it."

"In fact he didn't *faint* faint. Maybe he just slipped. But you ran over and caught him before he fell, because otherwise . . . otherwise, I don't know, he may have cracked his skull and . . . "

"Well, aside from the fact that that doesn't seem like such a fantastic feat to me, I don't think it actually happened."

"Of course it did! I saw it with my own two eyes. I remember it like it was yesterday."

"Oh really? So what was I wearing?"

Sandro doesn't answer her right away. He looks at Serena, focuses on her with all his strength as if he could see through time. He can't screw this one up. He has to stay calm and not screw this one up.

"Let's see, you were wearing the same kind of army pants you have on now, an undershirt and a button-down shirt; I can't remember whether that was army too or denim."

"Good guess. I've always dressed like that."

"Fine but that's not my fault. And see, I remember."

"No, actually, you don't," says Serena. Except she says it strangely. Her tone has changed. In fact Sandro catches it and stops studying her hips and looks back up into her eyes, which shine in the dark with a light he doesn't like anymore.

"Of course I do."

"No, that's not what I was wearing. I was in pajamas and gym socks that night."

"Yeah right, that's not true. No way you'd come to the dance in pajamas."

"My point exactly. I never went to the dance. I stayed home."

"What? That's impossible. I was there that year. Or maybe it was the year before—"

"Never went. I already had to see those losers at school; you can imagine my desire to run into them at night. Besides, the principal would announce the winner of Miss High School, and every year it was me. Do you think I had any interest in getting up on stage and . . . No, I'm sorry, you're mistaken.

Plus you're a fool. I mean, you liked me that much and didn't realize I never went to the dances?"

Sandro looks at her. He doesn't answer yes or no. He tries to come up with the right answer, although clearly there is none. Finally he throws up his hands and looks down. "I don't know, Serena, I never went either."

An infinitely long moment of silence. Then: "So why even say that crap?" Serena sits up, looks at him, and appears about to leave, but then stays. "'You know, in high school you did this beautiful thing that I'll never forget'—and then you make up some garbage about the end-of-year dance. What was the point? Are you making fun of me? Huh? Is this your idea of fun?"

Sandro doesn't answer, doesn't say anything, just looks at her. He's an imbecile and knows it. This fairy tale about the dance was totally pointless, it was bound to blow up in his face, yet he still said it to avoid saying how things really stand. That's his problem: for him, "how things stand" are meager and lousy, which is why he tries to boost himself up with other stuff, stuff he accumulates in the hopes of looking a little less sad. But then that stuff collapses and all that's left standing is the squalid truth, caked in dust from messes like this.

But not this time; this time things can't end that way. Sandro feels strange, out of breath. He sits with his back to the window and suddenly something crazy and frightening slips out of his mouth, like in that documentary where the guy goes to Costa Rica and eats a piece of fruit, inside of which is a kind of worm, and the insect grows in his body and one day out of nowhere he feels something in his throat, opens his mouth, and out comes this gigantic cockroach.

Well, the same things happens to Sandro now. Only out of his mouth comes this absurd thing called the truth.

"Listen, Serena," he says, trying to look her in the eye. "I'm a fool, but you already knew that, so please don't get mad. True, I made up that story about the dance, but only to tell you a specific day, a beautiful thing you once did. But it wasn't like that with you; you were always beautiful. Doing the occasional beautiful thing would be too easy. Take serial killers. When they're caught, the neighbors on TV always say that they can't believe it, that he was such a nice guy, this one time he lent them milk, another time he got their cat to climb down from the roof. One time, yep, then the day after he opened folks up with a chainsaw. Do you know how many people I'd run into on the street after school who would wave and smile, then the next morning in front of everyone else they'd make fun of me or draw dicks and swastikas on my Vespa. But not you, Serena. You were different because you were always the same. You were always you, every time I looked at you. And I looked at you a ton. One time I even thought about buying a tiny camera advertised in a magazine, the kind spies used, it said, to take photos of you. I'm not embarrassed to admit it. I mean, I am a little, but I'm telling you anyways: I thought about it. The only reason I didn't buy it was because they said it would take a month to arrive. It was May and school was almost out. At any rate, I wanted to take pictures of you, but not because you were pretty. I mean, you were pretty, you were beautiful, and you are now. It's absurd; you're even more beautiful now. That's true and you know it and don't deny it. But that's not the reason I wanted to take pictures of you. I didn't want to photograph your ass or your tits and jerk off to them at night. I mean, maybe that too, but that wasn't my number one motive. My motive was that I wanted to photograph what you looked like when you arrived at school, what you looked like when you left class, when the principal told you that you had to wear the Miss High School sash and you didn't even answer him. I wanted to take a photo of who you really are, always and only the way you wanted to be, everywhere and with everyone, not worrying about fitting in, not even noticing whether you did or not, and you went on gracing people with this beauty.

They may have been idiots and morons and imbeciles, but I promise you they were aware of your beauty. That's what I wanted to take a picture of, since a picture makes something that is really a moment and which you'll never encounter again last forever. In fact I never came across anything like it again, year after flat, indistinguishable year. Up until last winter, when I returned to school and met Luca. Luca was like that, just like you, and I may not have a dime but if I did, I'd bet it on Luna growing up to be like that too. You can already tell. You raised two amazing kids by yourself, without a father or anything, and that's how they turned out. What have I done? You got me. I haven't done dick. I can't even say that I succeeded in doing what I wanted to in life, because I didn't even try, I just put everything off. And I mean everything. On my desk is a letter from a kid in elementary school. I found it in the pine grove one day, attached to a balloon that took this crazy journey and landed there, and all it asked in return was a postcard. But after that long journey the balloon had the bad luck of ending up with a guy like me who brings it home and says, 'Tomorrow I'll buy a postcard and put it in the mail,' then tomorrow turns into the next day, then the next . . . Nine years have gone by, Serena, nine years! What would it have cost me to pick up a postcard and write, 'Get fucked,' and mail it? But no, all I did was put it off—the way I did with everything—until one day it's too late and you can't even try anymore, the thought alone makes you hang your head. You look around and find you have nothing that you wanted, you don't even know what it is you want. As a matter of fact, maybe I don't want anything. Scratch that. I know what it is I want, Serena. I want you."

There, Sandro said it, and now that he's out of words, he's out of breath. All he has left is the wild and relentless thump of his heart. That strange thing he felt in his throat has disappeared; he can breathe easier. It's as if, escaping his lips, those words had swept away all that had backed up and gotten lodged there. He lies down on his side, his back to Serena, facing away. He doesn't say anything, just silence, overwhelming after all those words, just silence and the crickets outside. And the rustle of Serena's clothes as she lies down too. Maybe she wants to sleep. Maybe, like him, she's pretending. Who knows. It doesn't matter.

What matters is, it went badly. Sandro had held out hope but it went badly. That happens when you take a chance on something. And now all he can do is force himself to stay still while he lies next to Serena and stares daggers sharp enough to carve a hole in the body of the car and infuriate Rambo.

Rambo must already be infuriated. He's called ten times tonight and sent a message saying, "Call me, it's a mess here," but Sandro didn't answer and didn't call him back. Because he's no friend, he's a shit who only thinks of himself and what he wants. Or what he wanted and now knows he can't have. Perhaps he ought to hop out of this goddamn jeep and call Rambo and find out what's going on and—

But there'll be none of that. Because that's talk, and talk is air. It fades the moment Sandro feels something light and delicate yet real, the way only things you can touch seem real. Touching *him*, rather. Someone caressing his arm, perhaps, a hand brushing against him. Serena's hand. Sandro turns to stone. A burning hot stone with his eyes wide open, trying to see behind him without turning over, without moving, because stones don't move. Besides, maybe it's an accident. Maybe Serena has already drifted off and rolled over in her sleep. That must be it. But he continues to feel it, this caress, this touch, and Sandro starts to think perhaps it's beckoning him. Even a rock would respond to the call of a hand that fabulous. Sandro turns abruptly, and Serena is right there, closing her bright eyes, her wonderful mouth, that half-smile that isn't a smile because it has been permanently affixed to her lips, now trembling and changing into something new and less sure of itself, which Sandro tries to look at but doesn't see anymore, because Serena's mouth is too close now, it's on his, just as she's on him, or he's on her, skin seeking other skin, rubbing together so hard they become one, salty and hot and alive.

They kiss, she bites his bottom lip then puts her tongue back in Sandro's mouth. He kisses it and doesn't really know what to do, because his lips are on her lips, and meanwhile his fingers explore her sides and Serena presses her leg between his . . . and suddenly Sandro's life becomes very interesting in more than one place. After years of indistinguishable days with nothing to rouse him, now there are important occasions all over that require his attention. Every once in a while she pulls herself off of him and says something, although perhaps they're not words but a warm sigh combined with a kind of moaning in Sandro's ear. He runs his mouth along her neck, to kiss and lick it but especially to open his eyes and take in this wonderful woman, even if the dim light only hints at her wonders. Women might like this dim light, the soft and romantic mood it creates, but not Sandro. He'd prefer the blazing noonday sun that burns ants in the street. He'd prefer mounting one of those lights that ships use to cast signals on the coast from thousands of miles away and aiming it straight at Serena. Because he's never laid hands on a woman this amazing—he may never have even laid eyes on one—so he'd like to see her fully. Every contour, every smooth and perfect spot that he can feel with his hands: he'd like to be able to film her and re-watch the tape endlessly, sit on a couch and spend his life in front of the screen and die with his eyes open, like Marino's mom.

Well, of course. How like Sandro to think of that. Just as he was running a hand over her cotton army shirt and arriving at the curve of her hips and sliding it up under her shirt, Sandro thinks of Marino's dead mom on the couch. Like when he was twenty and people told him that in order not to get off too quickly and last a little longer, he should think horrible thoughts about dead people or torn limbs or run-over dogs and cats or the bathroom at a nursing home at the end of the day. And so what if he was twenty at the time and now he's twice as old and the deal should be different? To make the difference there would have to have been ample experience in the interim. Yet there was no such experience, so Sandro has to keep thinking of dead Lidia while his hands crawl up Serena's back, bowed and shivering. He feels her legs enclose his, and in a second he flips her around so that now Serena is no longer on her side but on top of him, and they may still be wearing pants but those two wispy layers of jeans and military issue-whatever practically don't exist. Down below, Sandro's cock knows it and is delirious. Especially because Serena's stroking his neck with her hands, leaning into him, and Sandro feels her breasts brushing against his chest. She moves her pelvis up and down, up and down, and again he tries to think of Marino's dead and shriveled mom, her skin peeling off her rotten bones. But the skin of Serena, the scent of Serena, and the small noises she makes with her mouth are so hot even Marino's mom in the freezer becomes sensual and arousing.

So it dawns on Sandro that there's not much he can do. He grits his teeth and grabs hold of Serena's ass with both hands, fondling it and guiding it forward and back, forward and back, and at this point it's impossible to resist, impossible to restrain himself. Sandro could hurt himself, might tear it in two, so he removes his hands from Serena's hips and promises he'll be one second, just the time it takes to unbutton his jeans and . . .

In the meantime Serena whispers into his ear and asks for a blanket. Because Sandro may be burning up, but in fact it's damp inside the jeep and the windows are drafty. In lieu of a blanket there's a rubber sheet that Rambo keeps in case of tsunamis and sundry cataclysms, he tells her, and Serena reaches for it while remaining on top of him, arching her back and showing off the criminal beauty of her hips, all the more absurd under those army pants that were made for going to war or hunting or surviving in the woods and definitely not for that kind of splendor. She pushes aside the bags and rummages through the gear, in a long, grinding movement that Sandro feels fully, feels clearly, feels too much. And in order not to bring to an abrupt end this moment that should last forever, he delves back into the world's most horrific thoughts.

He pictures Marino's mom making love with the veggie mart man in the back of the shop, only now he's in the middle, and it turns into a hair-raising threesome. To make matters worse, Lidia is dead, and while Sandro and the veggie mart man take turns, her eyes fall out and worms and gigantic spiders crawl from the holes—

Yet even though Sandro has seen millions of horror movies and has a knack for imagining nasty stuff, nothing that comes to mind could compare with what really happens: when Serena finally finds the rubber sheet, wraps it over her shoulders, and leans up against him again, something falls from the sheet and slams against the hard aluminum floor of the jeep.

Sandro shrugs and returns to fondling her while Serena picks the thing up and is about to move it out of the way. Only she doesn't. She looks at it for a moment, and gradually her rhythm of grinding back and forth slows until she's stopped moving altogether.

And all of a sudden Sandro can't see her body anymore, her ass, the outline of her legs underneath her army pants. Nope, it's all blacked out by Serena's eyes, which are aimed at him, hard as two hammers.

"What the fuck is this," she says.

Sandro lifts himself up to look and an invisible hand reaches down into his throat, slides down the tube conveying air to his lungs, and chokes him.

"What the fuck is this?" says Serena, lifting that thing and waving it in the air as if she'd like to break it over his head. And wood that coarse and heavy could do real damage. It's the wood he tried to sculpt a stele statue from, with the bracelets attached, along with the hacksaw and other equipment Rambo had used to make a better one. Ancient stuff, from just the other day, but to him it seems to belong to another century, to another Sandro who doesn't exist anymore.

He fumbles for an explanation, to make Serena understand it's nothing, she should throw it away, ignore it, go back to loving him and grinding against him forever, as she was doing a moment ago. But it's all over, all of it, and Sandro is the only one who still doesn't understand that. Serena's eyes do, as do the air around them and the crickets outside that have stopped singing. Even Sandro's cock gets it. It has shriveled up and lies there lifeless, flaccid as a jellyfish smashed against the terrible cliffs of destiny.

END OF THE WORLD

T here, did you hear that?"
"No, what did he say?"
"I don't know, it sounded like . . . " Zot whispers, then
we go back to listening to Ferro sleep. We've been sitting
beside him for an hour. Maybe not exactly an hour, but, you
know, even ten minutes is a long time to spend listening to an
old man snore, and the noises he emits sometimes sound like a
man about to suffocate and other times like a broken car that
won't start. But earlier, amid all those noises, Ferro had said
something. We heard him loud and clear. He said, "The chestnut . . . under the chestnut . . . hurry . . . I'm waiting for you
under the V-shaped chestnut tree." Now, someone might say,
"Big deal, a lot of people talk in their sleep, it happens," but
you can tell that that someone wasn't here in the tent, because
otherwise she'd have heard how deep and clear and different
from Ferro's normal voice it was, and, like us, would have gotten goosebumps.

"It's not his voice," Zot had said. "He's under a spell!"
Because in Tages's day and during that whole beautiful past,
back when people would listen to nature and thunder and the
flight of birds, sometimes someone would get drunk or go
crazy and would start talking in a weird voice and saying really
weird things, and today they'd immediately send that person to
an insane asylum, but back then they'd stop to listen to him,
because his words were messages from the beyond and you
had to heed them.

Same as us. We're sitting here quietly, holding the flashlight, primed to hear that voice speak from Ferro's mouth again, in case it has something to add.

"There! There!" goes Zot again. "Did you hear it? He said 'chestnut.' I heard it clearly this time. Or maybe 'checkmate.' Whatever it was, I'm sure it was a word." We lean toward Ferro but there's only the noise of the broken car and the stink of Dry Death that makes my eyes sting. The tent is full of this smell, and if I think about how it's coming from Ferro's stomach, I stop breathing. I try to stand but the tent is low. I bump my head on the tent and the whole thing shakes.

"Careful, Luna. Did you hurt yourself?"

No, I didn't do anything to myself. But I can't stay in here any longer. My legs are burning under my skin; they really don't want to stay still. And neither do I.

"Enough, Zot, Ferro's got nothing else to say. Let's go."

"But where?"

"You heard the voice. We have to go under the V-shaped chestnut tree. He said to hurry."

"Okay. But, first of all, what is a V-shaped chestnut tree? And how are we going to find it in a forest brimming with chestnut trees?"

"I don't know, but if we stay here we definitely won't find it. We have to go."

I say so and as I say so I'm and convinced by what I hear. I look for the tent zipper by running my hand along the side but I can't find it. I thought it was right under here but it's not. So I start poking everywhere, harder and harder, more at random. I feel trapped. I feel locked in this plastic cage that stinks of mold and grappa. Then Zot gets up and I hear the sound of the zipper opening. It takes a moment and finally I stick my head outside, into the real world, with no stinks with no roofs and with a full moon up above bigger than I've ever seen.

"Are we going, Zot?"

"Frankly, Luna, I don't think it's a prudent idea."

"Me neither, obviously. But we're here. We were waiting for a sign and the sign has arrived. I heard it loud and clear and you heard it too. So if you're not coming, then this is goodbye, because I'm going." And I step out of the tent.

I pull on the hood of my sweatshirt and start walking. The stars above are so bright they sizzle in the sky. The truth is I don't see them very well, one by one. I see one whole light smeared across the blackness, but Mom and Luca always told me that they're actually like many tiny dots of light, and that must be beautiful but if you ask me it's even more beautiful the way I see it, as this single, magical immense thing.

Then a sound pulls me away from the sky. It's Zot, in his coat and scarf, tripping and stumbling but finally reaching me. "Wait up, Luna, I'm coming with you!"

I look at him and feel like smiling. Not because of the way he's dressed; I'm happy because he didn't leave me on my own. I signal to him to speak quietly because the jeep is a foot away, and if they hear us, Mom might not let us go. I'd rather she kept cool inside the car with Mister Sandro. And maybe they're sleeping but I hope not. I hope they're talking, explaining themselves, getting to know each other. I don't know what will happen, like if they'll become boyfriend-girlfriend, although I doubt it because Mom has never had a boyfriend, but you know, before when we were in church and Mom came in and I heard the rare sound of her laughter, I hadn't heard that sound in a long long time. So I'd rather have her stay in the jeep with Mister Sandro and learn how to make that sound more often.

Only I get closer to the car, and from inside there comes a different, very loud noise. It's still Mom but she's not laughing. Actually she's shouting. And I know I shouldn't but I lean against the back of the jeep and Zot does the same, and we start to listen.

It's sort of fun for me at first, like we're two spies listening in on super secret conversations in the heart of the night. I watch Zot and signal for him to be quiet, and he does the same to me, and we have to clamp our lips to keep from laughing.

Then I hear what they're saying in there, and laughing ceases to exist.

"No, Serena, I wouldn't follow them! They told me at catechism. You know how much Zot talks. He told me all the stories about things the sea carries, messages on the shore, the Luna people, Etruscan wizards, the statues in Pontremoli . . . "

"And you came up with this crap," says Mom, waving a dark object that I can't see. "Why? What the hell did you want?"

"Nothing, Serena, nothing bad, I swear! I only wanted them to come to Pontremoli."

"Why the hell should you care if they came to Pontremoli," asks Mom. And Sandro tells her he cares because he wanted to come with us, and with her.

"And that's why you attached the bracelets with our names?"

Sandro doesn't speak. Maybe he nods his head. Not even Mom speaks, and this silence hurts my ears. I breathe and feel this thing building up inside me, like I'm in a car winding through the mountains and from one moment to the next I have to get out because I feel I'm going to puke.

"You're sick, Sandro. You know that right? Look. You even made the eyes, the mouth . . . you do realize you're forty years old? At forty people work, people have families. You on the other hand, look at what you do. You even made little hands. You're really sick, Sandro. Sick in the head. Plain sick. You shouldn't be walking the streets. They should lock you up."

"Serena, I swear, I didn't mean to do anybody any harm. It all started by accident with that bone, which I swear I didn't place on purpose."

"What bone?"

"The whalebone that Luna found. Which actually came from a boar. I brought it to the hospital to give her as a present but she was asleep. I left it there and afterward I wanted to tell her it was a gift from me, but then you showed up and began hitting me and—"

"Oh right, so this is my fault!"

"No! Obviously not. I'm just saying I didn't mean to. It happened by accident."

"Of course it did. And by accident you took a piece of wood and made this little statue. By accident you stuck these bracelets with our names on it and planted it by the sea for them to find. Is that it? Do you realize what an asshole you are? Those two are children. They believe in this stuff with all their heart. What did they ever do to you?"

"Nothing! As a matter of fact I care for them and—"

"They're so innocent, a little weird maybe, but what's wrong with being weird? Nothing. What's wrong is dicks like you in the world who take advantage of them."

"But I didn't mean to—"

"So why did you make all this bullshit up, huh? What the hell did you want?!"

"Nothing, I . . . I wanted, see, I wanted you, Serena. I did it because I had to see you. I had to talk to you. I wanted to be with you. I did it for us."

Mom doesn't respond right away. A second goes by, maybe two, then her voice came crashing down like an avalanche: "*For us?* Fuck you. What the hell do you want from me? And what do you want from my kids? Leave us in peace, Sandro, leave us in peace. Disappear for good and get fucked!"

Sandro tries to say something but the words come out in pieces and then they don't come out at all. I cling to the jeep, my legs shake, my ear is flat against the glass, my eyes, through the tears, fix on Zot, and Zot's fix on me.

Of course they do. We can't look at anything else. There is nothing else. Brick by brick the world around us has collapsed and ceases to exist. Everything splits apart and crumbles. The earth gives way and disappears from beneath my feet. I feel myself falling into nothingness and in no time I'll be nothing too. Me and everything else, spinning in this vortex, like the drift that rolls around in the sea and is scattered here and there and wherever it ends up, it ends up by chance and for no good reason.

Fine then. It's fine to fall and disappear forever, the way the Etruscans disappeared forever and the cities of the Luna people and the way Tages disappeared and even my brother. I feel myself falling and want to latch onto something. I press the handle of the jeep real tight and pull, and the door opens.

I didn't mean to open it. Or maybe I did. I don't know. But I definitely don't want to look inside. I don't want them to see me. I open my mouth but nothing comes out. My lips curl and tremble. Because I have nothing to say, nothing. All I had to do was let myself fall and instead I'm here and I feel really stupid and all alone. And Mom opens her arms. She rises and wants to hug me, but I don't want her to, since all hugging does is squeeze you and keep you from moving, braced for the next cruelty, the next lie.

Mom says something but I don't hear her. Everyone speaks but their voices are faint and far off, while I tighten my hood and run, run with all the strength I have plus extra strength and where that comes from I don't know. I run toward the dark. That's my place, even if I wish it weren't. That's where I'm supposed to be. Where you can't see anything and nothing exists. Not even me.

THE DARK AHEAD

I run. I run real fast. I don't see where my feet fall or where I'm going. But I don't care. When you're running away, it doesn't matter where you go as long as it's far. Far from the jeep, from the nasty things I heard, from Sandro who wants to tell me he didn't do it on purpose and from Mom who wants to tell me she loves me even though I'm an idiot. I can hear them down there but I don't answer. I just run.

My foot lands in a hole. I almost fall and my ankle kills, but I ignore it, the way I ignore my breathing and my heart pounding so fast my eyes jut out. I grit my teeth and run into this wet, dark field, not wanting to stop, not ever.

But I nearly give up when the field ends and all of a sudden I find myself facing an enormous black wall.

Just like that the woods begin, out of nowhere, a million trees packed together, trunks and branches that entwine to form this one overwhelming thing that covers the sky and swallows the stars and the moon, and I swear I feel like I'm running into a wall.

Fine by me. If it's a wall, I want to slam my body into it. Or if it's something like a black hole, that's fine too. That way it can suck me up and shoot me out someplace in the universe, who knows where, as long as it's far away from the stele statues, from days of studying trash on the seashore, from Tages, from Ferro's voice as he sleeps, from the whalebone, from that junky wooden sculpture you'd have to be the dumbest of dummies to believe in, you'd have to be sick in the head, you'd have to be me.

So instead of stopping I pick up the pace. I reach the black woods and jump in. I close my eyes and pinch my nose, as if I were diving rather than jumping in, and when I touch down, there I am, floating in the dark, and nothing exists anymore. Only my legs that continue to run and my arms out in front of me dodging the trunks, although sometimes I don't manage well and scrape myself and carry on.

I want to live right here. I want to stay forever and never come out again. That's how stories are born about the ghost of a girl who can be seen wandering at night when there's a full moon, and if someone really were to bump into me they would run away in terror, and later say, "I saw her. I swear I saw her. She's all white with white hair and transparent eyes— a real ghost!" Because deep down that is what I am: a ghost that hasn't died yet. I don't have magic powers and can't foresee the future or talk with the Afterlife. And Mom and Miss Gemma and everyone else can keep telling me I'm a unique creature, I'm special, but it's not true. I'm not special. I'm just weird, I came out wrong, and the rest are all lies.

Grown-ups love that, telling lies. Like the story about Santa Claus, which I believed in until middle school, and after that I believed in Tages, in the people of Luna. I believed the sea bore me gifts . . . Fine, maybe I'm to blame for being stupid, but why do grown-ups get a kick out of telling these bogus stories?

I keep thinking about it, I keep running. Every once in a while my hair catches in a branch, every once in a while I run into a chestnut tree, but it doesn't hurt. Or maybe it does. I don't know, it doesn't matter.

Even Luca, even my fabulous big brother, what nonsense he used to make up! I was raised with his eyes, with his mouth describing the world to me. And it was all a marvel, miracles and magic happened in front of us every second: the mountains were friendly but severe giants with skin made of stone and trees that grew tall, like thick hairs, and they carried water down to the sea, which is our father, the sea that talks to us and calls to us and hugs us with its currents and waves . . . And yet none of it's true. The mountains are just stones. The sea doesn't bring me gifts. It's just a gigantic tub where people offload garbage and plastic bags and toxins. And the trees you can see for yourself: rotten and reeking of mold and mushrooms that I scrape past while I run, my heart leaking out of my ears and brain. In fact I don't believe in all that anymore, and I don't want to stop running, there's no place in this nasty world I want to stop, and—

And then I smack into a chestnut tree. It's gigantic but I swear I didn't see it. I hit it with my shoulder and luckily just a small part of my head, my ear and temple, and I fall to the ground that smells damp and muddy. I lean against the trunk to stand back up. My ear burns but in a moment I'll start running again, in a moment . . .

Suddenly I hear this loud noise above me, and in the silence of the woods it scares me to death. It sounds like an explosion, or several explosions in succession: two black wings beating the air and a sharp cry. A bat. Only totally huge. And because I'm a moron I think back to the vampire from Sandro's story, the one in Transylvania or the Apennines, and shield my neck. But it's not a vampire, it's an average bat, and instead of attacking me it flies off, ignores me entirely.

Bats don't see very well. They wander around in the dark. I'm like that, like a bat or a mole or those white worms that live at the bottom of caves—nice company, huh?

I feel those creatures crawling all over me and get goose bumps. But a moment later I hear something else and out of nowhere feel a rush of happiness.

"Ah! A vampire! SOS! SOS!" The cry is nervous, desperate.

I smile and squint to get a better look but can't see anything. "Zot!" I shout.

"Luna, is that you? Oh, thank Saint Genesius of Brescello! Luna, where are you?" he cries. But I'm already by his side.

"Hi Zot."

"Is that you, Luna?"

It is, I tell him. I should have said, "Of course it's me, who else would it be?" Only I was about to ask him the same question, so I just say yes. And Zot hugs me. I swear. Real hard. With a strength that, if you ask me, his arms don't have. And yet I can barely breathe. It's as if someone else were hugging him and me both. Though that's not the case—enough with the nonsense. It's just Zot and he's happy to have found me and I'm happy he's here. But he can forget about my going back to the grown-ups with him.

"Don't even think about it, Zot, I'm not going," I say. Going where, he asks.

"To the jeep. I'm not going back. I'm staying here. There's no point insisting."

Zot pulls away and looks at me even though we can't see one another in this dark. "Excuse me? Do you really think I want to go back there?"

"Yeah. I mean, I don't know. I think so."

"Well, you're wrong. You ran away but I ran away too. What happened hurts me as much as you, you know? Maybe you don't remember, but I also believed . . . in everything. Clearly I have no intention of returning to the jeep. You don't want to go back and you have your mother there; why would I, who have no one, want to?"

"That's not true. You have Ferro."

"I wouldn't count on it. Yesterday I asked him if we could have a big dinner for Christmas and he said if they haven't come to take me away by Christmas he's going to leave me in a dumpster."

We're silent for a moment, there's only the sound of our breathing, then we start walking together, moving forward.

Which is to say, we turn toward a random spot in the dark, decide that it is facing forward, and head out in that direction.

"Okay, Zot, but my feelings were more hurt than yours cause I thought it was my brother who wanted to speak to me, got it?"

"Me too! If your brother talked to you, maybe mine could tell me something one day."

"Since when do you have a brother?"

"You never know. A brother, a sister—anything's possible. Only my parents know. But I can't ask them because I don't know them either. I'm ashamed to admit it, Luna, but sometimes I almost wish that they were dead, because if they're alive, that means they care nothing for me."

"No, Zot, what are you saying? That isn't true. Your dad the violinist doesn't know he's your dad. And who can say what they did to your mom. You know how mean nobility can be."

"Please, Luna," says Zot. He stops walking and I stop too. "Please, not you too. Spare me the poppycock. Otherwise Mr. Sandro is right and we'll go on telling each other lies."

"It's not a lie. It's the truth. Isn't that what the nun told you?"

"You know what the truth is, Luna? The truth is, I don't know who or where my parents are. All I know is that when I was born they brought me to the nuns. Then the nuns brought me and some other kids to Italy and by the time they returned home they'd forgotten about us. Got it, Luna? That's the truth. At least you knew your brother and you loved each other for many years and you have a mom who loves you immensely too. I'm sorry about what happened, it grieves me, but look, I always listen to you and understand you, Luna. Every once in a while you could try to understand me too."

The voice is his but the words sound nothing like Zot. In the dark I almost doubt it's him. But it is him, I feel it, only I don't know what to say. I don't know what to do. I merely feel like crying, in part for myself and more for him. I don't want him to see me crying, so this time I'm the one to hug him, and he hugs me back, and all I manage to say is, "I'm sorry, Zot, I'm sorry."

"You don't have to apologize, Luna, but please remember that it is not always you versus the world. You're not always alone. Actually you're never alone. I am."

"Neither are you, Zot, you're not alone either."

"I know," he says and squeezes harder. "Not anymore."

We stay there, and I cry and laugh and nod, and even if I don't see him I know that Zot is doing the same. There's no point looking at one another or talking. The silence is total, like the dark, and it seems weird not to hear anything, not the wind in the leaves or the voices of the grown-ups calling us. Maybe they went looking for us in the wrong spot or maybe these woods are so dense that the sounds of the world, like the light, can't reach this far. In which case, this really is the perfect place for us.

"What do we do now?" Zot asks.

"Now . . . I propose that from now on we only believe what we see. Deal?"

"Consider it sacrosanct. Except I can't see anything," says Zot. For a while we don't talk, peering into the deep darkness of the woods.

But it's not that dark. Not like when I dove in. It's weird, even the tent seemed dark to me. Then I went out and discovered that the real darkness was in that field. Then I got to the woods and in comparison the field was showered in light. And now even this dark leaves me something to see. Maybe that's how it works. Maybe remaining in the real dark is impossible. The dark is always and only ahead of you, and when you reach it you realize it isn't as dark as you'd thought. You take one step forward and it's no longer there, it's moved a little farther on and is waiting for you to arrive so it can disappear again.

In fact now that I open my eyes I can recognize certain shapes. Shadows, darker patches, leaves. And off in the distance, something different and quivering, something neither black nor shadowy: an actual light.

"What is it?" asks Zot. His hand grips mine and we walk toward it slowly. Though it isn't easy to reach. The trees are more densely packed, and in the middle are these kinds of wires, brambles with thorns my sweater snags on, but they break off when I pull away. We get closer to the light, and from a few feet away we can see that it is round and sits high up, like a beacon in the sky, illuminating a precise spot. Because suddenly the mass of chestnuts vanishes and in the middle is a clearing with one lone tree underneath a light that shines down on the earth around it and its gigantic crown. Two crowns, actually, since there are two trunks. They were born attached but one climbs this way and the other that, each crooked in its own way, and together they form an incredible and gigantic V.

"Jesus, Mary, and Joseph," goes Zot. And we stand there, planted in the ground, more stationary than that dark, unreal tree. Only after a while do I manage to say, "I, I don't believe it." Cause what the freak, I don't want to believe it.

"Me neither, Luna. Yet I see it. Please tell me you don't see it."

"I do. Not well, but I see it."

Zot gasps and I gasp too. Just when we'd worked so hard not to believe anything anymore, there appears this V-shaped chestnut tree that Ferro's voice told us we had to hurry to. But why? What's waiting for us in the dark behind that tree? Why these woods? More importantly, why us? Do the people of Luna have something to tell us? Or does Tages himself? And what do they want? What . . . "

I don't know and maybe I don't want to know. I try to convince myself that it's all nonsense, that Zot and I should ignore it and continue on our way. But we don't have a way, and even if I don't want to, I think, well, maybe Luca is waiting for me down there. I don't know how or why, but it would be pretty easy to check; the chestnut is right there. So, without deciding, without wanting to, I start moving.

I keep going and Zot goes with me. We exit the woods and stop inside the light circling the tree, but underneath the tree it's dark and you can't see a thing. Another couple of steps, I squint, and there beside the trunks something emerges. Actually someone, a dark figure, standing there, waiting for us.

Zot gets a better look at it than I. He says it has a weird head, wide and rounded on top. "Maybe it's a hat, or maybe . . . " He spits out a kind of cry and claps his mouth and says through his fingers, "Heavenly Father, it's the people of Luna!"

Which is ridiculous, but heck, that is their head: round and shaped like a crescent moon. I open my mouth. Nothing comes out. I take another breath and try again. "Hello."

The figure doesn't answer me or move. It stands there staring at us.

"I, I'm Luna. And this is Zot. Were you waiting for us?"

Again, nothing. Only the wind makes the leaves tremble, although compared to us, they seem cool and calm. We take another step. Two, actually.

"Should we get closer?" says Zot. Not to me but to that person. "Or would you prefer to be left alone? We understand if so. We wouldn't dream . . . "

Silence again, again nothing. Enough already, freaking A, I'm going. I go and I don't know what will happen but it doesn't matter, since maybe it's a spirit of the people of Luna or maybe Tages has popped out from the underworld but it's definitely not Luca. My brother was way taller, way stronger, way handsomer. More importantly, Luca would have opened his arms and run to me and we would have hugged each other real hard. So if it's not him, who cares about the others. I'm going. End of story. Zot shouts at me to stop but he doesn't stop either and we arrive in front of the person waiting for us under the chestnut tree. But he doesn't move. He doesn't talk. It's not even a person.

"What is it?" I ask. "Is it a statue?"

I ask because this thing is hard, square, flat. Freaking A, maybe it really is a stele statue who stayed behind to protect the woods and has been on his own for thousands of years. Until the night we discovered him.

"No," says Zot. "It's a sign."

"What do you mean a sign?" I lean over and examine it. It says something I can't make out.

Zot reads, "SAPORI DELLA LUNA ROTISSERIE/ PIZZERIA, 2000 FT. And there's an arrow. Or there was an arrow. Someone's drawn a penis on top of it."

"Ah," is all I say. Any more than that I can't.

A sign. Just a sign. A crappy sign for a crappy rotisserie that's 2000 feet from this crappy chestnut tree that was born weird and grew into a V.

I sit down. I suddenly realize how badly my legs are shaking. All of a sudden, I feel exhausted, I can't stand on my feet another second. I sit on the ground with my back against this damn sign.

"You okay, Luna?"

"Yeah. But I'm tired."

"Me too," goes Zot, leaning against the fake statue and sitting beside me. "And cold. The damp is dreadful. I'm also a little hungry."

We stand side by side, our eyes aimed straight ahead, scanning the woods full of chestnut trees and bats and nothing but darkness. We stay that way for a time. I'm not sure how long, long enough for me to feel cold too.

"You know, Luna," says Zot finally, all bundled in his coat, "if it were up to me I would stay here forever. It's cold and we don't have anything to eat and who knows what we'll do when winter arrives with the snow. Well, I'm just fine here. But the grown-ups back at the jeep, what will they do without us?"

I don't say anything, although I was sort of thinking the same thing.

"Admit it. They're goners without us. Your mom is just starting to get better. Without you I fear she might shut herself up in the house and *addio*."

"True. Ferro, too; what would he do without you?"

"You think he'd miss me?"

"Are you kidding, Zot? He'd miss you a lot. He's not the kind of person who'd say so, but he would miss you."

"I think so too, you know. And Mr. Sandro."

"Yeah, I don't care about him."

"Me neither. But think about it, he's worse off than anybody."

I nod and we stop talking. Sitting there, chilled to the bone, we lean against a sign for a rotisserie with a penis for an arrow. Just a radioactive orphan and a bright white girl who believe in everything. Or used to believe. On the contrary, the truth is there's no sea bringing you gifts or mysterious people calling you, no magical powers of the Etruscans and no brothers who talk to you from the afterlife.

I lean against the sign and stand up. Zot does the same. We don't know where we're going. We don't even know where we are. Actually, that we do know: we're near a rotisserie.

"You know, Zot," I say, starting off in the direction of the arrow, "I don't think lies are the problem. The problem is the truth and the truth totally sucks."

W hat a dream, boys and girls," says Ferro, coiled in
the front seat. "*Maremma Cane*, what a dream."
As the car wended its way past the trees and fields,
Zot had asked if he happened to know anything about a V-
shaped chestnut tree. Ferro was silent for a second, then
whipped around: "Of course, of course! I even dreamt about
it last night! I spent the sixties boning this woman named
Giovanna. She was married to a guy who ran a bakery in the
hills of Giustagnana. At night he'd go make bread and we
would meet in the woods just outside of town, under this V-
shaped chestnut tree. There was a clearing there we'd lie in.
Actually, sometimes she'd be so frisky we wouldn't even lie
down, as soon as she got there she'd grab my—"

"Ferro," Mom interrupts. "Please."

"Hey, they asked. Those were some wild nights under that
tree, boys and girls, and that was one hell of a dream last night.
Clearly all those chestnuts must have jogged my memory.
Maremma Cane, Giovanna was a tramp in real life—just imagine what tricks she could perform in a dream."

Zot nods, without smiling or anything, then turns around
to push back part of the tent that knocks him on the head
every time the car brakes. It had taken us hours to assemble
and five minutes to disassemble. Sandro and Mom had woken
Ferro up and dragged him outside, then picked the tent off the
ground and threw it into the trunk as is. But that's all right.
The important thing was to leave immediately. Who cares if

now it looks like a pile of trash with bits of grass and leaves, and at every bend rolls this way and that and sounds like broken junk? I listen with my forehead pressed to the window, and all the stones and holes make my head buzz and help me think a little less.

"You two are morons, by the by," Ferro persists. "How the hell do you get lost in a forest of chestnut trees?"

I don't answer. Neither does Zot. Sandro, who had been quiet until then, butts in.

"It happens," he says, his voice all broken as if he were waiting to be told off after every word and is stunned when he's allowed to arrive at the next one. "Everybody gets lost; it's not a crime. Getting lost is the only way to discover the truly beautiful things. The day I got lost in the woods I found the largest porcini mushroom in the Apuan Alps."

"Quit yanking our chains," says Ferro. "The biggest porcini was found by two pensioners from Seravezza. They even wrote it up in *Il Tirreno.*"

"That's not true! They say they did but I'm the one who found it, I swear."

"At least spare us your swearing," says Mom. "At least spare us that."

"But I swear I did, Serena, I swear to God."

"You can't swear to God, Mr. Sandro," scolds Zot. "That's a sin. That's taking the name of God in vain. A catechist of all people ought to know that."

A minute of silence, then I say, "That's if this catechist stuff isn't a lie too."

I don't say it to him because I'm not talking to Sandro. I say it to the air in the jeep. But Sandro drives and doesn't answer, and his silence says it all.

Besides, it doesn't matter to me. Who cares if he's a catechist or not, if his name is really Sandro or if he made it up, if it's true he got lost in the woods and found that gigantic mushroom? All

I care about is that I got lost in the woods and found nothing aside from a sign for a rotisserie.

But I don't want to think about it. I press my head harder against the glass and the rattle of the road makes it so I can't think straightly. I'd like to close my eyes and sleep, dream about something beautiful or at least not dream at all. And even if I don't believe I can, in the end somehow I manage to.

"No, let's just go home, my head's killing me."

Ferro speaks but I'm not sure to whom he's talking or why. I open my eyes; we're stopped. I pull away from the glass and realize I've missed a lot of talk and miles of road. Because, although it's still dark out and I can't see anything, the air no longer tastes like leaves and dirt, I smell the salt and fresh sand and varnished wood. And that means we've arrived at the beach.

"Enough, Sandro, take us home," says Mom, more tired than angry.

"Yeah, sure, just give me a second while I get the keys. Then we'll go."

Ferro asks where the hell his keys are and Sandro answers that Rambo and Marino have them, here at the beach. Which ticks off Ferro, since they were supposed to be guarding the house. What are they doing at the beach at this hour?

Sandro hesitates a moment with the door half open then says he'll be right back, climbs out, and walks away.

We sit here, hushed, still in the jeep, and from Sandro's door comes the salt air along with the calm sound of the waves lapping at the shore. And, well, I swear I almost don't realize it when I open my door and climb out too.

"Can we go to the beach, too, Mom?" I don't know what she answers, whether she says yes or no or whether she's even heard me, since by the time I ask I'm already gone.

I can see next to nothing but I reach out my hand and touch

the oleander leaves, the pods of pittosporum and rows of stiff palm branches, and when those taper off it means you've reached the passageway to the sea. But I can't find it, and instead I feel a hand on my back that by now I know well. It's Zot, pushing me forward a little. "Now," he says, and we enter a passageway that smells like sand and stale cigarettes and pee. It's almost as dark and narrow as the night before when we got lost among the chestnuts in the woods of Filetto, only at the end of those woods all we found was a sign for a rotisserie with a penis drawn on it, while here we take a dozen steps and something marvelous happens: the tunnel ends abruptly, and at the end of that dark, narrow tube the world opens up before us, and there are no more walls or roofs or objects shielding our eyes. We're on the beach and around us there is only the sun and the sea, and I feel like an astronaut floating freely in empty space. Only I'm freer than them. I don't have to wear that huge white suit or a helmet on my head that looks like a goldfish bowl. As a matter of fact, I take my shoes off, walk on the cool sand, and start to run toward the shore, even if I can't see anything, but that's the point: everything is free and made for running where you please, toward the sky streaked with starlight and toward the sea, which is the same color and reflects that light, making it dance up and down on the waves.

"Luna! Wait for me, Luna! Wait!" It's Mom calling, along with Zot, and a cloud of curse words coming from Ferro's mouth. I stop but not to wait for them. I've reached the water, the black sea from which a white band occasionally rises, marking the edge of the slow, peaceful waves touching my feet, one by one.

But a little farther out in the water is another white thing, thrashing and tottering, and Sandro shouts at it to come ashore.

"What the hell are they doing on a paddle boat at this hour," says Ferro.

"They were . . . they went, you know, they went fishing for squid," says Sandro.

"And they're coming back now? When the fishing's good? Sunup is when you catch squid."

Ferro speaks and Zot touches my arm and points to something behind us. I turn around and at the far end of the sky there really does arrive this kind of light with the mountains silhouetted underneath, a line of several dark and pointy triangles. Not that I see them exactly, but Luca used to tell me about them all the time. He'd say the mountains at sunup look like dogfish teeth, and like dogfish those mountains out there are the first to wake in the morning. Actually, the dogfish doesn't wake, he never goes to sleep, because in order to breathe he must move constantly and draw water into his gills. If he stops he dies. So, even if just a little, the dogfish keeps going forward.

That's what Luca would tell me and I'd listen to him and like him I could kind of see this incredible and marvelous world. And now that my big brother is gone, I look back at the sea and the gentle waves, the noise they make comprised of thousands of different sounds mixed together, and in the middle of them all I seem to hear him still telling me his unbelievable tales from beyond the waves.

Yet now the voice I hear off the sea is different, a cry with nothing deep to say, only, "Hold still, moron—"

And immediately after that something happens that I can't see but the others can, since they all start shouting from the shore, and Ferro goes: "No, don't turn your side to the wave, don't—"

Then a splash in the water, a voice crying, "Help," another emitting a strange noise then breaking up and disappearing, the way Mom disappears. She had been by my side but suddenly she's not there anymore. She's out in front, with her army shirt whipping about and the dark water up to her waist before she dives in.

"What are you doing, you lunatic!" screams Ferro, and he runs into the sea too, kicking up sand and a dust cloud of curse words. Someone else dives behind us. It must be Sandro because Zot is still next to me. But I can't see him exactly, I only see the lights on the water ahead of us, trembling and dashing off like frogs in a stream when they hear you coming.

Here on the shore, I don't know what I'm supposed to do, so I do what a dogfish does: I keep going forward. The sand is increasingly wet, then a more powerful wave encircles my feet, and as it retreats carries me out to sea. I can actually feel it grabbing me and ushering me out, its hold so weird that for a moment it scares me: I'd been expecting to freeze, to die of cold, and instead I swear that in all my life I have never felt a sea as warm as this.

It comes up to my waist. I take off my sweatshirt and throw it toward the shore, where Zot is yelling at me to come back, that I'm crazy and I'll get sick again. Then I can't hear him anymore over my heavy breathing. I hold my breath and dive.

The sea is warm and slippery and soft. Maybe it's that I hadn't swum all summer, but I don't remember it being this gentle and smooth and friendly. I swim and it laps at my skin and makes me smile, as if it were tickling me, as if it were caressing me. Then I come back up and hear Mr. Marino far off saying in his broken voice, "My Lord, I thought I was going to die, thank you, Lord, I could have sworn I was going to die." To which Ferro replies, "Some loss," while from the beach Zot continues telling me that I'm going to wind up in the hospital again.

"But it's not cold," I say. "It's really warm!"

"Yeah, I bet not! Come back, Luna, please! For the love of God come back!"

"Coming," I grumble, and return to the shore. And in fact as soon as I exit the water the air is chilly and makes me shudder. "Help me, Zot, I have no strength left. I'm exhausted."

"There, you see? Those are the symptoms of hypothermia! Do you have the shakes? Let me see how pale you are." But he shuts up as soon as he realizes that last symptom doesn't work much with me. He merely takes my hand and tries to help me out. But I grab his arm and pull him backward with all the strength I have, and Zot falls into the water with me—coat, scarf, and all. He cries as he falls. He sinks under the water, comes back up, and screams again, thrashing his arms and trying to remove his shoes, which are seriously heavy and tight as a boa constrictor wrapped around your neck. When he can, he thrashes less, then stops altogether and looks around, baffled. Breathlessly, he goes, "Pardon me, Luna, why is it so warm?"

I laugh. I say nothing and laugh. Then I grab onto his coat and we swim over to the others, while all alone the paddleboat comes reeling into shore on the waves.

Us, on the other hand, the waves carry us up and down, up and down, we're bathing in the sea at the end of September with the sun emerging and the full moon hanging back a little longer to watch what happens, and the most absurd thing about it is that it seems totally normal to me. Here we are, only our heads sticking out, our feet touching the soft sand at the bottom and occasionally some harder bit: seashells and hermit crabs and crabs and all the life that lives down there, checking out our huge feet and thinking, "What's with these morons? What came over them this morning?" And they're retreating, shoving off, because, indeed, to them it's weird. But not to us. We're here, bathing in warm water, and I hope that the others feel the way I do, because I feel really good.

Mr. Marino not so much. Rambo and Sandro take him by his arms and he says his back hurts and he has to go ashore. "But first I have to thank you," he says to Mom. "You saved my life."

"Don't get carried away. Ferro deserves credit too."

"Yes, of course, thank you both. From the bottom of my heart, thanks."

"No sweat," says Ferro. "I'm a lifeguard, it's in my blood. Besides, if you had to count on your two queer pals here . . . ."

"That's it!" says Rambo. Yells Rambo. Really loudly. "You can't call me queer! That I won't accept."

"Easy, kid. You will accept it because that's what you are."

"No!" says Rambo, crying and punching the water hard. But he's not angry. He's not trying to hurt anyone. He's more like someone who has just stopped beating himself up and has really harmed himself. "I won't accept it because it's not true! Why are you all saying that? I hunt. I dig car rallies and guns. How can a guy like me be gay? I can change a tire on a truck. I'm good with my hands."

"Yeah, I bet the boys tell you that," says Ferro. And Rambo looks like he wants to say something back or tackle him or who knows what, but Mr. Marino makes this wailing sound, says his head is spinning and that he has to go ashore. So Rambo takes him by the arm, asks Sandro what he's doing, and Sandro says he'll be right there, but in the meantime he hangs back with us.

"Sure, leave us to fend for ourselves, bravo," says Rambo, walking backward in the water with Marino in his arms. "Look, just because I won't stoop to your level to be with a woman, just because I have a little bit of pride, that makes me a fag? Well then, you know what I have to say to you? Well then, yes, I'm gay. I'd rather be gay than a sorry-ass like you!"

"Yeah," says Ferro, "we heard you. Alert the press."

He doesn't say anything else and neither does Rambo, except for bits of broken words to himself that get drowned out by the waves and crash on the shore.

We stay here, in the water. A moment ago we were in the woods up in the mountains and now look at us, bathing in the sea, in this warm water, so strange and beautiful. It laps at my skin and makes me smile. Actually, it makes me feel like laughing, even though I don't want to. Because I'm angry and I clamp my mouth shut and try to hold this laughter in without them hearing me. Instead, a minute later, we hear this earth-shattering cry.

We look around to see what's happening, everyone but Sandro, since he's the one shouting and hopping about and trying to lift his foot to see what stung him. But that's not easy when you're neck-deep in water. All he manages to do is jump and wail. "It stings! It stings!"

"What's gotten into you?" asks Mom.

Sandro doesn't answer, just makes this muffled sound with his lips sealed. But I know what happened.

"A weever!" I say. Sandro nods, his eyes wide open, and hops again.

Ferro laughs and Mom does too, so finally I can laugh, and I laugh real loud because, with all the sea around us, somehow Mr. Sandro has managed to step right on a weever.

Weevers are small, dark fish that spend their lives buried in the sand with only their dorsal fins poking out from the surface: three black, poisonous spines that really hurt whomever steps on them.

"Argh! It burns! It burns! Fuck!"

"Is it lethal?" asks Zot. "Blessed Saint Christopher, I said that at the end of this adventure someone would pay with his life, I said that!"

"Way to go, kid, you were right," says Ferro, laughing along with me.

"Don't laugh—this really burns!" Sandro speaks, his teeth clenched from the pain.

"Of course it's going to burn in the water," says Ferro. "You have to put something hot on it. Hot sand would do it, that stuff's perfect. Only now it's cold."

"So then?"

"So then, tough luck."

"Or urine," says Mom. "Urine works, doesn't it? With jellyfish people use urine."

"Right," says Ferro, "urine would work too."

So I raise my arms to the sky and scream, "Yes! Come on, let's pee on Sandro!"

And he: "Ah! You of all people, Luna! First you won't speak to me and now you want to pee on me?"

"Yes! Right away, too, because I've got to go!" I say. I'm embarrassed to say it but I do, then I stop myself because I remember that I'm not talking to Sandro.

"All right," says Mom, "come on, everybody pee on Sandro!"

"Please, people," says Zot, his coat swollen with water and shrouding his mouth. "Honestly, I think this crosses the line of good taste."

"The kid's right," says Ferro. "No way I'm whipping it out in front of this guy. He'll fall in love and who knows what he'll do."

"You're joking, you're joking," says Sandro, his voice still choked with pain.

"Fine, listen," says Mom. "There's no warm sand, you don't want to be peed on—at least swim ashore and improvise."

"Yeah, I'm going," says Sandro. But he doesn't move.

"What are you waiting for? Aren't you going? Go ashore and have a look. The spine might still be stuck in it."

"Yeah, I'll go in a minute, not now."

"Why not?"

"Because I'm scared that if I go you won't want me back again. That despite this great trip together, because it ended the way it ended, now we'll never see each other again."

For a moment no one speaks. Then Mom goes: "Well, who can say. In my opinion the only person who can decide that is Luna."

And even though I don't see well, I can feel everyone looking at me now.

I don't speak because I don't know what to say, because I feel so happy in this warm water that I'm unable to stay mad at Mr. Sandro or anyone else in the world. And yet that's not fair and what should happen is that all the Etruscan gods and the people of Luna should arrive and unleash their rain of fire and killer locusts and every divine curse there is on Sandro. Then it occurs to me that something actually did happen—the weever struck. I look at Sandro waiting there for me to say something, trying to keep quiet and motionless while sounds of suffering escape his lips and every so often he hops on one foot. I feel like laughing again, like being happy, and so I keep totally quiet.

Luckily Zot thinks of something to say. Something, as usual, completely irrelevant. "Wait, but, is the weever going to die now?"

"Huh?"

"I was just asking myself whether weevers are like bees, and when they sting you their stinger tears off and they die?"

"Kid," says Ferro, "you won't be happy until someone dies, huh?"

"Yes. I mean, no. But it seems probable. Which makes me wonder, couldn't the weever have run away? Didn't it see the huge foot of Mr. Sandro coming?"

So Ferro starts to tell him about this one time a stingray stung him, and it could be the best story ever but I don't listen. I can't. Because out of nowhere this business about the weever not seeing Sandro reminds me of something else about Luca that, I swear, I hadn't thought about since it first happened.

It must have been last year, summertime. He and I were walking on the beach and we came to a place where the sand dies off, at the mouth of the Versilia River, where the water runs down the Apuan Alps and into the sea. There were some really big fish in the mouth of the river. I could only see the shadows of their fins but they were there, held in the current, facing the mountains.

And we snuck right up behind them, which seemed weird to me since the one thing fish—and all animals—know about humans is to run away when you see them. But those fish weren't running away. They stayed there, facing the current. Fish always do that, Luca told me. Because the current brings them bits of stuff and smaller fish to eat, as well as sticks, plastic bags, and larger fish to avoid. Really. That's how they live, always keeping their eyes out for what's coming. And whatever's going on behind them, even just a step away, they ignore.

"See, Luna, we're here, up close, watching them, but to them we don't exist."

"Can't they turn around to look?"

"Maybe. I don't know. But they don't turn around. Because the current is coming from over there. Everything, the good stuff and the bad, shows up in front of them. That's how fish live, Luna. They might imagine we're here, they might suspect so, but they stick to the current. They go on that way, they go on living."

Luca told me that last summer, but because I hadn't thought about it since, it kind of feels like he was telling me now, on this absurd morning when we're in the sea, all of us facing the sun coming up, and a light breeze off the shore drifts around the quiet houses and the shuttered stores and the empty streets and carries the smell of fresh-baked croissants from the bakeries along the coast, so powerful I can taste them. And inhaling is a little like eating.

I think of those fish in the mouth of the river and us just behind them while Ferro finishes telling his story about the stingray, which I don't understand because I wasn't listening, then Sandro says he has to go in because he can't feel his leg anymore, but he asks me again if, once he's recovered, he can come back.

I take a breath, look at Mom for a minute, and say no, it's not up to me, she's the one who must decide. Then Mom looks back at me and we both raise our arms to the sky and say, "Oh, who knows, we'll see!" And we laugh, we laugh a lot. But out of the water it's cold and our arms freeze, so we plunge back into the sea, into its warm, wonderful embrace.

Sandro limps back to shore, Ferro follows after him, and Zot, though not a very good swimmer, tries to swim behind the man he calls Grandfather and who in the end, if you ask me, really is his grandfather.

Mom and I hang back to watch the sun coming up and the sky brightening everything and the water sparkling with little reflectors of light.

"We going in, Luna?"

"No, please, Mom, it's too nice."

"We can't spend our whole lives here."

"No, but we can stay a little longer."

And we do. We tread close together and watch the sun rising in the sky up ahead.

And whatever is behind us we don't see, though something is there. The whole gigantic sea and the water that never rests and the waves that have always come and will always come, one after the other. They break on the shore and that seems to be the end of them. Only it's not. They withdraw so that the next one can rise and the next and the next, with a shove from who knows where, but it's there and it sends us up and down, up and down, sending us up and down, up and down, in this warm embrace that we don't need to face to feel, it's all around us, while we keep looking ahead, at what the current carries us, at the break of day, which looks like an enormous orange gift waiting to be opened.

A MONTH LATER

Ivan regards the rain and for a moment the rain regards him, then it spatters against the windshield and dies. But he doesn't give a damn. He tightens his grip on the throttle as if he wanted to break the handlebar, and maybe he really does want to break it, because that thing is the bane of his existence. Not the handlebar itself, mind you, but the entire Ape 50 pulsing under him on his way home from another hellish morning at school.

Hellish as his summer, which the other kids spent sleeping in and going to the public pool, or hanging around acting like idiots, or enjoying themselves anyways, the way you should during the summer you're sixteen years old. Ivan, on the other hand, would wake up at 6:30 and by 7 he was already in the square outside Alga Bibite loading cases of water and Coke onto the bed of an Ape and delivering drinks till evening to the families of Reggio Emilia, drenched in sweat and with one objective in mind: to purchase a scooter.

Practically everybody else had one, and they were acting all smooth and taking girls for rides. Ivan's father, however, told him times were tough and in this recession they couldn't afford anything, and so he understood that he had to take matters into his own hands. The whole break he worked his ass off and finally in September when he took his money to the dealership he found himself standing before *her* instead: a used Ape that looked brand new. He'd had fun cruising around in the Ape this summer, and come winter he would be

warm inside the cab rather than sucking fog all the way from
Villa Cadè to downtown Reggio. And when it rains, well, when
it rains there's no question how much better off you'd be inside
an Ape.

To cut a long story short, Ivan bought it, and for the first
time in his life he awaited the start of school as if it were a
party, a party to celebrate his new life as a stud on wheels.

When he arrived at school, he parked near the entrance,
opened the door, and climbed out, ready to be met by the
stares of the whole school, and in the expectation of general
applause Ivan headed for the courtyard, and toward his doom.

Yes, doom, because, just as Ivan had predicted, everybody
gathered around him and his vehicle, except they began to
laugh, to point at his splendid Ape and riddle it with disses.
"What the hell is that? A loaner from your grandpa? Did you
jack the janitor's car?" They were shouting and taking photos
with their cell phones, and the biggest dicks of all hugged each
other, happy to have a target that big and easy to ridicule.

And that target is him, Ivan, increasingly preyed upon in
the morning, increasingly depressed and humiliated. His last
hope had been for it to rain someday; he wanted to see what
the others would do then, shivery and soaking wet, while
inside his Ape he'd be dry and happy and finally cool, at least
a little.

Which explains why this morning, when he saw all that
water pouring down from the sky, Ivan's was the one happy
face at the yellow windows of Villa Cadè. He ran out of the
house, jumped into the Ape, and got to school, where he'd
imagined everyone else would be devastated and was confident
that at the end of the day the girls would come say, "We're
sorry, Ivan, we were wrong to make fun of you, would you
please take us home?" And he would have chosen the petti-
est, or maybe not the prettiest, maybe it was better to choose

the one with the biggest tits so that he could watch them jiggle on the way back.

Except when classes let out, no one, pretty or ugly, came. They simply climbed on the bus. Or the more spoiled kids got into their parents' cars. So Ivan was stuck offering a ride to his one friend, Maicol, who told him, "Thanks, Ivan, but in the Ape? Here in front of everybody? They already shit on me enough as it is . . . "

Ivan nodded, locked himself inside the solitude of his Ape, and stared past the foggy windows at his defeat. Then he switched on the engine and returned to Villa Cadè, where he's now docking this dilapidated ship in front of the house without locking it—I mean really, who would want to steal an Ape?

He enters and Dad tells him Mom is running late and if it's all right with him he'd prefer to wait, that way they only have to throw the pasta in once. Ivan says he's not hungry, tosses his bag on the couch, and goes to his room, but Dad hands him this weird package.

Flat, rectangular, all white. It's a paper envelope with a stamp on top and his name, Ivan Cilloni, written in ink above the address.

"What's this?"

"A letter."

"For me? How come?" He had never received a handwritten letter before.

"How should I know if you don't? It's from Forte dei Marmi."

Ivan nods even though he doesn't know anybody from Forte dei Marmi. Forte dei Marmi is where soccer players take those sluts they date on vacation; that's the extent of his knowledge.

He enters his room and closes the door behind him, hoping to shut out the rain, the Ape, the laughter of those bastards at school, thoughts of how dreary a summer he'd had while soccer players weren't doing dick and taking beautiful women to Forte dei Marmi and how they had enough money to buy a million Apes, and yet they wouldn't deign to buy them, since soccer players may not be smart but neither are they idiots.

He, on the other hand, is. He's a bona fide dumbass, and he dives on the bed like something to be disposed of. He tears open the envelope, looks inside, and finds four square postcards from Forte dei Marmi, one of which pictures a beach from up high with the sand and several colored circles for umbrellas, while in the others there are people crossing a lit-up bridge at sundown, and seagulls, and the surrounding sea.

He turns the postcards over. On the other side are several different messages in cramped, slightly crooked handwriting. And with the rain outside unrelenting, Ivan begins to read in bed.

Forte dei Marmi, October 22

SANDRO: Hey Ivan, You don't know me, but I found your note attached to a balloon that you released when you were in elementary school. Remember? I found it in the pine grove in Versilia, my hometown, and I know that nine years have gone by, and I could tell you that I've just discovered it again or that I've faced many hardships or lost it and didn't find it again until yesterday. But that wouldn't be the truth, so I won't. I'm writing you now because up until today I never decided to pick up a postcard and write you. See, I'm telling you how things really stand. If it's not pretty, I'm sorry, but my storytelling days are over. Maybe the one way to tell pretty stories is to begin living them. In fact, I'm beginning today by writing you. I'm not sure if you're still at this address, but I hope so. In your message you said that you would send a drawing of a rhinoceros to whomever wrote you back, but nine years have gone by and I understand if you no longer want to. It doesn't matter. I'm just glad to be finally mailing you this postcard. Cheers, Sandro

SERENA: I don't know why I'm expected to write to you too. Hi, pleasure to meet you, this has nothing to do with me. Sandro is the one who took a lifetime to write you back, and all of a sudden sending you these postcards is so important to him. I explained to him that you're sixteen years old now and couldn't care less, that you don't even remember this balloon business, but he wanted to mail them to you and he's mailing them to you, and it's important to him that I write you too, although I don't know why. I tried saying no, but that's not easy with this guy. He doesn't understand the meaning of the word No, *and he persists, and in the end sometimes you just have to say, 'Okay, listen, all right,' and see what happens. So there you have it. Now I've written you too. Bye, Ivan, be good. Actually, be whatever you feel like. It's better that way. S.*

FERRO: Look kid I don't know who you are nor do I care and I don't know anybody in Reggio Emilia although once there was a client from Reggio Emilia who used to come to the beach club. She was a coldhearted skank and in the mornings I'd take her to the cabanas. Don't worry. That was years ago and she couldn't have been your mother. Your grandmother at best. But that doesn't matter. All that matters is that you stay put and don't come here since I was perfectly fine on my own and now there are four of us, plus this moron Sandro who comes around in the evening to get on my tits. Bye kid, and do me a favor, stay put.

LUNA AND ZOT: Hi Ivan! Don't listen to Ferro. If you come see us we'd be super-happy and we'll find a room for you. We have a tent that we can set up in the yard. It's pretty and there are trees and Grandfather even took out the mines.

470 · FABIO GENOVESI

*We're waiting for you. If you come we'll take you to the sea.
We found a killer dinghy and we can sail it together. About
that rhinoceros you know how to draw so well. Well, if you
still have it we would be curious to see it, and we swear we'll
hang it up in our room. Bye. See you soon, Luna and Zot*

Ivan reads them through to the end, then rereads them
again, then turns the cards over and looks at the beach, the sea,
the bridge. He places them on his bed alongside the envelope
with his name on it and stares up at the ceiling.

And, well, he can't remember this business about a message
in a balloon. Sure, it's plausible; they made you do stupid
things like that all the time in elementary school. Paintings
with macaroni glued on for Mother's Day, letters to other kids
from Reggio Emilia's sister city in Calabria—that kind of junk.
But he doesn't remember the balloon. Or maybe he does. Nine
years have gone by, he was a kid, who knows?

No one. But Ivan thinks about it anyways, and while he
thinks about it he stands up and pulls out a flyer for a pizza
place he'd been handed outside school. He turns it over. The
reverse side is blank. He sets it on the blanket, takes a blue
marker, rests it on top, and starts moving it up and down.

With his other hand he reaches for the phone in his pants
pocket, checks to see if someone has sent him any messages or
anything at all. Nothing. So, out of curiosity, he looks up Forte
dei Marmi and the road to get there and he thinks about how
far that balloon had flown, from the Villa Cadè Kennedy
Elementary School way up to the top of the mountains, passing over them and descending to the coast, to the pine grove
on the shore. Then Ivan looks at the normal road, the one people have to take to get there, snaking through the Apennines,
and after that it's all downhill until you hit the plains on the
other side. Going on foot would be impossible, as would going
by bike, and who knows how cold it would be to ride a scooter

through the mountains. But the Ape could do it. If you ask Ivan, you could easily get there in the Ape, as long as you left enough time and didn't rush.

And as he follows the road and all its twists and turns, with his marker he traces the same twists and turns on the slip of paper. At first glance, they look like random lines, made up on the spur of the moment, aimless as a balloon in the sky.

But if you pull away from the sheet of paper and take a step back to get a better look, suddenly there it is in front of you, your rhinoceros.

Acknowledgments

This book took four years to write, and wonderful people during those years who kept me on my feet, more or less.

They are: Giulia Ichino, Marilena Rossi, Antonio Franchini, Riccardo Cavallero, Antonio Riccardi, Mario de Laurentiis, Marta Dosi, Giacomo Callo, Beppe Del Greco, Camilla Sica, Elisa Martini, Emanuela Canali, Nadia Focile, Francesca Gariazzo. They did amazing work and also put a ton of heart into it, which has nothing to do with work.

Isabella Macchiarulo, precious guide through the world of albinos.

Teresa Martini, Roberto Mancinelli, Francesca Giannelli, Carlotta and Edoardo Nesi, Michele Pellegrini, Giada Giannecchini, Matteo Raffaelli, Michael Moore, Debora Di Nero, Gipi, Sandro Veronesi, Teresa Ciabatti, Chiara Valerio, Antonio Troiano, Aldo Grasso, Mariarosa Mancuso, Federica Bosco, Simone Lenzi, Michele Boroni, Daniele Bresciani, Marta Caramelli, Mauro Corona, Fabio Guarnaccia, Michele Dalai.

My "pier" pals, for telling me often, "Lucky you, you don't do shit for a living."

And everyone who over the years has understood me, even if there was nothing to understand.

See you around.

About the Author

Fabio Genovesi was born in Forte dei Marmi in Versilia in 1974. He is the author of *Live Bait* (Other Press, 2014), which has been translated into over ten languages, an earlier novel, *Versilia Rock City*, the memoir *Morte Dei Marmi* (Laterza, 2012), and *The Breaking of a Wave*, winner of the Young Reader's Strega Prize.